A WARMTH BLOSSOMED INSIDE HER, AND A RESTLESS LONGING RACED THROUGH HER VEINS.

She should cover herself, she thought, yet she couldn't move as Max looked up at her with a heavy-lidded gaze and lightly traced her bottom lip with his forefinger.

With a bravery she did not know she possessed, she pressed a kiss to his finger and caught it with her tongue as she moistened her lips and leaned toward him.

Max's hand cupped her chin, holding her still, their lips a hairbreadth apart from one another. "Tempt me not, Jillian," he said on a ragged breath. "You are treading on dangerous ground."

"I'm not afraid, Max," she whispered as she leaned closer, her mouth brushing his.

"You should be," he groaned. And his mouth opened, covering hers.

TEMPT ME NOT

EVE BYRON

AVON BOOKS ◆ NEW YORK

TEMPT ME NOT is an original publication of Avon Books. This work has never before appeared in book form. This work is a novel. Any similarity to actual persons or events is purely coincidental.

AVON BOOKS
A division of
The Hearst Corporation
1350 Avenue of the Americas
New York, New York 10019

Copyright © 1995 by Connie Rinehold and Francie Stark
Published by arrangement with the authors
Library of Congress Catalog Card Number: 94-96687
ISBN: 0-380-77624-3

First Avon Books Printing: June 1995

AVON TRADEMARK REG. U.S. PAT. OFF. AND IN OTHER COUNTRIES, MARCA REGISTRADA, HECHO EN U.S.A.

Printed in the U.S.A.

RA   10   9   8   7   6   5   4   3   2   1

PART I

Prologue

Westbrook Court, Spring 1800

Her name was Jillian Nicole Forbes and Max hated her on first sight.

Her bald head was shaped like an egg and her eyes were the color of pond scum.

"Isn't she beautiful?" a hushed voice asked.

Keeping his true opinion of the infant to himself, Maxwell Hastings glanced at his best friend, Damien Forbes, and nodded in agreement.

Through narrowed eyes, he watched Damien lift his two-month-old sister from her cradle and coo softly to her. The reverence in his friend's manner embarrassed Max. How this infant had garnered such devotion from Damien was beyond him. Maybe it was because Damien didn't have his mother anymore. She'd died when Jillian was born two months ago. For that alone Damien's sister deserved to be hated. Damien's mother had been a nice lady, and he suspected that Damien had cried a lot over her loss. Even today, Damien's eyes were red and swollen.

Max didn't know what to do or say. He couldn't understand what it felt like to lose a mother, since he didn't remember his own. Nor did he understand the happiness Damien found in his new sister.

Now, if she were a boy, he could understand that. A brother might be a nice thing to have.

Yet, there seemed to be no possibility of that ever

happening. Max's father had said there was no reason for him to marry again since he had an heir, and Max had no intention of giving up the exalted position of heir to a dukedom.

"Do you want to hold her?" Damien asked.

Max folded his arms across his chest and shook his head. "I'll wait until she's bigger," he said, using the same excuse he'd used every day since her birth.

Damien wrinkled his nose suddenly. "She needs changing," he informed Max as he returned her to her cradle. "Will you watch her while I fetch LadyLou?"

Max wanted to volunteer to locate Damien's aunt, only something in Damien's eyes stopped him—a look that said he had guessed how Max felt and was offering him one last chance to accept his sister.

Resentment coiled inside Max. Ever since the baby had arrived, he'd had to fight for every moment spent with his best friend. His faith in friendship was slowly weakening, and it scared him. Friendship was the only thing that had never disappointed him, until now.

It was all her fault.

She was intruding in a centuries-old tradition of friendship between their families. His father, the Duke of Bassett, and Damien's father, the Duke of Westbrook, were best friends, just as Max and Damien were best friends. It had always been that way— Hastings and Forbes, guarding one another's backs since the reign of Henry III.

And she was botching it all up.

He wouldn't allow it. He didn't have to like her. All he had to do was pretend a polite interest and wait for Damien to grow bored with his latest toy. Max was becoming very good at controlling whatever threatened him, whether it was a person or a place that disrupted the parts of his life he could call his own.

Feeling much better, he smiled at Damien. "I'll watch her." *But that is all I will do,* he added silently.

Damien gave a relieved sigh, adjusted her blanket and left the room.

The baby whimpered and Max dutifully peered down at her to sure make all was well. She kicked the blanket away with one skinny leg. Careful not to touch her, he leaned over and gingerly grasped the edge of her blanket between his forefinger and thumb and tugged it back over her.

Her face screwed up and turned scarlet, yet she made no sound. The sight fascinated him, and he had an almost irresistible urge to remove the piece of charcoal from his pocket and draw side-whiskers on her so she'd look like the hated headmaster at school. But he had turned ten years old last week, and the age for drawing on offensive objects had passed.

Max cringed as she abruptly released an ear splitting wail. Desperate to calm her, he stroked and patted her cheeks. It worked with dogs.

To his surprise, her mouth latched onto his forefinger and sucked vigorously.

He stiffened as she grasped his finger with her tiny hand and made a contented baby noise. For some reason, he got a happy tickle in the pit of his stomach, like the one he used to feel when he knew his father was coming home.

That feeling was dangerous. Whenever it happened, he knew that as soon as it went away he'd be left with a lump in his throat that hurt ... or worse, he would cry. He snatched his finger away.

The baby wailed and tears ran from the corners of her eyes. He wondered if something might really be wrong and anxiously glanced toward the nursery door, then turned back to the baby. "Shhh," he murmured.

She stopped crying and her gaze seemed to focus on him. Captured by the intensity of her eyes, he stared back and realized that they had little flecks the exact green of Damien's eyes. And she really wasn't bald at all. Her head was actually dusted with fine, black hair and her eyebrows were arrow straight slashes just like Damien's. She looked like her brother.

Something cracked inside him and the dreaded lump formed in his throat anyway.

"What's wrong?" Damien said racing into the room, his aunt trailing behind him. "I heard her crying, but just as I found LadyLou, she stopped."

"She wanted to eat my finger and I wouldn't let her," Max explained.

Damien's aunt smiled at Max. "That's because she's hungry. Thank you for looking after her so well."

"Thank you ma'am," Max said stiffly. He hadn't decided yet if he liked the Lady Louise Forbes. She was Damien's father's sister, a bluestocking who, according to Damien, was quite on the shelf and shockingly independent. Without being asked, she'd announced that she would live here and raise the baby herself, acting as both mother and governess. Damien called her LadyLou. Max tried not to call her anything at all if he could help it.

"Along with you," she said. "I will look after her until her wet-nurse returns."

"But, Max and I can rock her to sleep," Damien protested.

No! Max wanted to shout. He knew what Damien was doing. They had always shared everything and Damien was trying to share his sister. But, she wasn't a favorite rock or garter snake in a box that he could take home and keep overnight. He didn't want to watch her or hold her or have any part of her.

"There will be plenty of time to see her later," Lady Louise said. "She needs her nurse before she can go to sleep." She smiled at Damien's downcast look. "Surely, the two of you can find something to occupy yourselves. The fish may be biting at the pond or perhaps there is a sea beast lurking beneath the surface of the water that needs to be vanquished."

Max's insides quickened at the way Damien's face suddenly brightened. It seemed like forever since his friend had wanted to do anything but spend time about the nursery. "Our swords are still hidden beneath a stone near the water," he said, knowing he was too old for such silly games. But Damien wasn't. He wouldn't be ten for a few months yet. Max would slay as many dragons as necessary if it would give him back his friend.

"Are you sure you don't need us, LadyLou?" Damien asked.

"I'm certain." She winked at Max. "I don't want to see either of you until dinner."

"Yes, ma'am," Damien said with a grin as he punched Max on the shoulder. "Race you."

Max knew he liked her then. And she was sort of pretty, with her black hair and light blue eyes. As he and Damien started for the door, he wondered what it would be like to have someone like her living at his house. He couldn't imagine her rapping Damien's knuckles for any reason. Max's last governess had nearly beaten his hands off.

"Damien," she called after them. "Don't forget your father is arriving this afternoon. He wants the family to dine together tonight."

Max's footsteps faltered and he felt the blood drain from his face. Damien's father was coming home. It meant that the dukes of Westbrook and Bassett, who spent the majority of their time together, had parted company for a while. "Father and I are going to dine together, too," he said.

Damien gave him a dubious look and Max felt ashamed. He was lying and Damien knew it. Max rarely knew when his father was coming to Bassett House. He had no idea where his father, the great Duke of Bassett, spent his time when he wasn't in London. He only knew it was not with him.

Chapter 1

Bassett House, Spring 1807

Max stared up at the stone face of the ancestral home of the Dukes of Bassett. The embodiment of the generations of men who had ruled over it, the house reflected arrogance and power with its wings bent like arms flexed in a show of strength that challenged man, the land—even heaven itself. The standard that heralded the presence of the master was not flying from the highest turret of Bassett House.

The duke had not yet arrived.

Max lingered in the coach, his posture languid against the squabs as he decided whether to wait for his father or go to Westbrook Court as he had originally intended. Yet, he knew he had no choice. His father had sent a missive to Max commanding that he return home as soon as the school holiday began. Even for the duke, six months was a long time to go without inspecting his heir.

The sound of the butler subtly clearing his throat dragged Max's attention to the staff standing at rigid attention on the broad portico, their eyes blank as they waited for him to emerge from the coach. Poor stiff-kneed bastards. They'd stand there and rot if he willed it, just as he would rot here if his father willed it.

Again the butler cleared his throat.

Max's lips thinned in irritation at the obvious signal that he had lingered too long. It was an impertinence that Burleigh would dare only with the sixteen-year-old heir.

Let them wait, he thought, as he flicked an imaginary speck of dust from his breeches, then deliberately dallied with his gloves, easing each finger into its sheath. They expected it—the arrogance and insouciance. Far be it from him to disappoint them.

He gave an imperious nod to signal his readiness. A footman opened the door of the coach and lowered the steps.

"Welcome home my lord," the butler said the instant Max's feet touched the cobbled drive.

"The duke?" Max asked curtly.

"Delayed, my lord."

Max nodded. The duke was always delayed for one reason or another. Squaring his shoulders he moved swiftly past the row of waiting servants, accepting every bow and curtsy with a brusque nod of his head as he climbed up the stone steps. A footman sprang forward and opened the heavy oak doors.

Max could not stop his sharp intake of breath as he stepped into the massive entrance hall of his father's home.

The interior was stunning in its beauty with fluted marble columns reaching up three stories to a vaulted ceiling carved and painted in ornate bas-relief. Everywhere Max looked were the treasures the duke had collected for as long as he could remember. He wondered what new priceless painting or piece of sculpture he might find if he took the time to explore the rooms. Given his father's latest obsession with Egyptian artifacts, he might well find a mummy standing sentinel with the medieval armor in the small dining room.

Museum or mausoleum? he wondered. It didn't really matter. Either way Bassett House was filled with lifeless memories and untouchable beauty.

He strode toward the stairs, intent on escaping to his chambers. There, he could move about freely and isolate himself from the oppressive atmosphere of the rest of the house. Not that his rooms were much better, but they were the only place where he would not find another priceless something or other to beware of.

"My lord," Burleigh called out.

Max halted with his foot on the first step and turned to meet the butler's gaze. Burleigh looked like a shade, his thin body seeming to sway, his aged, sunken features ghoulish, his one tuft of white hair sprouting from the top of his head like a plant that refused to die.

"His Grace ordered that you be moved to the west wing."

Disquiet rippled through Max, but he would not ask the reason and he would not dwell on being ejected from the room that had been his since he'd been allowed out of the nursery. He would simply accustom himself to his new surroundings as soon as he found out where they were.

"Are you going to tell me where, or have you left a string tied from my old bedpost to my new one so I might find my way?" he asked.

"The red suite, my Lord."

Max forced himself to contain his temper. The suite was an oriental horror of dragons and black lacquer furniture. Obviously, his chambers would no longer offer the safe haven of familiarity. "Have Sovereign saddled and brought to the front in five minutes," he ordered.

"But my Lord! His grace is expected this afternoon!" the butler said, clearly scandalized.

Another impertinence. Burleigh kept forgetting precisely whom he was addressing. Drawing himself up to his full height, Max stared down at the butler and with the hauteur of seven Dukes of Bassett behind him, spoke in perfect mimicry of his father. "When he arrives, you may inform his Grace that his lordship went riding."

Before Burleigh could pick up his chin from the floor, Max stalked up the stairs. It was too bad the duke had not witnessed the scene. He would have been proud of the arrogance his heir displayed. But then, the duke never witnessed his son's finer accomplishments.

Max rode hard and fast over the parkland, then reluctantly returned to Bassett a few hours later. Dismounting in front of the house, he tossed his reins to a footman. The turret was still bare. The duke still had not arrived.

Caught between impatience and relief, he closeted himself in his chambers. After he finished the meal delivered to his rooms on a tray, he made his way to the library in search of a book. He slipped soundlessly down the dimly lit hall and paused at the sound of voices echoing from nearby. He recognized the formal tone of Burleigh and the squeaky voice of his father's valet. It wasn't difficult to catch the gist of their conversation.

His father wasn't coming at all.

Shrugging, Max continued on his way. Now he was free to visit the inn, or more precisely, the golden-haired wench who worked there. Perhaps even Damien would indulge in the favors so freely offered by the maids. It was about time Damien gave up his virginity. After all, they were both almost seventeen and Max had been wenching for a full year.

As he passed the white drawing room, he ground to an abrupt halt. Someone on the staff had committed the gravest of errors. The room was forbidden, yet its doors were ajar.

He stepped inside, venturing no farther than the threshold. The room was cast in complete darkness, but he didn't need light to know what it looked like with its French furniture, priceless paintings and vases. Predominantly white and gold, the room was as cold as the unused grates in the white marble fireplace.

He hated this room.

At one time he had loved to come inside and simply admire the beauty here, until the duke had caught him.

"No one touches what is mine . . . no one," the duke had said in a voice Max had never forgotten.

From that moment on, he had understood quite clearly that he, too, fell into the same category as his father's possessions. Possessions that once acquired were displayed and occasionally inspected, yet never again touched by the duke.

Chapter 2

Westbrook Court, Spring 1807

*P*lease let father remember my birthday. Jillian silently repeated the wish over and over again as she burrowed her hands beneath the folds of her skirt and snapped her last wishbone. She'd used her first wishbone to ask that LadyLou come home in time for her seventh birthday. Soon after, Jillian had realized she'd asked for the wrong thing. Her aunt had slipped on the stairs at her friend's house and a broken arm couldn't be wished away. But as she sat beside Damien on the sofa in their father's study, she was certain that she was wishing for the right thing.

"When are you leaving for Westbrook Castle, Father?" Damien asked.

Jillian's hand clenched around the pieces of bone. *Please let him stay until tomorrow.*

"Within the hour," the duke replied.

Her heart sank, and she waited for Damien to speak. Her father firmly believed that she should be seen and not heard.

She used to get confused as to why they lived at Westbrook Court, when her father had a perfectly good castle. LadyLou had told her that Westbrook Castle, her father's duke's seat, was a long way from London and his other estates. Westbrook Court was more centrally located. Jillian hadn't understood that until LadyLou explained that all it meant was Westbrook Court was in the middle.

"I don't have to return to school for a few weeks," Damien said in a careful tone. "Jillian and I could go down with you and come back in a week or so. She's never been there."

Jillian's breath snagged in her throat. She could hardly believe he asked that. She had never been to Westbrook Castle, and wanted to go so desperately it made her feel all hungry inside. Hungry to be a part of her father's life. Hungry for her father's attention. She could see it on his face and in his eyes that Damien felt the same way. Besides, if they all went to the castle, her father would have to remember her birthday because Damien would remind him.

"Your sister has no reason to go there and one day you'll have more time at Westbrook than you want."

"Yes, sir," Damien said.

Jillian dropped her gaze to her lap, disappointment uncurling inside her. She had wished for the wrong thing again. Even though Father looked like her and Damien with his shiny black hair and green eyes, he was a stranger who made brief appearances to look them over and then went away as quickly as he came. Damien always pretended it didn't matter, but she knew it did.

Their voices droned around her as Damien and their father began discussing estates and tenants. Bored, Jillian wiggled her loose front tooth with the tip of her tongue and stuffed the pieces of bone into her pocket.

Sighing, she straightened the ruffles of her yellow muslin frock. She'd worn the dress specially for her father because it made her feel pretty and she'd wanted him to notice. He hadn't. Absently, she reached up and grasped her front tooth between her thumb and forefinger and gently worked it back and forth. It had to fall out today or Damien was going to tie a string to it and yank it out tonight. The thought made her shiver all over.

"Do you know how long Max's father plans to stay at Basset House?" Damien asked.

With her fingers still in her mouth, Jillian froze. Max's father was coming to Bassett House.

"What are you doing with your fingers in your mouth?" her father asked sternly.

Jillian snatched her hand away. "Nothing, sir."

"You may be excused."

Head bowed, Jillian climbed down from the sofa, her tummy twisting with hurt at being sent away. "Goodbye, sir," she said and gave him a nearly perfect curtsy.

"Behave yourself while I am away," her father said gruffly.

"Yes sir, I will," she said.

Damien touched her arm and smiled at her. "Wait for me at the swing," he said quietly.

The tummyache went away. She turned and ran toward the door, remembering too late LadyLou's rule about walking instead of running in the house. She paused and glanced back, waiting for a reprimand. Instead her father again mentioned Max and the Duke of Bassett. She closed the door and wandered around the hall.

Max's father was coming to Bassett House. That meant Max would not be spending his school holiday here and she would have her brother all to herself. She didn't like Damien's best friend, mostly because he didn't like her. When he was here, she had to fight for her brother's attention. If Max and Damien didn't hare off somewhere, Max tagged along with her and Damien, though he always stood apart from them. And she'd never seen him have any fun. Sometimes, he would laugh, but there was always a look on his face that made her feel sad.

She strolled down the short hallway to the door leading to the inner courtyard and stepped out into the sunshine. Her thoughts instantly turned toward her swing. Maybe today, Damien would push her high enough to touch the sky.

She hopscotched her way across the brick mosaic courtyard and through the rose garden watching her feet and wiggling her tooth with her tongue. She skipped around the garden wall.

"Be careful," a deep, irritated voice warned. Max's voice.

As she tried to catch her balance, hands shot out and grasped her shoulders. Her body twisted and her nose hit his leg, jamming her tongue hard against her tooth. It flew right out of her mouth, bounced off his knee and landed on the ground at her feet. She gasped and quickly covered her lower face with her hand to catch any blood and rub her wounded nose.

Still grasping her shoulders, Max gazed down at her. "Are you hurt?"

Too shocked by his appearance to speak, she shook her head. He wasn't supposed to be here. Now her birthday would be spoiled.

"Remove your hand and let me see," he ordered softly.

His tone stunned her. She hadn't known he could speak to her as nicely as Damien did. She lowered her hand. He cupped her chin and tilted her face up.

Jillian blinked and her mouth dropped open as she stared into his eyes. They were the same color as the Westbrook sapphires that LadyLou had shown her once. She'd thought the sapphires so pretty with all the gold around each jewel. With his blond hair and eyebrows, Max was all blue and gold and pretty, too.

Because it wasn't polite to stare, she'd never really looked at him before. But since *he* was staring she thought it might be all right. He had the same expression on his face that he sometimes had when he watched her and Damien. The look that made her feel so sad.

He released her abruptly and stepped back.

Dropping her gaze to her hands, she examined her fingers, vaguely surprised to see that they were clean. Losing a tooth was usually a messy business. "It didn't even bleed," she said.

"Your nose is a little red. I apologize. I did not mean to inflict any injury."

"Oh, you didn't hurt my nose, you knocked my tooth out," she lisped and bent to retrieve it from the grass. "See." She extended her hand to show him the tooth.

"Oh, my God," he muttered as he stared at the shiny, white pebble in her palm.

"It was already loose," she explained quickly. "I nearly had it out anyway. You just helped it along." She smiled widely so he could see what she was talking about.

A strange expression came over his face, making her feel as if he had walked away from her, though he hadn't moved.

She tucked her tooth into the pocket of her dress along with her broken wishbones. "I'm saving all my teeth," she confided.

"I see," he said, his voice seeming as far away as his expression. "If you will excuse me." He brushed past her and continued on his way.

Tears stung her eyes and she gulped them down hard. Maybe he was pretty on the outside, but he was ugly on the inside. It was just like LadyLou had always told her, "pretty is, as pretty does."

She ran after him, catching him as he rounded the corner of the garden wall. "Damien is with father," she said breathlessly. "They are leaving for Westbrook Castle in an hour."

The words were barely out of her mouth before Damien's voice thundered behind her. "Jillie, whatever possessed you to tell such a clanker?"

Her heart sank at being caught in such a terrible fib. And then she was mad because it was all Max's fault. He wasn't supposed to be here. She didn't want him here. She glared up at him and suddenly her throat hurt to see sadness creep into Max's pretty face.

"Answer me, Jillie," Damien said, moving around to stand beside Max.

"I thought you were leaving with Father," she fibbed outrageously and tried not to feel guilty about it.

"No," Damien corrected. "You should have been listening instead of fiddling with your tooth." He leaned over to peer at her mouth. "What happened to it?"

"I ran into Max and it fell out," she said.

"We collided at the garden wall," Max added, his voice as flat as peas without salt. He directed his attention to Damien. "Have you plans for the afternoon?"

"None, after giving Jillian a push on her swing," Damien said. "What are you doing here, Max?"

"The duke had matters to attend to elsewhere," Max said.

"I thought your father would come to Bassett for certain," Damien said. "It's been six months since you saw him last."

Jillian wondered how long six months was. She hated it when they talked about things that she didn't understand.

Max shrugged. "If I'm fortunate, it will be another half a year before he puts in an appearance."

Jillian could understand that. The Duke of Bassett was scary. He looked at her as if she was a bug that needed to be squashed. He looked at Max the same way. Still, half a year seemed a very long while to her. Absently, she ran her tongue over the empty sockets in her mouth as she tried to measure how much time that really was. A year lasted from one birthday to the next, but she had trouble with the half. "Damien, was Christmas a half a year ago?" she asked.

Damien ruffled her hair. "I imagine to you it seems

as if it was, but no, it's only been four months." He
took her hand. "Ready for your swing?"

She nodded and allowed him to lead her away, dazed
by what she had just learned. Christmas was forever
ago. It was beyond her comprehension that Max had
not seen his father since before then, that he had not
even seen him at Christmas. But Max had spent Christmas here. She had not understood what that meant until
now. Max would have spent Christmas alone if he
hadn't been here.

She glanced at Max over her shoulder. He had that
sad look on his face again. It sort of reminded her of
the way Damien had looked in the study earlier, and the
way she felt when she waited for her father to decide
whether to take her to Westbrook Castle . . . only it was
hungrier.

The look had a name and a feeling.

Hungry.

Poor Max. As little as she and Damien saw their father, she realized now that Max saw his even less. She
understood at last. She and Damien had each other.
Max had no one.

They reached the swing and as Jillian settled in the
seat, Max leaned against the tree and folded his arms
across his chest. She wanted to cry at how his eyes
looked like the sapphires when there was no light to
shine on them.

"What is it, Jillie? Why are you frowning so?"
Damien asked.

She thought and thought but she didn't know how to
explain. Max had never liked her, never even spoken to
her really, yet all of a sudden her heart hurt for him.
"Swing me high, Damien. I want to touch the sky.
Please."

"No. You'll fall."

"I'll hang on tight. Tighter than ever before. See,"
she said and gripped the ropes so hard her knuckles
turned white. "Please, please, please, Damien."

"All right," he relented. "But promise you won't squirm about in the seat."

"I promise," she said as her brother pulled up the seat of the swing.

"Ready?"

She nodded. Ready to fly.

Back and forth she sailed as Damien pushed her higher and higher. She loved the thrill of leaving her stomach hanging in midair each time she went backward.

Max moved away from the tree and stared up at her. "Higher," she cried.

She kicked out her legs as Damien laughed and sent her flying again. The swing arced through the air, going so high Max was a blur as she soared past him. All she could see was blue sky and fluffy white clouds. And then, for one glorious moment, she hung suspended in the air. "I'm touching the sky," she cried.

Suddenly, she lost her grip on the ropes and tumbled out face first. A scream tore from her throat as the ground hurtled up to meet her. All she could think about were birds she had seen fly into windows and fall down dead. Unable to look, she closed her eyes.

Her scream died as her breath whooshed out painfully and her chin slammed into her chest. She couldn't breathe for the pain squeezing her middle. So this was what it was like to die.

"I've got you," said a voice that was both harsh and gentle, and she knew it was Max.

Her eyes popped open and the first thing she saw was her feet dangling above the ground. She realized she was hanging in the air like a puppet on a string. She wasn't dying at all. Max had come from behind and caught her. The pain in her middle was only his hands holding her in an unbreakable grip.

Jillian began to shake. She twisted around to bury her face in his throat and wrap her arms around his neck. She could feel his heart pounding right along with hers.

"You're safe," he murmured, cupping the back of her head with his hand.

"Oh God. Is she hurt?" Damien asked. "Jillie, are you hurt?"

"No, she's just scared," Max answered. "You shouldn't have let her swing so high, Damien. What if I hadn't been there to catch her when she fell?"

"It was stupid, I know," Damien said.

"That does not even begin to cover it," Max bit out.

"Leave off Max. I won't do it again."

"Oh, please don't fight," she pleaded as she pushed away from Max to look from him to her brother and back again. Max's face was as white as Damien's and he was as scared as her brother and she knew then that Max cared.

Damien eased her from Max's hold and set her on the ground. "Never again will I allow you to go that high."

Jillian swiped a stray lock of hair away from her face. "But why? You can push me and now I know Max will catch me."

Max folded his arms across his chest, closing himself off from them. But it was too late. She was never going to let him do that again. He cared about her and he was her friend and she was never going to let him go.

"Max won't always be around to catch you," Damien said.

From the corner of her eye, she saw Max back away from them. She followed him and stood beside him. "Then I will never touch the sky unless he is with me."

"Um . . . yes . . . well, we will see." Damien bent and picked something up. "You lost your tooth again."

Jillian took the tooth from Damien, and held it out to Max, wanting to give him a part of herself. "Take it," she whispered. "So you remember the day you caught me."

He stared at her outstretched hand and shook his head. "Your collection won't be complete. You keep it, so you'll remember."

"I won't forget." Before he could stop her, she dropped the tooth in his coat pocket and grasped his hand. He frowned as she shifted her hold, snuggling her small fingers between his. Smiling up at him, she reached to her side and curled her other hand into her brother's palm, liking the thought that they were all connected together . . . like family.

"Damien?" she said softly, afraid she'd scare Max away if she spoke too loudly. "Can we have tea in the gazebo?"

"I suppose we could have it served there. What do you think, Max?"

"You must be very thirsty, Max," Jillian said quickly. "And cook has made cream cakes." Suddenly it seemed terribly important that the three of them stay together for a while longer. "Oh, please, Max. It is my very special place and I want to show it to you."

His frown smoothed out like the covers on her bed after her room had been tidied, and he nodded.

She took a step forward, wanting to get him to the gazebo before he changed his mind. She knew he wouldn't want to leave once they were inside. She never did.

Side by side with her brother and her new friend, she climbed the steps into the gazebo. It felt so right somehow. It even felt a little bit like magic, as if the world had grown around her and changed before her eyes.

And as she walked over to ring the bell that would summon a footman, she saw the corners of Max's mouth tip up, just a little. She'd hardly ever seen him smile, but she supposed she wouldn't smile either if she was as truly alone as Max.

But he didn't have to be alone. She could share her brother and her Christmases with him. She could make sure he walked beside her and Damien instead of behind them . . . if he would let her. She wished he wasn't so terribly stubborn.

Biting her lip, she willed the wish away. She only

had one left—the birthday wish she'd been saving for something really special.

She lifted her face toward heaven, forming her request carefully and whispering the words to make sure it was received. Then, satisfied that everything would be all right now, she settled back on the seat between Max and Damien.

"And what are you looking so smug about?" Damien asked his sister.

Max lounged back in the seat and watched Jillian, realizing that she did indeed look smug. But then why shouldn't she? he thought. She'd managed to get her way again. He tried to summon up some irritation and failed. He felt odd, almost content.

"I was making a birthday wish," Jillian said, a flush staining her cheeks.

"What did you wish for?" Damien asked.

"That Max was part of our family," she replied solemnly.

Damien smiled and drew her into an affectionate hug. "I think in a way, he is, Jillie."

Max felt as if he'd broken wide open and his soul was spilling onto the ground where everyone could see it. And, as he watched Damien and Jillian create a world within a hug, he glanced away and focused on a leaf peeking in through the latticework. "Your wish was wasted."

"No, it wasn't," Jillian said sweetly. "You have your own room at our house and dine with us all the time—"

"Don't be ridiculous," he said tightly as he rose and strode to the arched entrance. He had to get away from here, away from her logic that defied imagination.

"Careful, Max, before you go too far," Damien warned.

Before *he* went too far? Max thought as he glanced back at Damien and Jillian. He wasn't the one who gave away teeth and prattled on about touching the sky.

"It's all right, Damien," Jillian said gravely. "He

doesn't know he treats me the way his Father treats him."

Max froze. It was as if Jillian held up a looking glass and an image of his father reflected back at him.

Jillian approached him and took his hand. "It's all right, Max. You didn't know any better."

"No, I suppose I didn't," he said. He'd only known what he was taught and what he saw and now there was something more, and it made all the difference in the world. Instinctively, his fingers closed around hers. Bemused by the sense of comfort her small hand gave him, he allowed her to lead him back to the seat.

The footman arrived with their tea and Jillian clumsily served them, spilling more in their saucers than what actually landed in the cups.

"Have you learned any new myths lately?" Damien asked his sister.

"Oh yes. LadyLou told me about Pandora. Shall I tell you?"

Max stretched his legs out in front of him, prepared to endure her chatter. It surprised him to find that he was listening, charmed by the way her small nose puckered and her green eyes widened and sparkled with wonder as she recited a list of all the wicked things that flew out of Pandora's box.

Jillian smoothed out the ruffles of her dress. "LadyLou says I'm just like Pandora. Too curious for my own good. But there is hope for me."

"Are you quite certain?" Max asked with a curious lightness in his voice. The realization that he'd enjoyed the whole afternoon shocked him. He'd been at ease as he so rarely was, uncaring of propriety and of behaving the way the heir to a dukedom should. It had almost been like when he and Damien were children, slaying imaginary dragons or fishing in the pond. It was almost like being family.

As if she'd heard his thoughts, Jillian smiled a melting smile and hugged his arm, then reached for Damien's hand, linking herself to both of them.

Max stared at the small face turned up to his and felt a fierce new sense of belonging. Today, he had opened Pandora's box and discovered hope cowering at the bottom.

Chapter 3

All too soon, summer ended and it was time for Max and Damien to finish their final year in public school.

Jillian had given them both fierce hugs and promised she would write as soon as she learned to form all the letters in the alphabet. Max didn't give the promise any credence, doubting that she could sit still long enough to write a note, much less an entire letter.

As she always had done, LadyLou wrote Damien with detailed accounts of Jillian's life.

Jillian had painted her face with her water colors.

Jillian had lopped off five inches of her braid for no good reason.

Jillian was up to the letter *T* in the alphabet . . .

Max began to feel uneasy with his continued eagerness to hear Jillian's antics. With time and distance, his sense of belonging faded. Still, Max could not help but wonder about the toothless child. In spite of himself, he lay on his bed in their room at school with his arms folded behind his head, battling back anticipation as Damien opened his mail.

"Apparently Jillie has mastered the alphabet. We've letters from her," Damien said and tossed a folded piece of parchment toward Max.

Abruptly, Max sat up and caught the letter, staring in
disbelief at his name written across the front in wobbly
letters and runny ink. By God, she'd actually done it.
He couldn't imagine what a seven-year-old girl might
have to say in a letter. He couldn't believe that she had
written to him.

Flipping it over, he felt his lips twitch in amusement.
Jillian had obviously sealed it herself. He had never
seen such a great gob of wax. With a firm snap he
broke the seal and read:

> Dear Marquess Max,
> The cat had kittens. My hair is growing. I miss
> you. Your friend, Jillian.
>
> Lady Jillian

Damien chuckled as he read his own. "Short and
sweet."

"Yes," Max said.

"LadyLou says that Jillian used a pot of ink and
nearly every piece of parchment in the house," Damien
said.

Max re-read the words Jillian had so painstakingly
written, then stored the letter in the box beneath his bed
along with the tooth she had given him.

Near the end of the term, Max learned from Damien
that their fathers had purchased a yacht and would
spend the summer at sea, planning to return before Max
and Damien left for Oxford in the fall. Forbes and
Hastings men always attended Oxford. Even though
Max had not seen his father in eight months he wanted
to shout with laughter at the news that the duke had
found a new diversion, leaving him free to spend the
summer at Westbrook Court. It didn't bother him that
he'd found out from Damien what his father was up to.
That was nothing new.

The summer months slipped past, and for the first
time in his life Max began to fully appreciate the rou-

tine at Westbrook Court and enjoy the warmth of
Damien's family. Although he had shared countless
meals at the Westbrook table, he had never allowed
himself to join in the laughter and conversation because
Jillian had always been present. Once, he had wondered
why she was not banished to the nursery or her room to
eat her meal in solitude as were other children her age,
but now, he thoroughly enjoyed her excitement as she
told her aunt how she had spent her day.

Max and Damien took her fishing.

Max and Damien taught her to swim in the pond.

Max and Damien pushed her in her swing . . .

The Duke of Westbrook returned two weeks before
Max and Damien were to leave for Oxford. Max had no
idea where his own father was and knew better than to
ask.

A week later, the Duke of Bassett came home and
summoned Max to Bassett House. Dutifully Max returned to stand for the long-overdue inspection. As he
rode through the back gates, he saw a wagon filled with
long wooden crates being unloaded at the servants's entrance.

More treasure.

He dismounted and tossed his reins to a groom and
strode directly to his father's study. The duke sat behind
a massive mahogany desk, his head bent over a stack of
correspondence. He had acquired a healthy tan, and the
sun had lightened his blond hair to almost white. Max
subtly cleared his throat.

The duke raised his head. "You look fit," he said, his
brilliant blue eyes hard and probing.

"So do you, sir," Max replied. "The sea seems to
agree with you."

But the duke wasn't listening. His gaze was fixed on
Burleigh who stood in the open doorway of the study.
"Have the tapestries been unloaded?"

"Yes, your Grace. They're ready to be uncrated," the
butler replied.

The duke nodded at Max in curt dismissal and left

the room to oversee the placing of the Medieval tapestries he'd collected in France and Italy. Then, he was off again within the hour.

Three days later, Damien and Max left for Oxford.

The first few weeks were spent adjusting to university life and immersing themselves in their studies. They were the heirs to Bassett and Westbrook and at the age of eighteen, duty was firmly seated on their shoulders. Besides, the sooner they met their obligations to titles and learning, the sooner they could spend their free time wenching and consuming gallons of ale.

The usual establishment of who among the aristocracy was worth knowing and who wasn't was even more stringent than in public school. Damien and Max topped the list. After all, heirs to dukedoms didn't grow on trees.

Only one person didn't give a bloody damn that Max and Damien held the ranking titles. Bruce Palmerston, Viscount Channing, didn't give a bloody damn who anyone was, and he captured Max's attention with his outrageous sense of humor and irreverent manner.

One night, Max and Damien entered the billiard room just as Channing finished a game with Anthony Edgewater. Edgewater never bathed and, greasy hair and grimy fingernails aside, an offensive odor followed him into a room and lingered long after he departed. From the conversation, Max gathered that Edgewater had just wagered and lost his entire quarterly allowance on a game of billiards.

"If you agree to bathe at least once a week, I'll give you your money back," Channing said as he leaned one hip against the table, a cue stick in his hand. Edgewater's beady eyes had grown glassy with outrage.

"I sense that you don't care for my proposition," Channing said as he set his cue stick aside. "Very well. Precisely how much have I won from you?"

"Agreed," Edgewater bit out angrily, his face flushed red as he brushed past Max and Damien, leaving a trail of stench in his wake.

"We will all be grateful for that piece of work,

Channing," Max said and introduced himself and
Damien.

"I know who you are," Channing replied and cocked
an arrogant brow. "Call me Bruce. I'm a man, not a title."

As they spent more time together in the weeks that
followed, Max saw signs of gossip in silent nudges and
rapid whispers when he and Damien and Bruce walked
past. Max didn't bother to wonder what was being said.

But as they sat at a table in a tavern Max lost track
of the conversation he was having with Damien and
Bruce and focused his attention on the one going on behind him. It was damned cheeky to gossip about a man
when he was sitting within earshot.

". . . been his mistress forever. Channing's father left
the country. *My* father says he probably couldn't take it
anymore after ten years of wearing horns," said one stu-
dent.

"Can you imagine the earl leaving every time the
duke came to dally?"

"Well of course I can. The duke would merely say,
'move over old man, I've come to make love to your
wife.' What I can't imagine is having the same mistress
for ten years." Hoots of laughter followed as the two
students shoved back from the table and rose. They
paused as they came abreast of Max's table and grinned
slyly at Bruce. "Channing, what do you suppose your
father thinks of your new friend?"

"Why don't you write to him and inquire?" Bruce replied coldly. "Shall I give you his direction?"

There were more hoots of laughter as the idiots
turned and strode out the door. Max's head buzzed as
he met Bruce's steady gaze. ". . . *been his mistress
forever . . .*"

Bruce drained his glass. "I take it you have divined
from their talk that my mother is your father's mistress.
My father resides abroad for the obvious reason."

"Why didn't you tell me sooner?" Max asked,
numbed by what he had just learned.

Bruce gave a dry laugh and rose. "It's not something I care to advertise." He turned and stalked away.

Damien released a long breath. "One has to admire his honesty."

Max couldn't admire anything about Bruce Palmerston at the moment. Over the next four days, Max avoided Bruce and, thankfully, Damien didn't ask questions. Max needed time to digest the information. Now, he understood where his father spent his leisure time and felt rather stupid for not having figured it out sooner.

Ten years.

Bruce had probably spent more time with the duke than he ever had. Yet, Max could not find it in himself to be angry with Bruce. Because of the duke's presence at Blackwood, Bruce's father had abandoned him while Max had enjoyed *his* holidays with Damien and Jillian, free of his father's critical eye. Because of that, Max felt a certain kinship with Bruce. There was no reason why they should not be friends. They had no control over the affairs of their respective parents.

That decided, Max waited for Bruce outside a lecture hall. "Thought you might like to go for a glass."

Bruce nodded and they strolled in silence to the nearest tavern.

They never spoke of the duke over the course of the school term though Bruce did eventually speak of his mother, Countess Blackwood, and his eight-year-old sister, Kathy.

Max spoke of Jillian.

Jillian learned how to play chess.

Jillian collected words and more fallen teeth.

Jillian celebrated her ninth birthday. . . .

At the end of his first year at university, Max returned to Bassett for a brief audience with his father, then the duke left again—to Blackwood to see the countess, Max supposed.

Summer passed with Max readily falling in with Jillian's pretense of family. It was easy to do when he awoke to her bright green gaze peeking at him over the

edge of his bed at Westbrook every morning and her
sleepy eyes peering around her door when he and
Damien came in late at night.

Another school term began, and the friendship between Max and Bruce and Damien grew stronger. In the
time-honored fashion of Hastings and Forbes men, they
closed ranks around Bruce, and discreetly put it about
that the Countess of Blackwood was a forbidden subject for gossip.

Jillian wrote longer letters.

Jillian despaired of ever growing taller.

Jillian learned how to cheat at chess. . . .

Two years passed and Max reached his majority, celebrating the occasion with Damien and Bruce.

Max, Damien and Bruce graduated Oxford. Even
Max's father turned out for the event, looking stern and
powerful as he sat with LadyLou and the Duke of
Westbrook.

After the ceremony, his father congratulated him
tersely, then proceeded to inform Max of his responsi-
bilities now that he had reached his majority and finished his education. There was an inheritance left to
Max by his mother, as well as a large estate in Hamp-
shire. That said, the duke had turned and walked
straight toward a woman standing with Bruce.

She could be no one but the Countess of Blackwood.

Even from a distance, Max could see she had perfect
porcelain skin and fine bones and a glorious mane of
bright auburn hair only a bit lighter than Bruce's. She
smiled at Max and it was so warm and beautiful that
his breath stalled in his throat. Max understood why the
Duke had chosen her as his mistress. His father would
have never been able to look upon such beauty and not
claim it as his own, as he had with all the treasures in
his collection.

Bruce stared directly at Max for a moment, then
turned and disappeared into the crowd. At that moment
Max felt the weight of the world on his shoulders. And
he vowed that he would be a better man than his father.

PART II

Chapter 4

Westbrook Court, Spring 1817

She looked like an escapee from bedlam.

Jillian stared at her reflection in the looking glass and stifled a smile. From one moment to the next, the curls Clancy had set into her hair dropped and straightened, and with every stroke of the brush, strands crackled and clung to the air around her as if they would fly away from such torture. She could have told LadyLou that efforts to curl her hair would be futile. But LadyLou had it in her head that Jillian would have a cascade of curls tumbling down her back at her ball.

"I can try again my Lady," the maid offered.

"No," Jillian said. "Put the curling tongs away, Clancy. It is futile."

LadyLou sighed in defeat. "You shall be the only lady at your come-out with straight hair. Perhaps a simple chignon would suit you best," she said from her chair by the fireplace.

Jillian's stomach pitched as her excitement instantly reached a delicious, almost unbearable level. In a few hours, Max and Damien would arrive and tomorrow they would escort her to London. Then it would begin: settling in at the Forbes townhouse, fittings at the modiste, dance lessons, more fittings, and finally, her presentation at court and her come-out ball.

They would all be together in the same city with Max in his house just a few blocks from hers. She would see Damien and Max every day. Finally, she would become a part of their world.

She had not seen them in a month. Normally, they visited her every fortnight, but their business interests of late had made it impossible for Max and Damien to leave London—

"Jillian!" shouted a masculine voice.

She sprang to her feet, toppling her chair as she whirled from the dressing table and broke into a run. "They're early."

"Walk Jillian," LadyLou admonished. "Ladies do not run."

Jillian wrenched open the door and ran straight into what felt like a brick wall. Her hair flew about her face and the air in her lungs whooshed out in an unladylike grunt.

"Careful there, you will knock yourself out," an amused, male voice rumbled as a pair of strong arms enfolded her. "And I should not like to wait for hours until you regain consciousness to talk to you. It has already been too long since I saw you last."

"Damien," she breathed as she rolled to her tiptoes and wrapped her arms around his neck. "Oh, I have missed you."

She leaned back and tilted her head to look at him and to make sure he hadn't changed . . . that he was really here. He, too, angled back, his hands firm around her waist, balancing them both as he returned her perusal.

He hadn't changed. His smile was still as brilliant, his eyes still twinkling with good humor.

"Did I hurt you?" she asked.

"Hardly. It felt more like being pounced upon by a small black kitten."

"Hello Damien," LadyLou greeted as she walked toward them. "You and Max must have left London early this morning. We did not expect you for hours yet."

"Where is Max?" Jillian asked.

"Waiting downstairs."

"Why ever didn't he come up?"

"Because," LadyLou said, "Max is aware, if you are not, that his presence in your boudoir is inappropriate."

"I fail to see why," Jillian said as she lifted her skirt clear of her feet and bolted from the room.

"Walk Jillie," Damien called after her. "You cannot possibly see where you are going through that mop of hair hanging in your face."

She barely heard him as she raced down the hall. At the top of the staircase, she paused to swipe the hair from her eyes.

"Hello Pandora."

Her heart jumped into her throat and her hand stilled as she heard the deep baritone. Her gaze shot to the bottom of the stairs, finding Max, held by the sight of him standing with his legs braced apart, hands on his hips . . . smiling up at her.

Where Damien was a handsome man, Max was majestic and reminded her of a lion—tall and broad and ruling the space around him. His mane of golden hair and sapphire eyes took her breath away. She thought *him* the most handsome man alive.

"Max," she cried and made her descent at a decidedly unladylike pace. When she reached the last three steps, she hurled herself through the air, trusting that he would catch her. He plucked her from space as if she were a feather, holding her close and swinging her about. "It seems forever since I saw you last," she said.

"It has only been three months," Max said, setting her on her feet. He reached out and tweaked a glossy black lock. "Whatever have you done to yourself? Your hair is atrocious."

Jillian shrugged. "LadyLou thought to give me a new coif. It did not work."

"Obviously," Damien said as he strolled down the steps behind her. "What is wrong with your braids?"

Jillian glanced over her shoulder at Damien. "Braids are for school girls, not for ladies about to make their debut. I am seventeen years old you know."

"Surely you cannot be that old," Max teased as she turned back to him. "I have only just grown accustomed to my Pandora having all her teeth."

"How can you possibly see that she has teeth?" Damien said. "All I see is hair."

"That is because you are looking at the back of my head," Jillian retorted. She spun around and flashed him an overly wide smile. "See, not only do I have teeth, but eyes and a nose as well."

"So you do," Damien said and tucked her hand in the crook of his elbow. "Shall we repair to the drawing room? I have an urge to sit on something stationary. The coach ride was abominable."

Jillian shook her head and brushed an errant lock from her face. "I must have Clancy attend my hair. I will join you in a few minutes."

"Never mind that," Damien said as he placed her hand in the crook of his elbow. "I can braid it while we talk."

Jillian raised a doubtful brow. "Do you know how?"

Damien shrugged. "It cannot be any more difficult than unbraiding a lady's hair."

"Since when have you taken down a lady's hair?"

Color crept up Damien's neck as his gaze snapped to Max.

"Spilled the soup, did we?" Max said with a wicked chuckle.

"Oh really," Jillian said. "Is there a special lady in his life?"

"No," Max said and tucked her other hand in the crook of his elbow. "Damien was playing the gallant to a lady in distress."

"And how would taking down a lady's hair relieve any sort of distress?" Jillian asked as they walked arm-in-arm toward the drawing room.

"Since you seem to know exactly what happened, you explain, Max," Damien said.

"Very well," Max patted Jillian's hand. "Remember

how Damien and I found you tangled in a rose bush when you were ten?"

"Yes," Jillian said.

"Well, Damien found another lady trapped in a rose bush."

Damien sighed. "There was nothing for me to do but take her hair down to free her. She was most grateful."

Max nodded in solemn agreement. "Indeed she was."

Jillian glanced from Max to Damien. Judging from their twin expressions of thinly veiled amusement, she knew that they were selling her a bill of goods. It was something they were quite good at whenever she ventured into territory they felt unseemly for her young ears. But she was not so young anymore. She was a woman full grown. Of course she realized that Max and Damien had lady friends. They probably even stole a kiss on occasion. It was high time they realized that she no longer believed their flummery.

"I do wish," she said, in a sugary voice, "that if the two of you insist on telling me a Banbury Tale, that you would begin with 'once upon a time.'" Feeling her point was made, she tugged her hands free and marched toward the drawing room. Damien and Max trailed in behind her.

"God, Max. Was that the best you could do?" Damien muttered under his breath as he and Max strode across the room.

"Ungrateful sod." Max sprawled in a chair near the fireplace.

"I heard that," Jillian said with a trace of smugness.

Ignoring her comment, Damien sat in the chair opposite Max, and motioned to the space on the floor before him. "Sit here, Jillie."

Jillian sat down on the Aubusson rug and arranged the skirt of her yellow gown around her as she settled between her brother's knees.

Without hesitation he plunged his fingers into her unruly mane, combing through the tangles with awkward, less than gentle strokes. She'd wager that any lady who allowed him to take her hair down did not do so more than once. He snagged the fine hair at her nape.

"Ouch! You are pulling too hard." She flinched, reaching back to bat his hands away.

"I am not," Damien said.

Max cocked his head to one side. "Yes you are. From where I sit it looks as if you are kneading dough."

"Oh really," Damien said. "Should you like to give a try, Max? God knows you've had more practice than I."

Jillian stiffened at the comment, and something lurched in her chest. Suddenly, it hurt having Damien confirm what she had so recently speculated about. Inexplicably, her spirits sank to her feet. Inexplicably, it made her angry. She pinned Max with a hard stare. "And have you had more practice than Damien?"

Max glared at Damien and rose to his feet. "Your brother is teasing." He crossed the short distance between them. "Move, Damien. You're making a hash of things."

Jillian rolled her eyes as she was gouged in the back twice during the switch.

Damien strode to a small sideboard. "Brandy, Max?"

"No, thank you." Max brushed his hand over the hair cascading down her back. "I have my hands full at the moment."

A tingle swept from her head to her toes as his warm fingertips brushed the back of her neck and gathered her hair to one side. She blinked in surprise at the sensation.

"Lean back," Max ordered in a soft voice.

Jillian obeyed, her shoulders brushing the insides of his thighs, feeling the heat of him. Her gaze darted from side to side, and she was shockingly aware of doeskin stretched over solid muscle. She felt overwhelmed and surrounded by the strength of his thighs on either side of her shoulders, by the scent of fresh air that clung to him from the journey, by the very sound of his breathing.

Suddenly, he released his hold on her hair.

In her mind, she had an image of it spilling into his lap and over his thighs like black ink—running and spreading and being absorbed by his breeches, penetrating to the flesh. Another odd tingle swept through her and mysterious heat pooled low in her belly.

She shook off the feeling as her brother sat down in the chair directly in front of her. At the same moment, Max again gathered her hair, tugging at it a little as he shifted back in his seat. Fingertips whispered against her temple and grazed the curve of her ear. She sucked in her breath as a fierce quickening spread from her heart to the tops of her knees. Mercy. And she had thought her neck was sensitive.

His hands glided back to her temple and over the crown of her head, and it felt so wonderful she could scarcely stand it. He stroked and stroked as if he were taking as much pleasure from her as he was giving.

Damien took a sip from the glass in his hand. "Max and I saw the 'graces' last week."

Her brother's use of the name she had coined when she was twelve to refer to their collective fathers doused her strange mood.

And it created apprehension as she felt her sense of freedom slip away. Her father's presence meant that she would be subjected to his constant scrutiny. It was bad enough he would be watching her every move during the Season. The thought of having him directing her every move for the months before was more than she could bear.

"Is it not just a little early for the graces to have returned to London?" she asked.

"Apparently they have grown bored with house parties and hunts," Damien said wryly.

"The Season does not begin for a few months. Surely the graces won't remain in London that long." She couldn't imagine it. While the Duke of Westbrook would most certainly "do the proper thing" and present her at court, it was not his way to linger once his duty had been performed.

"No. They will be in town only as long as it takes to refit the yacht," Damien said.

Understanding dawned. "They are taking to the sea," she stated.

"By now, they are at sea," Max corrected, "engaging in a yacht race with Hogarth and Riley."

"Who knows where they will wind up," Damien added. "They do not expect to return until the Season begins." Damien stared into the amber liquid in his glass. "And they are off to Greece immediately after your come-out. I am to oversee the Season itself."

"I see," Jillian said on a sigh.

"Is that so very surprising?" Damien said.

"No, actually it is a relief," she admitted. Max's hands moved to the center of her back. She felt him deftly divide her hair into three sections. He most certainly had practiced, she thought, annoyed.

Damien sat farther back in his chair and crossed his ankles. "I had feared you would be disappointed."

"Perhaps a little. But now I can enjoy the Season without worrying that Father will marry me off at first opportunity."

Max's hands stilled in her hair. "Good God. Surely, he was not entertaining the idea that you would wed anytime soon. You are just a child."

Jillian stiffened. *A child?* Without conscious thought she looked down at her. Was Max blind? She was anything but a child and she certainly did not feel like one. She raised her gaze to her brother. But Damien was staring in open astonishment at her. Jillian bit back a grin as he blinked once, flushed a bright shade of red, and jerked his gaze away. Well, at least her brother had just realized she was not a child.

Damien raised the glass in his hand and drained it. "You know I would not have allowed father to wed you to just anyone, Jillie."

"I do not know why I was ever worried. The odds of father missing my Season were always greater than those of his being in attendance."

"The graces will probably miss their own funerals," Max said dryly.

"What a terrible thing to say," Jillian scolded.

"Nonetheless, true," Damien said.

"There." Max flipped a flat braid over Jillian's shoulder.

"Perfect," Damien pronounced, then grinned wickedly. "Allow me to compliment you on your skills at attending a lady's hair."

Jillian's stomach twisted. The subject no longer amused her. "Apparently, practice does make perfect," she said the words stinging her tongue like acid. Her face flushed with heat as Damien's eyes widened. But she couldn't help it; she had no wish to hear more about Max's expertise with ladies' hair or imagine another woman nestled between his thighs, feeling his warmth. In any case, it was a silly subject.

Abruptly, she pushed to her feet and took a seat on the sofa. "What else have you two been doing this past month?" she asked, deliberately changing the topic.

"Well," Damien said. "Max and I have a wager with Viscount Channing."

"Really, Damien," LadyLou said from the doorway. "You and Max must stop filling her head with such inappropriate information. She is already enough of a bluestocking."

"I believe it runs in the family, LadyLou," Damien said.

"Indeed it does," LadyLou said, a beaming smile on her face. "But at the moment, Jillian needs to cultivate the fine art of polite conversation rather than discussing business."

Jillian stifled a groan. "Surely, I do not have to guard my tongue around family?"

"No, but it will behoove you to practice on Max and me at every opportunity," Damien said.

"Or else your mouth will get you into more trouble than you can wiggle out of once you've made your bow," Max added.

Jillian glared at them in disgust. Really, if she had known about the layers upon layers of senseless rules and traditions she would be required to learn before she made her bow in society, she would have been sorely tempted to *bow out*. "And what should I talk about? The weather? Should I gossip about the best catches in England?" She rose to her feet and waved an imaginary fan. "Damien Forbes, Marquess of Hartford, and Maxwell Hastings, Marquess of Castleraugh, are of course the best catches of the Season."

"And what elevates them to that esteemed position?" Damien asked.

"Why I should think that is obvious. Every debutante aspires to be a duchess."

"Then I am afraid that puts Hartford and Castleraugh out of the running since their fathers are quite fit and unlikely to cock up their toes in the near future," Max said, his voice amused.

Their attitudes amazed Jillian. They never gave a moment's thought to the titles that would one day be theirs. But then, she admitted, she could not imagine their becoming the graces either. The titles belonged to their fathers and always would. Still, there was more to recommend them as prime catches than mere titles.

"It most certainly does not put them out of the running," Jillian said. "They are almost as dreadfully rich as the graces."

"Jillian!" LadyLou gasped. "You cannot refer to the dukes in that manner."

"Max and Damien do."

There was a light tap on the drawing room doors. At Damien's call to enter, the butler stepped inside.

"My lord," Stokes said, "Sir Riley and Baron Hogarth have arrived and asked to see you and Lord Castleraugh immediately."

"I thought they were sailing with the dukes," Jillian said, sending LadyLou a slanted glance.

Her aunt nodded approvingly at her proper form of address.

Damien shrugged. "Apparently they changed their minds. Show them in, Stokes. Perhaps they bear a message from the gra—our fathers."

"Probably," Max agreed. "It wouldn't surprise me if they have decided to sail to China."

Hogarth and Riley walked into the room, their faces equally white with a ghastly pallor, their gazes skipping from Max to Damien.

A frisson of alarm skittered up Jillian's spine and she unconsciously moved closer to Damien.

As if she, too, sensed trouble, LadyLou flanked Jillian on the other side.

Max acknowledged them with a curt nod of his head.

"Riley, Hogarth," Damien greeted both men in a neutral voice. "I thought you were sailing."

"My lords," Hogarth said, his voice cracking. "I'm afraid there has been an accident."

"We were caught in a storm," Sir Riley said, his words bumping into one another. "A wave capsized your fathers' yacht. They did not survive."

The room seemed to recede around Jillian. As if in a dream she took the few remaining steps toward her brother, needing his comfort and protection as the words sank into her heart.

The graces were dead.

Immediately, she glanced over at Max, wishing that he, too, were close enough to touch. But he stood frozen, his pose still indolent, his expression tight. She leaned forward as if she would go to him, but Damien and LadyLou were holding her.

"Max," she called to him as she held out her hand, reaching to draw him in the circle.

He stared past her to Hogarth and Riley. "It was good of you to come," he said, dismissing them with chilly indifference, then turned to stare out the window.

His coldness shocked her. Pain welled in her throat as tears flooded her eyes and trickled down her face. Damien released LadyLou and gathered Jillian close and she wept openly. "Shhh," he murmured.

"It isn't fair," she said.

"No," Damien said, his voice cracking.

"We've lost them. They won't be back. I always hoped they'd come back for us, take us with them someday."

Max propped his arm on the window sash. "They were never ours to lose," he said harshly. "We were the possessions to be arranged or packed away according to their whims."

"No," Damien said as if he were coming out of a trance. "No. There were times when Father was kind to us . . . when we knew he cared."

"Of course he cared," LadyLou said softly. "He would not have come home at all if he hadn't." She wiped tears from her cheeks and gazed at Damien.

Max pushed away from the window, his expression blank. "I must return to Bassett."

"Max, you must stay," Jillian said, again extending her hand, willing him to take it. Oddly, in that moment, she felt more grief for Max than for her own loss. Nothing had changed for Max since they were children. He still had nothing from his father—not even a need to grieve for his loss.

"Yes, you must," LadyLou said. "There are arrangements to be made."

"LadyLou is right, Max," Damien said. "It is fitting that a joint memorial service be held."

Jillian lowered her hand. "Please, Max."

His back rigid, Max halted at the door and sighed as if it were the only release he could find. "My God," he said, his voice almost a whisper in the silence of the room, "the graces really will miss their own funeral."

Chapter 5

"**C**rows and buzzards," Max muttered under his breath as the cream of British aristocracy filed out of Westminster, displaying their respect for the dead with proper expressions of sorrow, and the *de rigeur* drabness of expensively fashioned mourning attire of velvet and bombazine and crape. Even nature seemed to show respect with pewter-gray skies and the threat of rain.

The astute observation brought a grim smile to Jillian's mouth as she stood at his side near the coach and watched Damien and LadyLou accept condolences with solemn nods and murmured thanks. Max had refused to participate in the ritual, removing himself from the crowd as soon as the service concluded. Jillian remained by his side, refusing to allow him to be alone. It haunted her, how he had remained remote even as they had conferred over arrangements, how he'd grown cold and silent when she and Damien had slipped, from time to time, into reminiscences and sorrow.

Numb with exhaustion, she sighed and glanced around. Black coaches lined the street. Horses draped in black velvet pawed the ground and munched from feed bags. Footmen and coachmen, all liveried in black, stiffly maintained their positions, eyes forward and shoulders straight, prepared to whisk their employers away from the grim occasion.

None of it seemed quite real to her, and she felt as if this were some sort of macabre social ritual rather than

the result of personal tragedy. Other than the intona-
tions of the archbishop, there was nothing here to tie
the graces to the gathering. It was at Westbrook Court
that she felt her loss the most, the hollowness of knowing there were spaces in their lives that would forever
remain empty. That was the worst of it, knowing that
even hope was gone that someday, she would hear her
father voice approval or love. She knew, from the far-
away look that occasionally crept into her brother's
eyes that he, too, regretted opportunities that no longer
existed.

All that was left now was a feeling of profound
change in the air. Change that seemed to affect Max
most of all. Max, with whom she and Damien had
shared so much over the years had withdrawn from
them, sharing nothing but his presence. His thoughts remained closed and private as did his grief.

Jillian's chest tightened with apprehension as an
auburn-haired gentleman with a veiled lady clinging to
each arm walked toward them. She glanced at Max,
waiting for the glacial stare he bestowed on anyone
who dared approach him. It stunned her to see him nod
his head, to hear his voice warm with greeting.

"Bruce, it is good to see you."

"I thought you might appreciate a friendly face," the
gentleman said.

Jillian glanced at the man who had received the first
civil words Max had spoken outside the family, and
wondered who he was as she peered at him through the
distortion of her veil. Vaguely, she recognized that he
was handsome and rather tall, but she could not summon up enough energy to really look at him. As for the
two women, it was impossible to distinguish their features through the layers of netting shrouding their faces,
beyond that they were tall and slender.

"Bruce," one of the women prompted in a soft, trembling voice.

The man frowned slightly and stared down at the
woman on his left. "Max, allow me to present my

mother, Lady Blackwood and my sister, Lady Kathleen," he said.

"Lady Blackwood, Kathleen," Max said nodding toward each in turn. "Bruce speaks of you often."

The two women murmured polite, yet oddly strained, greetings.

Max turned to Jillian and introduced her to Bruce Palmerston, Viscount Channing, and his family.

"I am very sorry about your fathers," Lady Blackwood whispered, and leaned heavily into her son.

"Please excuse us. As you can see my mother is unwell," the viscount said, his brow furrowed in obvious concern.

"Then I am doubly grateful for your presence here, countess," Max said with rigid formality. "I'm sorry our first meeting is under such grim circumstances."

She leaned forward slightly, her hand fluttering up, and down again as if she had wanted to touch Max and thought better of it. "You are like your father," she said softly, then clutched her son's arm.

Max stiffened and said nothing as Bruce quickly guided his mother and sister toward the line of coaches.

Jillian frowned as she watched the small group walk away, puzzled at the way Max's gaze seemed to intensify on the Palmerstons. His manner with Bruce had been familiar, as if they were more than mere acquaintances. "He is your friend," she stated, as much to herself as to Max. It hadn't occurred to her before—that there were parts of Max's and Damien's lives that she was not privy to.

"Yes," Max said.

"He is the one you and Damien spoke of."

"Yes."

"You've known him for a long time then?"

"We were at university together."

"Yet, you hadn't met his family until today?" she persisted.

"No, I hadn't."

"Why not? Apparently the countess knew the graces."

"Didn't everyone?"

"Is her husband dead?"

"In a sense."

Why hadn't she noticed before how closely Max guarded his words? She folded her arms and glared up at him. "Max! I know you are capable of speaking more than one word at a time. I insist you do so."

He turned to her with a bemused smile and cocked his brow. "You're not going to stop the questions are you?"

"No." She beamed up at him, seeing for the first time since the graces had died the old, familiar Max. *Her* Max.

"All right, Pandora. I may as well. You'll hear it soon enough once you are out in society." He took a deep breath as if he were preparing to deliver a speech and began to recite a string of facts. "Bruce Palmerston, Viscount Channing, is the heir of the Earl of Blackwood. His mother and father are estranged. The earl has lived abroad for over a decade. He had no contact with his family—an arrangement that apparently suits everyone."

"I see," she said. And she did see all too clearly. No wonder Max had responded to Viscount Channing. They had much in common. "But, the countess is ill. Surely, their differences should be cast aside at such a time."

Max smiled. "Ah, Pandora, such idealism. Differences *can* be cast aside. Indifference is another matter entirely."

Jillian folded her arms over her waist, feeling chilled by Max's mockery and cynicism. It distressed her to think he would know so much about indifference.

"I believe we can make a graceful exit now," LadyLou said as she and Damien joined them. Jillian's aunt looked weary, her thick black hair more prominently silvered, the lines fanning out from her blue eyes more pronounced, her slim body seeming smaller than ever.

Jillian sighed in relief as Damien assisted her and LadyLou into the coach. But, before Damien and Max could climb in behind them, an elderly gentleman she recognized as her father's solicitor called out and hurried toward them. His expression solemn, he doffed his hat and performed a hasty bow.

"Allow me to extend my heartfelt sympathy, Your Grace . . . um . . . and Your Grace . . . ," he said, his gaze flicking from Damien to Max and back again, his face flushed in obvious embarrassment. "Forgive me. It is quite disconcerting to address two dukes at the same time."

Jillian watched Damien and Max accept the man's comments, both standing tall in their formal black attire, Max golden and broadly muscular and Damien dark and powerfully sleek, each commanding in his presence. The proceedings of the day suddenly took on new significance—something she had not comprehended until this moment.

Max and Damien were now the graces, and they were magnificent.

Chapter 6

London, Spring 1818

"**G**od, Jillie you weigh a ton," Damien groaned as he tugged on Jillian's arms in an effort to dislodge her from her seat in the carriage. "You could at least put forth a little effort."

"I am trying, but my foot is caught in this bloody hoop."

"Jillian!" LadyLou gasped.

"I will excuse your language," Damien said as he released her arms and shoved aside the voluminous skirt and hoops tangled about her legs and searched for her feet. "I realize your court presentation was a trying experience."

"You have no idea," Jillian muttered as her brother freed her slipper and proceeded to pry her from the carriage. Her headdress caught on the top of the carriage door, and an ostrich feather floated down to her feet. As soon as Damien set her down, she deliberately ground it under her heel. She hoped she never saw another ostrich feather in her life.

Taking extreme care to keep her ankles from showing, she lifted her skirts a scant inch and trudged up the front steps of the London house, leaving Damien and LadyLou behind.

She could not wait to change. If court protocol had not had to be obeyed to the letter, nothing could have induced her to garb herself in the hideous costume.

The high-waisted, white brocade gown was a nightmare of spangles and hoops and lace and dainty rosebud trim. Dainty rosebud trim complemented dainty bosoms wonderfully. Her bosoms were not dainty. She did not need them outlined in roses.

Her only comfort was that she doubted anyone noticed for the assorted bracelets and necklaces and broaches adorning her person. Again court protocol required that she wear as much jewelry as she could find places on her body to stick it, loop it, or hang it.

As soon as the footman opened the door, she brushed past him and headed directly for the stairs. She would have liked to run, but that particular habit had been drilled out of her during the past year. There had been precious little to do but refine her comportment while sequestered in mourning.

It had been a strange time, and their lives had changed even as they slowly returned to normal. Their fathers were gone, yet the only difference seemed to be in the finality of it. She and Damien no longer awaited word of their father's impending arrivals. Max appeared not to notice the difference at all. The most notable difference was in the ease with which she had ceased to think of their fathers as the graces. Since the day of the funeral a year ago, Max and Damien had irrevocably become synonymous with their titles. If nothing else, their fathers had prepared their sons well—

"Good God, Pandora, is it you?"

Mortified, she stopped in her tracks as she looked up to see Max in the doorway to the study. "Yes, I am in here somewhere," she said glumly as her heart sank to her feet.

The day only lacked this. If she had known that Max would return three days early from Bassett House, she would have used the servants's entrance. She looked a horror and he was breathtakingly handsome in his buckskins and coat of blue superfine molded over a body grown more muscular and defined in the past year. There were other changes, too. His hair had taken on a more burnished sheen and his sapphire eyes seemed clearer, sharper, more discerning. The sculpted planes of his face had become more refined, more arresting.

She wondered if she looked different. When she looked in the mirror all she saw was black hair and green eyes—nothing remarkable unless she was literally dressed to her eyebrows, she thought, acutely aware of Max's continued scrutiny.

A year ago, it would not have mattered if Max saw her dressed this way. She would have run to him and hurled herself into his arms with carefree abandon regardless of her appearance. But that was a year ago, and everything had changed.

She was in love with Max and she hated it.

For the past year, she had suffered agonies trying to understand how she could suddenly be "in" love with a man she had always loved.

The feelings his touch had awakened in her the day he'd braided her hair had intensified into a constant yearning, producing an ache in her heart that was pleasure when Max was near and pain when he was not.

"Do stop staring, Max," she warned. The amusement

in his eyes as he took in her costume devastated her. He had not seen her in a fortnight and all he could do was laugh at her.

"He can't, Jillie," Damien chuckled as he and LadyLou stepped into the entry hall. "Your display of all the Westbrook jewels is rather stunning."

"Actually, I had not noticed the jewelry," Max said, his mouth twitching with suppressed laughter. "I cannot seem to get past that flowered and feathered abomination on her head."

"Do not remind me," she said, wishing with all her heart that she were wearing one of the gowns the modiste had fashioned according to her specifications. Perhaps, then, Max would not find her appearance so laughable. She forced herself to smile, forced herself to respond in a familiar way. "Oh, Max you should have seen all the ladies waiting to make their curtsy. We all looked like great, fat bejeweled birds in our hoops and ostrich plumes."

Jillian started as a bark of laughter echoed through the room. A man appeared in the shadows behind Max, his height and breadth close enough to Max's that he seemed like Max's shadow.

Max glanced over his shoulder. "Oh Bruce, I apologize. I quite forgot about you."

"So did I," Damien admitted. "My apologies for being tardy. I hope you haven't been waiting long."

Jillian had an overwhelming urge to cosh her brother on the head. Why had he not told her Max was coming today? As for their additional guest—what was one more humiliation? When the stranger stepped into the light, she realized it was one humiliation too many.

"Jillian, you remember Viscount Channing do you not?" Max said.

"Of course I remember," she said. How could she forget the only man Max had been civil to at the funeral, nor could she forget how her curiosity about him had drawn Max out. She did not, however, remember his formidable stature or the way he filled out his coat.

Nor did she remember that he was handsome in the extreme, with rich, shining, auburn hair, and striking blue eyes that spoke volumes. If he had smiled that day, she most certainly would have remembered the air of mischief it imparted. She liked him for that mischief.

"It is a pleasure to see you again, my Lord," she said, summoning what pride she had left. "Please forgive my appearance. As you have no doubt guessed, I have just returned from my court presentation."

"So I gathered," Bruce said. "And how did you find Prinny?"

Jillian gave her answer careful consideration. Simpering seemed to be in order, but she could not bring herself to do it with this man. She had a feeling he appreciated honesty. But more importantly, she did not want Max to see her presenting herself as a brainless twit.

"Suffocating in his corset, my Lord."

LadyLou paled. "Jillian, you should not speak of the Prince in such a disrespectful manner."

"I am sure it was a mere slip of the tongue," Damien said.

Max stared at her thoughtfully, a hint of disapproval darkening his eyes. "Actually, I believe it was more a slip of her *willful* tongue." He sent Bruce a meaningful look. "Jillian has not yet grown out of the habit of speaking her mind."

"Or perhaps, it is a habit that I have finally grown into," Jillian retorted. His tone infuriated her. He spoke of her as if she were still a toothless child.

"And one that suits you admirably," Bruce said, his blue-gray eyes gleaming with amusement. Without taking his gaze from Jillian, he addressed LadyLou. "Lady Forbes, I have not yet responded to your invitation to attend Lady Jillian's ball next week. I would very much like to come."

"We will be pleased to have you in attendance, Lord Channing," LadyLou said.

"How extraordinary," Damien said with a thoughtful

frown. "I cannot recall the last time any of us attended a come-out."

"I can," Max said in a bored tone. "When the young lady made her grand entrance, her mama had the butler read her list of family connections and announce the size of her dowry. He droned on for half an hour or so."

"How terrible," Jillian said, her anxiety about making her own entrance multiplying tenfold. She shuddered at the prospect of being put on display and judged on nothing more than her money and bloodline. But, to have it publicly declared was too awful to contemplate. "The poor thing must have nearly expired from the humiliation."

"Did LadyLou not tell you, Jillie?" Max asked, his tone serious. "It is common practice, otherwise how are potential suitors to know if they should ask a lady to dance?"

"Stop teasing her, Max," LadyLou said. "She is nervous enough as it is."

Jillian sucked in her breath. How could she have been so gullible; no matter how briefly? Why was Max deliberately trying to humiliate her? In ten minutes time he had twice made her feel like a green girl. She might be green, but she was no girl, and it was high time he noticed. She resisted the urge to glare at him and smiled instead, determined to hide her discomfiture. "Sort of like putting a horse on the auction block?"

"That is how all the best horses are presented," he said with a smile. A slow, lazy smile, his sapphire eyes so eloquent with affection that her heart twisted in delight and ... anguish. She realized then that the problem was with her. Max was the same. His feelings were the same. He had not meant to embarrass her, but was merely indulging in their usual tomfoolery.

She knew she had to behave as if she hadn't changed or risk embarrassing them all. "Well this particular mare has no intention of making a grand entrance, unless of course a certain light bay stallion she is acquainted with should like to accompany her."

The smile on Max's face abruptly disappeared. His brows shot up, and his mouth opened as if he were going to speak, then clamped shut as his gaze jerked away from her.

Jillian inhaled sharply. She was not sure how she had done it, but she had finally managed to shake Max's composure, and it felt so very good. A bubble of laughter escaped her as she proudly glanced around at her audience.

LadyLou looked horrified.

Damien looked appalled.

And Viscount Channing looked as if he might explode into laughter at any moment. What had she said? It seemed obvious that she had committed a *faux pas,* yet she failed to see how. An ostrich feather floated past her eyes, reminding her that she was still wearing the hideous court costume. As Max continued to avoid her gaze, she wondered if the day could get any worse.

"Jillian, I believe it is time we allowed the gentlemen to get on with their meeting," LadyLou said, her voice halfway between a croak and a squeak. "And you must change for your dancing lesson."

Jillian seized upon the topic LadyLou provided. "Do you think it possible to cancel today?" she said in a tumble of words. "I cannot bear to waltz with Mr. Miller. He grows red in the face and stiff as a poker whenever we try."

Viscount Channing grinned and stared up at the ceiling.

LadyLou blinked.

Damien's mouth dropped open.

A deep frown creased Max's forehead.

Caught between frustration and embarrassment, Jillian lowered her gaze to the floor and kept it there. Apparently she'd done it again, though she still didn't know what she'd done. Perhaps she should give up speaking altogether. Perhaps it was the dress. How could anyone take her seriously when she looked like a fool?

"Oh dear," LadyLou finally managed. "I had not realized—"

"I believe it would be prudent to engage a new dance master," Damien said.

"Yes," LadyLou agreed. "I will send a note at once. Gentlemen, if you will excuse us." She touched Jillian's arm. "Come along dear."

"Gentlemen, shall we repair to my study?" Damien said.

Relieved that Damien and LadyLou had dismissed the matter so adroitly, Jillian remained rooted, listening to the sound of their boot heels clicking on the tile floor. She had no intention of making her exit until after the men made theirs. At the rate she was going, she would trip on her way out.

"It was a pleasure seeing you again, Lady Jillian," Bruce said in a smooth, deep voice.

Why had he not gone away with Max and Damien? Cheeks burning, she forced herself to meet his gaze.

"I look forward to attending your ball." He smiled as he grasped her hand and slowly raised it to his lips to gallantly kiss the air a proper half inch above her glove. Then, he backed away and gave her an audacious wink. "Perhaps you will save me a waltz."

Chapter 7

Perhaps you will save me a waltz.
    Yesterday, Viscount Channing had restored Jillian's frayed dignity and set her world to rights with those simple words. And he had looked at her—really

looked at her—as if he saw more than black hair and green eyes, as if he saw a woman rather than a girl.

If only Max would do the same.

Jillian stood in the empty ballroom, and wrapped her arms around herself as she imagined how the room would look in a week's time, filled with guests and music and flowers, how the candles in the crystal chandeliers would reflect in the mirrors on the walls and in the polished surface of the floor. She closed her eyes and wondered how it would feel to whirl around the ballroom in Max's arms . . .

"May I have this dance, my Lady?" she said in a husky voice as she sketched a bow, just as she'd seen Max do.

"You may have all my dances," she replied to the Max in her daydream. She curtsied deeply and lifted her hands in the air, fitting them to her vision of Max's height, the width of his shoulders. Lilting music floated through the air as she hummed a waltz and moved in slow circles about the room, executing the steps perfectly.

The lace-trimmed skirt of her lavender lawn dress fanned out around her as she whirled faster and faster, becoming lost in the dance and the images in her mind of Max smiling at her and telling her how beautiful she looked and how wonderfully she waltzed and—

A voice intruded into her fantasy. A real voice.

"Our Jillie is growing up, Max," Damien said with amusement. "She has progressed from pretend tea parties to dancing with imaginary partners."

"So I see," Max said.

She had been caught again.

Jillian stumbled and swayed on her feet and her hands dropped and pressed out at nothing more substantial than air to regain her balance. The room stopped spinning and her gaze focused on Damien and Max. How long had they been watching? Had she said Max's name aloud? He must think her a child.

"And what do you celebrate today, Pandora?" Max asked, his eyes gleaming with amused indulgence.

Why couldn't he look at her as Bruce had?

She drew herself up and thrust her chin in the air. "My ball actually. I was practicing my dance steps." She slanted a glance at Damien. "As you know I am without a dance master."

Max smiled and arched his brows. "Then I suppose it is left up to Damien and me to see that you do not disgrace yourself at your come-out."

"It did not look to me as if she needs further instruction," Damien said.

"It's a tricky thing, dancing with real men instead of air," Max said.

Blast them, Jillian thought, annoyed beyond measure at such condescension. They were speaking around her as if *she* were made of air. Didn't they see? Didn't they understand? If she were old enough to dance with real men, then she must be a real woman.

She drew herself to her full, lamentably inconsiderable height and clasped her hands behind her back, fully aware that the pose thrust out her bosom and pulled in her waist.

"Actually, you are correct, Damien. I don't require further lessons," she said. "Mr. Miller instructed me most thoroughly before he began to have such strange fits. I do hope he sees a doctor for his complaint."

Max snorted. Damien rolled his gaze to the ceiling.

She refused to ask what amused them so. She absolutely refused to care. "If you will excuse me, I shall leave you gentlemen to find other entertainment. LadyLou will be returning from her errands at any moment and we are expecting guests."

"Oh really," Damien said. "Who?"

Jillian wrinkled her nose. "Lady Arabella Seymour and her daughter, Melissa."

"Ye Gods, why the devil would LadyLou accept a call from them?" Damien said.

Jillian shrugged. "LadyLou only receives her when she is too embarrassed to return another card."

"Ah, yes, the calling ritual," Damien said. "She leaves her card and LadyLou answers with a card and so on and so forth until LadyLou caves in."

"Precisely," Jillian said. "It is all rather silly if you ask me. Receiving them would not be so bad if Lady Seymour gave me a chance to get to know Melissa."

"Ah yes, Melissa," Max said.

"You know her?" Jillian asked.

"Good God, no."

"Arabella spent the entire season before the graces died reminding us at every opportunity that her darling Melissa was making her bow," Damien explained.

"You have her name wrong, Damien," Max corrected. "It's Melissa, Darling."

Jillian stifled a giggle at their mockery of Lady Seymour. But she also felt a curious prickle of apprehension along her spine. Of course they would know the beautiful Lady Seymour, but they had not yet been introduced to Melissa since she had made her bow while they were in mourning.

They were in for a shock. Melissa was all pink roses and English cream. Blessed with high, finely molded cheekbones, china-blue eyes framed with dark, arched brows and an abundance of sun-gold hair, she was a true classic beauty in every way. Jillian was ashamed to admit it, but she was not in a great hurry for Max and Melissa to meet. Still, she had to find out sooner or later if Max liked pink roses and English cream.

"Will you join us?" she asked.

"Not on your life, Pandora," Max said. "Arabella Seymour rubs me the wrong way."

"It's a talent of hers," Jillian said as she turned and left the room, both disappointed and relieved that Max would not be present. Lady Seymour had a knack for shedding unfavorable light on her while enhancing the image of her daughter.

She hurried up the stairs, calling for Clancy as she

went. She would wear one of her new gowns. The deep rose would do nicely and was as close to the accepted pastels that looked so ghastly on her. Since she had promised LadyLou that she would closely guard her tongue and her manners when in Lady Seymour's company, she would give the woman as little excuse as possible to criticize her.

"Lady Jillian," Jacobs, their London butler, said as she crossed the entry hall after changing her gown. "The Seymours have arrived and Lady Louise has not yet returned from her errands."

"Oh dear," she muttered, then grinned with a sudden thought. Without LadyLou, she would be free to match Lady Seymour insult for insult. What LadyLou didn't know wouldn't hurt her, Jillian thought. It really was too bad she had a conscience. "Are the graces still here?" she asked, resigned to being cordial.

"Yes my Lady, the *dukes* are still in the ball room."

Jillian grinned at his subtle correction. "Show Lady Seymour and Lady Melissa to the drawing room and tell them I will be there shortly." She stepped past the butler and paused, "Jacobs, would you please have tea and cakes sent in?"

"Yes, my Lady," he said, frowning at the odd request. Refreshments were never served during a call. But Jillian hoped that Lady Seymour would not be able to talk so much if her mouth were full.

By the time Jillian arrived at the ballroom she felt as if she had been running for miles. Max and Damien stood in the center of the dance floor speaking in low tones as Max scribbled madly on a piece of paper. Taking the paper, Damien smiled broadly and nodded his head as Max swept his hand through the air in a wide arc.

"Excuse me," she called out politely.

They both started at the sound of her voice. Damien quickly folded the paper and stuffed it in his breast pocket.

"Lady Seymour and Melissa have arrived, and LadyLou is not here. I'm afraid you will have to do me the favor of making an appearance after all."

"That is not a favor," Damien said. "That is a sacrifice."

"How well I know it," Jillian said. "But I refuse to be sacrificed on the altar of the morning call alone."

"Can't say that I blame you," Damien said. "Damned woman drips venom."

Max scowled at Jillian. "Does Arabella sharpen her fangs on you?"

She rolled her eyes. "What do you think Max?"

A smile played about the corners of his mouth. "So, we are to play the gallant defenders."

"You begin to understand."

"And whom shall we defend, Pandora? You or Arabella?"

"Me, unfortunately," Jillian said. "LadyLou made me promise to play the sweetly silent ingenue."

Max chuckled. "I believe we have just found our new entertainment." He offered her his arm. "Shall we go?"

"If we must," Damien said and flanked Jillian on her other side. "Once again the Forbes' and Hastings' join forces to guard one another's backs."

Three abreast, they reached the drawing room. Max separated from them as Damien opened the doors and ushered Jillian in.

"Good afternoon ladies," Damien said, smoothly.

Lady Seymour smiled radiantly. In fact, Jillian had never seen her look so pleased. She did not spare Jillian a glance as she addressed Damien and then Max. "Your Grace . . . Your Grace . . . what an honor," she said in a breathy, triumphant voice. "It has been too long since we've seen you in society. I don't believe you've met my daughter. She made her bow while you were out of circulation."

Melissa rose and, unlike her mother, acknowledged Jillian with a smile as the introductions were made.

Jillian watched in fascination as Melissa executed a perfect curtsy and murmured a shy greeting to each man in a sweet, musical voice. How very perfect Melissa's demeanor was. Even her flush was a lovely petal-pink wash that enhanced her coloring. How on earth, Jillian wondered, did one control one's own blush? And how did one manage such a dewy shine in one's eyes?

"A pleasure, Lady Melissa," Damien said, his gaze skimming over her, then moving on.

"Yes, a pleasure." Max echoed Damien both in word and action, then tucked Jillian's hand in the crook of his elbow to saunter toward the settee.

She lowered her head, to hide her smug smile and resisted the urge to skip. Max didn't appear to be impressed by English roses and cream. In fact, Melissa could be invisible for all the notice Max—and even Damien—took of her.

Unfortunately, their lack of interest was obvious enough to catch Lady Seymour's attention, and her ire. She aimed a sharp look at Jillian.

Max made an elaborate show of seeing Jillian settled before taking a place beside her.

Lady Seymour watched him carefully. "My darling Melissa and I were discussing Jillian's ball before you joined us."

"Really," Damien said, his gaze bouncing off Melissa and landing on his nails, as if his manicure held more interest for him.

"Yes. Do you not agree that all the gentlemen will find it difficult to decide between Jillian and Melissa."

Jillian almost gasped aloud at Lady Seymour's blatant solicitation of a compliment for her daughter, and she wondered if that was the reason Melissa never looked directly at anyone.

Even Damien seemed taken aback as his expression changed subtly. "Yes it will," he said in a tone Jillian recognized as compassion. She felt it, too and wondered how a woman who looked as youthful and blondly pure as her daughter could be so ugly under the skin.

Lady Seymour must be a weighty cross for Melissa to bear.

"It is all so exciting," Lady Seymour began only to be interrupted by a sharp rap on the door. A footman entered carrying the tray Jillian requested.

"How thoughtful, your Grace," Lady Seymour gushed. "I should have known you would remember my sweet tooth."

"Thank my sister," Damien said dryly.

"Yes," Max said, "Jillian has a fondness for tea parties."

Jillian flashed him a grin.

The warmth Lady Seymour had shown Damien froze into a tight smile. "This was your idea, Jillian? How nice . . . though I do prefer coffee." She sighed wearily. "Oh well, tea will have to do."

Jillian reached for the silver server. "Cream and sugar?"

"Just lemon, dear."

Naturally, Jillian thought. Lady Seymour probably had one with each meal. After serving Lady Seymour, she turned to Melissa. "Tea, Melissa?"

"I would love a cup of tea, Jillian," she said quietly. "And it was very thoughtful of you." Jillian wanted to stand up and cheer. It was the first time in their short acquaintance that she had seen Melissa show any spirit.

"I believe I have already made that point, Melissa darling," Lady Seymour said frostily. Melissa sagged like a cushion that had lost its stuffing.

"Max, what will you take in your tea?" Jillian said.

"Tea?" he said.

"Perhaps you would prefer port instead," Damien suggested, then added under his breath, "I know I could use one."

"Allow me." Jillian rose and went to the low table that held crystal decanters of liquor. Changing her mind, she poured them both liberal glasses of whiskey. They deserved something more substantial.

Damien winked at her as she delivered his drink. "A far wiser choice, Jillie."

"Bless you," Max murmured as she returned to her place beside him. As soon as the glass was in his hand he raised it to his lips and drained half the liquid. His face contorted as the fiery substance slid down his unprepared throat.

Damien chuckled. "Don't you know whiskey from port, Max? Even the glasses are different."

Jillian's hand reached out to grasp his knee. "Oh, Max I am sorry."

His hand shot out and clasped around hers. "It's quite all right, Pandora," he rasped. "I should have expected mischief from you."

Jillian smiled. "Ah, so you know you deserve it," she shot back. Though she hadn't intended mischief, it pleased her to catch Max unaware. It happened so rarely.

"Pandora?" Lady Seymour said.

"A pet name," Damien answered.

"How quaint. I suppose there is a story behind it," she said with obvious distaste.

"Yes," Max said enigmatically.

"I'm intrigued," Lady Seymour said. "Really, you must share the tale with us."

"I don't think so," Max said pleasantly.

Damien shot a warning glance at Max and stepped smoothly into the breach. "Jillian has always had a fascination for myths."

"Ah, and since her aunt is an admitted bluestocking, it seems only natural that Jillian would follow suit. Melissa, on the other hand has devoted her time to learning the gentler arts suitable to a wife and mother."

"I assure you, Arabella, that Jillian is not lacking in the gentler arts," Damien said.

"Yes of course. And I'm sure offers for her hand will be adequate, given her enormous dowry and her brother's status as one of the most powerful dukes in England," she said, her gaze fixed on Jillian.

Adequate. Jillian's fingers dug into her palm, and the sweet memory of Max's touch withered from the sudden chill in her fingers.

"I should say they will be more than adequate," he returned as he pointedly glanced at Lady Seymour. "Jillian's dark beauty will be a refreshing change from the blonds that are so fashionable at the moment."

Jillian struggled to maintain her composure. He had complimented her. He thought she had dark beauty. It sounded wonderful. Did he really mean it?

"Her looks are ... ah ... certainly unique," Lady Seymour replied slyly. "But you surprise me, your Grace. Generally, you prefer the familiar to the exotic."

Exotic. Jillian rather liked the sound of that. It went rather well with dark beauty.

"I wasn't aware that you were privy to my tastes, Arabella," Max said.

Lady Seymour stared at them coldly. "You are very close to his Grace, aren't you, dear? Dare I surmise that an arrangement has been made? It would certainly explain your familiarity."

The muscles in Damien's jaw clenched as his gaze flickered over Max and Jillian.

Max stiffened.

"An arrangement?" Jillian parroted, too confused by the sudden change in Max and Damien to grasp the implications of the comment. There were always implications in the witch's conversation.

"Marriage, dear."

Jillian's breath seemed to freeze in her throat. Marriage? To Max? How frightening. How wonderful. Her gaze shot to her brother. She did not dare look at Max. She could not bear it if he were finding amusement at the prospect.

The tension eased as Damien laughed. "What—and ruin a beautiful friendship?" He shook his head. "Our families have watched one another's backs for centuries, and we have had the good sense to keep marriage contracts out of it."

Warming to the possibility, Jillian had an urge to ask why the idea was so absurd. Marriage to Max seemed the height of good sense.

Lady Seymour smiled. "Yes, I see what you mean. Loyalty and marriage so seldom mix."

"Mother, how can you say so?" Melissa asked. "You and father were devoted to one another."

"We were the exception, Melissa darling," Lady Seymour said as she patted her daughter's hand.

"I, too, shall marry for love," Melissa announced.

Lady Seymour gave an aggrieved sigh. "I wish that for you, but still you must be cognizant of the realities."

Realities? Jillian held her breath as she leaned forward, for once, wanting to hear what the countess had to say. But Lady Seymour seemed content to sip her tea and nibble at a cake from the tray.

Damien cleared his throat and shot up from his chair to refresh his drink.

Impatient with the sudden lull in what she considered to be a very important conversation, Jillian wondered if she and Melissa were supposed to guess the nature of such realities? The only reality Jillian was certain of was that she, too, wanted to marry the person she loved. She wanted to marry Max. It was all so simple, and so very complicated.

She wanted desperately to look at him, to see his expression. There was a stillness about him that disturbed her. She could feel the tension surrounding him, see it in the tightness of his thighs and the rigid control he seemed to be exerting. Was the idea of a marriage between them so inconceivable to him? Or perhaps he was simply angry with Arabella. He'd made it quite clear that he had no liking for her. Of course. That had to be it.

The doors flew open and LadyLou bustled into the room on a wave of navy blue taffeta and profuse apologies. As she settled into a chair, Max rose to his feet.

"Damien, I have an appointment later this afternoon, and we still have business to discuss. Ladies, if you will excuse us . . . ?"

"Yes, of course, Max," Damien replied and drained his glass in one swallow. "Arabella, Lady Melissa, I expect our paths will cross during the season."

Just that quickly Damien and Max were gone. Max hadn't been able to leave the room fast enough. She had to believe that Lady Seymour rather than the subject of marriage drove him away.

"Goddamn Arabella Seymour," Max said as he firmly closed the door of the study behind him. "We should have kept Jillian in the bloody country."

"Things had to change, Max." With a heavy sigh, Damien sat down behind his desk. "Arabella only spoke aloud what others will whisper. Until now, we've refused to recognize it."

"Let them whisper," Max said, pacing the length of Damien's study. "After a time they will all come to realize that Jillian is like a sister to me."

"No, they won't," Damien said softly. "If they don't, as Arabella so delicately phrased it, 'assume there is an arrangement', they will view your relationship with Jillian as something sordid." He steepled his fingers, his gaze tracking Max across the floor. "You do have a certain reputation. Your attraction to widows and discontented wives has labelled you a rake."

"So speaks Saint Damien. Your fondness for opera singers and actresses is legend."

Damien shook his head. "Regardless of our differences in taste, my reputation will not affect Jillian. There are too many like Arabella who feed off innocents for breakfast and spit them out before luncheon. The ton is fond of making matches where none exist. More than one marriage has been made that way, and as much as I value our friendship, I could not and would not countenance a match between you and my sister."

"God forbid," Max said, silently cursing the "public," and how its appetite for scandal had the power to change his life. "As much as it galls me to admit it, you are right." He halted by the window and propped his arm on the frame, stroking his chin with his fist. "You needn't worry, Damien. Jillian deserves some young pup whose ideals match hers, and when the time comes I will wed someone with a respectable fortune and name who will expect the same things from marriage that I do." Abruptly, he strode toward the door. He'd had enough of this.

"And what do you expect?"

Max paused with his hand on the knob. "Aside from the requisite heir, nothing."

"The tragedy is that I know you are serious," Damien said wearily.

"Never doubt it. And I shall make every effort to see that the ton doesn't doubt it as well."

Damien leaned back in his chair. "No doubt you will." He held up the rough sketch Max had made an hour ago. "I'll have this taken care of."

Max paused and glanced over his shoulder at the drawing. A gift for Jillian at her come-out. The idea had come to him when he had seen her dancing alone in the ballroom with an imaginary partner. He had thought to make her smile and just for one night allow her to believe that pretend things could become real. Perhaps for just one night, he wanted to forget that reality would be just as vicious for Jillian as it was for the rest of mankind.

Chapter 8

"Jillian, the guests will be arriving soon. Are you sure you do not wish to make a grand entrance?" LadyLou asked.

"Quite sure," Jillian said. "I have no desire to embarrass you by tripping over my feet."

"I am certain that would not happen."

Jillian was not certain of anything anymore. She had been trying very hard not to think about Lady Seymour's comments of a week ago. It shouldn't have been that difficult since no one had been around to remind her. Damien seemed preoccupied. She hadn't seen Max at all.

But she would see him tonight. And he would see her. They would waltz and exchange witty repartee, and he would realize that Lady Seymour's comments weren't so absurd after all.

"May I look now, please?" she asked, staring at the linen-draped mirror.

"Not yet," LadyLou said as she turned to the maid. "Clancy, the pearls."

Jillian groaned. The anticipation was unbearable. LadyLou and Damien were torturing her with all their secrets and high drama. She was banished from the ballroom, and for three days workers had scurried in and out with a lot of fuss and bother. She could have slipped in any number of times, but she hated to spoil Damien's surprise.

The final frustration was in having LadyLou and

Clancy tugging and tweaking her and she couldn't even see what they were doing. It was so ridiculous. She knew what she looked like and she'd seen her gown at least half a dozen times. But the ritual seemed important to LadyLou, so she stifled her rather childish urge to stomp her foot in protest.

"You may look now," LadyLou said.

"I feel like a statue that is about to be unveiled." Jillian sucked in her breath as Clancy slowly lifted the cloth from the glass. "I—" she broke off, unable to finish as her attention fastened on her full-length reflection.

She looked like someone else. Someone whose eyes flashed a brilliant emerald green. The black slashes of her brows that marked her a born-and-bred Forbes had never seemed more dramatic. Her inky hair was swept away from her face and pulled into a simple chignon. The neckline of her ivory silk gown framed a long neck with a wide portrait collar that skimmed her shoulders and fell over the tops of her arms. As she had hoped, the bodice fit to the midriff, drawing attention from her generous bosom and defining her small waist. Free of any embellishment, the gown flowed to the floor in soft, wispy folds.

"Is that me?" she whispered.

"Yes, Lady Jillian, it is you," LadyLou said softly.

Lady Jillian. The woman in the looking glass was a lady—the most elegant looking creature Jillian had ever beheld. A lady who knew how to execute a perfect throne-room curtsy and how to peek over her fan and dance gracefully.

Jillian could only hope that she would live up to the image in front of her—a reflection of all that she wanted to be.

If only the reflection could step out of the mirror and become a part of her, present to the whole world the illusion of Lady Jillian rather than plain Jillie. She was almost glad that she hadn't seen Max in over a week. She wanted to look as new to him as she did to herself.

Perhaps he would experience the same sense of magic that she felt at this moment.

Jillian slipped her arm around LadyLou's waist, careful not to crush the bronze silk of her aunt's gown. "Did I ever thank you for making me spend countless hours walking around with a book on my head?"

"No," LadyLou said as she brushed Jillian's cheek with the back of her hand. "But you have now, and you're very welcome." She stepped back and gave Jillian a gentle nudge toward the door. "Along with you. Damien is waiting for you. I will come shortly."

"And Max," Jillian added, her heart turning over at the thought.

"Yes," LadyLou agreed. "And Max as well."

The corridor to the ballroom had never seemed so long, but she supposed that it always took a long time to journey into the future. Jillian walked at a sedate pace, occasionally glancing down at her gown and the way it drifted with every movement, savoring her excitement and anticipation, committing the feelings to memory.

Her brother stood at the entrance to the ballroom, the doors closed behind him, his expectant smile fading to bemusement as his gaze swept over her from head to foot, silently inspecting her as if he'd never seen her before. Seconds passed and still all he did was look at her.

"Blast it, Damien, say something."

He nodded his head. "You will do."

"Is that all you have to say? Do I not look like a different person?"

"No, you look like Jillie in a pretty dress. The hair is nice. You were right to not curl it. You would look silly with all that fluff hanging about your face." He straightened his coat. "How do I look?"

Many things came to mind: dashing in his formal black evening attire; dangerous with his jet-black hair and deep green eyes; handsome with his straight blade of a nose and aristocratic carriage. Of course she had no intention of telling him that. "You will do," she said, nodding her head as he had done.

Damien chuckled. "Then I suggest we see if the ballroom will do us both justice."

"Oh yes," Jillian said. "I am most anxious to know what all those workers were building."

"Come and see for yourself," Damien said and pushed open the doors.

Jillian gasped. The center of the ballroom was covered by a massive canopy of white latticework twined with roses and supported by four ivy-covered pillars. Openings had been left in the top to accommodate a chandelier that glittered like a brilliant sun.

"Max and I stepped through the portals of a gazebo to enter your world," Damien said, his voice suddenly thick. "We thought it appropriate that you enter our world in the same way."

Emotion swelled in her throat and burned behind her eyes. "You and Max did this for me." It was not a question, but rather a simple statement, an acknowledgment of memories that would never disappear, of bonds that could not be broken. It reassured her as nothing else could that Max was still hers.

"Oh now, do not get weepy," Damien said. "You will ruin your face and no one will ask you to dance and I will be forced to take the floor with you every time to keep you from being a wallflower."

She blinked back the tears and gave her brother a weak smile. "You won't have to. Max can relieve you every other turn. You know I have permission to waltz."

"No, he can't, Jillie. You know the rules. You are only allowed two dances with any gentleman."

"But Max is not just any gentleman," she protested. "He is family."

Damien shook his head. "To us, he is like family, but society views him as—"

"What do you mean *like* family?" Jillian interrupted. "How can you say such a thing? He is part of us. He should be here now." She glanced about in panic, feeling as if something very precious were slipping away from her. "Where is he?"

"I did not wish him to be here for this discussion," he ground out, then his voice softened.

"Jillie, listen to me. Max is *not* family. Tonight you must not display any favoritism toward him."

Apprehension chilled her. Had Damien and Max guessed how she felt? "I do not treat Max any differently than I do you."

"That is the point," Damien said. "Society will not understand your relationship with Max. Any open familiarity between you two will be considered more than friendship."

"But it is more than friendship," Jillian blurted, then clamped her mouth shut. "I cannot pretend otherwise."

"When you are out in public with Max, you must do exactly that."

He captured her hand in both of his, as if he thought she might snatch it away. "Tonight, things will change, Jillie. The world you are about to enter is as structured as the props in this ballroom. You must tread carefully or it will all collapse about you."

"Are you saying that I must peer at Max over my fan and simper because society is too shallow to recognize friendship?" she asked, though inside, she knew the answer. Everything had been all right until Arabella had spread her poison.

Damien raked his hand through his hair. "Are you deliberately being obtuse? Any displays of affection between you and Max will immediately be interpreted as courtship, or worse."

"Have you and Max discussed this?" She watched Damien shift on his feet, his gaze skipping over her, his mouth tightening with impatience.

"Yes."

"And I take it he shares your views?" Every word she uttered seemed to burn in her throat.

"He does . . . Jillie—"

"Of course he does." She cut him off, not wanting to hear anymore. Now, she had to accept what she had been trying to ignore all week. Both Damien and Max found the idea of a match between her and Max so absurd as to be embarrassing. "It was kind of Max to spare me the humiliation of discussing this with me himself." She forced herself to smile, to keep her voice light.

Damien slanted a grin at her in obvious relief. "Thank God you understand." His expression became serious once more. "Jillie, you are my sister, and he is my best friend. I don't want eyebrows raised because of your relationship with him. All I'm asking is that you be discreet when in the public eye."

Jillian nodded. She understood very well. Neither the depth of her friendship with Max nor the newer, more consuming emotions she felt for him were to be revealed. There was too much to lose. Damien knew it. Max knew it. And now, she knew it. Her feelings were to be sacrificed to spare the sensibilities of a shallow society.

If she allowed it.

There was a light tap on the ballroom door. The butler hovered at the entrance. "Your Grace, the musicians have arrived."

"Has my aunt been informed?"

"Yes, I have," LadyLou said, bustling into the room, trailed by a group of men, carrying instrument cases of assorted sizes.

Absently, Jillian watched the members of the orchestra take their places. It was nearly time. She glanced at the gazebo, remembering her brother's words. With bittersweet sorrow, she accepted that this was where yesterday ended and tomorrow began. The past was simply something to be cherished like a favorite story about people living in a time that no longer existed.

The tale had ended. Damien and Max were the ones who refused to close the chapter on her childhood.

She, on the other hand, had every intention of beginning a new one.

Jillian stood in the receiving line, feeling as if her smile had frozen on her face as she graciously nodded and secretly cringed when each male bowed over her hand, assessing first her jewels, then her body. Even the women seemed to calculate her worth, both in economic and social terms, before turning their scrutiny on Damien.

The butler's voice droned on and on as he announced each guest. With every arrival Jillian's anticipation peaked. Each time her disappointment multiplied when Max failed to appear.

"I cannot understand why Max has not yet arrived," Damien whispered into her ear.

"Perhaps he has decided it is best if he does not come at all," she said as she stared straight ahead, her face aching from the smile she could not seem to drop.

"Something must have happened, Jillie," Damien said. "He would not be late tonight."

Jillian nodded, unable to reply as the pain in her throat became almost unbearable. Her heart reached out and snatched the reassurance Damien offered and held it close. Forcefully, she reminded herself that Max had never missed a significant event in her life, so how could she believe for an instant that he would miss her come-out?

Again, the butler paused. Her gaze darted toward the entrance as her chest expanded with a burst of hope and the faith that Max would not do this to her, that the years between them could not be destroyed in one afternoon. Every emotion inside her melted together and became a burning knot of resentment as Lady Seymour and Melissa stepped inside the ballroom.

Each was perfectly coiffed and bejeweled. Lady Seymour was gorgeous in brilliant green silk. Melissa looked like an angel in a frothy pink confection shot through with silver threads. All she required were wings and a halo to complete the effect.

"Lady Seymour . . . Lady Melissa," Damien said with a perfunctory dip of his head.

"Good evening, your Grace," Lady Seymour said, in the breathy voice that Jillian had come to associate only with her. "Jillian, how interesting you look tonight."

"How very kind of you to say so." Jillian stared past her and wondered how it felt to be like Lady Seymour, to gain pleasure from hurting other people. She told herself that trading insults with this woman would accomplish nothing. She was not worth the effort. At least that's what LadyLou had told her.

Lady Seymour gave her a bored look and turned her attention to LadyLou. "Louise, how lovely everything looks tonight. The gazebo in the center of the room is a charming idea, darling, but is it not a bit of a hazard?"

Jillian's hands clenched at her sides as the countess's remark lit a spark of anger. "Why don't you ask my brother?" she said coldly. "He had it constructed."

"Really?" Lady Seymour said, then turned her smile on Damien. "It was very clever of you to create such a memorable setting for Jillian. Sometimes it is necessary to utilize whatever means is at our disposal to make a debutante stand out on the marriage mart."

Damien stiffened, and Jillian laid a hand on his arm, squeezing slightly to stay his anger at the blatant dig. Her mouth twisted in the suggestion of a smile. Lady Seymour thought herself a veritable master of the veiled insult. How foolish she was. "Really," Jillian said, feeling no remorse for what she was about to do. "That explains why you chose to wear green tonight. The color compliments Melissa's gown perfectly . . . like a stem enhances a pink rose. All that is required is for someone to dig a hole in the earth and plant you."

Lady Seymour's smile vanished. A flush stole across her face as she struggled to formulate a rejoinder.

LadyLou had been wrong. Lady Seymour was definitely worth the effort.

Melissa hastily turned her head and raised her fan to cover the lower half of her face.

Damien didn't bother to hide his amusement.

"Arabella, there are other guests still waiting to be received," LadyLou said quickly, shooting a warning glance at Jillian.

Lady Seymour gave an icy smile. "Come away, Melissa, darling, it appears we are holding up progress."

Jillian made it a point to look completely bored.

"Hello, Jillian," Melissa said softly as she passed. "You look very beautiful tonight."

"Thank you, Melissa, so do you." Jillian replied and felt a pang of regret at having used Melissa to insult Lady Seymour. She should have just told Lady Seymour she looked like a toad and been done with it.

"How do you suppose a harridan of the first water gave birth to an angel of the first water?" Damien asked as Lady Seymour and Melissa walked way.

"I thought you didn't care for Melissa," Jillian said.

"I don't have to like her to admire her graciousness," Damien said off-handedly, and turned his attention to the next guest in the seemingly endless stream.

Names and faces became a blur to Jillian as more people drifted past and the anger she had felt toward Lady Seymour found a new target.

Max.

Was he so afraid that she would forget herself and be overcome with a display of affection for him that he would deliberately miss her ball? Did he not have more faith in her than that? And as the thoughts tumbled through her mind it seemed that the people passing before her were not even human beings, but only a parade of exotic feathers, fine fabrics and precious jewels.

She shifted from one foot to the other and mentally counted the guests still waiting to be received. Only a few more . . .

Only a few more and Max was not one of them.

So be it.

If he came, she would demonstrate fully to him that his fears were groundless. He would not see Jillian but, rather, Lady Jillian the cool and elegant woman reflected in the full-length mirror earlier this evening.

Bruce Palmerston, Viscount Channing was announced.

She had to admire how handsome he looked in his pitch-black evening suit. But what captured her attention was the way his blue eyes twinkled wickedly as he perused her thoroughly while being carried toward her on the last wave of guests. That he thought she looked much better than "interesting" was obvious and Jillian reveled in the first genuine rush of pleasure she had felt since the evening had begun.

"Lord Channing, how nice to see you again," she said.

He gave her a slow, lazy smile. "So you are real, Lady Jillian. I had begun to doubt my perceptions." He bowed and moved on before she could formulate a reply.

It was a jolt in her heartbeat, a chill up her spine as she stared after him. Viscount Channing had seen it and somehow she knew that it was so. She was real—not an image in the mirror at all. She was Lady Jillian.

Max should have been the one to see it first.

A few more faces floated past and then there were no more, and she and Damien and LadyLou stood alone.

"Damien, the guests wait for the ball to open," LadyLou prompted softly.

"There is no hurry," Damien said. "It will not hurt to delay the first dance a little longer."

"No," Jillian said softly. "Let us get on with it."

"He will be here, Jillie. He would not miss the most important moment of your life."

"Apparently he would." With her head held high, she allowed Damien to lead her to the center of the floor. He gestured to the musicians. She took her brother's hand and fell into the graceful steps of a minuet. Other couples joined them on the floor and the dance seemed to go on forever as she mechanically turned and nodded her way through the line. The colors of the ladies' gowns were an indistinct blur, the music flat to her ears, the conversation just babble.

There was no shine to the evening, no glitter to the moments.

Max wasn't here.

Then, suddenly it was over and Damien was leading her off the floor. "What is it Jillie? You seem too pensive for such an occasion."

"I am quite all right, Damien. I was simply thinking about this being the most important night of my life. If that is so, then what is there to look forward to?"

"His Grace, the Duke of Bassett."

A hush swept through the ballroom at the butler's announcement. All heads turned. Damien muttered under his breath as Jillian gazed toward the entrance.

Max stood beneath the threshold, a stunning portrait of light and dark with his tawny hair a dramatic contrast to his black coat, breeches and waistcoat, his strength and vitality making the other men present seem faded and threadbare in comparison—her lion in all his majesty.

His gaze met hers as he sauntered toward them, his eyes a startling flash of sapphire blue glinting in the light of a thousand candles.

"Good God, Pandora, is it you?"

Chapter 9

She *couldn't* be his Pandora, who wore braids and ran through life at full tilt. My God, she looked beautiful with her hair swept back from her face displaying her creamy skin and high cheekbones, her straight brows and jewel-green eyes. He'd never realized how small her ears were—too small almost for the pearl earrings she wore. Nor had he been aware that her neck was so gracefully long—long enough for the five-strand choker of pearls at her throat. But, as he studied the silk and elegance of her, he told himself that she was still a little girl playing dress up, that the sudden stir of warmth in his body was due to the heat of the room.

"Your Grace," she said, and it filled him with sudden, inexplicable grief. Is that what she saw? One nobleman among others? What had happened to Max? More importantly—where was his Pandora?

All he saw was Lady Jillian Forbes.

"I believe, Max, that it is customary for the *ladies* to make a grand entrance," Damien said. "Was it contrived or were you detained?"

"Detained," Max said. "My carriage broke an axle."

"I suspected as much," Damien said, "though Jillie had quite given up on you."

It was another shock, stunning him into silence as he waited for her to deny the statement, to make some teasing comment that would take away the sting. He faced Jillian, staring at her for a moment as he searched for the mischievous twinkle that was so much a part of her. Instead, she favored him with a somber gaze.

"Did you, Pandora?" he finally asked. "It is not like you to give up on anything."

"I simply accepted your absence tonight, Max. I would not have tolerated such a breach from you again."

Relief brought laughter and he gave it free rein. Damien joined in. His Pandora was here after all.

"If your 'graces' will look about," Jillian said, nodding toward the gaping crowd, "you will find that we are the objects of approximately three hundred pairs of eyes. Shall we observe the proprieties now?"

"Bloody hell," Damien murmured.

Max bit off his laughter, but he could not banish his smile. Now he understood. Damien had spoken to her, repeating the warnings he'd given Max a week ago. How ironic that Jillian was the one to take heed while he and Damien made a hash of it. And leave it to Jillian to bash them over the head with it.

Max took her hand and bowed, breathing the suggestion of a kiss over her gloved fingers, then regarded her with false solemnity.

Jillian nodded and sketched a small curtsy, accepting his gesture as her due.

"Shall we dance, your Grace?" she asked, her voice so low Max barely heard her.

"You forget yourself, Jillian," Damien said benignly from the side of his mouth. "It is customary for the gentleman to ask the lady to dance."

"It is quite all right, Damien, as long as she does not forget herself with anyone but me," Max said, frowning as his gaze skipped from Damien to Jillian. Damien didn't seem perturbed by his slip, and Jillian's expression showed no recognition that there might be a deeper meaning beneath the words. He would have preferred a reaction from them. It would have meant that he was not jumping at shadows and feeling a self-consciousness that did not belong in their relationship.

Shaking off his discomfort, Max offered his arm and
Jillian placed her hand lightly on his elbow. As they approached the gazebo, the crowd scattered and suddenly
conversations provided an undertone to the music.

The orchestra struck a waltz and Jillian drifted into
his arms.

They danced in silence, yet sensation was eloquent
on his body, in the slide of silk under his fingers at her
waist, the weight of her hand on his shoulder, the subtle
drift of her scent—jasmine, he concluded—surrounding
him as they whirled and glided to the music. He'd
touched her a thousand times, but he had only noticed
angular bones and wriggling energy. Now they were
buried beneath an unfamiliar softness and grace. Conversation had always been easy between them. Now he
could think of nothing to say. He'd taught her to climb
trees and skip rocks. Yet she had learned to dance without him.

"I love the gazebo, Max. It's perfect."

"Damien has outdone himself," Max replied, again
feeling strain. It had always seemed so natural to do
things for Jillian, to try and make her moments special.
What had been a spontaneous thought on his part had
become, in his mind, the symbol of a fool in the wake
of Damien's admonishments.

"It was your idea."

"Was it?"

She smiled at him, "Thank you, Max. I will never
forget it."

He returned the smile, no longer feeling the fool. Her
pleasure in the gazebo had made it special again. "And
I will never forget the sight of you standing beneath the
canopy."

"I wondered if you had noticed how I look."

"How could I not? You dare much, Pandora, with a
gown that fits where it should billow," Max said.
"Whatever were you thinking to make such a bold
statement?" And whatever was he thinking, Max wondered, to point out what he would rather ignore?

"I wasn't thinking at all, beyond how absurd I would appear dressed like the others."

They danced past Damien and his partner. "And so you have unwittingly made them appear absurd instead," Max said. "Look at poor Damien, he is smothering in all those ribbons and curls."

"Damien admires Melissa's graciousness, and I think she is beautiful."

"A veritable feast for the eye," he said mockingly. "I am surprised that Arabella has not stuck an apple in her mouth."

"You target the wrong Seymour, Max. Lady Seymour is the one who needs an apple in her mouth. Then she would not be able to use her wicked tongue."

The movement of Jillian's mouth caught his gaze, and he felt a familiar pull in his midsection, a stirring of awareness. But, for Jillian? Suddenly, their innocent quips seemed like flirtation and innuendo. What they had shared in private had always been whole and clean. Public scrutiny had somehow blurred his own vision of their relationship, as if he were seeing it through a dirty window. "Perhaps we should take care to see that Arabella never has cause to inflict her wicked tongue on us," he said, hearing the strain in his voice, the urgency to find some balance between past and present.

"If we do not give Lady Seymour cause, she will simply fabricate one," Jillian said.

"Perhaps our challenge will be to bore her into silence."

Jillian arched her neck and laughed, a rich, throaty sound that invited all who heard to join in her pleasure. Max felt it as he always did—her joy in life that seemed to spill like water on a linen tablecloth, spreading over and under and through him, lingering until it became his own.

He didn't want to let her go as the music ended on a light note and, reluctantly, he willed himself to release her, to lead her back to LadyLou's side. His steps slowed as he saw the queue of hopeful suitors waiting to claim Jillian's attention. They were vultures who saw only opportunity, uncaring that she was so much more than beauty and wealth and position.

Not one of them was the sort Max wanted courting Jillian.

But the ballroom was only so large and all too soon they reached LadyLou and Damien.

"Is it not wonderful?" Jillian said, her cheeks flushed and eyes glowing with excitement as she turned to sweep her admirers with her gaze.

"Wonderful," Max said dryly as he tamped down the hostility he felt for every man present.

Scowling, Damien met his gaze over Jillian's head. His friend saw it, too—their shallow concerns and lack of worthiness. Max smiled grimly as he studied each of England's finest, posing and primping himself with a cocky assurance that he would be the one to win Jillian's approval. They hadn't yet realized that they first must win the approval of the Dukes of Bassett and Westbrook.

His insides tightened in revulsion as the Honorable Jasper Reynolds approached with Viscount Nunnley on his heels.

"L-Lady J-J-Jillian," Reynolds stammered. "Could I-I—"

"Lady Jillian," Nunnley cut in smoothly. "May I have the honor?" He cast Reynolds a disdainful look. "By the time the Honorable Reynolds finishes his request, the dance will be over."

Jillian gave Nunnley a frosty smile. "Mister Reynolds was here first," she said evenly. Her smile warmed on him as she placed her gloved hand on Reynolds's arm and allowed him to lead her into the steps of a quadrille.

His gaze trained on the couple, Max shifted impatiently as he watched Jillian favor Reynolds with a smile. If the fop didn't close his mouth he would trip over his own tongue. Irritation changed to pity as Reynolds stumbled over his own feet. Damn fool would fare better if he took his eyes off Jillian's neckline. Still, Reynolds was the better of the two, being shy and awkward as opposed to Nunnley and his overblown opinion of himself.

"Do the two of you intend to stand guard for the remainder of the evening?" LadyLou inquired blandly.

Before they could reply, the dance ended and Reynolds escorted Jillian to her aunt's side. He and Damien remained at her back as she turned to stare out at the dancers. Nunnley and Lord John Blaylock closed in. Max glared at them through narrowed eyes. They stopped in their tracks and veered off in another direction. The next dance began and Max felt a twinge of guilt when no one approached Jillian.

Nearby a flock of apprehensive suitors hung back, alternately casting longing looks at Jillian and wary glances at Max and Damien. The dance ended and another one began. The knot of eligible bachelors nervously murmured among themselves as they seemed to collectively advance a step, then pause. Max watched with a mixture of satisfaction and contempt. They were not only fools, but cowards as well.

Damien snorted and tossed a knowing look at Max.

A third dance was struck and still, no one approached Jillian.

Jillian stood unmoving in front of them, a proud statue with her head held high.

Suddenly, the flock parted and Bruce Palmerston strode through, ignoring the men around him, his full attention on Jillian. "Lady Jillian, I have come to collect my waltz." He nodded at Damien. "With your permission."

Damien nodded his head curtly.

Max's jaw ached with the effort of stifling his protest.

Bruce tucked Jillian's hand into the crook of his arm and led her way.

"Arrogant sod," Max muttered.

"At least he has a spine," Damien replied as he glowered at the line of disappointed suitors.

LadyLou turned to give them a glacial stare. "I believe the two of you have made your point," she said in a furious hiss. "You are ruining Jillian's chances of making a successful debut, and humiliating her in the process."

Something lurched in Max's chest as Damien cursed under his breath.

LadyLou softened her attack. "I know there are undesirables from whom you would wish to protect Jillian, but you are also frightening away perfectly acceptable suitors."

Privately, Max thought that acceptable suitors would not be so easily frightened. On the other hand, he considered Bruce to be the worst of the lot with his cynicism and his casual attitude toward propriety—any propriety. Damn, but he hated this.

"Your point is well taken, LadyLou," Damien said, "but still, Jillian's admirers must be vetted."

LadyLou sighed in obvious exasperation. "*My point,* Damien, is that your diligence is a bit overwhelming. I suggest you both make yourselves scarce for the remainder of the evening and leave the chaperoning to me. Your presence alone is enough to keep the rakes and scoundrels away."

"It appears we are being dismissed," Damien said. "Shall we enjoy ourselves?"

"As much as we can," Max qualified, torn between relief and annoyance at being banished. It was bloody hell watching every man in the place drool over Jillian. She was too young for this, too innocent.

Damien made a sound that was part laugh and part groan, as they turned their backs on Jillian for the first time all evening, "I suppose we'll eventually grow accustomed to gentlemen looking at her as if she were the last cherry tart on the table."

"I sincerely doubt it," said Max, glancing back at Jillian one last time. Perhaps Bruce was the safest one for her to be with after all, he thought, reversing his earlier opinion. Like him, Bruce had no taste for innocents, and if he should develop one, Max would see to it that their mutual business interests required Bruce's presence on another continent.

Jillian mechanically followed Lord Channing through the steps of the waltz. Humiliated, she kept her gaze focused on his shoulder, grateful that he didn't seem to require conversation. She was afraid to speak, afraid that she would make a cake of herself, and even he would seek more satisfying company. It was bad enough to think that he was being kind to her because of his friendship with Max and Damien.

She was a failure, a wallflower at her own ball.

"It appears as if your champions have withdrawn the gauntlet."

"Pardon me?" Jillian lifted her gaze in confusion, startled by the sudden intrusion of Lord Channing's voice into her thoughts.

"Damien and Max," he said.

Jillian glanced toward the sidelines and saw only LadyLou. Damien and Max were nowhere to be seen. "I don't understand," she said.

"They were scaring off every potential dance partner that glanced your way. Actually scaring is too mild a word. Terrifying is more apt."

Her eyes widened. "Oh no," she gasped. "Really?" She grinned as comprehension dawned. They hadn't been rejecting her, but rather avoiding Damien and Max. Pleasure curled in her stomach at the thought of Max *wanting* to scare away her suitors. She straightened her spine and lifted her head, meeting Lord Channing's gaze with an arch look. "They didn't scare you, my Lord."

The music ended just then, and though they stopped dancing, Lord Channing continued to stand in the middle of the dance floor with her. "I don't frighten easily and let us dispense with the lord and lady business. I am merely Bruce."

"And I am merely Jillian," she responded, pleased that he had expressed a wish for less formality between them.

"Merely?" Bruce said as he escorted her from the floor. "To describe you as 'merely' anything is like saying a Gainsborough is merely a painting."

Suddenly her earlier sense of enchantment returned as her feet seemed to leave the floor. She was floating in a drift of ivory silk and renewed pride—not a failure at all. And though she wished that the compliment had come from Max, she refused to dwell on what was missing when there was so much magic in the air.

As the evening progressed she took to the floor with one partner after another, basking in their admiration. If so many found her pleasing then surely Max did, too. She chose to believe it as she caught him watching her more than once, his expression serious and intent, oblivious to the women who cast inviting glances his way. At least she seemed to be the sole object of his attention, even if he had yet to claim his second dance.

Conversely, she chose not to dwell on his oversight, indulging instead in feeling flattered that so many men requested permission to call on her, though she wondered what she was going to do if they all came. It was difficult enough to focus her attention on only one man during a short dance. She'd never realized that men preferred to conduct one-sided conversations, questioning and answering without any help from her. She listened and smiled till her face hurt.

And then it was over. The last guest departed, and only the scuff marks on the polished floor proved they had been there at all. Wilted flowers lined the walls, and burned-down candles dripped wax in the chandeliers. The gazebo leaned a little to the side, as if it, too, were tired.

LadyLou took to her bed, leaving Jillian alone in the ballroom with Damien and Max. Bleary-eyed, she gazed at her gazebo and felt a touch of melancholy. To-morrow, the ballroom would be stripped bare and the echoes of a magic night would fade into nothing.

"Tired, Pandora?" Max said.

"Yes," she sighed. "But I don't want this to end. I don't want to let it go. . . ." She shook her head, unable to express the feelings that weighed her down.

"There will be plenty of other balls," Max said as he slipped up behind her and she felt the warmth and strength of his hands on her shoulders.

"Yes," Damien said. "Tomorrow night, you get to do it all over again,"

"I am not sure I will be up to it," she said, and shifted uncomfortably, her feet burning and aching in her slippers. "In fact I know I will not be up to it."

"There are other entertainments, Pandora," Max said. "The theater, the opera—"

His hands fell away as she turned to face him, then regretted that she had moved at all. "LadyLou said we would attend the opera later in the season."

Max shrugged. "We could go tomorrow night."

Damien's mouth twisted in distaste. "Wouldn't you rather go to the theater?"

Jillian grinned. Damien hated the opera. Max loved it and so did she. "Shall we vote?" she teased. Damien scowled at her. "You do not have to attend, Damien. Max can escort me." Jillian gave an exaggerated sigh as Max and Damien frowned. "Propriety is such a nuisance. I didn't even get my second dance with Max, and now there is no orchestra."

Their expressions cleared and Max arched a brow at Damien. "With your permission?"

Damien nodded.

Max opened his arms and smiled. "Come," he said softly, so softly it became an intimate thing between them.

His expression nearly undid her with its open display of all the affection that he had given her for more than ten years. Everything inside her fluttered and her knees trembled and her feet seemed to be a foot above the floor as she went to him, felt the firmness of his grip on her hand, the pressure of his fingers splayed at her waist, the quick brush of his thigh against hers as he drew her close.

"Hum, Damien," he commanded as he spun her into a waltz.

Chapter 10

"L-Lady J-Jillian, I do hope y-you w-will ... " Jasper Reynolds broke off and flushed as he struggled to express himself. He took a deep breath. ". . . s-save a dance for me tonight."

"I will certainly reserve a dance for you the next time we meet," Jillian said.

A befuddled look flickered across Reynolds's earnest face at her vague reply, and Jillian felt a pang of guilt. He couldn't be more than twenty-one years of age, with the soul of a poet and the sensitivity of a child. She always had the urge to offer him a sweet. She did not, however, entertain an urge to tell him of her plans to attend the opera with Damien and Max that evening.

Max. She was again caught by the memory of last night and her last dance with Max. Those moments had been like a fantasy come to life as he'd embraced her in the dance, his gaze locked with hers as if only she existed in his world. The gazebo again had seemed new and the fading light of the candles had cast a dreamy glow over the room. They had laughed with the exhilaration of it all as Max spun her about faster and faster, and then their laughter had faded to smiles as Max held her after they had stopped, and gently tucked a stray tendril behind her ear. She'd gone to sleep with the memory of his touch on her cheek, her forehead warm and tingling where he'd kissed her, the husky, intimate sound of his voice when he bid her, "Sweet dreams, Pandora." She'd discovered then that Max was the only magic she needed.

"I do hope I am the reason for your captivating smile," Nunnley said as he elbowed Reynolds out of his way.

Jillian stepped back at the harsh intrusion into her reverie. Nunnley stood far too close to her for comfort. Handsome as he was with his coffee-colored hair and eyes, she did not like him in the least. Truth to tell, she was not especially impressed with any of the gentlemen gathered in the drawing room, and after only one afternoon she was heartily sick of taking calls. The room had seemed to close in on her almost immediately after the first group of visitors had arrived, and now the air was thick and cloying with the combined odors of the colognes and hair pomades that dandies favored.

"Don't tell me I have struck you speechless as well," Nunnley smirked.

Oh my, Jillian thought, but he was impressed with himself. "Actually, I was thinking of the evening ahead," she said.

"Ah yes, the Dudley's ball," Nunnley said with an air of supreme boredom. "I had not planned to attend, but I might put in an appearance if it will make you happy."

"How very considerate of you." Jillian bit back a grin. "But I plan to attend the opera. You may, of course, put in an appearance there if it will make *you* happy."

Suddenly, every man in the room clustered around her, leaning forward and jostling one another for a better position. Jillian did not realize until Nunnley sent his cronies a satisfied lift of his chin at their obvious belief that it appeared she had shared some secret with him, thereby showing him special favor.

She could not let that stand and, in the end, felt inclined to share her schedule for the evening with everyone present when all she wanted to do was make a ringing announcement that they were all wasting their time calling on her.

Instead, she excused herself to join LadyLou and whisper in her ear. "I am going to fetch my shawl." Her aunt nodded her permission and Jillian slipped quietly from the drawing room.

Her gaze darted about furtively as she made her way to a small sitting room at the end of the hall. Just as she reached her destination, the door knocker sounded, announcing yet another caller. She ducked inside and waited to see who else had come to plague her.

"What the devil is going on, Jacobs?" Max demanded. "Both sides of the street are lined with coaches. It looks as if the circus has come to town."

"Callers for Lady Jillian, your Grace," the butler explained.

At the sound of his voice, her stomach fluttered—a lovely sensation that had become as familiar to her as Max. What had seemed to be torture a few moments ago now took on a different aspect. The flutter turned to a delicious warmth in the pit of her belly as she peered around the corner and saw him standing tall and golden in the foyer. Her heart pounding, she stepped into the entry hall. "Max, have you come to rescue me?"

"From what?"

"The circus," she said, waving her arm toward the drawing room. "Is it always like this?"

Max shifted on his feet and glanced about, his brow creased in a frown. "I wouldn't know," he said evenly. "I have never called on a young lady."

That statement pleased her immensely. Then confusion set in. How many times had she speculated about him stealing a kiss from a lady? After all, he had been a part of this society for as long as he'd been a part of her life. She had always assumed that he participated in the courting ritual. "Never?" she asked. "Do you simply dance with the ladies as you did last night and that is that?"

His gaze snagged on her at that and his smile was quick and dry. "Not precisely. I simply go about things a bit differently."

"How so?" Jillian asked. "I would certainly like to know why I must receive calls when you are not required to make them."

Max gave her a conspiratorial wink. "Then don't receive them."

"You mean there is a choice?" she asked hopefully, then scowled as his mouth twitched. She knew that look. "You're teasing me."

"I am," he admitted and sighed. "As unfair as it may seem, Jillian, there are different rules for men and women. And while those for women are rigid, those for men are rather flexible."

She barely heard anything he said beyond his coupling of her proper name with the word "women." He had, by implication, called her a woman. At last. The rules didn't seem so important, nor so irritating now.

LadyLou dashed out of the drawing room, closing the doors behind her with a solid thump. "Jillian what are you doing? You cannot abandon your guests."

"Oh please, LadyLou, send them all home. Tell them I am indisposed. Tell them I eloped to Gretna Green with a footman."

"I shall not. I expect you to return in precisely five minutes." LadyLou whirled about, then paused to glance back over her shoulder. "Oh, Max. I am sorry. I didn't realize you were here."

"That is quite all right. You seem to have your hands full at the moment."

"If you will excuse me, I must get back." With a last meaningful look at Jillian, she disappeared inside the drawing room.

Jillian closed her eyes and drew several long, deep breaths.

"There now," Max said with a placating tone as he chucked her under her chin. "I'm sure it is not as bad as all that."

"How would you know if you have never paid a call?" she grumbled, then grasped his hand and tugged. "Come inside with me, Max. Perhaps you can steer them toward more stimulating topics ... or better yet, chase them away with your most formidable ducal glare."

He pulled his hand away and glanced toward Damien's study. "Not today, Pandora. I can't imagine anything worse than being hemmed up in a room full of overeager swains." He turned toward the butler. "Is Damien in his study?"

"He is out, your Grace," Jacobs replied.

Max had done it again—spoken to her as if she were a woman, then treated her like a child. Instead of fixing a ducal glare on her suitors, he had given her a ducal dismissal. She was beginning to wonder if he knew the difference between Jillian and Pandora. Heaven knew she was confused.

"He has gone to meet with his solicitor and Baron Fillmore," Jillian said. "It looks as if the baron may be willing to sell the land adjoining Westbrook."

Max gave a quick tip of his head. "Yes, he told me about that. It slipped my mind that their meeting was today."

The knocker sounded, and she grinned as Jacobs admitted Bruce Palmerston. The afternoon was shaping up nicely after all. "Bruce," she said happily. "Will *you* rescue me?"

Bruce cocked a thoughtful brow at Max, then slid his gaze to Jillian. "Do you need rescuing?"

"I most certainly do," Jillian replied.

"Really," Bruce said, his voice laced with curiosity. "Is Max chasing off your admirers again?"

"What are you doing here?" Max asked, abruptly ending the exchange.

Bruce smiled at Jillian and handed over his hat and gloves to Jacobs. "I should think that is obvious. I came to call on Jillian."

Max stiffened. "You cannot be serious."

"Why wouldn't I be?" Bruce asked.

Jillian silently echoed the sentiment. What was so unbelievable about a man like Bruce paying a call on her? Drawing herself up with offended pride, Jillian faced Bruce, giving Max a view of her back. "I am so glad you came, but I must warn you the drawing room is full. I feel like a cornered fox."

Bruce chuckled. "Now that sounds like something my sister would say. I have a feeling the two of you would get along well together. The next time she visits me, I would very much like to bring her around to meet you."

"Lady Kathleen," Jillian said. "I remember meeting her at the graces memorial services. I did not realize we were of the same age."

"You are exactly the same age," Bruce clarified.

That bit of information unleashed a tumble of questions in Jillian's mind and a curious excitement. It would be nice to have a friend her own age, and if Bruce's sister were anything like Bruce, she knew they would indeed get on famously together. Thus far, she had met no ladies with whom she had a thing in common. She had given up on having more than a nodding acquaintance with Melissa and the other debutantes were more interested in attracting Max's and Damien's attention than cultivating her friendship.

"If we are the same age, why is she not here for the Season?"

"She has delayed her come-out," Bruce said, a melancholy frown briefly knitting his brow. "Our mother has not been well this past year."

"I thought she was improving," Max said, speaking for the first time in the past five minutes.

"She has some good days."

"Please give her my best wishes," Max said.

Jillian stared at the tips of her slippers peeking out from her hem. She would have liked to ask for further details, but didn't know what to say beyond echoing Max's sentiment.

"Jillian," LadyLou hissed from the drawing room door.

"Oh," Jillian said with a start. "I quite forgot about my guests. I must return."

Bruce offered her his arm. "Perhaps that is because they are all so forgettable."

With a chuckle, she took his arm. "Are you sure you don't wish to join us, Max?"

"No," Max said. "I'm off to Tatt's."

"Oh. I'll see you later then," she said, anxious to remind him of their plans for the opera. If he would forget Damien's meeting this afternoon, he could just as easily forget her. "And do be ready when we come around to collect you. I don't want to be late."

Abruptly, Max turned on his heel and strode out the Forbes townhouse before he gave in to the urge to yank Jillian away from Bruce. "Tattersall's," he barked at his driver as he climbed into his coach.

His sister indeed, he thought sourly. One would think Bruce could be more original than that. He couldn't imagine why Damien had given permission for Bruce to pay his addresses to Jillian. It was more likely that Bruce had given himself permission.

Bruce was too experienced for her. Worse was Jillian's naiveté in falling for such a weak ploy. But then, Jillian had fallen for Max's feigned lapse in memory. He had known very well that Damien had a meeting this afternoon. It was the reason he had decided to come and check up on Jillian, and to see how many of the bumbling fops that had surrounded her last night would actually call.

Too damned many, judging from the number of

horses and carriages outside Damien's townhouse. The only thing that had kept him from joining Jillian in the drawing room was the memory of LadyLou's set down the night before. God knew what he would have done if he'd found Nunnley and Reynolds hovering about.

It had been all he could do to make his exit. He hadn't counted on having to deal with Bruce. Having Bruce call on Jillian was as inappropriate as Lady Seymour's assumption that there was an arrangement between Jillian and himself. Bruce was the same age as he and Damien—a friend who had danced with her out of respect. Or so Max had thought.

He didn't like it one bit—not Bruce's apparent interest in Jillian nor Jillian's obvious pleasure in Bruce's company.

Neither did he like any of the horseflesh at Tatt's. All he could think of was Jillian as each beast was led to the auction block. Why hadn't he considered before what her debut would mean? Even Jillian made the connection sooner than he had. Though the furnishings were more elegant than a stable yard, the balls of the Season were nonetheless auctions of flesh and property.

It turned his stomach.

Irritated at his lack of interest in the stallion he'd had his eye on, Max retreated to his club, settled at his usual table and ordered a glass of brandy, determined to drive away the strange mood that had engulfed him since last night. He had not realized until now how hard it would be to watch Jillian surrounded by men, to come to grips with the knowledge that she would inevitably slip into a life in which he would have no place. His hand clenched around the bowl of his snifter and he took a swallow, willing the brandy to soothe him. He was thinking nonsense. Jillian would always be a part of his life, as Damien would always be. The bonds that held the Forbes's and Hastings's friendship had never been breached and never would be, regardless of Jillian's new status.

Dimly he heard the hum of conversation around him.

Needing diversion, he listened, separating voices and exchanges. The prime subject of the day seemed to center on a dilemma concerning attendance at the opera as opposed to the Dudley's ball. His ears pricked suddenly when Jillian's name was mentioned. He focused on the low voices directly behind him and recognized that of John Blaylock.

"She is spectacular, I tell you. Her figure alone set my blood to boiling."

"Indeed, she is," Nunnley agreed. "And the size of her dowry and family connections make her all the more attractive."

Max ground his teeth together as Nunnley continued. "I would have offered for her today if her brother had been home."

"Wouldn't have done you any good," Blaylock said. "She would have turned you down flat."

"As long as her brother doesn't turn me down, I don't see a problem."

"He won't give his consent unless she gives hers. She has him wrapped around her finger."

Nunnley laughed derisively. "There are ways around that."

A number of images crossed Max's mind—of seduction and compromise and cold-blooded manipulation. Nunnley was capable of those and worse. Max shoved his chair back and abruptly rose, reaching their table in two long strides. "What ways?" he inquired, employing a soft, menacing tone meant to intimidate.

Nunnley and Blaylock paled. Their cocksure arrogance evaporated under Max's regard.

"Your Grace! We didn't realize you were here," Blaylock said, his voice wavering.

"What ways?" Max repeated, his attention riveted on Nunnley.

"You know how it is," Nunnley blustered. "We merely—"

"I know that if the two of you wish to see another sunrise," Max said, enunciating each word slowly and precisely, "you will do well to keep your comments concerning Lady Forbes to yourself. If you are wise, you will also keep your distance. Do you understand?" he snapped.

"Yes, your Grace," Blaylock answered as Nunnley nodded.

"I require a verbal response, Nunnley."

"Yes, your Grace," Nunnley ground out and rose. "I understand perfectly."

"Good," Max said and turned on his heel to return to his solitude.

Evidently, peace was not to be his fortune in the foreseeable future. Bruce Palmerston sat in the chair opposite Max's, his ankle propped on his knee. Good enough, Max thought in grim satisfaction. He might as well make a clean sweep of Jillian's most unsuitable suitors.

"Well done," Bruce drawled. "You certainly know how to clear a room." He smiled as Nunnley and Blaylock hastened out the door. "Between your threats and Jillian's subtle rebukes, Nunnley's pride ought to be dragging in the dust."

"I'd prefer to see Nunnley dragging in the dust," Max said as he took his chair.

"Didn't expect to see you here, Max. Your visit to Tatt's must have been a quick one."

"As quick as your call on Jillian," Max said.

"I know the proprieties—fifteen minutes per call," Bruce replied with a touch of amusement that irritated Max. "I wouldn't want to set out on the wrong foot with her."

"When did your taste start running to children?" Max inquired smoothly.

Bruce cocked a brow. "If you are referring to Jillian, she is hardly a child."

"And not yet a woman. Does Damien know you are calling on her?"

"Not that it is any of your concern Max, but I'm not such a cad that I wouldn't ask his permission first."

"Jillian has been my concern for over ten years," Max said, rankled that Bruce would presume to instruct him on his concerns.

"My mistake. I forget your position as her devoted protector," Bruce said. "I suppose I must suffer this conversation sooner or later."

"I'm glad we understand one another." Max took another draught of brandy and wished that all he had to worry about was soothing Jillian's skinned knees and freeing her braids from the rosebushes. He found the idea of having to protect her from opportunists like Nunnley and rakes like Bruce unnerving. It didn't help that Bruce was his friend. "Now, tell me: what possible interest could you have in her?" Max asked abruptly.

"The irresistible combination of money, brains and beauty," Bruce replied with an indulgent grin.

Max glared at Bruce. It wasn't bloody funny. If he were having this conversation with anyone but Bruce, he would have long since dispatched his smile with a well-aimed fist. But Bruce's irreverence was legend and one of the reasons Max liked him.

Ignoring what could not be stifled, Max continued his interrogation. "I have never known of money or brains attracting you to a woman, so it must be Jillian's beauty." He frowned at that. Of course he knew Jillian was beautiful. He'd thought so when she'd only had a handful of teeth to fill out her smile. But, he knew what Bruce's, and Nunnley's, and Blaylock's—and hell, a host of others'—concept of beauty was and their concept of beauty had nothing to do with her mischief and smiles and her honesty and intelligence.

"You know there is more to her than that," Bruce said.

"Yes, I do know," Max said.

Bruce's expression suddenly became serious. "And you should know better than anyone that it is possible to develop a friendship with a member of the opposite sex."

"Is friendship what you are striving for?"

"For the moment." Bruce leaned back and stretched his legs out in front of him.

"Don't trifle with her, Bruce. Exercise your whims on someone else."

Bruce sighed in exaggerated patience. "Have done, Max. From what I have observed, I suspect her heart belongs to another."

The revelation came at Max like a rapier prick, drawing blood long before he realized he'd been hit. He understood the meaning of Bruce's words, yet he couldn't link them with Jillian. It was too soon. She'd barely made her debut. She hadn't said anything to him. Surely, he would have been the first—or the second—to know. And yet, Bruce would not toss out such a statement unless he had observed something that he and Damien had missed.

"Who?" Max asked bluntly.

"If you want to know, you should pay more attention," Bruce said as he fussed with his cuff.

"You're wrong, Bruce. Jillian has no interest in anyone."

"I suppose it's possible that I am wrong," Bruce said with a familiar, enigmatic chuckle that drove Max to distraction. It was Bruce's standard reply when he knew something that he was not quite ready to reveal. But then, in all the years Max had known Bruce, he had always felt as if Bruce carried a secret he was waiting to drop at precisely the right moment for maximum effect.

Bruce shrugged. "At any rate, only time will tell."

"Because you won't," Max said, knowing that Bruce had his fun and would say no more on the subject. In any event, Max wasn't entirely certain he wanted to know. It wasn't any easier to contemplate the possibility of Jillian caring for an unknown man than it was to worry about Bruce corrupting her. Either way, it was a double-edged sword.

"May I go now, your Grace? I have to dress for the opera." Belying his question, Bruce rose, nodded his head and walked away.

The opera! Max consulted his timepiece and frowned. He, too, had to dress for the evening. He glanced around, dimly aware of Jillian's name entering into the debates concerning the Dudley's ball and the opera. Then, one by one and in groups, the others began to leave, their conversations turning toward the merits of the current diva. . . .

Good God. They were *all* going to the opera.

"I have never seen such a turnout at the opera this early in the season," LadyLou said as she scanned the crowd with her opera glasses. "Every eligible gentleman in the ton is here."

"Really?" Jillian said absently, fascinated by the large, empty stage that didn't seem empty at all with painted figures on either side and on the ceiling and crimson curtain. She thought that the performance itself would have to be grand indeed to compete with its ornate trappings. She studied the tiers upon tiers of private boxes, then the pit below where a number of familiar faces gazed upward through lorgnettes and opera glasses. Wondering who had captured their attention, she glanced around and wished that she could see into the boxes to either side without leaning forward and craning her neck in blatant curiosity. LadyLou would never approve and no doubt Max would glare at her in disapproval.

Ever since they had called for him, he'd been quiet and brooding. He'd propped himself against the squabs in the corner of the carriage and exchanged polite civilities with her and LadyLou before turning to Damien to launch a discussion on business. And when they'd arrived at the Royal Opera House, he had completely ignored the grand way in which she'd stepped out of her cloak and stood before him in all her finery. It was all she could do not to twirl in front of him, showing off her peach silk gown with its ecru lace overlay. But his glance had simply passed over her as he'd handed the clerk his cape and top hat and accepted a program.

She'd hated to see the cape and hat disappear into the cloakroom. There had been something dramatic and dangerous about Max in the solid black cape lined with white satin. Now, he looked dashing and dangerous in his black trousers and cutaway coat, his white embroidered waistcoat and stark white linen.

He sat beside her, his attention riveted on folding the program into a neat square.

She almost wished that he had gone off with Damien to mingle with his cronies ... almost, but not quite. Max was right where she wanted him.

She wanted to captivate and charm him out of his foul mood with her poise and maturity. Still, she was beginning to feel awkward with his silence and distressed by his mood. With what she thought might be studied nonchalance, she glanced about and sighed. "I wonder if the Dudleys' canceled their ball."

"Perhaps everyone plans to attend after the opera," LadyLou mused.

"Only if Jillian announces her intentions of doing so," Bruce said from behind her. "She seems to be setting the pace this Season."

Jillian turned in her seat and smiled up at him, relieved that Damien had thought to bring him to their box. If Max wouldn't talk to her, she knew Bruce and Damien would. "Bruce, how wonderful to see you." Her smile faded as she grasped what Bruce had said. "What do you mean I am setting the pace? What pace?"

"Look about you," Bruce ordered softly. "What do you see?"

"The same faces I saw last night and this afternoon."

"And you have no idea why they're here?"

"They like the opera too," she ventured.

"A possibility," Bruce said in an amused voice. "But actually, they're here because you are. Today, at my club, the sole topic of conversation was whether to attend the Dudleys' or come here, thanks to your announcement that you had chosen the Barber of Seville over another ball. Obviously, they all found the opera to be the greater attraction."

Jillian stared at Bruce in stunned silence for a moment, then glanced around at the occupants of the theater. "Oh dear," she said, heat rushing to her cheeks.

Abruptly, Max crushed the program in his hand and sat up straight in his chair. "It appears that if Jillian announced her intent to jump off a cliff, they would line up behind her."

"That's ridiculous, Max," Jillian said as she wondered at his sudden interest in conversation. Until Bruce had come in, he had been remote at best. She glanced from Bruce to Max to the collection of bachelors down below. Now that she thought about it, Max had seemed inordinately preoccupied by the assemblage.

"Were you at the club this afternoon, Max?" she asked ingenuously.

"I was," he replied shortly.

"Oh," she said as a thought began to tickle in the back of her mind. "You didn't tell me that you were coming here tonight, Bruce."

"Damien, are you going to stand in the doorway during the performance?" Max cut in.

"I hadn't planned on attending until I realized how interesting the performance would be," Bruce said as if Max hadn't spoken.

"I am waiting for another chair to be delivered," Damien replied. "Bruce is joining us for the performance."

"Good," Jillian said. "I was about to suggest it myself."

Max's mouth tightened as he glared at her from the corner of his eye and the tickle in her mind became an itch. The chair was delivered and she scooted hers closer to Max, hemming him in between herself and the wall. "Here, Bruce," she said, pointing to space on her other side. "There is just enough room."

"Actually, I believe he would be more comfortable

over here," LadyLou said as she cast a reproving look at Jillian and smoothly moved into the extra chair.

At that, Max appeared to relax. The itch was replaced by an intriguing notion in Jillian's mind. To test her theory, she smiled down at a group of young men. Max scowled as they nodded her way and raised their glasses to see her more clearly. She leaned over to whisper in LadyLou's ear and Max's expression eased. It seemed that the more attention she received from the gentlemen of the ton, the more Max reacted. The discovery was stunning and thrilling, and filled her with a sudden sense of power that hummed like a live thing inside her.

It wasn't precisely how she wanted to gain his attention, but it would do for now, and she intended to use it to her fullest advantage.

The orchestra struck a chord and the curtain raised. The buzz of conversation faded and the predominantly male audience settled into their places, though their attention still focused upward.

Taking his seat, Damien leaned toward Bruce with a good-natured grin. "How does it feel to be the envy of every eligible bachelor in England?"

"Unbelievable," Damien muttered as he and Max indulged in a nightcap in Damien's study. "Jillian has captured the attention of every male between the ages of eighteen and eighty. Even Bruce has fallen prey. I thought he would lose interest once I granted permission for him to call."

"Shouldn't you be concerned that he hasn't lost interest? You know as well as I do what Bruce is," Max said, trying to relax after a night of listening to the flowery nonsense spouted to Jillian by the scores of bachelors who stormed their box during intermission and the bleating of second-rate performers on the stage. Thankfully, Jillian and LadyLou had retired almost immediately after they'd returned from the opera.

"I do," Damien agreed. "But for the moment he

amuses Jillian. If he follows his usual pattern, he will find a new interest before her feelings become involved."

Max rubbed the bridge of his nose. Damned if he wasn't getting a megrim. He'd felt tight and confined since hearing the buzz at his club that afternoon. Bruce's assertion that Jillian had already found someone of interest had scattered his thoughts into a dozen disturbing directions. It didn't make sense. She'd only made her bow last night, and heaven knew how she could have found any redeeming qualities in any man in the mobs besieging her since. It was getting so he couldn't take a bloody step without tripping over one drooling fop or another.

It had become worse when Jillian had stepped out of her cloak with the grace of a woman confident in her power. She'd been incredibly beautiful in peach silk and ecru lace. She'd even smelled of damned peaches. He wouldn't have been surprised if one of her admirers hadn't tried to take a bite out of her. The thought had certainly crossed his mind once or twice.

He'd reminded himself that she was only a little girl playing dress-up, but it had been difficult to believe as he'd witnessed the effect she had on all the court dandies. It boggled his mind that a man of Bruce's sophistication would find her so fascinating . . . which brought Max back to the matter at hand. "What if Bruce doesn't lose interest?"

"I'm watching, Max. Bruce is no fool. He knows that I will not tolerate any misstep on his part. On the other hand, Jillie just might engage his affections."

"You would approve?" Max said, hearing the incredulous edge to his voice. "You know Bruce cannot be trusted."

"Can't he? Then why is he our friend? Why are we in business with him?"

That pulled Max's thoughts into some kind of order. What was he doing? What was he thinking? Of course Bruce was his friend. Of course Bruce could be trusted. Still, Jillian was not business and he wasn't convinced that Bruce's interest in her was platonic. "You know Bruce's reputation—"

"Which will make Bruce all the more wary with Jillian," Damien cut in. "Besides, if he or any of those bumbling fools hurt my sister, I'll kill them," he said with a good-natured grin.

Now that was a solution Max could live with. Reassured, he held up his glass in a toast. "I do like the way you think." And as Damien met his gaze over the rim of his own glass, he reinforced Damien's pledge with one of his own.

He, too would be watching.

Chapter 11

"I've had ten offers for her hand," Damien said, *though Max could not see him.*

"Who?" he asked, his voice swallowed by the mist surrounding him.

"Guess." The word echoed as Damien's voice drifted farther and farther away.

And then Jillian was there, the mist playing about her feet as she stood beneath the canopy of the gazebo, her gaze inviting and her arms open to receive him as he moved toward her. Wordlessly, he swept her into a waltz, his hand sliding down to grip her bottom. They whirled faster and faster, her braids swirling around them, silken ropes binding him to her. They sank to the floor, and the other couples waltzing around them began to drift away.

"Why have you braided your hair, Pandora?"

"I didn't Max; you did."

Why? he wondered. It looked absurd with her ball gown. "Sit here, Pandora, and let me take down your hair."

She settled between his knees, her bottom a sweet pressure against him, stirring him to arousal. He eased his fingers into each plait, releasing strands that spilled onto his lap, the heat and vibrancy of her hair soaking into him, drenching him with her fragrance . . . jasmine . . . peaches . . . and jasmine again. He gathered the tresses and swept them over her shoulder, fascinated by the exposed nape of her neck and the dark, fine hairs that curled against the creamy whiteness of her skin. He kissed her there as he stroked her hair, combing his fingers through the strands, drawing them toward him once more to spread them over her shoulders.

She turned to face him, her legs wrapping around his waist. Their lips met and his tongue urged her lips to part. He did not have to coax or seduce her. She opened her mouth, receiving him, accepting the stroke of his tongue, sipping from him as he sipped from her.

And then, he was naked above her, his hips thrusting, searching for entrance, hampered by her clothes. He eased her skirts upward, his hands lingering on her flesh, exploring and discovering her, finding her hot and wet and ready for him. Her legs spread wider, and her hips arched up to meet him, to invite him in—

He stopped himself then as he saw her pink muslin frock with a ruffle around the hem, not a ball gown at all.

He drew back to stare at Jillian. Her hair was wild around her head.

Suddenly the mist thickened and rose about them, distorting his vision, confusing him. He watched her face flush with pleasure as her lips parted in a smile.

She had no teeth.

He held a woman, yet saw a child.

Max awakened with a shout. An eager one.

"Your Grace, are you all right?"

Max blinked and jerked upright in his bed, the dream vivid in his mind, his manhood throbbing against his belly. His valet, Harley stood at the window, his hand still grasping the cord of the draperies he had just opened.

Max squinted against the bright sunlight pouring into the room. At least last night's storm had passed.

"Your Grace?" Harley said again.

Max lay back down, struggling to slow his breathing and calm the pounding in his chest. "I am fine, Harley. Is my bath ready?"

"Yes, your Grace. Are you ready for coffee?"

"I'll attend myself, Harley. Leave me." He bounded out of bed and stepped into the bath, scrubbing himself vigorously. He felt dirty and disgusted with himself, disturbed beyond bearing that he had dreamed of Jillian, of being naked with Jillian. At least his mind had the decency to leave her clothed.

But even Jillian clothed disturbed him now, with her woman's gowns and woman's jewels and woman's coif. He could no longer remember her ruffled dresses enhanced with smudges of dirt and a dab of preserves on her face—

An immediate image of himself licking a cherry sweet from her chin intruded on his sanity. His body quickened as the thought progressed from her chin to her mouth. Abruptly, he stepped from the tub and stood naked in the chill morning air and forced his thoughts to toothless grins and shrieks of childish laughter as he pushed her in her swing higher and higher until she declared that she could touch the sky.

It had been getting worse over the past two weeks, seeing her in her ball gowns, standing by while she smiled and danced and played her fan as if it were a musical instrument and yawned when no one was looking, convincing him that it was all smoke and mirrors. And then he'd remember how she looked with her eyes glowing in the candlelight, her skin soft and creamy and ethereal, not his Pandora at all. And when he began to doubt, as he always did when she wasn't near, he felt compelled to see her again, to reassure himself that she was the same. That it was not possible for her to transform herself in two weeks's time to the image of a woman fully grown.

A woman who inspired a dream so carnal it seemed to him a nightmare.

But the dream was his and it had ended as it should. Bruce was wrong. She treated all her admirers the same. She still smiled with mischief rather than stars in her eyes. There was no man in her heart. Jillian was honest in her emotions. If she were infatuated with someone, Max would see it.

He rushed through donning his clothes and stood at the mirror to brush his hair. He would go to see her before another round of social madness began her day. He needed to wipe the dream from his mind, to see her with the sleep barely rubbed from her eyes, her face scrubbed and shiny as she skipped down the stairs to fling herself at him, his Pandora once more.

Yet he hesitated. The hour was still early. It wasn't proper for him to appear at the door unannounced. He slammed down his hairbrush at such absurd concerns. Propriety be damned. Damien's home had always been open to him, just as his was open to Damien and Jillian. There would be nothing unusual about him showing up for breakfast unannounced. And if they were still abed, he would wait. After two killing weeks of routs and balls and senseless ritual, it was time for the three of them to be together without five hundred people milling about scrutinizing their every move. Only he had to know that he would be there to see Jillian.

Jillian drew herself up short in the doorway to the dining room, holding onto the frame as she tried to catch her breath and stop her heart from skipping about in her chest. She blinked, certain that her eyes deceived her. Max sat alone at the table flipping through the pages of the *Post* and absently sipping a cup of coffee, not at all the stranger who'd stood at a distance these past weeks, watching her every move with a scowl of disapproval.

It had been so long since Max had come to begin the day with her and Damien.

He didn't know she was there and his expression was clear, giving her the perfect opportunity to study him, to note that his face had not yet lost the shine produced by a fresh shave and his hair was still damp around the edges. A familiar and maddening awareness tingled over her skin. She'd hoped that she'd become accustomed to the heightened senses and chaotic responses of her body whenever he was near. Instead, the feelings had grown until they happened on a thought or a memory, and at times she felt as if she were suffering from a perpetual case of the vapors.

The paper rattled as Max turned the page. Suddenly, he paused, tilted his head, then met her stare. For a moment he seemed startled by her presence, but then his gaze sharpened on her, studying her thoroughly from hair to shoes and back again. She felt captive by his perusal, unable to move though the urge was strong to squirm under his regard. He'd never stared at her so intently before, as if he were searching for something, as if he didn't quite recognize her ... staring at her as she so often stared at him.

Her heart jumped into her throat at the thought. Was her plan working? Had the attentions of other men forced Max to see her in a new light, to perhaps think of her in a new way?

Abruptly, Max snapped the paper shut and shifted in his chair as if he had seen enough.

Catching herself before she raised her hand to smooth her hair, she stepped into the room. Why had she not put it up instead of wearing it in a loose braid down her back? She wished she had chosen another gown. Anything but a plain blue frock.

"I see you survived the Moreland musicale last night," he said, a cross edge to his voice.

"And good morning to you too, Max," she said as she went to the sideboard. After filling a cup with coffee she took a place across from Max. "You are out and about awfully early. Do you and Damien have plans for today?"

"No. It is not unusual for me to be here for breakfast," he said evenly, turning his attention back to his newspaper.

"I did not say it was," she responded just as evenly, refusing to ask how she could be in the suds when she had barely spoken a word to him. He wouldn't tell her anyway.

"Then what are you saying?" he asked.

"Only that you are normally still abed at this time."

"And how would you know that?"

"Because, I have had years to observe your habits," she said with an impatient sigh.

Max's mouth tightened, and he looked at her as if she had somehow invaded his privacy. He must have forgotten how she used to sneak into his room and watch him sleep. At least she had until LadyLou caught her and that had been the end of that.

"Oh for goodness sake, Max. Damien told me," she added, determined to put an end to such an insane conversation. One would think Max was actually trying to pick a fight with her.

"Damien told you what?" her brother said, strolling into the room, head down as he read the missive in his hand.

Relieved for once to have a chaperone between her and Max, Jillian smiled brightly up at Damien. "That Max is cross as a crab when he stays up too late and rises too early."

"Not human before noon," Damien agreed and took a seat beside Jillian. He picked up her coffee cup and took a sip. "The storm yesterday damaged the roof on the east wing at Westbrook Court," he said without preamble. "Stokes believes the whole thing needs to be replaced. I need to go to Westbrook." He glanced up at Max. "Will you look after Jillie while I am away?"

Jillian's immediate sense of affront that Damien spoke of her as if she required a nanny gave way to anticipation. She rather liked the idea of Max looking after her. At least she would if he'd make up his mind whether to be country Max or city Max. She grinned at her own cleverness in discovering why Max's manner had altered so drastically. Hadn't he made it clear on more than one occasion that he had no use for London society?

"Why don't I go instead?" Max said. "If the storm did damage at Westbrook, it probably did the same at Bassett House. I can, as they say, kill two birds with one stone."

Jillian felt a strange sense of rejection. She understood Damien feeling that he needed to go to Westbrook and see for himself what havoc the storm had wreaked. But it was no secret that Max was not overly fond of Bassett House, and had given Burleigh, his butler, the authority to see to any problems. Even though it was only an hour's ride from Westbrook, Max never stayed there if he could help it. Jillian could well understand that. After visiting Bassett House with Damien a few times, she had decided that it was the most beautiful estate in England, and it was the coldest.

It hurt to think he preferred Bassett House to her.

If Damien thought it odd that Max would volunteer, he gave no sign. "Actually, I would appreciate it. I wouldn't want anyone carrying Jillie off in my absence."

Max pushed away from the table and rose. "I'll leave within the hour."

Jillian's head spun with the speed with which the men had reached a decision and dispatched her in the process. This was not at all what she had envisioned. "Wait, Max. When will you return?"

"In a few days," Max replied as he strode out the door.

"Oh," she said as he disappeared down the hall. This wasn't at all how her plan was supposed to work. How could Max "discover" her if he wasn't here? On the other hand, she mused, maybe the poets were right. Maybe absence would make the heart grow fonder.

Max should have known that the storm would leave Bassett House unscathed. Nothing ever touched Bassett House. It was inviolate, sealing all within its grasp in a vacuum.

When he'd left London yesterday, Max had thought Bassett the ideal escape. He'd reasoned that all he needed was time away from Jillian to put himself to rights. He had to purge himself of thoughts he should not be having, of a dream that was both arousing and profane. They could have no future, Max would only end up hurting her. Matrimony for him was as cold as Basset House.

And still the dream plagued him. Seeing her yesterday morning in braids and a simple frock had made no difference. Sharing breakfast with her as he'd done so many times in the past hadn't helped. It had been awkward and disconcerting as Jillian sat across from him in complete familiarity. She'd been irrepressible and as artless as always.

He'd been a complete ass.

"Damnit," Max muttered as he set the breakfast tray aside. Jillian wouldn't allow him to escape, but followed him about, invading his thoughts wherever he went at Bassett, where no one was welcome, not even the master.

Precisely on cue, a maid knocked and slipped into his quarters to whisk the dishes away. He knew that as soon as he left, that the same maid would return the book he had begun reading last night back in the library and obliterate the signs of his presence from the room. Tonight, a dinner tray would be sent and after he finished his solitary meal, he would go back to the library and retrieve his book. It was rather like chasing one's own shadow.

Burleigh still ran the house like an army barracks.

Max didn't care enough to stop him.

Looking neither left nor right, Max rose and left the room and made his way down the massive staircase. As he reached the bottom, another maid emerged from the white drawing room, a feather duster tucked under her arm. She shut the double doors with a firm thump, then whirled around, her head down and her short legs carrying her toward him at maximum speed. She collided headlong into Max. He grabbed for her but caught only a handful of plumage as she sprawled on the floor in a shower of feathers.

She stared up at him, horror etched in her cherubic face. "Oh! Pardon me, yer Grace," she bawled and plucked feathers from the air as she scrambled to her feet, backing away and clutching the remains of the duster to her chest.

Bemused, Max gazed at her through narrowed eyes. Burleigh's sharp, disapproving voice cut in before Max could utter a word.

"Miss Woodhouse, if you're quite through mopping the floor with your person, I suggest you get on with your other duties."

Wide-eyed and babbling incoherent apologies, the maid continued to gape at Max as if he had a tail and horns and she fully expected him to eat her.

"At once!" Burleigh snapped, then glared at her feet. "Miss Woodhouse, were you wearing your shoes in the white drawing room?"

The girl raised her skirt and looked down at her feet as she began to blubber.

"You know the rules. You are not to enter that room unless you remove your shoes."

"Yes sir. I'm sorry, sir. I forgot, sir."

"Do so again and you will be dismissed without a reference."

Her head bobbing up and down, Miss Woodhouse scurried away on her tiptoes, holding her skirt still hiked up above her ankles.

"Burleigh," Max said as he stared after the girl, then glanced at his butler. "You are an ass."

"Yes, your Grace," Burleigh replied.

Max strode across the entry hall and paused at the doors to the white drawing room.

"Do you require anything, your Grace?"

Max almost jumped out of his skin. "Damnit, Burleigh!" he swore. "Stop shadowing every move I make in this house. And yes, I *require* that this room be closed permanently."

"As you wish."

Max stalked away. He hated this house and its hollow echoes and pristine rooms and the older servants who moved about like living corpses. *He* felt like a corpse when he was here. "And have Sovereign brought around, and order my carriage prepared to leave for London by this afternoon," he rapped out. He had to escape this place where memories of Jillian contrasted so sharply with the bareness of existence here, where the differences between the two parts of his life seemed to take on a new significance. He refused to think about such disparities. What was the point? They existed, just as hot and cold existed.

Sovereign snorted and pawed the ground. Max vaulted into the saddle and spurred his mount across the parkland at a full run toward Westbrook Court.

There wasn't a room in Westbrook that was not warm and inviting. At Westbrook he was more comfortable with memories of innocent mischief and laughter.

And once at Westbrook he found those memories corrupted by the storm.

A limb had fallen from a tree and crashed through the roof of the gazebo. He couldn't imagine Westbrook without a gazebo.

"Stokes, why was the duke not informed of this?" he asked Damien's butler in a deliberately soft voice. If he spoke any louder, he would surely lose control and bellow in frustration.

"I apologize, your Grace. In light of the damage to the manor house, it did not seem significant."

He gave Stokes orders concerning repairs to the manor and the gazebo, then took to his saddle once more. Of course Stokes would not consider the gazebo significant. It was after all, a mere embellishment that was popularly referred to as a "folly." But the gazebo was all important to Max, symbolizing every profound change in his life. It was here that he had learned the meaning of family from a precocious little girl who used her imagination to fashion a more hospitable world for herself. And two weeks ago, he had seen his Pandora standing beneath the canopy of yet another gazebo, transformed into Lady Jillian.

He'd been shocked and comforted by turns ever since, as his view of her shifted from moment to moment. More often than not, she remained his Pandora when they were alone with Damien or LadyLou. But then she would turn to a roomful of callers or a group of potential dance partners and suddenly, unquestionably, disturbingly, she became an elegant creature of society.

He'd discovered then the necessity of employing his own imagination to recognize the part of her that matched his memories and to ignore the woman who visited his dreams.

He kicked his horse into a hard gallop in an effort to outrun the image. He would not, could not, think of her as a potential mate.

A felled tree came into his line of vision, its gnarled branches reaching up from the ground like the hands of a monster. He pulled up hard on the reins, knowing Sovereign would break a leg if he became entangled in the limbs.

The horse reared and screamed in alarm as Max struggled to keep his seat. Sovereign pawed the sky once more, then twisted out from under his rider. Max's teeth jarred together and he felt as if his spine were being jammed through his skull as he hit the ground, his left foot twisting beneath him before he rolled away from the horse's hooves.

"Bloody hell," he said as fiery pain shot through his ankle. Groaning, he leaned back on his elbows and stared up at the sky as he labored to catch his breath. Sovereign might have been spared, but Max knew he was not going to be so fortunate. But then, he supposed such things were to be expected when one tried to escape headlong in two different directions.

Chapter 12

"**E**scaping from Nunnley again, Jillian?" Bruce Palmerston drawled as he peered through a break in the foliage.

Jillian started and pressed her hand to her chest as she backed farther into the corner behind a large potted palm where she'd taken refuge from the crush at— Jillian frowned, who's ballroom was she in? *The Wiltshires? No that was last night, or was it the night before? Oh, what difference did it make?* The past few weeks were an indistinct blur in her mind. The endless round of social events had become a chore since Max's departure. She didn't understand why he wasn't here. Surely a sprained ankle was no reason to retire to the country. She could name any number of men present this very night who were limping about on gouty feet.

Jillian sighed and leaned against the wall. It didn't surprise her in the least that Bruce had known exactly

what she was doing. Bruce was too observant.
"Nunnley is the bane of my existence," she said
glumly. "He is entirely too fond of airing his vocabu-
lary with arrogant babblings about *his* estates, *his* ward-
robe, and *his* interests."

"Take heart, Jillian. I suspect Nunnley's attentions
will last only as long as Max's absence."

The ripple of excitement that inevitably ran through
her at the sound of Max's name ebbed as she registered
what Bruce had said. "Whatever do you mean?"

As if he hadn't heard her, Bruce pointed to a matron
who passed by. "Have you noticed Mrs. Fitchley's sudden penchant for turbans?" he asked, nodding toward
the lady as he joined her behind the palm.

Jillian knew better than to pursue the topic. When
Bruce ignored a question, it was because he had no intention of answering. "Yes," Jillian replied, resigned to
following wherever Bruce lead her. Besides, she'd
wanted respite from the stifling discussions going on
around her, and Bruce always had some entertaining bit
of gossip for her.

He wasted no time in dropping the other shoe. "She
tried a new dye that had turned her hair from gray to
green."

"And how, may I ask, did you come by this information?"

Bruce grinned. "I hear things."

"You eavesdrop and are utterly shameless about it,"
she said as she gave him a fond smile. He was all that
had made these last two weeks bearable. She liked him
immensely and prayed that his feelings for her went no
deeper. Friendship was all she had to offer him, and he
seemed to be content with that.

"Well, I shall be on my best behavior for the next
fortnight. Kathy is—"

The palm fronds rustled and two pair of eyes stared
at her through the leaves. "Why Jillian . . . *and Bruce.*
I had wondered where you'd gone off to."

"As you can see, Arabella, we are merely taking advantage of the only quiet corner in the room," Bruce said with an air of boredom.

"Hello Jillian," Melissa said with a sweet smile.

"Just a warning, dear," Lady Seymour said, ignoring her daughter and Jillian's attempt to respond. "You really shouldn't stray from your aunt's side. It is so easy to set tongues to wagging."

Especially yours. Jillian opened her mouth to deliver the acerbic comment, then shut it again as her gaze met Damien's over Lady Seymour's shoulder.

"How nice of you to be concerned over Jillian's welfare," Damien said, frost coating his words.

"Of course," Lady Seymour said. "Since Louise is too indulgent of Jillian's whims to properly control her, I feel it is the least I can do to remind her that every misstep she makes signifies disaster."

"You overstate such significance, Lady Seymour," Jillian said as she deliberately stared down her nose at Lady Seymour. "I fail to see how disaster is possible with my aunt, my brother, and several hundred guests watching my every move."

Lady Seymour's bosom seemed to inflate as she drew herself up in indignation. "Perhaps," she addressed Damien, "you should explain the power of gossip to your sister."

"Damien," Bruce stepped in as Damien crossed his arms and gave Lady Seymour his most imperious glare. "Have you any word from Max? I heard that the physician has predicted that he won't have a limp."

Lady Seymour's expression went from avid interest at the mention of Max to horror at the mention of a limp.

Melissa seemed to come alive then, and she leaned forward, her eyes wide with alarm. "But I thought it was a simple riding accident—a sprained ankle."

Damien glanced away and swallowed convulsively. Astonished, Jillian skipped her gaze from Damien to Lady Seymour, then caught Bruce's surreptitious wink. "What are you—"

"What happened? You must tell me everything." Lady Seymour said as she neatly elbowed her daughter out of the way.

With an exaggerated sigh, Damien unfolded his arms. "Max doesn't want the details of his mishap bandied about, Bruce."

"I apologize," Bruce said and gravely shook his head. "I know how fond he was of his horse."

Recognizing mischief when she saw it, Jillian again leaned against the wall and waited to see what the devils would do next. Lady Seymour was so up in the boughs, she was almost trembling.

"Jillian, LadyLou is not well," Damien said, smoothly changing the subject. "I've called for the carriage."

"But what of Max's horse?" Lady Seymour asked.

"I'll walk you out," Bruce said and stood aside to let Jillian precede him.

"Witch," Jillian muttered as they wound their way through the crowd, leaving Lady Seymour with her mouth flapping like laundry in the breeze.

"Yes, but in this case she is an accurate witch, Jillian," Damien said, using her full name to indicate his displeasure. "Do you have a yen to be the current subject of gossip?"

"Thanks to you and Bruce, that is no longer a problem ... what was the purpose of that nonsense about Max?"

"To illustrate how easily gossip grows from the trivial to the disastrous," Bruce said, then turned to her brother. "I apologize, Damien, for hiding in the bushes with your sister. I know better."

Jillian halted in the middle of the staircase leading to the entrance foyer. Below, LadyLou stood with a footman who held their cloaks. "I cannot comprehend why you are apologizing, Bruce. I certainly don't intend to."

"I suggest that you listen carefully to the gossip that will surround Max in the next few days, Jillie. Perhaps

then you will comprehend," Damien said and took her
arm to escort her down the staircase.

They reached LadyLou's side, giving Jillian no opportunity to respond.

Chapter 13

The tickle was irritating in the extreme. It felt like
a fly crawling across the sole of her bare foot.
Jillian cracked one sleep-heavy lid, then closed it at
once to shut out the sunlight streaming through her
windows. She was not yet ready to wake up.

The fly did a ballet across her arch. Blindly, she slid
her legs across the sheet searching for cover. She found
none and flicked her ankle in an attempt to drive the
pest away.

The fly grasped her big toe, not an insect at all. "Go
away, Damien," she mumbled.

"Oh, you're awake. Good, I need to talk to you."

She pulled a pillow over her head. "Not now. I have
not finished sleeping," she said.

"Too bad. It is hours past breakfast and I must leave
shortly for an appointment. Sit up and listen to me."

"I'm listening," she said, from beneath the pillow.

"LadyLou is still not feeling well."

Jillian thrust the pillow aside. "What?" she said, as
she pushed her hair out of her face. Damien stood at the
foot of her bed, his hands on his hips. "LadyLou has a
cold," he enunciated slowly, as if she did not understand English. "And I should be surprised if you don't
catch one as well. What are your covers doing on the

floor?" He strode to the side of the bed and hauled her quilt and sheet from the floor.

Heat climbed up her face. She'd been thinking about Max kissing her before she fell asleep. "I was hot," she said. "You are sure that LadyLou only has a cold?"

"Quite certain," Damien said, sitting down on the foot of the bed. "Her head is stuffed and she is sneezing continuously. I told her to spend the day in bed."

"Should we call in a physician?" she asked around a yawn.

"LadyLou insists that she will be fine with a little rest," Damien said. "I have a full agenda today," he continued. "That leaves you without a chaperone. I am sorry, but you cannot receive callers."

Jillian hid a smile. She wasn't sorry at all. Unless Max was here to notice her popularity, she really didn't see the point. "I shall treat it as a holiday. It is very tiresome to make conversation with gentlemen you have nothing in common with save the weather."

"Come now, do you not enjoy discussing the abnormally wet spring we have been having?" Damien teased.

Jillian stretched and yawned again. "Not in the least."

Damien arched his brows. "What, precisely, are your requirements in a suitor?"

Jillian had never given that any consideration. Not that it was necessary. Strength, honor, a sense of humor—Max's attributes. "That they not pad their coats."

"Pardon me?"

Jillian grinned. "Most of the men wear so much padding beneath their coats, I have the urge to plump them."

"I see," Damien said, his lips twitching.

"What about you? What are your requirements in a lady?"

"Kindness, gentleness, honesty, courage," Damien said without hesitation.

"What about beauty?"

He smiled. "An added bonus."

Suddenly distressed, Jillian plucked at her covers. Thoughts of Damien falling in love immediately led to thoughts of Max falling in love with someone besides herself. Contrary to her expectations when she'd come to London, Jillian had had so little time with him that he could meet a woman and become engaged before she even knew about it. "Shall I send a note to the Leightons informing them that we will not be attending their ball tonight?"

"Why wouldn't we attend?"

"LadyLou is ill," Jillian reminded him.

"I can chaperone you," Damien said.

Jillian smiled in spite of her glum mood. "It is rather amusing to think of the Duke of Westbrook standing with all the single ladies and their mamas."

"I'm looking forward to it," Damien chuckled. "I'll be the envy of every gentleman there, for having the privilege of spending the evening surrounded by pretty young ladies." Before she had time to respond, he planted a quick kiss on her forehead. "Be a good girl today. I will see you later."

He paused at the door. "I thought you might like to have luncheon with LadyLou. I've ordered a tray to be served in her room."

After Damien left the room, she reached for the bell-pull to summon Clancy, and begin another day without Max.

Jillian crossed the hall to her aunt's room, and tapped lightly on the closed door.

"Come in," LadyLou called, her nasal tone punctuated by a sneeze.

Jillian stepped inside. Luncheon had already been delivered, and her aunt sat at a small table set for two. "LadyLou why are you not in bed?"

"Because I feel ghastly no matter where I am,"

LadyLou replied, rubbing at her nose with a handkerchief. "Can't stand to take illness lying down."

"You might recover more quickly if you did," Jillian said as she sat in the chair opposite her aunt and uncovered the soup tureen.

LadyLou sniffed and frowned in disgust as the aroma of chicken soup wafted through the air on a puff of steam.

Careful not to show her amusement, Jillian spooned a serving into a bowl. Not only did LadyLou take illness badly lying down, but she didn't take it well sitting up either.

"I knew I was taking ill yesterday," LadyLou said as she speared a slice of ham. "But not to worry, Damien will look after you tonight at the Leighton ball."

"Yes, he told me," Jillian said, taking a sip of soup.

LadyLou sighed. "It's too bad you cannot receive your callers today. Who knows, someone might have caught your fancy."

"Most of them are very nice, but . . ." Jillian trailed off with a shrug.

"Sometimes I believe Damien and Max have ruined you," LadyLou groused. "You measure every man you meet against them. With the exception of Bruce Palmerston, they all fall short . . . though as far as I can see, you only consider him to be a friend."

Jillian nearly choked on her soup. "Is there anything you do not see?"

"Very little," LadyLou said proudly.

Thanking the fates that there was one thing LadyLou did not see, Jillian pushed back her chair. "You really should try and take a nap."

After seeing LadyLou to bed, Jillian pressed a kiss to her forehead and left the room. Restless and searching for distraction, she made her way downstairs, wishing that she'd had the chance to hear what Bruce had begun to tell her about his sister the night before. It would be lovely if Kathy would come to London. She would like to have a female friend.

The knocker on the door sounded. She ducked out of sight and listened as the butler turned away a gentleman caller. Once he was gone, Jillian continued on to the library. Before she reached her destination, someone else rapped on the door. She paused and listened as the butler turned away Viscount Nunnley, who sounded extremely annoyed when the butler informed him she was not at home. Jillian rather enjoyed that, considering how much the arrogant Nunnley annoyed her. She could not help but wonder who else might call and realized that she had found her distraction.

After finding the book she wanted, Jillian slipped into the small sitting room near the front entrance.

Leaving the door to the sitting room open, she curled up on the sofa at the far end of the room, alternately reading her book and counting callers. A running list formed in her mind as she noted their attributes. It was much more interesting than counting sheep, and certainly more fun than reading Shakespeare. As her mental list grew longer, it became more difficult to keep the gentlemen and their distinct characteristics separate. With a mischievous smile, she abandoned her book and took out pen and paper from the small desk in the corner to begin a list.

Henry Newcomb, rich, heir to an earldom, too short, pads his coat.

The Honorable Jasper Reynolds, rich, very nice, pads his coat.

Robert Abercromby . . .

Jillian paused, tapping her index finger on the desk as she listened to his deep, baritone voice. It reminded her of Max.

. . . pleasing voice, handsome, pads his coat.

In between callers she wrote in Max's name at the top of the list with a great flourish, resisting the urge to draw a heart around it. That would be childish. She could not resist, however, writing "Jillie loves Max" along the side. When she'd embellished Max's name to her satisfaction, she placed Nunnley at the bottom of her list—

Arrogant, handsome, pads his coat, wears his pantaloons too tight.

Her head jerked upright on number fourteen, and she pushed back from the desk. She most certainly would receive this caller—if she could get him past the butler. Jacobs was a stickler for propriety. Her list fluttered to the floor as, in her haste, her skirt brushed the desk. Ignoring it, she hurried into the entry hall.

"Bruce, how nice to see you," she called out to his retreating back.

He halted and glanced over his shoulder. A wicked grin spread across his face. Suddenly, he turned to the butler. "Shame on you Jacobs," he chided. "I thought you said Lady Jillian was not at home."

The butler cleared his throat and maintained a rigid stance with his hands folded behind his back. "She isn't, my Lord."

Unholy amusement glinted in Bruce's eyes. "Have you any notion as to when she will return?"

The butler's jaw clenched. "No, my Lord."

Jillian struggled to maintain a dignified expression. Now was not the time for Bruce to poke fun at the difference between not being at home, and not being *socially* at home. "It's all right Jacobs. Viscount Channing is expected," she said pitching a measure of authority into her voice, acting as if it was a normal occurrence to receive Bruce.

The butler drew himself up and thrust his chin forward. "Shall I rouse Lady Forbes from her bed, my Lady?" he inquired.

"That will not be necessary," she replied, knowing that drastic measures were called for. She crossed her fingers behind her back. "Damien will be home at any moment."

In the full spirit of things, Bruce thrust his hat and gloves into Jacobs's hand. "When his Grace arrives, please send him in."

Before the butler could protest, Bruce covered the short distance to the sitting room, grasped Jillian by the arm and led her inside, leaving the door gaping open behind them. Jillian broke away from him and closed it with a firm thump.

Bruce glanced warily around the empty room and then back at the closed door. "You're pressing our luck aren't you?"

Jillian shrugged. "I want to finish the discussion we began last night."

Bruce tilted his head to one side. "Which one?"

"Your sister. I'm hoping you were about to tell me that she is coming to London."

"Yes, she is," Bruce said as he stooped to pick up a sheet of paper from the floor. His gaze flickered over it before she reached him and snatched it from his hand.

She shouldn't have done it, shouldn't have put her secret in writing. She didn't want anyone to know— ever. She couldn't look at Bruce as she laid the sheet on the desk and picked up the quill to blacken all the incriminating words until the paper tore from her effort.

"It won't do you any good, Jillian," Bruce said.

She breathed deeply and straightened from the desk, feeling as if she'd relinquished control by leaving her emotions laying about for anyone to see. "Will you be a gentleman about this?" she asked stiffly, still unable to look at him.

"Jillian," he chided, "you should know by now that I am no gentleman."

She knew he was teasing her, but she was in no mood for it. Of course he was a gentleman, far more so than the other men who came to call. "A friend then. As a friend can I trust you to keep this to yourself?"

"I haven't told anyone yet, have I?"

She whirled on him, but kept her hands on the desk, an anchor to keep from sinking through the floor. "What do you mean? You can't possibly have known."

"I have eyes, Jillian. That," he pointed to the paper, "merely confirms my suspicions."

Oh God, had she been so obvious? All the admonitions Damien had given her concerning the proprieties rushed through her mind with humiliating force. Was that why her brother had made such a point of warning her—because Damien knew . . . because Max knew? It made sense. Why else would Max's manner have changed toward her? Why else would he stay away from her? She cleared her throat. "And do Damien and Max have such keen eyes as well?"

"Of course they do."

Her spirits plummeted to her feet as Bruce shrugged. "But they only see what they want to see." He chucked her under the chin. "Don't worry. Your secret is safe."

His gesture, coupled with an indulgent expression comforted her, and she imagined that he would do such a thing with his sister. She lowered her head a moment to collect herself and absorb what Bruce had said. "Max and Damien are your friends. Is not your first loyalty to them?"

The mischief returned to his eyes. "Far be it from me to presume to enlighten two such formidable men when they have chosen to ignore the obvious."

"Formidable . . . yes," she realized. "And becoming more so every day." She hadn't thought of Damien and Max in that way before, yet it perfectly described Max's distance in the weeks following her come-out and the anger she'd sensed lurking beneath the surface as they'd sat across the breakfast table from one another the day he'd left for Bassett House. Though she couldn't imagine ever being cowed by her brother, everything about Max and her feelings for him were intimidating. "I don't know whether to resent you or thank you for pointing that out to me."

Bruce gave her a cheeky grin. "Better the devil you know," he said, then sobered. "I should be going before someone discovers us. Propriety, you know." He reached the door just as it was opened from the other side.

Damien and Max stood in the threshold. Their gazes swept the room once and settled on Bruce.

Max's eyes turned to hard flint.

Damien's mouth tightened.

Panic squeezed Jillian's chest. She swallowed hard, her gaze flickering between Max and Damien. Assaulted by a barrage of conflicting emotions, she had the insane urge to run and find a pen and paper to write them down so she could sort them out. Her first instinct was to hurl herself into Max's arms, but his glare stopped her. His cold reception prompted indignation followed by misery. At Damien's scowl, guilt crept in at being caught breaking the rules. She wanted to run, and she wanted to stay. It had been two long weeks without Max, but facing his displeasure made her wish he had waited just one more hour to make an appearance.

And yet the impact of seeing Max held her rooted, doing nothing at all as love and longing sang through her veins. She opened her mouth to speak but she could not make a sound.

"Damien, Max," Bruce greeted them smoothly, then turned to Damien. "You're late for our meeting. Fortunately, Jillian was here to keep me company."

"How thoughtful of her," Max said acidly, then stalked past Bruce to lean against the desk, his arms folded across his chest.

Jillian drew herself up and lifted her chin, refusing to give in to the tears that burned behind her eyes. He'd left with barely a word to her and after being gone two weeks, he couldn't even bring himself to issue a polite acknowledgment of her presence. Well, she at least had good manners. "Max, it's good to have you back. When did you return?"

"Last night," he clipped out, then addressed Bruce. "Shall we get on with the meeting?"

"Why don't we reschedule for next week?" Damien said as he pinned Jillian with his gaze. "I'll send a note around and let you know the time and place."

"Certainly," Bruce said, clearing his throat and diverting his attention to Max. "I'm glad to see you've recovered."

Max nodded with a short jerk of his head and stationed himself at the window.

Bruce retrieved his timepiece from his pocket and opened it with a flourish. "I believe I'll toddle along now."

Jillian nearly collapsed with relief as Bruce left the room. It was short-lived.

"What the devil were you thinking to receive Bruce without being adequately chaperoned?" Damien snapped, his face taut with anger.

"He'd barely arrived," she said, suppressing the impulse to defend herself further.

"I know how long he's been here. Jacobs has been standing outside the door the entire time."

"We did nothing wrong," she said.

"I've told you before, Jillie. It's not what you do, but what people think you do," Damien said. "In the future, do not exercise such poor judgment."

Max turned from the window. "Do you intend to let Bruce off as easily?"

"I asked Bruce to accompany me in here," Jillian cut in. She would not have them think that Bruce had lured her into disgrace, either real or imagined. "He did nothing improper and I did nothing improper."

Impatiently, Damien rubbed the back of his neck. "I will not give this incident more significance than it deserves."

"More significance than it deserves?" Max said incredulously. Striding to the desk, he snatched up a piece of paper and thrust it toward Damien. "I would say it is very significant considering that Bruce is the only one not on her list. The only one who doesn't pad his coat, although he does wear his breeches a bit too tight."

Jillian stared in confusion as Damien eased down in a chair to look over the paper. It took a moment to re-

alize that it was her now-infamous list. How had he
seen it? But then, she remembered that Max had been
leaning against the desk. It made no difference how. He
had seen it and read it. Her fists clenched at her sides
as she faced Max. "That is mine. You had no right—"

"What is this about, Jillie?" Damien interrupted.

"Nothing," she said. "I was simply passing the time."

"Was Bruce the only one you wished to pass the time
with privately?" Max asked, his tone caustic and accus-
ing.

"Why no, Max. There have been times—in the
past—when I actually wished to pass the time with you
. . . *privately,*" she said, suddenly angry.

"Aren't you overreacting a trifle, Max," Damien said
quietly.

"Had it been anyone but me standing beside you
when the door opened, she would be compromised,"
Max said.

"But it was you. No harm was done," Damien said
reasonably. "And had circumstances warranted, Bruce
would have done the honorable thing."

Max's jaw clenched and the tendons in his neck
stood out as angry red color stained his neck. "The
honorable thing is not necessarily the right thing," he
said through clenched teeth. "She deserves to have her
bottom thoroughly spanked for her behavior." He
walked toward her, a pulse throbbing at his temple.
"And I am just the person for the task."

In a flash, she took refuge behind her brother's chair,
shaken to her very core by the depth of Max's rage. A
chill ran through her as she glanced from her brother to
Max, each as formidable as the other. Max had never
spoken to her with such anger. She pressed one arm to
her waist, restraining herself, holding in the pain until
she could be alone.

Damien bolted to his feet. "You overstep, Max.
Jillian is a member of my family and therefore my responsibility."

Max's brows pulled together and his head jerked

back as if he had been struck. Raw pain glittered in his eyes for a heartbeat, then his gaze narrowed as he stepped back.

Jillian's chest constricted as his expression became flat and hard and empty as if something had died inside of him.

"Leave us, Jillie," Damien said softly.

She barely heard him as she stared at Max, hating his remote expression. Never had he seemed so far away from her, so much a stranger to her.

"Now, Jillie," Damien barked.

With the last shreds of her pride, she walked stiffly to the door and shut it with a soft click. Turning back, she looked from one to the other, surprised that her mouth did not tremble when she spoke.

"I wish to stay," she said not liking what she saw or, rather, didn't see in Max's eyes.

Chapter 14

Max took slow deep breaths and struggled to contain his fury. He felt as if he had been hurled into a brick wall and his head had cracked open, scattering his wits on the carpet. He couldn't think and his vision blurred as he watched Damien stride to a low table to pour two liberal draughts of brandy. Silently, he pressed the snifter into Max's hand.

Without comment, Max accepted the drink, and with slow, deliberately placed steps made his way to the sofa and sagged into the cushions before draining the full measure of brandy. As the silence spun out, he rested his head against the back of the sofa, waiting for the liquor to take effect.

And with the calm came an insane urge to laugh.

He was the world's biggest fool.

Somehow in the past ten years he had come to believe that Jillian was as much his as Damien's. That his rights were equal to Damien's, and the three of them were a family. But they weren't and he'd had to slam into the invisible and impenetrable line of blood Damien shared with Jillian before he fully comprehended his place in their lives. He was not family. He was a friend *of* the family.

"How is your ankle, Max?" Jillian asked, startling him from this thoughts.

"Fine," he replied shortly. The urge to laugh grew stronger at her question. This *was* insane. A few moments ago he and Damien had been about to come to blows and now the subject of their battle was inquiring into his health.

"I can't imagine how you managed such an injury. You're such an accomplished rider."

"Apparently not accomplished enough," he said staring into his glass to hide the flush he felt climbing his face. He would be cursed with his own Pandora, who opened boxes of trouble faster than he could get them shut. During the past fortnight he'd succeeded in putting the dream from his mind, and now she brought it all back with a simple question. He couldn't tell her that he'd lost his seat on his horse because he'd been preoccupied with thoughts of the erotic fantasy that had sent him flying off to the country in the first place.

"We missed you," she said simply, artlessly, and it was more trouble flying out at him from a box he'd slammed the lid on.

He'd missed her, too, though he'd tried like the devil to put her from his mind. Instead it had taken all of his energy not to acknowledge that he'd missed her more acutely than ever before. The effort had been futile. Being lame and confined in a cold pile of stones, trapped by his own indecision, had only encouraged thoughts of mischief and laughter and belonging ... thoughts of Jillian. But there was no mischief in her eyes, no laughter in her voice now.

And he no longer felt as if he belonged.

He rose from the chair. "I have matters to attend to at home."

"Sit down, Max," Jillian ordered as she crossed her arms and leaned against the door.

Fascinated in spite of himself, Max stared at her, noting every nuance of her expression. Her color was high, her mouth was tight, and her glare was boring a hole through him. He'd never seen Jillian in high dudgeon before.

And he'd never felt quite so intimidated before.

Damien's brows snapped together. "What are you about, Jillie?"

"I was about to ask you the same thing."

"Meaning?"

"Meaning that I realize I shouldn't have received Bruce, but surely my breach of etiquette did not warrant such a display from the two of you."

"Does it not?" Damien said as he rose to splash more brandy in Max's glass and then his own. "Max was correct. If anyone else had been with me today, your conduct would have *warranted* marriage."

"To Bruce?" Max said. "Over my dead body." He downed his drink and sat back.

"And what is wrong with Bruce?" Jillian asked.

"Nothing," Damien replied.

Max snorted.

"Answer me, Max," Jillian insisted. "I did not realize that you had so little regard for a man who has been such a staunch friend to you through the years."

"My friendship with Bruce has nothing to do with it."

"Then what does?"

"Must I spell it out?"

"If I must suffer your ill temper every time he makes

an appearance, then yes, I have a right to know why."
She looked for all the world like a nanny about to administer discipline.

Good God, Max thought as his gaze focused on the rustle of her hem. She was actually tapping her foot.

"Fine. In all of my years as Bruce's friend, I have never known his interest in a woman to last more than a month," he said.

"All that signifies is that the right woman has not appeared in his life," Damien interjected.

Max glared at him. Sometimes, he forgot that Damien was almost as idealistic as Jillian. "There is no right woman for men such as Bruce beyond the usual advantages of money, title, and convenience."

"But you leave out the possibility of love," Jillian said, her eyes wide with shock.

Cynicism rose like gall into Max's throat as he tossed Damien a grim smile.

Tilting his head, Damien regarded him thoughtfully. "It does happen, you know."

"No I don't know. I've never suffered the emotion, and if I had I wouldn't trust it."

"Why Max?" she asked with a note of distress.

"Because," he said with his last grain of patience, "from what I've observed, the type of love you speak of is short-lived."

Jillian pushed away from the door and made her way to a chair in the corner, sitting back as far as she could, her hands curled around the arms, her expression pensive, her anger gone. "Yet it is what you want for me," she said, her voice a near whisper now, tentative somehow, as if she were reluctant to hear his reply.

Max suddenly felt as if he were inhaling shards of glass that shredded his insides and left little intact. He cupped his snifter in both hands and stared at his hands distorted through the crystal, moving as little as possible as the answer sliced through his mind. Yes, damnit, it was what he wanted for Jillian. For her, he wanted every dream she had to come true, no matter how unlikely. Better to wish for a bloody miracle. "I want you to be happy," he muttered.

"Is that why you object to Bruce?" Jillian asked. "You don't believe he would make me happy?"

"No." Max's jaw ached with the effort to keep from saying more. He shouldn't have to explain himself to a girl barely out of the schoolroom. Yet, she persisted in hammering at him, insisting that he do just that. He'd seen her do it before, when she'd pick apart a flower and shred the stem, studying each little particle, certain she would discover something wondrous at its core. But he was not a flower and she could pick him apart only if he allowed it. He set the snifter on the table and lurched to his feet. "I've had enough."

Her hands gripped the arms of her chair as she leaned forward, her green eyes studying him until he felt stripped to the soul. "Answer me, Max."

Feeling hunted and knowing it showed, he glanced at Damien looking for an ally.

Damien stared back at him, his gaze every bit as probing as Jillian's. "Since Bruce seems to be at the core of our problem, I would like to know, too."

"I object to Bruce," Max snapped with a brutal edge to his voice, "because he is too much like me. I don't imagine that he expects any more from marriage than I do."

Steepling his fingers, Damien gave him a hard stare. "And you expect nothing from marriage but the requisite heir, as you so succinctly put it," he said musingly, as if he had stumbled upon a truth that had been eluding him.

"Finally, you begin to understand," Max said, his insides churning at the words. He rose to pace the floor, hesitating as he came up against Jillian's suddenly pale countenance and distressed expression.

"How awful for you, Max," she whispered so only he could hear.

He veered away from her, avoiding the sadness he saw in her eyes. He couldn't credit such an emotion

over what he considered to be a blessing. It should be
the other way around, for he knew what to expect from
life and was prepared for it. Jillian was not. He caught
a glimpse of her in his restless wanderings around the
room. Again he hesitated, marveling at her resilience as
she seemed to recover herself between one moment and
the next.

"You're right, Max," she said, her gaze pinning him,
searching for . . . what? "Bruce is like you, and that is
precisely why I like him." She smiled then, a warm,
melting smile that had always had the power to set the
world to rights.

Yet, too much had changed in the past few weeks,
and his anger was too cold to be thawed with a simple
smile and an even simpler statement. It was a double-
edged sword—that statement. If she were to be believed, he could infer that her feelings for Bruce were
as platonic as her feelings for himself. He should be reassured by that, yet it drew blood instead, draining him
with the fear that the best things in his life were running ahead of him, leaving him behind to drown in his
own cynicism.

Shifting on his feet, he stared blindly ahead, refusing
to show a reaction, to give in to the impulse to pick up
his empty glass and fling it at the fireplace. How had he
become entangled in such a discussion in the first
place? Dimly, he heard Damien's voice, interrupting the
silence, his jocular tone an attempt, Max knew, to dissolve the tension in the room.

"There, you see, Max? If Jillie views Bruce in the
same light as she does you, then it follows that he is
merely a friend to her."

Against his will Max glanced at Jillian for confirmation.

"He is a friend, Max, nothing more," she said with a
gentle note as she continued to watch him, her head
tilted slightly, her eyes questioning. "I received him to
inquire whether his sister would be coming to London."

He nodded shortly. "I'm glad to hear it. If that is all,

may I be excused now?" he added, with a touch of sarcasm. It sounded churlish, but he had to get away, to think and make sense of it all.

"No," she said. "That is not all."

Max saw the slight tremble in her hands as she adjusted the folds of her skirt with studied care. That, more than anything betrayed the full measure of her distress, and it held him as surely as the memory of Jillian dancing in his arms, holding him with her smile, enchanting him with her maturity, intoxicating him with her scent and the warmth of her body.

Wordlessly, he walked to the table holding an array of crystal decanters and poured himself a fresh snifter of brandy, then set it down again. Drink was just another means to evade thought, and he was all too aware that it was too late to run. Sighing, he turned to her, trying to smile and failing. "All right, Pandora. I'm listening."

Her gaze slid from him to Damien. Oddly enough, she addressed her brother. "Damien, you shouldn't argue with Max over me. We're family."

"Families argue, too, Jillie," Damien said.

It was another slice of the sword, hearing Jillian and Damien talk of family so soon after Damien's reminder that they were not bound by anything but choice. Choices, he knew, could be reversed or discarded for more favorable options. His father had done it often enough, electing to return home to see to his son, then just as quickly haring off to more pleasurable pursuits. Max frowned, wondering where that thought came from. He seldom dwelled on circumstances he could not change.

"We never have," Jillian replied. "Yet, suddenly, the two of you are squabbling over *my* future as if I were a piece of property to be parceled off. You hurt me with your show of temper and insult me with your implications that I am not competent to make my own decisions."

Damien shifted in his chair. "Now, Jillie, you're imagining—"

"I don't think so, Damien. It is you and Max who seem to be given to flights of fancy. I spend a few minutes speaking with Bruce about his sister and suddenly you two are fighting one another over my honor and speaking of marriage." Again, she smoothed her skirt. "Yet, I have the queer feeling that Bruce has little to do with your objections."

Max had the queer feeling that she had directed that comment to him. Her sidelong glance did nothing to allay his suspicion. There was something in the look she gave him, something knowing in the way her lips turned up at the corners, her mouth parted in an attitude of expectation.

She was doing it again, he thought sourly—trying to pry open the lid of another box. A box so deep it would swallow them all. It was up to him to stop her before she completely upended their lives. It occurred to him then that only when they slipped into their old ways with one another did Jillian behave in the manner to which he was accustomed. Only when his manner was different with anger or impatience did she slip past his defenses to reveal his weaknesses.

Damien grasped the arms of his chair and pushed himself to his feet. "Well I for one am heartily tired of discussing Bruce." He clapped Max on the shoulder. "Max, are you still planning to collect Jillie and me for the Leighton ball?"

"Of course," Max responded, grateful that Damien had finally deigned to step in and remove him from this coil and restore them all to some semblance of normalcy. Yet his relief was short-lived as he smiled at Jillian and received a womanly-wise smile that maddened him with its eloquence.

It was as if she knew that the patterns of his life, his beliefs, were collapsing as surely as the old gazebo at Westbrook had collapsed in the storm. The blasted dream, so full of erotic images and sweet memories, had been enough to convince him that more than Jillian had changed.

Chapter 15

English roses and cream. Why had she never noticed how many members of the ton were blond? Jillian wondered as the elite of society gathered around Max and Damien, and by default, herself. Of course there were more women than men, and with a full dozen ladies circled around them, she felt like the dark center of a yellow daisy.

"By God, Bassett, heard you had broken your leg in a riding accident," Peckham said as he peered at Max's leg through a quizzing glass.

"I understand that, as usual, the gossips have made a mountain out of a molehill. As you can see, my limb is quite whole," Max said trying not to stare at how exactly the man's coat matched his yellowed complexion.

"Damned gossips," Peckham grumbled, then clapped Max on the back. "Too bad about your horse though."

"My horse?" Max said, staring after Peckham's retreating back.

Damien shot Jillian an amused look.

Two blond ladies moved closer into the inner circle. Unable to recall their names, Jillian resorted to identifying them by the colors they wore—a yellow lady and a pink lady.

"Yes," the pink lady said as she and the yellow lady swooped in. "We all know how much value you placed on Sovereign."

"How awful it must have been for you to be pinned beneath your horse for all that time," the yellow lady added in a breathy voice as she nodded her head in sympathy, her ash-blond tresses bouncing saucily. "The same thing happened to me on a fox hunt, fortunately I was thrown clear. But I vow I had nightmares for months afterward."

"It is true," the pink lady said toying with the fat, golden curl nestled at her shoulder. "Deborah found that talking about it helped. If you ever feel the need, please seek me out. I am a good listener."

"Indeed she is," the yellow lady agreed and smiled sweetly at her companion. "But perhaps it would be better to seek me out, since I am the one intimately familiar with the shock one suffers from such an ordeal."

"It was very brave of you to put the poor beast out of his misery," Mrs. Fitchley said, fussing with her turban. Jillian wondered if her hair was really green, as Bruce had said, and she wondered why Mrs. Fitchley would try to change the color of her hair. Maybe she was a brunette and wanted to fit in.

"It's a wonder you weren't crushed," her husband said to Max. "Although, I suppose that shooting him saved you from being mauled by his writhing about on top of you. Quick thinking, your Grace."

"Your concern is appreciated," Max said smoothly. "Please excuse me. We should be moving along." He tugged on Jillian's arm. "Good God," he muttered as they wound their way through the crush. "Why didn't the two of you set everyone straight?"

Damien chuckled and slanted an I-told-you-so glance at Jillian. "You know gossip cannot be stopped once started."

She grinned back at him. For the space of a thought she was tempted to tell Max exactly how the gossip had started in the first place, but she decided that one set-to between Max, Damien, and Bruce was enough for one day. Still, she mused, one discovered some very interesting things during a quarrel. In a way it had been gratifying to learn that she'd been right in surmising that the more attention paid to her by other men, the more Max reacted. Surely it was a good sign. On the other hand, she'd been distressed by his admission that he'd never "suffered" love before. What was it they shared, if not love? She knew firsthand that their friendship was not a thing to be "suffered." But then, considering Max's anger lately, perhaps he was suffering.

Lady Cornelia Thurston, who was not blond, and her sister Lady Judith Cecil, who was blond, stepped up to them.

"It is good to see you have recovered your Grace," Lady Cornelia said. "Sprains are very painful. Did your physician tell you that your ankle would be weak for a time?"

"Yes, he did," Max replied. "I see you had the good sense not to listen to gossip, Lady Cornelia."

Jillian wondered if Cornelia's good sense stemmed from her dark brown hair.

"My sister and I knew your injury could not be serious," Lady Judith interjected, staring at Max as if he were a Greek god stepped down from Olympus.

"And how did you determine that?" Max inquired.

Lady Judith nodded at Jillian. "Because Jillian and the Duke of Westbrook would have been at your side."

"I see sensibility runs in the family," Max said, his gaze drifting lazily over Lady Judith. "It is an admirable quality.'"

Lady Judith sucked in her breath and pushed two of her other qualities into prominence. "I had not realized that you had taken note of my attributes."

Jillian blinked as she thought she saw Max glance briefly at the two pillows of flesh rising above Lady Judith's square-cut bodice.

Jealousy stabbed at Jillian, and she suddenly had the most disgraceful desire to have Max study her bosom. Biting the corner of her lip, she flicked a glance down at her own chest, took a deep breath and straightened her shoulders a bit more.

He did not notice at all. He was too busy fawning over Lady Judith's hand in farewell, and staring at the tumble of silvery blond curls trailing down her back as she walked away.

"There's Fillmore," Damien said, diverting Max's attention. "I need to have a word with him. He keeps changing his mind about selling me that property."

"Just let it go Damien," Max advised.

Damien shook his head. "It's become a quest now. I intend to have that property and at a price I can live with."

Max shrugged. "Very well, but you know Fillmore is as fickle as a woman."

"I resent that," Jillian said.

Max grinned at her. "No offense Pandora. You don't qualify."

Jillian nearly choked on indignation at such a comment. Her face burned as if it were on fire and she knew she had gone scarlet. That afternoon, he'd been in a dither over her maidenly honor and now he again reduced her to the status of a child. And he had the gall to say women were fickle. She opened her mouth to say so, but Max and Damien had turned away from her to watch Fillmore's progress across the ballroom.

Damien brightened as the baron disappeared inside the card room. "Max, will you look after Jillie for a while?"

Max scowled. "Can you not wait until tomorrow to speak with him? It is not proper form for me to chaperone Jillian."

"I know," Damien agreed, "but since I am on the premises I believe we can squeak by this once . . . particularly if you dance with her."

Jillian's ire increased as they spoke above her head as if she were not present. How dare they bend the rules at their convenience and give her a royal set-down when she did the same? Why didn't they just send her to the ladies' retiring room where she would be out of sight and out of mind?

"Very well," Max said. "I will do it this once."

Damien nodded and strode away. Irate at being so summarily disregarded, Jillian stared after him, her lips parted, the nasty comment she was itching to deliver still lodged in her throat. From the corner of her eye she spied Lady Judith smiling at Max . . . and Max was smiling at her in return. The orchestra struck a waltz.

"Let us dance Jillian, so everyone will know I am not lame," Max said.

"Why don't you ask Judith?" Jillian said, hearing the petulance in her voice and not caring. She was tired of hiding her feelings when everyone else was free to show theirs.

"Judith Cecil?" Max asked, glancing at her with a puzzled expression.

"Oh, never mind," she said quickly as she saw Lady Seymour and Melissa approach—two more beautiful blonds. "Are we going to dance or not?" she asked abruptly.

Max rolled his eyes, then bowed, his manner a bit too patronizing for her taste. But Lady Seymour was advancing on them at an alarming rate, spurring Jillian to take his arm and walk beside him onto the dance floor.

"Are you going to tell me what that was all about?" he asked as he swept her into the waltz.

Jillian sighed, her irritation fading at the concern she saw in his eyes. This was the Max she knew. The Max who cared about her feelings. She'd missed him. Besides, he had given her the perfect opportunity to find out precisely what he thought of her. None of the other ladies seemed to be shy in their solicitation of his time or his compliments. "I am feeling sorry for myself," she admitted bluntly. "Until tonight, I had not realized that I am beyond the pale—literally."

"Whatever are you talking about?" Max asked, genuinely puzzled.

"I feel like a chimney sweep among all these fair-haired standards of English pulchritude."

"What rubbish!" Max said as he narrowed his gaze on her face. "You're quite beautiful, you know."

How she wished she could believe he was serious. But they had tossed such banter back and forth too many times before. "Really, Max, there is no need for platitudes," she said, flustered by the compliment in spite of herself.

"Describe the two most beautiful ladies here. Don't tell me their names," he instructed. "Just tell me what they look like."

Images of Lady Judith and Melissa instantly formed in Jillian's mind. "They both have blond hair and blue eyes."

"What else?" he prodded.

She hesitated for a long moment as her mind's eye searched the faces that it had conjured up for distinctive differences.

"Rather like trying to describe a pond full of white swans," Max provided.

"Yes it is," she agreed, meeting his gaze. He was staring at her intently, studying every feature, lingering at each point of interest, as if he were taking a leisurely stroll and was pleased with his surroundings.

"You are very lucky to be a black swan," he said and it felt like silk sliding over her skin.

Her knees turned to pudding and she couldn't seem to get enough air. He saw her—really saw her. Her blood felt like warm honey as she closed her eyes, savoring the joy and the sheer wonder of such a moment as she drifted in Max's arms, an elegant black swan gliding and floating above the others, unique in his eyes.

"Is that really how you see me?" she said, her voice a mere whisper of sound.

The final notes of the waltz drifted through the air and Max jerked his gaze from hers, his expression disoriented, as if he had taken a wrong turn and emerged in the wrong place. Abruptly, he released her and stepped away. "Yes. It makes it easier to find you in the crush."

She, too, stepped back, feeling the enchantment Max had so briefly cast over her fade and shrivel in the shadow of his sudden rejection. Her face ached with the effort to maintain a bland smile as she accepted his escort from the floor. All she wanted to do was run, to find a dark, quiet place where she could think in peace.

Max's face was stiff, his posture rigid, and he looked neither left nor right, acknowledging only those in his direct line of vision with a perfunctory nod of his head. Jillian felt the tightness of his muscles beneath her gloved hand, saw the whiteness of his knuckles as his clenched fist rested near his midsection. A lump of regret formed in her throat. It wasn't supposed to be this way—one fleeting moment of magic blotted out as quickly as she had blotted out his name from the top of her list earlier in the day.

They paused so Max could reply to yet another query concerning his foot. She kept her smile fixed as her temper began to blossom at the ease with which he neatly turned the gossip against its bearer with a single droll statement and patronizing lift of his brow. Why hadn't she noticed before that it was exactly the way he treated her of late? He listened to her with only one ear while speaking to her from both sides of his mouth. That afternoon, he'd spoken of her as a woman in imminent danger of being compromised, and then he'd treated her like a child to be spanked and sent from the room. Then this evening, he'd treated her like a woman for a few special moments, then recoiled from her as if she had jam on her face and threatened to smear it on his clothes.

She heartily wished he'd make up his mind and meant to tell him so.

But as they drew nearer to the chaperone's corner her spirits began to sink again at the sight of Mr. Nunnley advancing on them. She looked frantically about, hoping to attract the attention of someone tame like Reynolds or Blaylock. There was something about Nunnley that repulsed her.

Scowling, Max paused for barely a moment, staring straight ahead. Nunnley, too, hesitated, his gaze fixed on her and Max like an animal hypnotized by the light of a hunter's torch. She didn't bother to dwell on the peculiarity of Nunnley's actions as he veered away from her and disappeared into the crowd.

She had enough to do with dwelling on the peculiarities of Max's behavior.

Max smiled derisively at Nunnley's retreating back. The young viscount had made a wise decision. In his present mood, he would take great pleasure in planting the young Corinthian headfirst alongside the nearest potted plant.

On the other hand, Max thought that he himself might be the one who needed planting before his brain turned completely to feathers and his mouth ran away with his good intentions.

A black swan.

What was he thinking spouting nonsense that certainly was not appropriate conversation for him and Jillian to be having? He had only meant to bolster her confidence. But the dance had captured him with memories of a dream he couldn't forget, binding him with her nearness, her scent, her smile. Instead, there had been a glow in her eyes that he had never seen before. Actually, he had seen it before, but not from Jillian.

In the eyes of any other woman, he would call it seduction . . . the possibility for momentary pleasure. In Jillian's eyes, it still seemed like seduction . . . the probability of doom.

Damnit! Why couldn't she practice her wiles on someone else?

Of course the answer was quite clear. He was her friend. He was safe.

Jasper Reynolds approached and requested Jillian's

company for a dance. Max nodded his approval and she was swept away from him. He forced himself not to watch her drift in the arms of another man and wished he could repair to the next room for a drink. But, he didn't dare leave his post lest Jillian return, and if he took a drink every time she unsettled him, his wits would be pickled beyond recall and he would become as liverish as Peckham. Sighing impatiently, he propped his shoulder against a column and schooled himself to calmly wait for Reynolds to bring Jillian back to him.

The dance ended and another began, but Jillian was nowhere in sight. He told himself she was with Damien as he witnessed Reynolds bowing before Melissa Seymour. Perhaps Jillian had slipped away to the ladies' retiring room.

Max shifted from one foot to the other debating whether to search for Damien or remain where Jillian would be sure to find him. He cursed under his breath at his own indecision.

Suddenly, Bruce appeared at his side, leaning toward him in an attitude of confidentiality. "Thought you might like to know that Jillian has taken a stroll on the terrace."

"What?" Max said. "Why didn't you stop her?"

"She doesn't need my permission to leave the ballroom," Bruce said with an air of long-suffering censure. "And by the by, Nunnley slithered out behind her."

"Bloody hell," Max muttered. It didn't take any imagination to know what Nunnley had in mind. Where the hell was Damien? Exasperated, he started forward, Bruce at his side.

"Don't," Max ground out tightly, "follow me."

"God you're testy," Bruce drawled, unperturbed as he shrugged and strolled away.

Anger clashed with foreboding as Max pushed through the crowd, shaking off the hands that clapped him on the back and ignoring the overtures of the female population. If he survived Jillian's Season, he would seriously consider becoming a monk.

He stepped onto the balcony, looking left and then right, spotting his prey creeping stealthily toward a giant marble urn. "Nunnley," Max barked. The viscount jumped and spun around. In three long strides Max caught up with him and grasped the back of his collar, bunching it in his hand until Nunnley gasped for mercy. "Go back inside before I toss you over the balcony," Max said in a low, menacing voice.

Max waited until Nunnley disappeared. "Jillian," he hissed into the shadows, his fury growing with every minute spent searching for her among the statuary and pots of bushes.

A stifled giggle floated from behind the urn, then Jillian stepped out and flopped down on a stone bench by the balustrade. "Nunnley is so annoying. I'm glad you frightened the wits out of him."

She laughed then and it was enough to send him hurtling toward the edge. "Are you determined to ruin your life?" Max exploded, his hands clenched as he paced in front of her. "Your lack of judgment in coming out here alone amazes me." He planted his hands firmly on his hips. "Twice today you've put your head in the lion's mouth."

Toying with her fan, Jillian tilted her head to the side, her mouth a provocative curve as she looked him up and down. "How fortunate that the lion is too fond of me to bite my head off."

He glowered at her as he caught her meaning. She was deliberately misunderstanding him, intentionally turning his words back on him. He was not the one at fault here, damnit. "I can't follow you around to protect you from your own foolishness," he said, raking his hand through his hair.

"I do not remember asking it of you," she said with a politeness that drove him further over the edge of reason until he felt as if he were hanging on by his fingertips.

There was no reasoning with her. She was spouting

nonsense and making it sound like logic. "Go back inside, Jillian, I've wasted enough time with you today."

A moment passed, of awkward awareness and charged silence. He could see from the way her expression crumpled that he had succeeded admirably in finally getting her attention. He'd also hurt her. He'd always found it compelling how she thrust out her chin to defy pain, yet there was the barest hint of a tremble to give her away as she mustered her defenses. It never failed to touch him when she refused to back down, like a small terrier trying to bark a bear into submission.

He waited for her to speak, to deliver the last word. She always did.

But, her lips remained pressed together, her body stiff as she rose to her feet. Somehow, it shamed him to realize that she was not going to dignify his dressing-down with a comment. If he were in a mood to be rational, he would admit it didn't deserve comment.

She whirled around and her body pitched forward. She cried out in pained surprise as her shins collided with the stone bench. His hands shot out and found purchase in the silk of her dress.

But she had already fallen too far, and the fabric gave way as her hands slapped hard against the marble seat. Numbly, Max stared at the swatch of shimmering emerald silk in his hand, then lifted his head to watch Jillian's struggle to right herself. But her arms folded beneath her as she whimpered and sank to her knees on the cold marble of the terrace.

That whimper undid him. He tossed the cloth aside, lifted her into his arms and sat down on the bench, cradling her, rocking her gently, absorbing the shudders that ran through her body. She buried her face in his coat, stifling a moan of pain. He knew it hurt. And he knew she wouldn't cry. He'd rarely seen her cry, and even then she'd fought tears to the bitter end.

"Jillian," he whispered. "Where does it hurt?"

"My—my shins," she gasped. "Oh, but that bloody hurts."

"Let me see," he said pushing her skirt up to her knees and trailing his fingers down one leg and then the other. "You've a nasty bump growing on each shin," he said.

He felt her nod against his chest and heard her teeth grind. Stubborn girl. She'd no doubt feel better if she did cry. "Can you walk? We should find Damien and get you home."

"I can't," she said, her voice muffled by his coat. "The back of my dress is missing."

"The back of your dress is missing?" Max echoed in a strange croak. He stared down at her, the significance of the white knuckled grip she had on the front of her gown dawning on him.

Panic swelled and threatened to choke him as he glanced down at the swatch of silk laying at his feet, looking for all the world like a coquettishly dropped handkerchief. Dimly, he realized that the buzz in his ears was in fact the cacophony of music and two hundred voices coming from the ballroom.

In one motion he stood, set her on her feet and spun her around. Her back was exposed to the waist except for the dubious protection of her lawn chemise. The full impact of their predicament hit him, nearly doubling him over with calamitous implications.

He had to get Jillian out of here before they were discovered.

Whipping off his coat, he thrust it at her. "Put this on," he commanded and cast a searching glance around the balcony. With a sinking sensation in the pit of his stomach, he realized there was no exit other than through the main ballroom or down the stairway that led into the gardens and hedge maze—a stairway utilized by couples engaging in a moment's dalliance. He leaned over the stone balustrade and looked directly down, judging the distance to be no more than six feet.

"What are we going to do?" Jillian whispered at his side. He sent her a slantwise glance and almost laughed at the comic picture she presented. His coat hung past her knees, and she had rolled the sleeves so many times it looked as if she had a muff on each arm.

"Do you remember the time you fell from your swing?" he asked thoughtfully.

Jillian answered with a soft and melting smile. "How could I forget? You caught me."

"Yes, I did," he whispered, caught by the memory. "Do you trust me to catch you again?"

"You know I do."

Yes, he knew, yet hearing such certainty in her voice added weight to the knowledge, making it both a burden and a blessing.

Something was amiss.

Bruce Palmerston took care to step softly as he moved with inborn stealth along the dark balcony. Max and Jillian had never returned to the ballroom, nor had Nunnley. Then, ten minutes ago Arabella and Melissa had slipped out through the French doors.

Bruce had no idea where Max and Jillian were, but he had a feeling that when he located Nunnley and the Ladies Seymour, he'd find his missing friends as well.

Suddenly, he stopped dead in his tracks and ducked behind a stone column. Standing in the shadows, not more than fifteen feet away from him Melissa stood with her hands clutched beneath her perfect bosom. Her eyes were closed and her perfect face was contorted in an expression of perfect misery. Ye Gods, she was beautiful, even if she was decidedly bare in the brainbox.

A stone's throw away from her Arabella and Nunnley were peeking around the corner of a giant marble urn like two spiders waiting for a potential meal to blunder into their web. Unless he missed his guess, the hapless prey had already been caught.

"Melissa, stay well away," Arabella hissed. "I do not want you to witness any more of their indecent behavior."

Melissa raised her gaze toward heaven as if in supplication. "Yes, mother," she whispered.

Well and truly caught, Bruce thought. It must be bad if Melissa had been sent to stand in the corner to protect her maidenly sensibilities.

It was time to take a look for himself. Gingerly, he edged to the right and peered in the direction of Nunnley's and Arabella's gaze. He squinted and blinked and squinted again, not quite believing what he saw.

In the distance Max—indecently garbed in shirtsleeves, waistcoat and trousers—led Jillian down the shadowy terrace, with what was presumably Max's topcoat flapping about her slight frame.

"I would not have believed it were I not seeing it with my own eyes," Nunnley murmured. "He actually had his hands up her dress"—he broke off and snorted—"or what was left of it."

What the bloody hell had happened? Bruce wondered. Even though he had no idea precisely what had transpired, he knew that where gossip was concerned one could only rely on half of what one saw and none of what one heard. Arabella and Nunnley were proficient in the language of conjecture and small-minded assumptions.

"Do not speak of it," Arabella cautioned, her tone low and self-righteous. "My daughter has already been shocked enough tonight."

"Everyone will be speaking of it soon," Nunnley replied darkly. "He actually had the gall to threaten me earlier when I happened to walk out for a breath of fresh air."

Thoughtfully, Bruce tilted his head. Of course, Arabella and Nunnley couldn't be allowed to give their sordid version of what was likely an innocent escapade. He had no notion of how Damien might react to their tale. This was his sister's reputation that was about to be blackened. There would be a forced marriage of course . . . if Damien didn't kill Max first. And although Bruce knew Jillian would have no objections to the marriage, Max would surely have a few hundred or so. At this stage, he wasn't even willing to admit he was attracted to Jillian.

This had the power to destroy a friendship that had sustained Max his entire life. Already, Max had been denied too much. Bruce wouldn't allow Damien and Jillian to be taken from him as well.

"Her brother must be informed immediately. They mustn't be allowed to escape," Arabella said.

"Most certainly," Nunnley agreed. "His Grace, the Duke of Westbrook should know that his sister and his best friend are making a fool of him."

Bruce tensed at the blatant vindictiveness of Arabella and Nunnley. They would not stop at mere gossip. They wanted absolute annihilation, and Jillian would be their victim. Bruce's mind raced as he took in the scene, performing a quick study of the players in the sordid little melodrama.

He needed a plan—fast.

"Please don't Mother," Melissa implored. "I'm sure there is a logical explanation."

Melissa's defense of Jillian brought Bruce up short. He would have never thought her capable of such a thing much less stringing two sentences together.

He peeked around the corner at Melissa. Her perfect little hands were clutched in adorable little fists. "Jillian fell," she said. "It did not look as if his Grace meant to tear her gown."

Bruce smiled. Bless Melissa's heart. In one fell swoop, she'd given him the gist of what had really happened and a plan. A plan that was so wonderfully outrageous that there was no chance of it failing. If the situation weren't so dire, he might feel guilty for what he was about to do.

"I will not discuss this with you further," Arabella said. "Come along."

Bruce stepped into the open. "You would be wise to listen to your daughter, Arabella," he said smoothly. "And Nunnley, if I were you I would consider it very carefully before I crossed the Dukes of Bassett and Westbrook."

Arabella's eyes widened in surprise. "You saw as well?"

"Yes," Bruce lied.

"Then you know Jillian Forbes should not be allowed to associate with decent people." As if that were her final word on the subject, Arabella surged forward leading with her chin and leaving Nunnley behind. "Come along, Melissa," she said as she swept past Bruce.

Excellent, Bruce thought.

Melissa followed her mother. As she came abreast of Bruce, he flashed her a sunny smile and reached out and ripped off one little puffed sleeve from her gown.

Melissa blinked and stared down, her luscious mouth wide open in silent shock.

"Melissa!" Arabella whirled, her lips puckered as if she were ready to blister her daughter's ears. Seeing the tear in Melissa's gown, her mouth opened on a long intake of breath and from deep in her throat came a high pitched squeak.

"Nunnley did it," Bruce provided.

Arabella's outraged gaze jerked to Nunnley. It seemed the only part of her body she could move.

"That is not true!" Nunnley strode forward. "I wasn't anywhere near her."

Bruce reached out and yanked the end of Nunnley's intricately tied cravat. Naturally, Nunnley glanced down and when he did Bruce plowed his hand down the viscount's head effectively mussing his meticulously combed hair.

"This is scandalous!" Arabella sputtered. She moved to Melissa's side and ripped off her shawl to cover her daughter's torn gown.

"Why don't you give her your topcoat, Nunnley?" Bruce suggested pleasantly.

"What the hell are you about?" Nunnley rasped, trying desperately to retie his cravat.

"I'm trying to save your life, you fool," Bruce snapped. "You breathe one word of the exchange between Lady Forbes and the Duke of Bassett, and he and the Duke of Westbrook will have your guts for garters."

"I can't be seen this way," Melissa choked, her gorgeous eyes shimmering with tears.

Bruce shoved a twinge of guilt aside and concentrated on seeing this out to the end. "Forget what you saw. If you or Arabella speak of it, I'll see that you find yourself wed to Melissa in a trice."

Oh, it was delicious to witness the twin expressions of horror that statement invoked. He couldn't look at Melissa. If she found herself wed to Nunnley, Bruce would make sure she never lacked for anything. The creditors were beating down both Arabella's and Nunnley's doors. Not many people knew that, but Bruce made it his business to know everything about everyone. A forced match between Nunnley and Melissa was a disaster too terrible to contemplate.

"Arabella, take Melissa back inside the ballroom and leave at once. No one will notice her disrepair as long she keeps the shawl hugged close."

Arabella shot him a venomous glare and gripped Melissa's arm. "You bastard," she spat.

"So true," Bruce said with a shrug. "Now, begone and remember not a word or you know what will happen."

"Dry your face, Melissa," Arabella snapped as she gripped her daughter's arm and drove her forward. "Smile. We are just returning from a stroll on the terrace . . ."

"And what about me?" Nunnley asked. "How am I to escape here. I don't have my coach. I came with Blaylock."

The dunce didn't own a coach, Bruce knew. His creditors had repossessed it last week. "Walk down the stairs and through the garden," Bruce instructed, struggling to hang on to his patience. "Circle around to the front of the house and call for my coach. Wait inside until I come."

"But what if I'm spotted? Thanks to you I'm rather a mess," Nunnley said petulantly.

Bruce fought the urge to roll his eyes. The man was a complete blockhead. "The bushes are full of couples engaging a moment's dalliance. If you are seen, it will be assumed that you dallied a little too long."

Nunnley brightened visibly. "They'll believe I've made a conquest. I can keep them guessing for weeks at the club as to whom it might have been."

Apprehension shot up Bruce's spine. He wasn't at all sure Nunnley could keep his mouth shut. The fool could inadvertently reveal something if it increased his popularity with the young bloods of his set. Perhaps it was a good thing that Bruce was stuck with seeing the idiot home. It would allow him time to impress upon him more fully the necessity of absolute discretion.

"That you can," Bruce agreed and clapped him on the back. "Get to the coach. I'll catch up with you later."

As Nunnley walked away, Bruce released a long sigh of relief. With any luck, disaster had been averted at least from this end of the balcony. But Max and Jillian still might need help.

Who said chivalry was dead?

Chapter 16

Jillian teetered precariously on the narrow ledge of the terrace. She should never have left the ballroom.

Though he hadn't raised his voice nor directed his ducal glare at her since she'd toppled over the bench, she knew Max was furious with her. Not that she blamed him, she was well aware of how serious their predicament was. They had to escape before they were discovered.

She held tightly to the rail with one hand and used the other to grip Max's coat securely around her throat. Her foot slipped and with only a one-handed grip on the balustrade she swayed in midair like the Union Jack flapping in the breeze.

Max reached out to steady her. "Turn loose of the bloody coat and use both hands to hang on. And don't you dare try to recapture it once you jump. I don't want your elbows driven into my throat."

"You don't understand," she explained and wrapped her arm more securely around the rail. "The back of my dress held up the front."

He rolled his eyes and released a long suffering sigh. "I promise I won't look," he said and leaped to the ground, landing nimbly on his feet. He grinned up at her.

"Ready?"

She raised her chin and planted both hands on the rail, not daring to look down at herself. With only her chemise for coverage, she felt naked. Drawing a deep breath, she turned and felt the chemise grow taut as her chest pushed out. Embarrassment heating her face, she looked down at Max.

He stood with his legs braced wide apart, his arms outstretched, smiling at her. He didn't notice, she thought, thank God, he didn't notice.

"Jump," he commanded with a reassuring smile.

The distance to his arms didn't look so very far, and his outstretched arms were certainly more inviting than her precarious perch on the narrow ledge. Without hesitation, she locked her gaze with his and jumped. The coat billowed up behind her, slowing her descent. Cool air sliced through the thin fabric of her smallclothes, chilling her. She laughed at the freedom and exhilaration of it. Who'd have thought she would have such an adventure in the midst of a stuffy ball?

Her body collided with his. The breath whooshed out of her as he collapsed under her weight like a castle of sand, landing them both on the ground with bone-jarring force, with her on top of him. She emitted a ragged high pitched sound as she panted for air and shook with mirth at the same time. Propping herself up with her hands flat on either side of him, she angled up from his chest and grinned down at him. Apparently he hadn't taken into account that she had grown since she'd fallen from her swing.

A split second before she'd landed on him, the smile had evaporated from Max's face, replaced by an expression of utter bewilderment as he stared at her chest. He was still staring at her with a look that was simply priceless.

Max lay flat on the ground, staring up at Jillian as he gulped in air, the image of two magnificent breasts hurtling through the air toward him stunning him more effectively than the impact of her body.

A woman's body, fully grown.

No wonder he'd been so bloody confused. His body had noticed what his mind had been reluctant to accept. She *had* grown up, and he'd literally had to be slapped in the face with the evidence as she'd landed on top of him. And as she angled the upper half of her body upward, he could no longer deny it . . . not with her hips pressing into his, provoking him to swell and harden beneath his trousers. Not with those magnificent breasts staring back at him.

He had the insane urge to touch her and taste her . . .

And he tried to think on saner lines.

Jillian's body began to shake.

"Are you hurt?" he asked urgently.

She shook her head and made a sputtering sound. He gripped her shoulders and rolled her over, reversing their positions so he could see her face. Unfortunately he still had an excellent view of her upper body. His coat hung drunkenly off one of her shoulders and the bodice of her gown drooped to her waist. A waist that his hands had spanned hundreds, probably thousands, of times and he had never noticed how minuscule it was in comparison to tantalizing hips and what was indeed a glorious bosom.

He couldn't take his eyes off of the translucent chemise or the dark outline of taut nipples. He grew harder, straining against his trousers, aching with the awareness of having a beautiful, half-naked woman beneath him.

And she was laughing, damnit!

"I believe her funny bone may be shattered," Bruce Palmerston's calm voice said from the shadows.

It was like being thrust into an icy stream. Max's senses returned, sharp and alert. God, what was he doing just lying on top of Jillian like an idiot? They had to escape, though he knew that it was too late to escape discovery. The best he could hope for now was to avoid complete humiliation.

Compromised. She was bloody well compromised.

Had it been just this afternoon that he had lectured Damien about Bruce's conduct toward Jillian? The irony of it was laughable.

"Bruce," Jillian gasped and tried to raise up on her elbows and pull the edges of the coat together at the same time. But Max stopped her, maintaining a firm grip on her arms. She turned her head, craning to see Bruce over Max's shoulders. "I tore my gown. We had to jump from the balcony."

Bruce's mouth twitched. "How fortunate that Max was here to break your fall."

Protective fury shot through Max at the possibility that Bruce may have witnessed Jillian plunging through the air like the carved prow of a ship riding the waves, his frock coat billowing above her like a mainsail. That Bruce might have also seen the perfection of her body enraged Max even more. "How long have you been standing there?" he bit out.

"Not long enough, obviously. I would have loved to witness what ... ah ... dropped you into this mess in the first place."

Max's anger intensified at Bruce's flippancy. "Get up," he barked at Jillian and yanked his coat more securely over her shoulders.

Jillian gave him a startled look and tried to scramble out from under him, her knee pressing into his groin, nearly unmanning him. He sucked in his midsection and rolled off of her, then stumbled to his feet, dragging her up with him.

"I'm sorry I laughed, Max," she said, her voice a breathless babble, "but you had the oddest expression on your face." She clutched the coat in a death grip, bunching it over her chest. A thick lock of hair hung over her cheek and with the coat hanging on her like a sack, she looked as small and ingenuous as she had when she was eight years old. But it was too late. He'd already seen what the coat concealed. He'd seen what he'd refused to see in the past few weeks, wanted what he knew he should not—could not—have.

"Did you forget, Max, that I have gained a few stone since the last time you had to catch me?" she said with a frown, her attention focused on the coat that she could find no way to fasten.

Oh God, how he wanted to forget.

"A few stone in the most intriguing places," Bruce agreed, his eyes gleaming with suppressed amusement.

Clamping his teeth together so hard his jaw ached, Max spun her around to face him, her back to Bruce. He snatched a diamond stickpin from his cravat and took over the task of preserving Jillian's modesty himself while glaring murderously at the amused face behind her.

"Max," Jillian said in a strangled voice and pushed at his hands.

He looked down. He had the coat pulled so tightly

around her neck, he was almost choking her. "Sorry," he muttered and released his grip on the collar.

"I'll do it," Jillian said as she turned out the lapels, lapped them neatly about her neck and pinned them together.

Max nodded his satisfaction that her body was at last securely enshrouded.

Bruce crossed his arms and shook with silent laughter.

Heat rose in Max's face. If he didn't need Bruce's assistance he would kill him and toss his body into the Thames. "Do you think you can contrive to have my coach brought to the back of the alley?" he snarled.

"Certainly," Bruce said amiably. "Do you think you can contrive to get Jillian there without mishap?"

"Do you think you two can stop shooting poison darts at each other?" Jillian hissed. "I should very much like to go home before someone sees me."

"I'll get the coach," Bruce mumbled.

"Thank you," Jillian called softly as he disappeared around the corner.

Max grasped Jillian's arm. "Don't say a word. If we are lucky, we will get away from here without the whole bloody ton coming out to watch us."

It was lucky for them that the Leightons had a fondness for bushes. Max dragged Jillian from one to the next, zigzagging through the gardens and around to the alley behind the house. Still, his temper grew shorter as branches slapped him in the face and insects buzzed annoyingly around him. At least Jillian had the good sense to keep her mouth shut.

They didn't see a soul as they crept across the stable yard and slipped through the small rear gate, and Max began to hope that he and Jillian might actually escape disaster. He was even able to marshal enough magnanimity to be grateful that it had been Bruce who had come upon them. For all Bruce's odd wit and easygoing attitude, his loyalty to a friend was unquestionable.

He glanced down the alley one way then another as he listened for the rumble of a coach and four.

The carriage was nowhere in sight.

Max cursed under his breath and pulled Jillian behind a clump of weeds.

"Bloody damn rosebush," Jillian muttered and absently rubbed her arm.

"Mind your mouth," he chastised, exerting all his control to hold his temper in check. He did not think she even realized the seriousness of their situation.

"Well it stings," she groused and held up her arm for his inspection. The sleeve of his coat slid past her elbow.

Max licked his finger and washed off the blood sluggishly oozing from a small scratch. "You're fine."

As she had many times before when he'd soothed her hurts, she nodded and smiled up at him in complete trust. As he'd done many times before, he looked her over, searching her for further injury. But this wasn't like those other times and his gaze snagged at her chest and waist and hips, aware of what lay beneath the folds of his coat. He frowned and glanced away, scanning the alley for some sign of the carriage.

He still saw those magnificent breasts.

He needed a drink.

"What is it?" she asked and captured his hand and twined their fingers together in another gesture of faith that he would make everything all right.

"Nothing," Max said wearily. Nothing was all right and he had little confidence that it ever would be again. Everything had changed. In his heart and in his mind he had broken the trust they'd always shared. His desire for her was real, no longer a dream, corrupting the simplicity of friendship.

The creak of approaching carriage wheels carried through the night. Max waited, not daring to emerge from their hiding place until Bruce emerged from the interior, glancing in both directions down the alley before motioning for them to come.

Max grasped Jillian's arm and ran for the coach. He lifted her inside and climbed in after her. Bruce slammed the door behind them and leaned in the open window. "There you are, all tucked up safe and sound. May I be of any further service?" he offered with exaggerated gallantry.

"Bruce, I've about had—" Max began in a low icy voice, then broke off as practicality cut through the haze of insanity surrounding him. "Inform Damien that I have escorted Jillian home and will explain everything to him when he arrives. And Bruce, not a word to anyone," he added, knowing the warning was unnecessary.

"Discretion is my middle name," Bruce said blithely as he turned and walked away.

"Max?" Jillian called hesitantly from the shadows inside the coach.

"Do not say a word," Max warned as he prepared himself for what was to come. He leaned his head heavily against the squabs and rubbed the bridge of his nose. Damien's warnings hadn't been enough to avert disaster.

And now it was too late. Even now, his manhood was swollen and his flesh burned with desire as he sat next to Jillian in the coach, not touching, yet feeling her gaze, absorbing her nearness. He could no longer deny the truth.

He wanted her as he had never wanted anything in his life.

And he knew that her ruin would also mean his own.

Chapter 17

Jillian trudged into the drawing room behind Max. He had not spoken a word to her since they had slinked away from the Leighton's ball almost an hour ago. She watched him closely as he strode to the sideboard and poured himself a liberal glass of brandy, drained it, and poured himself another. She'd never seen him so disheveled and it occurred to her that it had been years since she'd seen him in shirtsleeves and with his hair mussed, a forelock hanging over his brow from the constant raking of his fingers.

She liked him this way, with his neck a strong column above his skewed neckcloth and his broad shoulders extending beyond the armholes of his waistcoat. This was the way he'd looked when he'd shared picnics with her and Damien, yet lately all she saw was the aloof Duke of Bassett. She'd never seen him so furiously silent, as if to voice his anger was to unleash more than even he could control.

He had good reason to be agitated, but his anger seemed overblown under the circumstances. She couldn't believe that the situation was as dire as his mood indicated. Technically, she supposed she had been compromised, but they had not been discovered by anyone but Bruce. They were safe.

It appeared that it was up to her to point that out to Max. "Bruce will not betray us," she said.

"Bruce is the least of my concerns," he said tightly. "Your brother will have my head."

"I will explain to Damien." Even as she said it, panic thrust sharply into her thoughts. How, she wondered, could she justify her torn gown, not to mention rolling about on the Leighton's lawn with Max?

"What is there to explain, Jillian?" he barked, the tendons on his neck standing out and a pulse throbbing at his temple. "You are compromised and I am the guilty party. It seems quite clear to me."

Jillian flinched and took a shuddering breath. Max was right and she knew it. Yet, she had faith in her brother's ability to discern truth from supposition. Hadn't he said that very afternoon that he would not give an incident more significance than it deserved? The irony of it was that, in her mind, the incident was indeed significant. She wanted Max and this was the perfect opportunity to have him . . . if she were willing to exploit it. There was the rub. She didn't want Max through coercion. She wanted him willing. She wanted him to love her.

"It was an accident," she said quietly. "Damien will understand."

"Damien will understand nothing but that your reputation is at risk. He will do anything to protect you."

Anything. She knew what he was talking about, though he wouldn't say it outright. Again, panic gripped her. Right here, right now, she could know the true nature of Max's sentiments toward her. Yet she was afraid. Until now, her feelings for him had been private and safe. Every wistful thought of him had been a dream to be nurtured. To know would be to either realize the dream or to have it shatter at her feet.

Heaven help her, but she had to know.

"Damien won't force us to wed if that's what you are worried about."

Max stiffened as she said it, and she thought of a frayed wire stretched to the limit—in danger of snapping if pulled too tight, the ends lashing out dangerously from the abrupt release.

"You had better pray that does not happen Jillian," Max ground out in a low voice.

"Would it be so awful?" she asked. "Most married couples I have observed are barely able to tolerate each other. At least we are friends."

Max laughed without humor. "God, are you actually warming to the idea?"

"I am merely pointing out that if we did find ourselves in a position where marriage is necessary, that we have more to base it on than most."

"Didn't you listen to me and Damien earlier? Don't you understand that all I want from a wife is a legal heir? I want more for you, things I can't give you."

Suddenly and painfully she realized the import of what he had revealed that afternoon. He and Bruce were alike, and there was no right woman for men such as them. If Max objected to Bruce as a husband for her, then it followed that he would also object to himself. She held her breath for a moment as one thought led to another, making everything clear. Max wanted her to be happy. He was not rejecting her at all. He was rejecting himself.

"You've always made me happy, Max. I don't see why marriage would change that."

"You naive little fool." He hurled his glass against the fireplace. "What makes you think you could make *me* happy?" Rounding on her, he glared at her with a glacial expression. "What makes you think I would want you to try?"

The words slammed into her, numbing her with their cold cruelty. Then pain set in, like blood running back into a smashed digit, or a crushed heart. It was an agony like she had never felt before, nearly doubling her over.

He didn't want her.

The walls seemed to recede and she felt as if she were shrinking with humiliation. She *was* a naive fool. He didn't want her. She covered her mouth with her hand to keep from crying out. But a whimper escaped her, a small, wretched sound that hung in the air between them.

He didn't want her.

Max's scent surrounded her and she was dimly aware that he was jerking her toward him, crushing her against his body, then urging her toward the settee. Her eyes dry and burning, she flailed out blindly, trying to escape him.

"Oh God, Pandora," he murmured as he lowered her to the cushions and sat down beside her. He cradled her head with one hand, and pressed her cheek against his chest. "I'm sorry."

She buried her face in his throat and wrapped her arms around his neck. She was sorry, too. Sorry that their friendship was slipping through her fingers because she had dared to reach for more. She had to hold on, to protect what they shared. Their friendship was too precious to sacrifice for a foolish dream. "Please don't hate me."

"Shhh," he soothed and pressed a kiss near her ear. "I could never hate you."

Startled by the intimate caress, Jillian shivered and pulled back to look at him. His head was bent, his attention focused on her chest. Following his gaze she saw that his coat had come unfastened and her breasts were clearly visible through her thin chemise. She stared at herself, fascinated by the way her breasts seemed to swell and her nipples puckered and pushed at the cloth. A warmth blossomed inside her, and restless longing raced through her veins.

She should cover herself, she thought, yet she couldn't move as Max looked up at her with a heavy-lidded gaze and lightly traced her bottom lip with his forefinger.

With a bravery she did not know she possessed, she pressed a kiss to his finger and caught it with her tongue as she moistened her lips and leaned toward him.

Max's hand cupped her chin, holding her still, their

lips a hairbreadth apart from one another. "Tempt me not, Jillian," he said on a ragged breath, "you are treading on dangerous ground."

She knew. She didn't care. Warmth became heat and longing turned to a delicious ache in the pit of her belly. Something was happening and she had to know what it was . . . what it meant. "I'm not afraid, Max," she whispered as she leaned closer, her mouth brushing his.

"You should be," he groaned and his mouth opened, covering hers.

Her heart skipped a beat then pounded harder. Her entire body felt like a pulse, and her breath shuddered in her throat as sensation followed sensation as she parted her lips and gasped when his hands cradled her head and his tongue brushed her lips, skimmed her teeth, then plunged inside her mouth, shocking her, thrilling her.

She rose to her knees, needing to get closer to him, to feel more as he drew on her mouth. Her hands tangled in his hair as he drew back and she touched his lips with the tip of her tongue, becoming intoxicated by the flavor of brandy and Max. Her breasts pressed against his chest and urgency gripped her as every part of her seemed to tremble inside and out.

And still their mouths clung until she didn't know where one kiss ended and another began. Over and over their tongues met and teased and stroked as his head angled one way and then the other in a hard demand that carried her on waves of need. She could not get enough of him, could not get close enough to him as pleasure burned hot and reckless inside her. She wanted to melt into him, become part of him. She twisted around to face him, her knees on either side of his thighs. His hands worked at her hair, freeing the strands to fall over her face, to cloak them both in a private world of discovery.

His hands skimmed down her sides to grasp her waist and his mouth slid away from hers. She moaned aloud at the loss, then arched her neck as his lips sketched a path from her collarbone to her ear, nipping the lobe and tracing the shell with his tongue. Urgency swept through her and it was hot, so hot—

A door slammed.

Max's hands tightened on her waist. Jillian's gaze jerked toward the sound, her hair whipping about her head and sticking to her mouth. She swiped it away and focused on the doorway.

Damien stood there, his face washed of all color, his green eyes blazing with rage, as if he were ready to commit mayhem on the first thing that moved.

"Damien?" Jillian said on a labored breath, unable to form a coherent thought for the shock of being so quickly plucked from the fiery sensation of Max's kisses and plunged into cold fear at her brother's expression.

A deathly silence fell over the room. She stared at Damien and knew that Max, too, was trapped in his furious glare.

Then, with precise, deliberate motions, Max lifted Jillian off his lap, set her on her feet, rose, and immediately stepped away. With his legs braced apart, he straightened his shoulders and folded his hands behind his back.

All she could do was fight for balance on a floor that seemed to be more liquid than solid and search for words that didn't seem to exist.

"Cover yourself," Damien said in a flat voice she'd never heard before. He was a stranger wearing Damien's features and Damien's clothes.

She clutched Max's coat over her chest, ignoring the strands of her hair tangled in her fingers. She had to say something—anything—to bring her brother back to her. "Damien, you don't understand."

"I understand perfectly," Damien said woodenly. "I left you in Max's care and he seduced you."

"That is not what happened," she cried, then cringed as Damien's gaze swept from her hair to the front of

Max's coat. She raised her hand and tried to smooth her hair back, belatedly realizing how disarranged she must look. She *felt* disarranged.

With a snarl, Damien covered the distance between himself and Max and seized Max by his waistcoat, twisting the cloth in his fists. Before Jillian understood what she saw, Damien hauled Max up until they were toe-to-toe and chest-to-chest.

Saying nothing, Max kept his hands at his sides, meeting Damien's gaze full on, unflinching as Damien hurled accusations at him.

"You bastard," he said, his voice low and vicious. "You weren't satisfied with having every willing woman in the ton falling at your feet. You had to ruin my sister." He released Max with a shove and abruptly veered away from him. "Goddamn me for a fool. I trusted you."

Why didn't Max say something? Jillian wondered frantically. Why did he stand so passively, a blank expression on his face as if he weren't really there.

"No, Damien. Max would never seduce me," she said.

Damien turned on her, pointing his finger at her. "You know nothing. He collects hearts like most men collect horses and with less conscience. He has no regard for women—"

She batted his finger away. "No more than you, Damien. I can't imagine that you have never kissed a woman."

He grasped her arms and frog walked her to the mirror hanging by the door. "Look at yourself," he grated, "and tell me that we are talking about a mere kiss."

She stared. Her hair was wild about her head. Her eyes were wide, her skin pale ... She raised her hand to touch her mouth. It was red and swollen, the flesh around her lips and down her neck chafed from the scrape of whiskers. The fabric of her chemise showed through where Max's coat parted below her hand, and the sheer white lawn was shaded by the color of her flesh beneath. Shaking her head, she tried to back away but Damien stood behind her, holding her firm.

Lowering her head, she averted her own gaze, feeling shame for the first time. Shame because she was nearly naked and her brother had seen her this way. Shame because the feelings she had for Max, the wild sensations and reckless needs she experienced with him seemed all too obvious in her appearance. The privacy of her mind and heart had been violated.

She lifted her chin and met Damien's cold stare in the mirror, then saw Max's image apart from theirs, standing alone and isolated in the center of the room. She wouldn't have it. Max belonged with her.

"It was a kiss, Damien," she said firmly. "And it was my choice."

"You defend his actions, Jillie?"

"No. I justify them. He didn't seduce me. I was willing."

"Shut up, Jillian," Max said, straining the words through clenched teeth. "There is no justification for this predicament." His gaze focused on Damien. "Nor is there any recourse."

Jillian twisted from Damien's hold to turn and face Max, but she couldn't think past Max's angry words. He'd never spoken to her like that before. That he'd done so after kissing her with such earthshaking intensity was an indignity too great to bear.

"I told you once that I will not allow a match between you and Jillian," Damien snarled.

"The two of you have discussed this before," Jillian blurted, shocked by the revelation.

"Certainly, and the feelings are mutual," Max said in a cruel, silky voice. "But, have we a choice, Damien?"

"There are always choices," Damien said. "Pistols at dawn being one of them."

A duel? It couldn't be happening—not to Damien and Max. Not to her. "No," she said, and it sounded as weak and frightened as she felt. She gulped in air and let it out, forcing herself to remain calm. Someone had to be calm. "You cannot mean it. It was only a kiss."

"No, he doesn't mean it," Max said, his voice as blank as his expression. "At least not until he is certain no one but Bruce witnessed tonight's folly. Otherwise he will need me to salvage your reputation." His mouth twisted into a savage smile. "Isn't that correct, Damien?"

"Goddamn you," Damien said bitterly. "If disaster can be averted this night, you are a dead man."

"Cease with your threats, Damien," Max said, his blue eyes glittering with barely suppressed rage. "We both know that a duel will accomplish precisely what you are trying to avoid. If the gossips do not catch wind of this, a duel will certainly gain their attention." He straightened his shoulders a little more and assumed a broader stance, as if he were issuing a challenge or bracing himself to accept one. "I assume you will notify me of the outcome."

Damien hesitated, watching Max with grim deliberation, then nodded curtly. "And if marriage between you and Jillian is not required, you will not come near her again . . . ever. All connections between us will be severed."

Jillian backed into the wall, feeling as if she were collapsing from the inside out, crumbling into a thousand pieces that would never fit together again. The clock on the mantle chimed the hour, proclaiming half past midnight as the exact time that life as she had known it drew to an end.

Without a word, Max strode toward the door and walked out.

Chapter 18

Jillian had never felt so isolated in her life as she sat in the window seat, each memory and emotion splintering inside her, inflicting its own wound in a different part of her heart, each creating its own unique pain.

How many hours had it been since her family disintegrated around her, leaving her feeling alone and unconnected?

She stared out at the sky and noted that the moon had made its arc from one horizon to the next since Max had walked away and Damien had sent her to her room. She rubbed her burning eyes and tried once again to sort her tumbled thoughts. Yet, she could only grab hold of one: They were all separate now and, for the first time in years, unable to reach out to one another for comfort.

She couldn't seem to get past it, to do more than absorb the misery and hope it would go away so she could think again.

A loud crash followed by a sudden, muffled thump and murmured voices came from the hall. She scrambled from the window seat and hurried to the door.

Damien lay amidst the remains of a small table, his valet bent over him.

"He is all right, my Lady," the valet whispered.

"Overindulged," Damien muttered drunkenly.

Jillian stared at him unable to comprehend what was happening. Damien never drank himself insensible.

The valet grasped Damien under the arms and tried to heave him to his feet. "Here we go, your Grace. It's only a few steps to your room." But the man was too small to pull Damien up to his full height and Damien's legs buckled, dragging the servant down with another crash.

Frowning, she glanced down the hall to LadyLou's bedroom. The door was shut and all was dark. It appeared that her aunt had slept through the commotion ... so far. But if Damien was not put to bed immediately, the entire household would witness his indignity. "All right, Gibbs, you get on one side and I'll take the other," she said as she looped Damien's arm around her shoulder. "That's it ... now walk slowly or we'll be dragging him down the hall."

"I c'n walk," Damien slurred. "Don't need ass ... assist ... help."

"Straighten your legs," Jillian ordered. "Good. Now put your right foot in front of your left."

They made it to his door, Damien taking the steps as if the floor was rolling beneath him. Gibbs reached out to turn the knob and they all three lurched across Damien's room, dropping him facedown on his bed.

With Gibbs on one side and Jillian on the other, they managed to turn him, but gave up on trying to shove him toward the headboard so his feet did not dangle over the edge. The valet busied himself with removing Damien's shoes.

Damien blinked and stared up at her as she stuffed a pillow under his head. "Betrayed me ... both of you ... who c'n I trust now?" His voice trailed off and his head lolled to the side as his eyes drifted shut.

Miserably, she stared at her brother as she brushed his hair from his forehead and lightly smoothed her fingers over the dark circles beneath his eyes. She loved him so much, and he was hurting so badly. As badly as Max must be hurting.

She pressed a kiss to his brow, then turned and ran back to her room.

Jillian closed her door and sank to the nearest chair. She couldn't bear knowing that Damien felt betrayed, that he didn't feel he could trust her. It was another splinter piercing her and her heart twisted in her chest, closing around the pain. And as it had every time her thoughts became too anguished to bear since Max had walked away earlier, her mind escaped to the most profound experience of her life.

Max had kissed her.

Oh God, that kiss. As many times as she had dreamed of such a moment, she had never realized how wondrous, how magical, it would be. She'd wanted it to go on forever. Even now, her lips tingled with the memory of his mouth covering hers, and the taste of him still lingered on her tongue.

Then Damien had walked in and the dream had become a nightmare so horrible that her mind could not even begin to grasp the meaning of it all.

She raised her hands to cover her mouth and shook her head over and over as she tried to blot out the images racing through her mind. Damien's accusations and rage. Max's withdrawal. Her pain at being forsaken by them both.

It was her fault. She never should have gone to the balcony alone. She never should have ignored Max's warning and kissed him. Yet, he had been as breathless and consumed by the moment as she.

And she might never feel Max's arms around her again.

Impatiently, she dashed a stray tear from her cheek and lunged to her feet to quarter the room at a frenzied pace. Weeping would do no good when there was so much to sort through and understand.

That was the problem. She understood nothing of the thoughts chasing about in her head, tangling themselves in a hopeless knot. Her mind raced faster and faster in one direction then another.

She'd been compromised.

Max had been banished.

Damien was wallowing in his cups.

Blast it! If she didn't straighten things out, no one would.

Yet, short of marrying Max, nothing else came to mind. She ground to a halt, captured by the thought. Marriage ... to Max. If she and Max were legally bound, Damien and Max would have to be friends again and everything would be as it was. The ideal solution.

Yet, Max had made it clear that was the last thing he wanted.

She almost wished she had been ruined, but she was sure no one had seen them—a miracle under the circumstances, and one that she was not sure she wanted. Yet, as much as she wanted Max, this was not the way she had envisioned it happening. She wanted the dream—Max loving her as much as she loved him ... Max asking for her hand ... Max sweeping her away to be a part of his life. Yet, Max and Damien had dashed her hopes of that ever coming to pass ... unless she was indeed ruined.

And she was not.

Yet.

The thought jarred her from her confusion. Stunned by the simplicity of it, she backed up to sink onto a chair. There was more than one way to make a dream come true.

It all depended on what was more important to her, her reputation or her future, to live without Max or to live with his anger. Besides, Max had never remained angry with her for very long. The choice was easy to make. The sacrifice no sacrifice at all. Her reputation was a small price to pay for a lifetime as Max's wife.

It was her only chance to have Max ... to keep her family intact ... but more importantly, she truly believed that she and Max belonged together.

She grinned with sheer relief at finally knowing what must be done ... and how. She rushed into her dressing room and quickly exchanged her nightclothes for a simple, dark gown. As she pulled the gown into place, she saw Max's coat draped over a slipper chair in the corner. She picked it up and held it close, smoothing it as she breathed in Max's scent, remembering that for a few moments, Max had wanted her touch. Sighing, she neatly laid the coat back over the chair. She had to hurry. There was much to do before the night was over.

She paused at the heap of emerald silk laying in her path on the floor, a visible reminder of what had been lost that night. The friendship between Max and Damien that had been the foundation of her life. The trust that had been implicit between the three of them until now. Her courage faltered as panic closed in on her, smothering her resolve. She was about to betray her brother and the man she loved. She could lose everything . . . everyone.

Closing her eyes, she breathed deeply, forcing away fear and doubt. If she didn't take the risk, everything was lost anyway. If she was careful, Max and Damien would never know what she had done.

She bent down to pick up the ruined gown, shaking it out, then laying it beside Max's coat on the chair, laying aside her doubts as well. Then, she left her chambers to creep stealthily from the house, praying that she would find Bruce at home.

He was the only person she trusted to make sure her ruin was accomplished.

"Don't wanna marry Melissha," Nunnley slurred drunkenly. "Too bloody poor."

Bruce remained silent. It had been hours since he had arrived home from the Leighton's with Nunnley in tow. Hours of plying him with liquor and repeating the threats over and over. Bruce intended to keep him here until morning and impress upon him once more the importance of discretion. That should do the trick.

"I ain't gonna marry Melissha," Nunnley repeated. "I could've loved Jillian."

And all her splendid money, Bruce thought. "Better to have loved and lost than to be dead," he warned.

Nunnley emptied his empty glass. "Would you stop say'n that? I ain't gonna say a word."

"Just remember there is a better than fair chance your new lodgings will be under six feet of dirt if you repeat anything you saw tonight." Bruce cautioned for what seemed like the hundredth time in the past few hours. "Or maybe you won't," he added thoughtfully. "I suppose it's possible that you might survive a duel with the Duke of Westbrook. But then after that there would always be the Duke of Bassett to contend with." Bruce paused for effect. "He doesn't like you much, does he?"

"Whersh the necessary?" Nunnley said, his face becoming more green by the second as he attempted to lurch to his feet and failed.

"Smithy," Bruce called to the footman stationed outside the sitting room door. He doubted Nunnley could walk much less find his way through the house. "Escort Viscount Nunnley to the necessary would you."

Nunnley levered himself up, and with the aid of the footman, staggered to the door. Abruptly, he lurched to a stop, his expression horrified as he glanced from the footman to Bruce. "He's been out there the whole time? He won't say nothin' will he? Backstairs gossip and all."

"No," Bruce assured. "Smithy is the soul of discretion."

Nunnley sighed and leaned heavily against the footman and allowed himself to be led out. "Don't wanna be dead. Don't wanna marry Melissha."

Bruce shook his head in disbelief. It amazed him that Nunnley found the prospect of marriage to Melissa as much of a threat as retribution from Damien and Max. If he weren't sick of the sight of Nunnley, he might find the situation amusing. With any luck at all Smithy would return with the news that Nunnley had lost consciousness and been put to bed.

But it wasn't to be. All too soon he was back. "Ever had a virgin before?" Nunnley asked as he slumped in his chair.

"No," Bruce replied bluntly, wondering if the man was ever going to pass out. "More brandy?"

Nunnley's head bobbed as he held out his empty glass. "Never had a virgin," he muttered. "Every man needs one to his credit."

Oh God, Bruce thought in disgust. He hated these sorts of conversations. "I suppose it depends upon the man."

"Don't know what you're missing. My mother's cook's assishstant was a tashty morshel." He chortled wickedly and drained his glass. "Even gonna have myself a bashtard in the bargain." He laughed loudly as he looked up, waiting, Bruce imagined, for him to appreciate his word play.

Bruce glared at him with utter contempt.

Nunnley frowned and his eyelids drooped. "Get it, the cook's assishtant was a tashty morshel," he explained.

"How clever you are," Bruce said softly. "And what do you intend to do about your bastard?"

"Why nothin . . ." Nunnley's head lolled to one side and his eyelids flickered as the last glass of brandy he had downed seemed to take hold . . . finally.

Bruce's gorge rose as the empty snifter slipped through Nunnley's fingers and thumped to the floor. Any man who would father a child and make no provision for him deserved to be horsewhipped. He was tempted to let Max and Damien have him.

"Smithy, put this overdressed rodent to bed," he ordered, his loathing for the man increasing with every breath he took. "Take him to the room at the farthest end of the hall—the drafty one with the lumpy mattress—and make sure he doesn't have enough blankets."

"Righto, milord," the footman said as he roughly

yanked Nunnley from the chair and hefted him over his shoulder like a sack of feed.

Bruce watched him stalk from the room, muttering about swells who belonged in the gutter. He'd expected a more violent reaction from Smithy to Nunnley's comments. Smithy was one of those bastards fathered by a nobleman such as his drunk guest. There had always been Nunnleys in the world and always would be. Hopefully there would also be people like himself and Smithy to make their lives as uncomfortable as possible.

Sighing, Bruce rested his head against the back of his chair, allowing himself to relax for the first time in hours.

Max and Damien owed him for this night's work, even if they would never know it. He had no intention of telling them that Arabella and Nunnley had seen the whole thing. As it was, Damien had been angry enough when Bruce had tracked him down and related what had happened between Max and Jillian on the balcony.

"Goddamnit," Damien had muttered harshly and then rapped out the most important question. "Were there any witnesses besides yourself?"

"Not that I am aware of," Bruce had lied. He had not cared for Damien's mood. The truth would only add fuel to the fire.

Damien had nodded thoughtfully for a moment before pinning Bruce with a deadly gaze. "I assume I can rely on your complete discretion. It would distress me greatly to have to call you out after you have so gallantly aided my sister."

It had been hard not to plant his fist in Damien's gullet. But the part of him that understood the lengths a person would go to protect family had stepped in to reason with him.

The clanging of the door knocker startled him from his reverie, and his gaze skipped to the clock on the mantel. It was three o'clock in the morning and calls at this hour could not bode well. Had his mother or Kathy taken ill?

He lurched from the chair, strode to the door, and wrenched it open.

White-faced, Jillian stood before him, a hand pressed to her side as she fought for breath. "Thank God, you're up," she gasped.

His thoughts careened in a dozen different directions as questions piled up in his mind. He blinked and forced himself to focus on the most immediate. "Are you hurt?" he demanded to know.

She shook her head. "It never seemed so far in the daylight."

"What never seemed so far in the daylight?" he asked, trying to make sense out of her sudden appearance.

"The distance to your house. It's so dark out there."

She was scared to death, he realized. And he had a horrible suspicion why as he stared over her shoulder and saw no sign of a carriage, or a hired hack, or a chaperone.

"I came alone," she said.

"On foot?" he asked incredulously, though he knew the answer. Her small nod only confirmed it. There was also the little matter of no chaperone. Did she never learn? "You know this is not a good idea, Jillian. It is only two hours before dawn. Should you be observed—"

She interrupted him with a laugh. "Then I will be the only woman in history to be compromised twice in the same night by two different men." She sobered suddenly. "Damien drank himself into a stupor and LadyLou is ill. No one is aware that I left the house."

Again, a dozen different questions ricocheted through his mind. Again, he focused on the most immediate problem, and grabbed her arm, nearly jerking her off her feet as he pulled her into the house and shut the door behind her.

Shifting his weight to one leg, he propped his hand

on his waist, trying to appear sanguine and unconcerned as visions of dueling fields and angry dukes flashed before his eyes. "I take it things did not go well when Damien arrived home."

"That is an understatement," Jillian said as her breathing eased and the color returned to her face. "Damien has forbidden me to ever see Max again."

All he had done had been for naught? What had happened? Suddenly exhausted, Bruce felt as if the weight of the entire night were sitting on his shoulders. And it wasn't over yet. Jillian wouldn't be here if it was. He needed to sit down. "I sense a long tale coming on," he said, helping her shed her cape and setting it on a bench by the door. "Shall we retire to more comfortable surroundings?" He led her down a short hall to the sitting room.

Smithy was inside gathering glasses and tidying up.

Jillian paused at the door and shot Bruce a worried frown.

"It's all right," Bruce said and gestured toward one of the sofas, inviting her to sit down. He took a seat opposite her.

He waited until Smithy left the room. "What happened?" he asked gently.

Color rose on Jillian's face as she dropped her gaze to her lap. "Max and I were kissing when Damien walked in."

Shock rendered him speechless for a moment. How could Max have been stupid enough to get caught? "Surely a kiss is no cause for such drastic action," he said, finding his voice and struggling to keep it even.

The flush on Jillian's face deepened as she swallowed convulsively. "We were in a rather awkward position on the sofa."

He felt his lips twitch. So, Max had finally cracked under the pressure of Jillian's charms. "I, ah, believe I understand."

"No, you don't," Jillian said on a long shuddering

breath. "You see it was all my fault. Max tried to warn me and I wouldn't listen. I forced myself on him."

He nearly exploded into laughter at her guileless confession. He no more believed she had forced herself on Max than he believed the moon was made of green cheese. But the laughter died in his throat as the story tumbled out of her. She told him of the disarray in which Damien had found her and Max, and how Max's banishment hinged on whether or not she was ruined. She spoke of how they were all torn apart. Finally, she trailed off into silence and wiped her hands across her lap leaving damp smears on the dark blue gown.

Bruce stared at her bent head, fighting the urge to applaud her for her courage in making such admissions to him. "I see," he said simply.

"Good," she said, "because I must make things right and I can't do it alone."

"And what would you have me do?"

She scooted back against the cushions as if she needed all the support she could find. She gazed at him squarely and her voice did not falter as she spoke. "You are very adept at spreading gossip. Make sure I am ruined."

Bruce had believed life held no more surprises for him. He'd thought he'd heard it all and seen it all. "Do you know what you are asking?"

"Yes, but there is no other way. I will not let Max go."

"You love him that much?" Bruce asked, even though he knew the answer. He could see it in her eyes, hear it in the desperation of her voice. His mother had loved a man that much.

"Yes," she said fiercely.

"And what of how Max feels?"

Her face softened. "He loves me, Bruce. If I did not believe that with all my heart, I would not ask this of you."

After hearing Jillian's tale, Bruce believed it, too. His suspicions were confirmed. Nothing short of love would have lured Max into such a compromising situation. "There are other considerations, Jillian" he said, knowing he had to try to turn her away from such a disastrous course. "Once done it cannot be undone. Have you thought of the repercussions if you are found out?"

"I have been over and over it in my mind. Damien is my brother. He will not stop loving me. I don't believe Max will, either, and if he does, it will only be for a short while." She pleated her skirt with her fingers. "He does that you know, comes closer and then backs away."

Bruce did know. It was one of the many things he and Max had in common. But where Max simply removed himself from the field of conflict, Bruce kept his distance by diverting the battle into other directions.

"He frightened me tonight," Jillian whispered, cutting into his thoughts. "There were moments when Max seemed to disappear and his father was standing there instead."

A chill rolled over Bruce. "You know, I have never purposely set out to ruin a lady before," he said, deliberately changing the subject before he made his own comments about the late and unlamented Duke of Bassett, "especially one whose brother had promised violence against my person should I breathe a word. I'm rather attached to my person."

"Damien threatened you, too? I had not realized—" She broke and frowned pensively.

Bruce shrugged. "I would have done the same thing had it been my sister."

"And would you actually follow through if the situation were reversed?"

"Yes," Bruce admitted.

"Then I withdraw my request," she said as she stared into the fire. "I will find another way, even if I have to go to Max's house in the middle of the night and invite the whole of London to watch."

She was serious, Bruce realized and experienced a pang of envy for the man who'd been his friend for so long. She loved Max enough to sacrifice her reputation and risk her brother's goodwill. A sense of rightness dissolved the envy. Max needed that kind of love. In that respect he was just like his father, for only in the company of Bruce's mother did the late Duke smile with contentment.

From what Bruce had observed, Jillian might be the only person in the world with whom Max might find contentment. In any case, she was the only female in England Max had a genuine liking for as well as a genuine interest in her welfare.

Marriage would be good for Max. It was time he had a family he could call his own.

Hell, he might even discover that he had a heart.

God, he was going to do it, Bruce realized. He was going to see that Jillian was ruined in some high-flown hope that Max might be saved from himself. It was arrogant and insane. Yet, if he didn't, Jillian would, and no doubt botch the thing with her innocence and honesty. It appeared that while he was playing the guardian angel, he might as well save Jillian from herself, too.

In for a penny; in for a pound; if he failed, the price would be the same.

He even knew how he would accomplish it. He needn't even leave home. With a smile, he focused on Jillian. "I have shown you how easy it is to drop tidbits of information and watch them grow. No one ever knows where they originate."

She stopped wringing her skirt in her hands. "You're going to do it."

He nodded.

"You're not afraid."

"I told you once that Max and Damien don't frighten me, remember?"

She relaxed at that and her mouth curved into a half smile. "At my come-out ball, when no one asked me to dance."

For a long moment, neither of them spoke. There was nothing left to say. And during the silence Bruce wondered why Jillian had spoken so freely with him. Courage and desperation aside, not only had she revealed her deepest feelings, but spoken of intimacies that most women refused to admit were even possible.

"Why me? Why do you trust me with all this?"

"Because, next to Damien, Max trusts you more than anyone else in the world," she said without hesitation. "But more than that, because you are like Max and there is nothing I cannot trust him with."

"It is good to know that my noble character is so easy to discern," Bruce said smoothly.

"Your home has a woman's touch," Jillian said as if she sought to move on to a lighter subject.

"Kathy and my mother," Bruce said, glancing around at the floral print sofas and brightly upholstered chairs.

"You never did tell me when your sister was arriving."

"In a week's time," he said.

"I look forward to seeing her again," she said as she rose from the sofa and smoothed her skirts. "I must go."

"I'll call for my carriage," he said and stood to ring for Smithy.

"I'd rather walk. I don't want to risk being seen getting out of your coach at dawn."

"All right," Bruce reluctantly agreed, seeing the wisdom of her reasoning. He escorted her out of the room, then picked up her cape and held it open for her. "Don't panic if you spot a man trailing you from a distance. It will be Smithy, my footman. Call out to him if need be."

"I will," she promised and donned her cape as if she were going on a stroll, when in truth, she was walking into ruin with her eyes wide open.

"You are a most amazing woman, Jillian. Anyone else would view a soiled reputation as a disaster, yet you only see opportunity."

"No, not opportunity," she said with fatalistic calm,

"but hope. I have to believe that God does indeed look after fools and lovers."

"I thought it was fools and drunks," Bruce said as Smithy appeared already wearing his hat and coat, as if he'd divined Bruce's next order.

She stepped outside and turned slightly to give him a sad smile. "I think I prefer my version to yours."

Bruce smothered a grin as he sat at the breakfast table and watched Nunnley creep into the dining room at noon the following day.

He looked as if he were dying with his pasty skin and bloodshot eyes. He'd retched himself inside out earlier, according to the footman Bruce had sent to rouse him out of bed and inform him that he was expected at breakfast.

On the other hand, Bruce felt wonderful, even if he hadn't slept in a good twenty-four hours. He couldn't help but relish the challenge of undoing his own handiwork. It was a simple matter really. All he needed to do was free Nunnley from his fears of marriage to Melissa, assure him there would be no retribution from Max and Damien, and make him angry enough with Bruce to gossip out of spite.

With the aid of Smithy, Bruce had every faith that it could be accomplished before Nunnley finished his coffee. Every word and action Smithy and Bruce would exchange had been planned and rehearsed. At the moment, Smithy was standing outside a door at the opposite end of the dining room waiting for his cue to enter. All that was missing were chalk marks on the floor.

Nunnley shuffled just inside the doorway and stopped, his expression sullen with resentment.

Bruce had been counting on that. Things always did look different in the morning. "I'm surprised you're still alive," Bruce said cheerfully. "Come and join me."

Nunnley began to shake his head and thought better of it. "I haven't time. I should be going," he said.

How rude, Bruce thought. Nunnley didn't even deem

it necessary to thank him for his hospitality. And he was making a hash of it all. He was supposed to come in and sit down.

"Make time," Bruce said. "We need to discuss last night one more time."

"There is nothing more to discuss," Nunnley said stubbornly. "You have made my options quite clear."

"Let us go through them again over a cup of coffee."

"No, thank you. I don't care for the stuff."

Oh wonderful. Nunnley was already blowing his lines, but that was easily rectified. "Tea then?" Bruce asked, stalling Nunnley in order to allow Smithy time to circle around to the other door and make his entrance. Actually, now that he thought about it, Nunnley would be able to better hear Bruce's planned conversation with his footman if he remained where he was.

Nunnley opened his mouth to reply and closed it at the sound of approaching footsteps. He turned just as Smithy appeared in the doorway behind him.

"May I have a word with you, milord?" Smithy asked, his hat clasped respectfully in his hands.

"Right now?" Bruce asked. "Can it not wait until after my guest has left?"

"It's important, milord," Smithy said. "I just came from Lady Seymour's."

"Lady Seymour's?" Bruce echoed, narrowing his eyes for effect. "What were you doing there?"

"It's me day off, milord. I'm right friendly with Lady Seymour's parlor maid. On account of what happened last night I thought you might want to know what she told me." The footman twisted his hat distractedly as he tilted his head slightly to one side to give Nunnley a full view of his wary expression.

Nice touch, Bruce thought as he schooled his features to annoyed impatience. "Excuse me, Nunnley," he said and rose, tossing the napkin on his lap to the table. He strode past the bewildered viscount and stepped to the side and away from the door with Smithy, yet still close enough for Nunnley to hear. "What is it?"

The wariness on Smithy's face intensified. The man definitely had a flair for the dramatic. "Lady Seymour's had three callers and they're all talking about Lady Forbes—"

"That bitch!" Bruce thundered, deliberately cutting Smithy off. There was no need to say more. That should be enough to convince Nunnley that Arabella had not heeded Bruce's threats.

Smithy hung his head. "Just thought you'd want to know, milord," he said in a quiet voice.

Bruce remained silent for a long, unrehearsed, moment, keeping a straight face through sheer force of will. Smithy should be on the stage. "Yes, thank you, Smithy. You may go."

Feigning anger, Bruce stalked back to his chair in the dining room.

Nunnley had turned crimson with white splotches on his face. "What are you going to do?"

Bruce propped his elbows on the table and laced his fingers. This was the tricky part. Everything had to be played by ear. By the time it was finished, Nunnley had to be outraged and humiliated enough to seek his own petty revenge and reclaim a smattering of his pride.

He stared at Nunnley consideringly and said nothing, allowing time for fear and panic to work their magic. He wanted Nunnley to beg.

"You cannot mean to do it," Nunnley said and stumbled forward. "I stuck to my end of the bargain. I cannot wed Melissa."

"So don't do it. My quarrel is not with you anymore. It is with Arabella."

"If you ruin Melissa, I'll have no choice," Nunnley said. "My mother will force me. You know how pious she is."

Bruce laughed loud and long, then. Indeed he did know. Nunnley had just delivered his most important line perfectly. Now, it was time to convince Nunnley that there would be no forced match with Melissa. "Just go home, Nunnley, and forget everything. Arabella knows me too well."

"But it ain't fair, I tell you—" Nunnley broke off abruptly. "What did you say?"

"Go home," Bruce said, dismissing him with a wave of his hand. "You are off the hook. Arabella called my bluff."

Nunnley's chin dropped to his chest. "You were bluffing?"

Bruce shrugged. "Of course I was bluffing, you nodcock. But you were pleading so prettily I couldn't resist bamboozling you a bit longer."

Nunnley's brows jerked together and his chin began to quiver as he lifted it from his chest. Higher and higher it rose until his Adam's apple was as prominent as his nose. "I should call you out for this."

"Go ahead," Bruce said. "I won't come, and *my* mother won't force me."

"You will regret this," Nunnley said as he turned and stalked from the room.

Bruce couldn't imagine why. The only thing he might regret was if Max and Jillian were miserable together, but he didn't think that was probable. Still, doubt niggled at him. He hated it when he had second thoughts, especially when it was too late to turn back. It was a weighty responsibility, manipulating someone's life for their own good.

Especially a bloody duke.

Especially this duke.

Max could grind Bruce to dust if he chose.

Yet, Bruce was certain Jillian loved Max and just as certain that Max needed that love.

How romantic.

At least it would be if Max opened his eyes and paid attention. How could he not see that Jillian was in love with him? The man was blind, and it would take a miracle for him to regain his sight. Bruce rather liked the idea of being a miracle worker. The title went nicely with his self-assumed role of guardian angel.

Besides, there was a certain satisfaction in knowing he might have the last laugh on the old Duke of Bassett by ruining his efforts to fashion his heir in his cold and dispassionate image. On second thought, Bruce concluded, there was *immense* satisfaction in having the last laugh on the old duke.

He had done the right thing.

Chapter 19

What a monumental fool he had been, Max thought as he sprawled on the oversize sofa in his library, his hands behind his head, his ankles crossed. He was vaguely aware of the rap on his front door, but didn't bother to stir. He had been officially "not at home" to callers since leaving Jillian and Damien two nights ago.

The only person he had any interest in seeing was Bruce, and that was impossible. Bruce's mother had taken ill and Bruce had sent a note around yesterday, informing Max that he would be at Blackwood indefinitely, and giving him authority to make any decisions necessary in their joint ventures. Max supposed it was just as well. While he might enjoy Bruce's irreverence, he really was in no mood to hear Bruce spout wisdom that always seemed to hit annoyingly close to the mark. He certainly didn't need to hear Bruce's opinions on the balcony incident.

And Max had no intention of telling Bruce that the "incident" had become a full-scale catastrophe by the end of the evening.

Closing his eyes, Max wished he could block out his memory as easily as he could block out his sight.

To allow himself to be seduced by an ingenue was bad enough, but to so mindlessly cross a forbidden line with Jillian was beyond insanity. God, but he hadn't expected her lips to part on a sigh. He hadn't expected her to respond as if they'd kissed thousands of times in a way that was not at all platonic. He hadn't expected his lust to rise and his blood to burn, reducing his wits to ashes.

He had to admit it now, had to face a truth he'd chosen to ignore until now.

Jillian had become a desirable woman when he wasn't looking, completely and magnificently.

He should have been looking. Once again, she had literally dropped into his life and disturbed the order of his existence, just as she had when she was seven years old. Until then he'd been comfortable with his isolation . . . until she'd shown him another way to live. And until now, he'd thought her harmless, letting down his guard, allowing himself to need her in his life. He'd forgotten that need often led to disappointment.

He wouldn't forget again.

Shifting on the sofa, he stared about the room without seeing the rich appointments of mahogany and sandalwood, the well-worn furnishings of leather and velvet. For the past two days, he had not left the house, existing in a state of limbo as he waited to learn which path fate would choose for him. It made no difference. Both routes led to hell.

Wed Jillian and be damned.

Or, be denied the friendship of the two people he cared most about in the world.

He felt betrayed.

How could Damien assume the worst and believe Max had purposely seduced Jillian? How could he discard a lifetime of trust so easily?

Yet, how could he not?

It always came back to that—the logic that justified

Damien's reaction to the scene he'd witnessed, the bitter reason that reminded Max of his own complicity. He'd wanted Jillian. He could have stopped it and hadn't. It was a simple truth that one could not be seduced unless one was willing. Unfortunately, Max had not realized until two nights ago that the truth applied to men as well as women.

Jillian was a woman.

He wanted her.

Again someone rapped on the front door and he heard the low murmur of indistinguishable voices in the entry hall. One presumably belonged to Ripley, his London butler, who had strict orders not to disturb him unless Damien called. And Damien would call only because the ill wind of gossip had blown through the ton.

The door swung open and sunlight spilled in from the windows in the foyer and backlit the form of a man.

Damien.

Think of an avenging angel and he was bound to flutter his wings, Max thought derisively. There could be only one reason for this visit.

"I take it you have brought news of my impending nuptials," Max said blandly, avoiding the social preliminaries.

"I have," Damien said coldly. "You and Jillian did not go unobserved at the Leighton's ball."

It had been too much to hope for, yet still the news surprised Max.

Suddenly, he realized that he did have a preference into which hell he was cast. He would rather go alone instead of dragging Jillian with him. And it undoubtedly would be hell with Jillian caught between himself and Damien.

Damien, the idealist, who believed that love was good and everlasting and wanted it for his sister. Damien, his friend, who was both betrayer and betrayed.

"Are you certain there is no other way?" Max asked as he stood, preferring to meet fate on his feet.

Damien stalked into the room. "You could refuse to do the honorable thing and ruin my sister completely."

Max's insides clenched into a burning knot of anger. "Are you questioning my integrity, Damien?" he asked in a low, controlled voice.

"I have many questions. For instance: Why did you not tell me of your run-in with Nunnley on the terrace?"

"Nunnley," Max muttered. "Quite frankly, I forgot about it. I had my hands full protecting your sister from her own foolishness. A responsibility you foisted on me while you conducted your business."

"You call what you did 'protecting her'?" Damien slammed his fist down on Max's desk.

"What I did," Max grated, "was to prevent Nunnley from trapping Jillian in the bushes." Pausing, Max stared thoughtfully into space as his fury found a new target. "I assume Nunnley is the one spreading gossip?"

"With a vengeance. He saw everything and the tale has been embellished to the point where it is as sordid as the scene I witnessed in the drawing room." Damien glanced away then, as if he could not bear to look at Max. "Why Jillian, Max? Of all the beautiful women available to you, *why Jillian?*"

Why Jillian? Max, too, turned his face away. He couldn't answer that any more than he could reason out why she changed her perfume every day. How could he have known that the same young woman who had laughed as she sailed through the air would suddenly change into a voluptuous temptress before his eyes. For all his experience he had never encountered a woman who had tried to consume him. He'd never thought he would be so willing to be consumed.

He'd been willing.

The admission was a jolt inside him every bit as stunning as what he'd felt when she'd pressed her mouth against his. It had been there all along, the awareness he had refused to think about every time he felt her hand on his arm or caught the scent of her perfume. She was like her fragrance and he never knew what he was going to get on any given day—roses or jasmine, ingenue or siren.

Why Jillian? He could not explain to Damien what he did not understand himself. "I will do the honorable thing Damien. Do not ask more than that."

"Damn you, Max. You're the one who said that the honorable thing is not necessarily the right thing. What will happen to her after you're wed? Will you abandon her and leave her to rot at Bassett House as your father left you?"

Max shook with the effort to restrain his outrage at the question. His jaw ached with the strain of replying calmly. "Jillian will be free to seek her own happiness. I will expect nothing from her."

"That is, after she delivers your requisite heir," Damien spat out.

Bile rose in his throat at having Damien poison his own words and serve them back to him. He'd dug his own grave with that statement, and apparently Jillian's as well. He did not want to marry her, yet he had no choice, thanks to Nunnley.

Nunnley. Now there was a man Max would relish dragging down with him. He and Damien had nothing left to say, and he'd be damned if he would engage in a battle of words with his old friend. All had been said and done. The only thing left to do was stuff Nunnley's malice down his throat, discreetly, of course. The urge was strong to shoot the man on the dueling field, but the same logic he had used on Damien still applied. Jillian's honor would suffer all the more for such flagrant actions.

For all he knew, Nunnley had witnessed nothing more than Max lifting Jillian's skirts to inspect her injured shins. But that was damning enough in a society where a leg was prudishly referred to as a limb. It was his own fault for not heeding Damien's warnings, and for selfishly clinging to a relationship that had changed in everyone's minds but his own.

Nunnley was guilty of nothing but indulging in the time-honored tradition of spiteful gossip and petty revenge.

But, Max wasn't willing to be that reasonable. "If you will excuse me Damien, I need to see Nunnley."

"You're too late," Damien said. "Apparently he slithered out the servants's entrance while I stood at his front door arguing with his butler. By now, he is no doubt halfway across the Channel."

"Slimy bastard," Max muttered. "I will have my pound of flesh from Nunnley."

"And one day, I shall have mine from you, Max."

"But not today," Max said. "At the moment I suggest that we give Jillian the *glorious* news that she is to be my duchess." He strode from the library and called for his coach. He didn't give a bloody damn if Damien followed or not.

"Lady Jillian, his Grace and the Duke of Bassett request your presence in the drawing room," Jacobs said in a subdued tone.

Jillian started and glanced quickly at LadyLou. Damien and Max here, together. It could mean only one thing.

It was done.

Her aunt closed her eyes for a brief moment. She, too, understood the significance of the butler's announcement. Since Damien had informed LadyLou of the situation, they had all waited together in the silence of their own private thoughts. During the last two days, Jillian had felt overwhelmed by the weight of her actions. Whatever happened now would irrevocably alter the lives of those she cared about. The responsibility of it crushed her spirits and threatened to smother her optimism for the future.

It was done and could not be taken back.

"Shall I go with you?" LadyLou asked.

"No," Jillian said, barely managing the word as panic again closed in on her. She'd been jumping at shadows since returning from Bruce's two mornings ago. Her only comfort had been LadyLou's steady presence. Oddly, the only comment her aunt had made on the subject had been, "I should have seen," and then she'd nodded as if to confirm some inner thought. Jillian hadn't questioned the remark. Her mind was full enough.

She laid aside the needlepoint she'd been holding for hours and rose from her chair. Her hands felt cramped though she hadn't sewn a single stitch. LadyLou rose also and circled her, adjusting the folds of Jillian's jade-green dress. Then, she stood in front of Jillian and smoothed back her hair with a tender hand. "You have great strength, Jillian, and you know what you want from life. Don't forget it for one moment."

LadyLou's advice carried Jillian across the upper hall and down the stairs with a single thought repeating itself in her mind. Her aunt knew how she felt. It gave her confidence and propped up her resolve.

Unfortunately, her courage was sagging miserably by the time she arrived at the drawing room.

Damien leaned against the window, staring out at the street, his mouth tight and his jaw rigid in profile.

Across the room, Max stood at the fireplace, arms folded across his chest, presenting another grim profile as he stared down into the cold grate. It was not supposed to be this way. She wanted to run, to deny the sight of a Forbes and a Hastings with their backs turned against one another. But she couldn't run. She had started this and she would have to finish it.

She had done the right thing, she assured herself. They were in the same room together because of her. She had to believe that, through her, they might forget their anger, not for her sake but for their own.

Jillian stepped into the room with her head held high and her knees shaking beneath her skirts. "You summoned me," she said formally, reminding herself that they loved her, that love did not die so easily.

Damien turned from the window, and Max lifted his

head—the panther and the lion, so still and watchful, prepared to pounce should she threaten them in word or deed. Their wariness calmed her, reassured her that she was not without power, that maybe they were meeting on equal ground.

"Sit down, Jillian," Damien ordered.

She obeyed without comment and met Max's gaze directly for the first time since entering the room. There was no familiar twinkle in his eyes, no fond smile on his lips, no sense of ease or pleasure in his manner. She smiled at him, a small, consoling smile meant to reassure him that everything would be fine.

He turned his face away from her.

"You and Max will be wed," Damien said.

Her blood raced in her veins and she heard the rush of it in her ears. Though she'd been expecting Damien's announcement, it still shocked her to have it put in so few words. She'd anticipated a certain amount of anger from Max, but not the sharp stab of rejection. Her skin tingled from her scalp to her toes as everything around her seemed to recede for a moment. And then the sensations faded and she simply felt numb from Max's coldness and Damien's bluntness. She folded her hands in her lap, willing them not to clench, willing herself to concentrate on the matter at hand. Later, she would have time to lick her wounds.

"I am not a piece of furniture to be shuffled about to suit propriety," she said carefully. She must be convincing. She must play her role well. "I have not been disgraced and I will not behave as if I have."

"Yes, you have," Damien said. "In the eyes of society you are ruined. No decent house in England will receive you unless you marry."

"And marrying for the sole purpose of placating the ton is not indecent?" she asked.

"We are not debating the injustices of civilization, Jillian," Damien rebuked. "We are discussing what must be done to ensure your place in society."

"I don't care what society thinks or says."

"You will care," Max said evenly, "when you are dropped from every guest list and people cross to the other side of the street to avoid you. You will care when the ladies stare at you and whisper about you behind their fans." He broke off with an impatient gesture and met her gaze. "Your reputation is destroyed, Jillian."

She absorbed the information. Bruce had been thorough, making sure there was no recourse. Still, she must not give in too soon. "My brother is the Duke of Westbrook," she argued. "No one would dare cut me."

Uncertainty flickered across Damien's features and her stomach clenched in alarm. Had she overplayed her hand?

Slowly, Damien shook his head. "I cannot take that chance."

Struggling to contain her sigh of relief, Jillian lowered her gaze to her hands folded so primly in her lap. She frowned, wondering if she should protest further. She'd said enough, she decided. It would not do for her to protest too much. She feigned a shuddering breath and nodded.

"I'm sorry, Jillian," Damien said roughly. "I would not condemn you to this if there were any other way. Max will procure a special license and the marriage will take place immediately. After a respectable amount of time has passed and your place in society is secure, you and Max can lead separate lives."

Jillian flinched. She did not want to lead separate lives. But how could she tell Damien that when he stared at her with such stark grief in his eyes? Guilt swelled inside her until she thought she might die of it. She felt torn in half, caught between the certainty of what she'd done and regret that it had been accomplished at her brother's expense.

A tense silence fell over the room as Damien and Max waited for her response. She didn't know what to do. She only knew that she had to comfort her brother, and giving him the answer she knew he wanted seemed to be the only way. "All right, Damien," she said softly.

"Now that you two have determined we will have a marriage of convenience, shall we plan the wedding?" Max said with a slight edge to his voice.

"The wedding will be small and discreet," Damien said as he assumed a protective stance in front of her, blocking her view of Max.

"I think not," Max shot back. "A clandestine marriage will only make matters worse."

"What do you suggest?" Damien asked peevishly.

Max pushed away from the mantel and paced to the far end of the room, putting furniture as well as distance between himself and Damien, and her. At least now she had a clear view of him. He clasped his hands behind his back. "I suggest that we meet lies with lies. Arabella Seymour has already remarked on our close relationship, and has no doubt made her suspicions public. All Jillian and I need do is display a marked amount of affection for one another to prove Arabella right."

The words hurt all the more for his reasonable tone. "Are you saying we should pretend to be in love?" Jillian asked.

"Yes," Max said in that same calm voice. "If they are convinced that we are in love, they will forgive us our indiscretion rather than condemn for our lack of morals."

"Your logic is faulty, Max," Damien snapped. "A man does not compromise the woman he loves."

"Precisely," Max said with exaggerated patience. "After a few appearances we will announce our engagement. By then, if we play our parts well, everyone will believe what Arabella suspected: that there has been an understanding between us for quite some time. We can use the invitations already issued to keep Jillian socially visible."

Jillian scooted back in the chair as if she could escape the wave of sudden doubt threatening to drown her. What had she done? Max spoke of pretending love for her as if she were of no consequence. He planned their future with the same dispassionate attention to detail he would employ if he were planning a new wing for Bassett House. The more he said, the more she began to think her emotions rather than her reputation had been compromised. She sat very still, feeling her face crumple and struggling to keep it from showing.

Damien glanced at her with a worried frown. "You've destroyed her and now you want to throw her to the carnivores of the ton," he said. "You will not humiliate her further."

"I have no intention of humiliating her," Max grated. "If all goes well, they will be forced to accept her back into their ranks, especially after our engagement is announced. No one would dare cut the future Duchess of Bassett."

Suddenly, Damien's body became rigid and seemed to vibrate like a bowstring. He opened his mouth, then clamped it shut. She could see his inner struggle, his desire to protect her warring with his hostility toward Max.

Her heart skipped a beat. Until now, she had not realized that Damien hadn't understood how drastically their lives were about to change. Max was being logical and methodical, devising a plan and executing it where Damien was running on pure emotion. Max had reduced the situation to its simplest form. She'd been compromised. Max would do the honorable thing. Max had accepted that. Damien had not.

"It could work, Damien," she said.

"It *will* work," Max stated forcefully.

Damien stared from one to the other. "You don't know what it will be like, Jillie."

She saw the wavering of his expression, as if it reflected the wavering in his mind. She had to convince him that Max was right. "I know exactly what I'm in for," she said firmly, then softened her voice. "I can endure anything if you and Max are beside me."

"If it weren't for Max you wouldn't have to endure anything."

Jillian pressed her fingertips to her temples. "Stop it, Damien. It wasn't just Max. I was there, too."

Max sliced the air with his hand. "Oh, for God's sake. I've had quite enough of your accusations, Damien. It's done. I suggest you learn to live with it," he said acerbically, then glowered at Jillian. "And I certainly don't need you to defend me. I'm aware of my part in this and have made it clear that I will accept the consequences."

It happened again and she couldn't stop it as she felt her expression collapse, everything inside her dissolving only to be frozen into a shapeless mass by Max's coldness. He spoke of their marriage as if it were a consequence to be endured.

She tightened her lips against a sudden tremor. She didn't dare move for fear that she would shatter like the icicles that used to fall on the cobbles at Westbrook Court.

She didn't want to be a consequence.

"Be very careful of the way you speak to her, Max," Damien warned as he again stepped in front of Jillian, a solid barrier between her and Max. "The prospect of making her a widow holds a certain appeal."

"Stop it!" Jillian cried as she lurched from her seat, knowing that if she heard one more word from either of them she would confess all to keep them from destroying what little remained between them. "Is there not enough strife to suit you both?" She fled from the room, refusing to let Max see that he had hurt her so deeply, refusing to let him see her struggle to control a pain that had no wound to be soothed and bandaged.

She ran into LadyLou's sitting room and slammed the door behind her.

"Jillian, what happened?" LadyLou asked rising to her feet.

"Nothing that we did not expect," Jillian said as she paced the floor. "Max is angry and patronizing. Damien is angry and patronizing. Max and I are getting married. Nothing will ever be the same." She stopped in the middle of the room, facing her aunt, yet not seeing her. She'd been a fool to think that she could make things right again, that Damien and Max would carry on as if nothing had happened. It had been sheer folly to think that she could force Max to marry her and he would simply fall into her plans with a smile on his face.

"Nothing has been the same for you for a long time, has it Jillian?"

Jillian blinked as she remembered her aunt's earlier comment. "You really do see, don't you?"

"Yes," LadyLou said as she sank down on the sofa and patted the space beside her.

Jillian went to her, needing to sort through her confusion and knowing she couldn't do it alone. It had all seemed so clear for the past year, until her feelings had gone beyond dreamy musings and become overwhelmingly real.

LadyLou gathered her close and hugged her tightly.

"I've always loved him," Jillian whispered, forcing herself to reveal the secret she hadn't wanted to share with anyone but Max. "But, it has never hurt before. Oh, why does it hurt so very much?"

"It's not being in love that hurts, Jillie, but wanting desperately to be loved back."

"But I know he loves me. He has since I was seven years old."

"Yes, he does, but remember Jillian, it is very easy to give your love and a small part of your life to a child, or to a friend. You still belong to yourself. It is a far more difficult adjustment to fall in love as an adult and realize that another person has become your life and that you have become his. Suddenly, you're accountable to someone besides yourself. It is, I think, easier for a woman to accept than it is for a man, particularly a man accustomed to being alone."

Alone. Jillian closed her eyes and concentrated on the thoughts that finally seemed to be falling into some kind of order. Max knew far more of her life than she had ever known of his. She hadn't known how closely he guarded himself until their fathers had died. He'd been so remote then, as if he had purposely stepped away from closeness and sharing. Since she'd come to London, she'd seen him do it time and time again— stepping away when she would draw him closer.

It hadn't occurred to her that he might choose to be alone. And now, she had taken the choice away from him.

"Jillie," LadyLou said as if she knew which path Jillian's thoughts had taken. "Most marriages are based on less than the friendship you share with Max."

"We used to be friends, now I don't know what we are."

"You are betrothed," Damien said, striding into the room. "The wedding will take place in six weeks time at Westminster."

Westminster. The cathedral where the ton had gathered to pay homage to the memory of the graces. "No," she said firmly, raising her head to meet her brother's gaze. "No," she repeated, sure now of what needed to be done. "I wish to be married in the chapel at Westbrook Court."

"It's too small, Jillie," Damien said shortly. "I've already instructed my secretary to order five hundred invitations from the engravers."

"Why? So that we can gather five hundred regrets?" she said. "I will perform for the amusement of the ton for the rest of the Season if I must. I will smile and dance and fawn to salvage the family pride if that is what you wish. But Max and I will be married at home." *Where it all began,* she finished silently. Home ... where, possibly, she would teach Max how not to be alone ... where she and Max might begin again.

Chapter 20

The play was written, the roles were cast, the stage was set.

Max stood in the anteroom with Jillian, Damien and LadyLou, waiting for the right moment to allow the butler to announce their presence. Conversation was a steady, congenial buzz on the other side of the threshold leading into the Garwood's ballroom. By contrast, the foyer was deserted and silent. Max had planned it this way, thinking that if they were going to bluff the ton, they would begin with a stunning entrance.

Jillian alone could do that with her subtle flaunting of the rules of dress. Though her gown was the required pastel, it was more vivid than the washed out shades the other debutantes wore. Though the rich sky blue fabric was an airy silk, it had an iridescence that shimmered with every brush of light and air. And though she usually wore a minimum of jewels, tonight she was adorned at neck, ears and wrists with her mother's *parure* of matched sapphires.

She was breathtaking, magnificent.

She stood before Max with a solemn expression that belied the color in her cheeks and the brightness of her eyes.

Damnit! Even after his and Damien's warnings, she still didn't know what she was in for. He should tell her, but couldn't bring himself to do it. Knowing Jillian, she wouldn't take him seriously. She'd always approached peril with a blithe confidence that if she should fall, he would certainly be there to catch her. Given recent events, he hadn't done anything to prove her wrong.

Damnit! She had no business trusting him that much.

And damnit, he had no business encouraging her to trust him, especially now when his affection for her had been corrupted by lust. He turned his head toward the ballroom and sighed. He'd courted danger by his very proximity to Jillian. And now he would willingly marry her, knowing that they might both be destroyed by such a union.

"Shall I announce you now, your Grace?" the butler asked.

Max nodded and offered LadyLou his arm.

"Wait," LadyLou said as she reached for Jillian and drew her forward, placing her hand on Max's arm. She stood back to study them, then motioned Damien forward to stand on Jillian's other side. "There. Much better." She shook her head as Damien opened his mouth to protest. "If ever there was a need for the three of you to present a united front, it is now. Any hint of hostility between the families would be interpreted as confirmation of the gossip."

"She's right, Damien," Max said. "If we are to make a statement then it should be a bold one."

Looking as if he'd swallowed something vile, Damien breathed deeply and tucked his sister's hand into the crook of his arm.

"Let the performance begin," Max said dryly as he glanced at Damien over Jillian's head.

"It's not too late, Jillie," Damien said. "You can be married quietly and they will all forget in time."

"No," Jillian murmured. "I have always wondered what it would be like to star in a melodrama."

Max again nodded at the butler.

"His Grace, the Duke of Westbrook, Lady Jillian Forbes, his Grace the Duke of Bassett . . ."

A hush fell over the Garwood's ballroom at the announcement. All heads turned. All eyes widened at seeing the unexpected. They must present quite a shocking sight, Max thought, as they stood three abreast, arm in arm, Forbes and Hastings united as they had always been.

The silence swelled, a soundless crescendo, announcing that the curtain had gone up. The atmosphere was charged with a tangible air of expectation as, collectively, the audience seemed to lean forward slightly, waiting for the play to commence, watching for the first sign of forgotten lines.

Slowly, they began to descend the shallow steps into the ballroom.

"Lady Louise Forbes," the butler intoned.

Max heard the rustle of LadyLou's skirts behind them and regretted that she had to enter the ballroom alone. Yet she had been right to insist that the combined power of Westbrook and Bassett be concentrated in one impenetrable line, just as Jillian had been right to flaunt it with her dress and the most impressive of the family jewels.

Jillian's obvious control chafed his nerves. He wanted to snarl at her composure. Didn't she understand that one misstep would lead them into doom rather than salvation?

"Are we to charm the ton or scare them to death?" Jillian asked from the side of her mouth. "Your scowl makes you look quite uncivilized."

"And what would you suggest?" he asked under his breath.

"Nothing more ferocious than arrogance," she replied in the same manner. "You're beginning to frighten even me."

He wanted to frighten her. But as he glared down at her, he saw the twinkle in her eyes and knew it was futile. She always did this to him, diluting his anger with her pluck, reducing him to tender feelings when he would rather bellow with rage.

With a sigh of frustration, he fixed his expression

into one of casual indifference as he stared out at the crowd.

As they took the next step, whispers flew from one person to another, a hissing sound, as if they had disturbed a nest of vipers. He had to force himself to move forward, knowing that whatever steps he took now could never be retraced—a betrothal that could not be broken, a role he would have to play for a lifetime in a marriage that should not be.

Repressing his contempt for the farce, he raised his hand to cover Jillian's where it rested in the crook of his elbow, applying light pressure as he glanced down at her, willing warmth into his smile, reminding himself that she was not to blame for this.

His breath stalled in his throat as she peered up at him from beneath lowered lashes, her smile shy at first, then curving into an expression that beguiled and promised at the same time. A smile that brought him face to face with the erotic dream that haunted his memories as persistently as it had disturbed his sleep.

A collective gasp rippled through the assemblage, startling him, snatching him back to reality. Annoyed that Jillian could so easily and so completely seduce him into believing they were not creating an illusion, he reminded himself that he was the one who had insisted on pretense.

"I see Arabella Seymour whispering to Melissa," LadyLou said as she joined them in the thick of things.

"Shall we make her our first stop?" Damien suggested.

"She is as good a place as any to start," Max said.

"I will mingle with the ladies," LadyLou said. "I have a feeling they are hungry for any tidbits I might drop."

Jillian nodded and tried to slip free from his hold, out of habit, he supposed. Always before, Jillian's place had been with her aunt on the sidelines, holding court over the cream of British manhood. She didn't yet understand. The sidelines were forbidden to her. There would be no suitors bidding for her attention.

Acutely aware of the two hundred faces watching them, he leaned down to whisper in Jillian's ear, providing the next *on dit* for their amusement. "You remain with me. Don't forget that we are supposed to be madly in love."

She turned her head abruptly, and her cheek brushed his, filling him with an awareness of her scent—a new one he couldn't quite identify, both spicy and sweet and a shade too bold for an ingenue. Her eyes were wide and her look could be construed as adoring.

"How could I forget?" she whispered back.

The speculative murmurs of the crowd turned to shocked titterings and there was a general shifting, as if each person could not wait to spread their comments to the others.

"Forget what?" Damien asked.

"That Arabella Seymour has been edging her way toward us and is about to *accidentally* bump into us," Max replied evasively, unwilling to report to Damien every word he exchanged with Jillian.

"How considerate of her to save us the trouble of accidentally bumping into her," Jillian said brightly.

It unnerved him to see how well she performed for the benefit of the crowd even as he felt a fierce pride for the way she met adversity with a spirit of adventure. He resented her for her optimism even as he struggled to find some within himself. Gathering his scattered wits, he forced a bark of laughter and playfully tapped the tip of her nose. "You are outrageous," he chided.

"Isn't that what they expect?" she asked with a look of wide-eyed innocence as she nodded toward the body of spectators.

Again, a babble of shocked whispers rose from the crowd.

Damien's gaze sharpened on Max, the annoyance in his eyes belying his pleasant smile, but before he could say a word Arabella swooped in front of them, her eyes glittering in anticipation of the kill. "How wonderful to see the Duke of Bassett and the Duke of Westbrook together again," she said, pointedly ignoring Jillian.

"Hello, Melissa," Jillian said.

Melissa opened her mouth but not a sound came out as she frantically looked at her mother.

"Aren't you going to greet the gentlemen, Melissa, darling?" Arabella asked in a warning tone.

Still saying nothing, Melissa curtsied, then directed her gaze at the floor.

Jillian's fingers dug into the flesh of his arm at Melissa's rebuff.

Arabella stepped slightly in front of her daughter to more fully face Max and Damien while managing to avoid Jillian. "Where have you two been hiding these last few days?"

"Damien and I have been occupied with other matters," Max said, hoping to keep Arabella too busy to notice Jillian.

Arabella smiled slyly. "So I have heard. Your absence at the Bingham's musicale and the Peterson's masquerade was a matter of universal speculation."

"The ton is always speculating about something," Max said with an indifferent shrug.

"True. But some people enjoy creating speculation," Damien said glaring at Max.

Max frowned back at him. What was Damien doing with such a display of disapproval? But then he recognized the message in Damien's eyes and his tension eased. How many times through the years had they played off one another, communicating with unspoken words?

He let the moment spin out as he formulated his reply. Arabella's gaze skipped from one to the other, her perfect brows haughtily arched. Jillian's grip on his arm tightened even more beneath his hand. Max massaged the back of her hand with the pad of his thumb, and she gave him a bemused, slightly wistful look. He would swear that she'd caught her breath at his touch.

Arabella's gaze dipped and rested on their hands.

Max leaned closer to Damien and lowered his voice to a conspiratorial whisper. "We have been over this countless times, Damien. You agreed to allow us to move the date up."

"I know what I agreed to," Damien said, "but this is not the place to discuss it."

"Since you have agreed, there is nothing to discuss," Max replied and cast a sidelong glance at Arabella, then nodded curtly at Damien, abruptly ending the exchange.

Arabella snapped her fan closed, and although her lofty expression did not waver, she could hide neither the curiosity lurking in her gaze nor the disappointed curl of her mouth when neither he nor Damien offered more information.

Satisfied that they'd planted enough seeds, Max gave her a look of benign indifference.

She responded by behaving as if they had never ignored her in favor of private conversation. "I really only stopped to extend a personal invitation to a small *soiree* I'm giving next week. Of course formal invitations are forthcoming. I do hope the two of you will attend."

Max stiffened at Arabella's daring. To cut Jillian was one thing, but to do so without any attempt at discretion in the presence of her brother was stepping over the line. "My regrets, Arabella," he said, then stared down at Jillian with calculated adoration, "but I will be otherwise engaged."

"As will I," Damien said.

"Well," Arabella said with a careless lift of her shoulders. "Should you change you mind, my door is open to you both. Come along Melissa darling."

"So that is the cut direct," Jillian said as she watched the two women disappear into the crush. "That wasn't so awful. I have always longed for Lady Seymour to ignore me."

"No, Jillie, that was the cut *indirect*," Damien said. "You have yet to see the worst of it."

Max remained silent. So far, Jillian was holding up nicely, but he was well aware that the situation could change at any moment.

As one, they strolled through the ballroom and came face to face with Lady Judith Cecil and Lady Cornelia Thurston. Cornelia's arm shot out to stop her sister's forward momentum. They turned and walked away.

Jillian's body shook with a barely controlled tremor.

One person after another greeted Damien and himself and ignored Jillian. The flock of suitors that had vied for her attention a mere week ago went out of their way to avoid her, giving her the cut direct. And each time, he felt Jillian's body sag a little more, saw her smile become more strained, her eyes a little more glazed. The atmosphere of malice was beginning to affect Jillian, and she was beginning to comprehend the meaning of human cruelty.

It was best this way, he supposed. After their encounter in Damien's drawing room he'd known that her innocence had to die. He preferred that it not be by his hand alone.

Her hand was limp on his arm, and she seemed to lose a little more of her stuffing with each cut delivered by the ton. "Oh ..." she said and it sounded like a whimper as she stopped short in the midst of the crowd.

Max glanced at her sharply. Her face had blanched of color and she held her eyes open wide, as if she were fighting tears. It could not be. Jillian rarely cried and when she did, it was over something monumental, like a death in the family.

He followed her gaze to see Jasper Reynolds standing a few feet away, staring at Jillian with a mixture of accusation and disgust, the expression both pathetic and ugly. He didn't turn away as the others had done, but remained in place, glaring at her until people trickled into the space and eventually obscured Reynolds from view.

Jillian seemed to shrink beside him and her smile was so stiff Max feared her face would crack. She was still pale, her gaze fixed and Max knew that she was dying inside.

Beside her, Damien clenched his fists and narrowed his eyes at the place where Reynolds had been, as if he could part the crowd and turn Reynolds to stone with his glare.

"Let us dance, Jillian," Max said, unsure of how long Damien and Jillian would be able to control themselves.

"Please," she said, her voice strained, her color high. "Not a *contredanse*. Can we not wait for a waltz? I don't want to be separated from you, Max."

He contrived a lover's smile of amused indulgence as he shifted to stand in front of her, cutting off her vision of everything and everyone but him. "Ignore them," he said. "Take their power away from them with your pride."

She shivered slightly and her gaze lifted to his. "I did not know it would be so terrible."

"You and your damned plan," Damien said under cover of a genial smile. "We're getting Jillian out of here."

Max ignored him. Damnit, Damien should know that it was too late to walk away. One misstep at this stage in his plan would only lead Jillian deeper into ruin.

She raised her head, her gaze darting about the ballroom, her mouth pinched with her effort to hide its tremble. With his lover's smile in place, he held her gaze, knowing he had to exploit the trust she had in him before she gave in to defeat.

"Look at me, Jillian," he coaxed in a soft, low voice as he stroked the line of her cheek with his forefinger. "Only at me."

Her eyes glittered as she focused on him with a stare so intense he felt as if he were drowning in her misery.

"Smile, Jillian," he said in a calculated whisper. "Smile only for me."

Her lashes fluttered as if she were awakening from a nightmare. Her body shuddered again as if she were shedding her unhappiness like a new skin that didn't fit quite right, and donning the strength that was so much a part of her. As she looked up at him with a trace of the familiar dazzle in her emerald eyes, he saw them change between one moment and the next, becoming less naive, more worldly. His mouth suddenly became dry as sand and his chest constricted as her smile brought back memories of how she'd responded to his mouth and hands.

The more she regained her composure, the faster his began to slip away.

He stepped back as he struggled for control, angry that he should lose it so easily, angry with himself, angry with Jillian. "We must dance," he said, relieved that his voice did not betray him.

"All right, Max. I'm ready." She sighed and lifted her head, leading with her chin as they stepped into the dance.

Several couples left the floor when Max and Jillian joined in the line of a *contredanse*.

Those that remained watched and whispered, and several of the men appeared discomfited at having to take Jillian's hand in order to pass her down the row. One gentleman was so flustered when Jillian reached him, that he paused midstep and stumbled. Recovering himself, he shook his head and walked off the floor, leaving his wife to flounder around the other couples without a partner. The woman glared at Jillian as if she alone were responsible for upsetting the symmetry of the line.

Jillian stared back at the woman without flinching.

Her ability to rally and step back into the role he'd demanded she play tonight was just one more irritation among many.

Needing a deserving target for his anger, Max reached for the woman's hand and whirled her around, then released her at the end of the formation where there was no partner waiting for her. She stood in humiliated silence as the dancers went on without her, trapping her at the edge of the floor until the music ended.

As they came together to promenade down the row of rigidly postured aristocrats, Jillian frowned at him in reproach, yet there was the slightest curve to her lips. The music ended and she curtsied to his required bow. "That was beastly of you, Max," she murmured.

"And eminently satisfying," he replied with a brutal edge to his voice as he escorted her back to Damien.

Max was saved from further conversation as Damien immediately escorted her back out onto the floor. It was easier to deal with her at a distance, without her damnable eyes searching his, without her touch on his arm and her bold perfume drifting about him. He forced himself to watch her every move with a proprietary air, and every time Jillian whirled past, he mustered a smile for the benefit of the crowd.

She stared back at him, as if no one else were in the room, her lips parted in silent promise.

He snapped his gaze away from her as warmth stirred in his groin. Every time she was near, his thoughts turned to treacle. How had she done it? he wondered. How had she made the leap from artless ingenue to alluring woman in the space of a few days?

It unsettled him to realize that he was becoming more familiar with this Jillian than with the one he'd always known.

But then he told himself that she was simply playing her role to the hilt, pretending so well that even he couldn't distinguish between reality and illusion. He should know better than to become ensnared by private smiles and starry eyes. He'd seen enough of them in the expressions of one infatuated debutante or another. His gaze skimmed the crowd, searching for her black hair and shimmering gown, and found her regarding him with all the adoration of a lovesick debutante. He'd seen that look before—the night he'd called her a black swan.

Horror crawled up his spine and the floor seemed to

pitch and roll beneath him as he recognized her look for what it was.

Infatuation. Jillian was infatuated with him.

She was not pretending.

Damnit! Why him? They were friends, the only kind of relationship he'd ever trusted. Yet, she had sacrificed their friendship for a maiden's foolish dreams of love. It occurred to him, then, that their present dilemma hadn't begun on the terrace at all. Thinking back on that night, he realized that he had shown her a man's desire and in her naiveté she would believe his response to her came from the heat and not from the flesh.

He grimaced at the image of Jillian pressing her mouth against his, of his half-hearted warning before they'd both become consumed in a kiss that was beyond her experience. Her first kiss should have been a chaste peck on the lips, not a carnal plunge with him into the depths of physical desire. If only he had separated himself from her months ago, her illusions would have died a natural death in time. Their friendship might have survived.

He shifted on his feet, battling impatience, helplessness, frustration. It was far too late for such useless hindsight. It was too late to preserve what he had held dear for so much of his life.

He couldn't even reassure himself that a young woman's fancy underwent as many cycles as the moon. What good was that when Jillian would be his wife, living with him, elaborating on her illusions?

His wife and lover. His friend. In his experience the roles were mutually exclusive. The only common bond he'd observed in the marriages around him was indifference. He'd experienced it himself in his relationships, growing bored and restless after the novelty wore off ... or when his partner began to cling and make declarations of love.

He'd never wanted that kind of love from anyone ... especially not from Jillian.

He focused on the couples dancing past him, willing

the color and movement to blur his thoughts. But, again, it was futile as he saw Jillian's smile, her beauty, her courage as she whirled in her brother's arms.

How long would her courage survive after her dreams were destroyed? How often would she smile in the face of his inevitable indifference?

Jillian would be hurt. How much remained to be seen. His jaw clenched as he forced himself to think of the future rather than the past. There had to be a way to make it easier for them both. He had only to find it. Jillian, like Bassett House—and his father when he lived—was something he could not rid himself of, but he could control her effect on him and on his life. More importantly he could control his effect on her. He could not allow her to enter this marriage with her foolish dreams intact. Her delusions must be shattered before she walked down the aisle. He had to make her understand that the kiss they had shared that night in Damien's drawing room had been nothing more than an act of lust.

As Damien returned Jillian to his side, Max learned the true meaning of grief—for Jillian and her ideals, for the friendships that would be irreparably broken, and for the warmth he might never know again.

He felt her hand on his arm and forced himself to harden himself against her, against his own regrets. He had already been cast as the villain in this melodrama. Now, it was time to play the role as if he had invented it.

He covered her hand with his and turned to her, once again giving her the indulgent smile of a lover. "Shall we have one more dance?" he asked, determined to see the farce he had instigated out to the end.

She responded with a nod and a beaming smile that normally would have melted his heart, yet it did not affect him at all.

As he led her back on the floor and took her into his arms, he bid a silent farewell to his Pandora.

Chapter 21

Tomorrow, Max would formally ask her to be his
wife.

Jillian knew she should be happy, yet she was miserable as she sat at her dressing table and carefully plaited her hair. She couldn't sleep with so many conflicting emotions rolling about inside her.

The Garwood's ball had been torture. Now Jillian knew how pickpockets sentenced to the pillory felt. She wouldn't have been surprised if someone had hurled a piece of fruit at her. How naive she had been to believe that it would not hurt to be ostracized.

Of course she had been warned, not only by Max and Damien but by Bruce as well. She'd missed Bruce's presence, yet at the same time had been relieved that he had stayed away. Still, she would have thought he'd want to be on hand to view the results of his handiwork. More than once she'd wanted to ask Damien or Max about Bruce, yet she hadn't dared. She and Bruce were both better off for his absence. If Max or Damien ever found out that she had asked Bruce to ruin her reputation, the misery she'd suffered at the ball would be for naught.

She could not have endured it if not for Max's tender smiles and softly voiced commands to *"look at me . . . only at me . . . smile for me . . . only for me . . ."* He'd touched her and whispered to her and smiled at her and every action was another weapon against the malice of the ton, protecting her . . . only her.

She'd floated through the rest of the evening, secure in having her belief confirmed that Max did love her.

And then, they'd left the ball and she'd shivered beneath his icy regard in the coach.

Max and Damien had retreated to opposite corners, sitting stiffly against the squabs, their faces turned away from one another as they stared out the coach windows. Jillian and LadyLou had also sat in silence, staring out their own windows until the coachman had halted the team in front of Max's townhouse.

"Damien, with your permission, I would like to call on Jillian tomorrow," Max requested formally after he had descended to the walkway.

"For what purpose?" Damien asked.

"It is customary to give one's fiancée a ring," Max replied.

"Permission granted," Damien said shortly.

She'd hated the formality between them. Even worse was the probing look Max had given her before he turned and stalked away. She could have sworn she'd seen fury and betrayal burning in his eyes.

She would have preferred the polite nod he'd given LadyLou. Perhaps then she would not feel so guilty about what she'd done. Perhaps then she wouldn't be so terrified that Max suspected her culpability in the scheme that had led them to this point.

But as she secured her braids, she realized that her imagination had run away with her. The light had been dim; all she'd seen was the natural brilliance of Max's eyes in the moonlight. As for his withdrawn manner in the coach, he had behaved no differently than anyone else. The evening had been a strain for all of them. Hadn't she felt like a rag that had seen too many washings by the time they had left the ball? Hadn't Damien wearily shaken his head and retired to his room when she would have spoken to him? Even LadyLou complained of exhaustion as she'd climbed the stairs beside Jillian, offering little more than a squeeze of her hand before seeking her own bed.

Of course, Jillian assured herself, Max couldn't possibly suspect a thing. He was coming to give her a ring and ask her to marry him. Sighing, she stepped into her closet and surveyed her gowns. She wanted to look perfect for Max. Black-swan perfect. And she wanted to look different for him. After all, he would only propose to her once and she wanted his memory of the moment to be as special for him as it would be for her. She fingered the wispy lawn overskirt of a white gown embroidered with gracefully curved leaves in deep green. The gown would be perfect with her new jade combs.

Yes! This was the look she wanted, all drifty and soft and romantic.

But every romantic image she'd ever seen included curls, she thought as she fingered a braid. How she wished her hair would retain the corkscrews left by the plaits long enough for Max to see her black tresses ripple around her face and shoulders.

Enthused over the image, she unwound an inch of braid and fingered the limp spiral. It flattened out before she could braid it again. Determined to have curls, she walked over to the wash stand and doused her braids with water, hoping that if they dried, the spirals would be more firmly set.

Convinced that it would work out nicely, she climbed into bed and lay on her back, her dripping braids carefully arranged above her head, her arms straight over the covers as she dreamily watched the muslin bed curtains sway in the soft breeze coming in from the open window.

It was perfect. Her gown seemed to float around her as she moved, the green silk embroidery glistening in the light as if they were touched with dew. With every brush of air, the scent of tea roses surrounded her and complemented the roses in her cheeks. How lovely that she'd awakened with high color and bright eyes. And *her hair* ... Why had she never done this before? she wondered as she turned and craned her neck to see how it wreathed her head and cascaded down her back in soft corkscrew curls. But then if she had, she would not look special for Max today.

And she was certain she did look special. Clancy had told her so. She stared at her reflection in the mirror. Perhaps she should solicit a third opinion.

She sought out LadyLou in the drawing room.

"Jillian," LadyLou said, laying her book aside. "You look lovely. How ever did you—" She broke off as Damien walked into the room, with Max behind him.

Jillian wasn't listening anyway. All she could do was admire the way Max's dark blue coat fit his shoulders and his fawn breeches and high black boots conformed to his long legs. His cravat was perfectly tied, snowy white against his tanned face, emphasizing his dark, depthless blue eyes.

He was so handsome, so perfect.

And he was hers.

Jillian was afraid to move for fear the flutters and tingles in her body would somehow disturb her appearance before Max noticed her.

But Max entered the room only a step and stood by the door, a remoteness about him that alarmed her. "I should like to do this without an audience," he said, glancing pointedly at LadyLou, then Damien.

Damien glared at Max. "You expect me to leave you alone with my sister?"

Jillian cringed at Damien's hostility.

"Damien," LadyLou said softly. "The worst has already happened. It will do no harm to give them some privacy."

Damien jerked his head in a semblance of a nod. "You have fifteen minutes," he said, then turned on his heel and stalked out of the room.

LadyLou gave Jillian a reassuring peck on the cheek before following Damien out and quietly shutting the door behind her.

In the sudden silence, Max regarded Jillian dispassionately, and she wondered if he could see her at all through the ice of his gaze.

What was it? she wondered. Did he hate her curls? Perhaps she should have stood near the window so the light would pick up the pattern in her dress. Couldn't he smell the tea roses?

But then, her anxiety disappeared and anticipation fluttered its wings in her throat as he pulled a small velvet box from his waistcoat pocket. She stared at the box, trying to imagine the kind of ring Max would choose for her. Was it an emerald? A ruby? Were there diamonds and filigreed gold? She didn't really care as long as it came from Max.

Her gaze met his and she felt as if her heartbeat and breathing were at odds with one another. He was going to walk toward her, take a ring from the box, slide it on her finger as he looked into her eyes and asked her to be his wife. He would smile and his arms would enfold her in a possessive embrace and whisper something sweet about the softness of her skin, the vibrancy of her hair.

He might even kiss her.

She hoped so. Kissing Max was the most thrilling experience she'd ever known.

He took a step and placed the box on the table by a chair. "Your ring."

Where was the Max who had treated her with such devotion the night before? Where were the secret smiles and lazy looks he'd lavished on her in full view of the ton? "I don't understand," she said, feeling as if she were choking on her disappointment.

"What is there to understand?" he inquired blandly. "You must have a betrothal ring. I have brought you one."

She shook her head in confusion. Something was terribly wrong. He was a stranger, a cold, dispassionate man she'd never seen before. A man who cared so little that he couldn't exert the smallest emotion. It shouldn't be this way when everything had fallen so neatly into place. "Why are you behaving like this, Max?"

"We are alone. There is no need to pretend," he said.

Pretend? The word sounded foreign to her, yet the implication was brutally clear. He'd been pretending the night before. Only his remoteness in the carriage had been real. She couldn't accept that, could not believe that all the years that had gone before could be so easily and quickly forgotten. Not when he had been so wonderful to her the night before.

She looked up at him, taking care to keep her voice even and controlled. "We are friends, Max. Nothing has changed."

"Everything has changed," he said as casually as if he were flicking lint from his coat. "In the eyes of the world we are lovers escaping disgrace."

"Better you than Nunnley," Jillian flared before she could stop herself. She wasn't sure what distressed her the most—the indifference in his tone or the apathy that smoothed all traces of animation from his features.

"I beg your pardon?"

The flicker of his eyelids and the barest hint of anger in his voice alerted her. She had accidentally found a spark of life in him and she was not going to let it go. She stood her ground and raised her chin. "I would rather have you as a lover than Nunnley," she said, carefully enunciating each word, hoping to provoke more emotion from him.

His mouth twisted into a cynical smile. "I am neither a gentle lover nor a patient one."

"I don't believe that for an instant," she scoffed.

"Really?" Max asked, his eyes taking on a feral gleam she had never seen before. "Perhaps I can change your mind." He crossed the distance separating them, and grasped the back of her head, his fingers tangling in her hair as he dragged her toward him. His hand cupped her chin forcing her lips to part. His mouth ground down on hers, his tongue thrusting inside in a hard and relentless rhythm. This was nothing like the last time he had kissed her. This wasn't warm and exciting. This was nothing intimate or personal.

She felt like a victim being picked apart and consumed by an indifferent predator.

His hand slid from her chin, down over the side of her breast, around her waist and down, spreading over her bottom, pressing her belly firmly against him.

She stiffened in shock and gasped against his mouth. Outrage such as she had never felt before cleared her head and gave her strength. He wasn't kissing her; he was punishing her.

She clutched a handful of his hair and jerked his head back, holding him so that they were nose to nose. "*Never* do that to me again. That is not the way you kiss a lover."

"What do you know of how lovers kiss?" Max said as he glared at her, his mouth slanted in a grimace, his breath labored and erratic on her face.

An instinct that seemed to awaken in that moment told her that he had lost control, and it was because of her. Maybe she shouldn't have pulled away. Maybe in a moment or two his lips would have softened and he would have kissed her as he had before.

"I know what you taught me, Max—the other night in this very room." Following that same instinct, she twined her arms around his neck and sifted her fingers through the hair at his nape. "You may kiss me as a friend or as a lover, but never as you did a moment ago."

He wrenched away from her. "Not bloody likely," he said as he picked up the velvet box from the table and shoved it into her hand. "Wear it," he commanded. "In a few days, the announcement will appear in the *Gazette*. In the meantime, I want people to see the ring on your hand. It will give them something else to speculate about tonight."

She backed away a step, as if putting even that small distance between them would somehow lessen the pain of his rejection. "I am not going anywhere," she said.

"If wedding invitations do not redeem me in the eyes of the ton, nothing will."

"Yes, you are going, and you will continue to attend every function I deem necessary until society understands precisely who you are."

"And who am I?"

"The future Duchess of Bassett."

It sounded so cold and mercenary as he reduced her place in his life to nothing more than the counterpart to his title. She was no longer Jillian or Pandora, but an acquisition for his estate. She wouldn't have it, wouldn't allow him to diminish all that they had shared over the years. At the very least, she wanted him to acknowledge her by asking her to be his wife rather than telling her that she was to be his duchess. Somehow, it seemed to her to be more important than kisses and a ring. "You cannot say it, can you? You cannot ask me properly to be your wife."

Max arched his brows. "Why ever would I do that?" he said, his voice patronizing. "Proposals are made when one wishes to have a wife." He smiled as she had seen him smile at Arabella and Nunnley and others he merely tolerated. "And if I were in the market for a wife, you would never be my choice. Unfortunately, I have no choice."

She covered her ears with her hands, refusing to listen to any more. "Max, stop. Don't—"

He wrapped his fingers around her wrists and wrenched her arms down, pinning them to her sides. "Don't what? Tell the truth? Would you have me continue this farce even with you?"

Yes! she wanted to shout. Anything but his cold and bitter cruelty. Anything to chase away the guilt such truth evoked. She tried to free herself from his grip, but he gave no quarter with his powerful hold. Always before, he'd used his strength to help her. But now he used his strength against her with an ease that terrified her. It hadn't occurred to her that she would ever be the cause of such a change in him.

She couldn't do this to him.

Words she'd pushed aside along with doubts she'd ignored came to the surface, choking her as she spit them out. "Then, I will end the farce, Max. I release you. There will be no marriage."

"Oh, yes, there will be a marriage, Jillian. Like me, you have no choice. But make no mistake: My life will be my own as will your life be your own. I want nothing from you." He let her go so abruptly, she stumbled back a step, and groped for the table to regain her balance.

He turned and strode from the room as if having delivered that statement, he had no further reason to remain. But then he paused at the door and glanced at her over his shoulder. "And Jillian, you went too far last night with your displays of affection," he said offhandedly. "In the coming weeks, I suggest you cease staring at me with adolescent cow eyes. An occasional sweet smile and silent acquiescence to my wishes would be more seemly."

Before Jillian could raise her hand to her mouth, he disappeared into the hall and she heard the front door close. What a fool she'd been to have worn her heart on her sleeve for him to see.

What a fool she'd been all around, dreaming of romance and happily-ever-after scenes. They were her dreams, not Max's. He was willing to marry her only to save her reputation. He didn't want a wife. *He didn't want her.* He'd told her before and she hadn't listened.

She should have listened.

But, she'd wanted to save their friendship, to love him as he had never been loved. She'd wanted to keep them together—a family. Nothing else had mattered.

She'd been so certain that what she'd done was right for both of them.

But it was too late now. Her plan had worked so well they truly had no choice.

She stared blindly at the small velvet box. She'd been so excited at the thought of receiving a ring from

Max, thinking of it as a promise and a symbol of the future they would share. How idiotic she'd been with her vanity and her expectations. She didn't want to touch the box, didn't want to see what he had chosen to symbolize yet another pretense.

Yet, she wasn't pretending. She had told Bruce that she loved Max enough for both of them. Little had she known that it would be put to the test, that it would be all she had to hang on to as she endured the weeks ahead.

With trembling hands she reached for the box and opened it. She inhaled sharply at the single, unconventional diamond set in a plain gold band. It was magnificent and brilliant, pure white and cold.

She hated it.

Things had gone quite well, Max reflected as he entered the library in his townhouse fifteen minutes after leaving Jillian alone with her disillusionment. Perhaps now, she would see her groom for what he was—a man who wanted neither to give nor to receive love. If she didn't, then he had ample time before the wedding to further convince her.

He poured himself a liberal brandy and, snifter in hand, strolled to his desk and sprawled in the worn leather chair. All in all, he felt nothing but relief at what had passed between him and Jillian. The only part of their confrontation that disturbed him was his appalling lack of control when he'd kissed her.

Why had he allowed her to provoke him with all that bilge about preferring him as a lover to Nunnley? Given her less than complimentary feelings about her erstwhile suitor, she would undoubtedly prefer almost anyone to Nunnley. Yet, he'd kissed her as if she'd issued a challenge. Perhaps she had, he mused as he leaned back and propped his feet on the desk. From the moment he walked into the room, she'd thrown him off balance.

He'd never seen her as she'd been today, with her

hair rippling down her back in shining black spirals, and her gown that defied the current loose style by fitting here and draping there.

And, she'd smelled of goddamn tea roses.

The minute he'd touched her and felt the heat of her body pressed against his, he'd lost control. It wouldn't happen again.

Until the wedding, he would further illustrate to her the futility of her infatuation for him. He'd made a good start today and, lust aside, felt nothing but an impatience to be done with the whole thing so he could get on with his life.

During the past few weeks, Jillian's behavior had been everything he could have wished for, Max reflected as he sat in his club, waiting for Damien to study his cards. She followed his directions to the letter, behaving with perfect decorum and a subdued manner. The stars in her eyes had faded and her smiles were controlled as if every response was rehearsed.

It was gratifying to know that he had succeeded in clarifying the situation for her. At least now, he had no doubts that she would walk down the aisle with her eyes wide open. And perhaps when the inevitable indifference came, they might go their separate ways without hatred. It was the most he dared hope for.

Max nodded to a footman to refill his and Damien's glasses. Damien studied his cards as if he had wagered all his wealth on this one hand. Only the most discerning observer would notice that their usual banter and easy camaraderie had been replaced with forced congeniality. Society could hardly believe he had compromised Jillian when he and her brother appeared together daily in carefully contrived displays of continued friendship.

Jillian's blackened reputation had been washed clean. The very people who had cut her so mercilessly now clamored for her favor. What had begun as a scandal was now considered by the ton to be the "love match of the decade."

And now, only one week before the wedding, Max's only complaint was that Jillian had adamantly refused to have a large, pretentious ceremony in town. Once again, she had thrown the aristocracy into an uproar by excluding the majority of the ton from her wedding.

Sighing, Max leaned back in his chair as Damien played his next card. They spoke little these days, but Max didn't mind. There was really nothing left for them to talk about beyond protecting Jillian's interests. Everything else had been said with hard finality weeks ago.

"There you are, Westbrook," Baron Fillmore said heartily as he approached their table. "My solicitor informs me that the transaction for the land is complete." He flushed slightly as he glanced from Damien to Max. "Sorry it took so long for me to make up my dashed mind, but that property has been in my family for generations."

"I quite understand," Damien said mildly.

The baron wiped his hand over the back of his neck. "Yes, well, it is done now. If it is all right with you, my wife and I will be in the area next week to see to the removal of a few personal items from the house."

"That will be fine," Damien said.

Fillmore fussed with his cravat and turned his attention to Max. "Have I offered my congratulations on your forthcoming marriage?"

Max quirked a brow. Of course he was fishing for a wedding invitation. Everyone was. It amused Max to know that, for the baron, an invitation to his wedding was as valuable as a parcel of land. The same land that Damien had been pursuing at the Leighton's ball rather than looking after his sister. "On more than one occasion, Fillmore."

The baron harrumphed and walked away.

A footman approached, bearing a familiar silver tray. "Your Grace, this just arrived for you."

Max frowned. Although it was a normal occurrence for members to receive missives here, Max had never received one. Most messages were from family members. Damien's gaze narrowed as Max took the note from the tray.

It was from Bruce.

Quickly he broke the seal and read, sucking in his breath as the words sank in.

"What is it?" Damien asked.

"The Countess of Blackwood is dead. Bruce regrets that he will not be able to stand up with me at the wedding. He and his sister are in seclusion and request that we not travel to Blackwood to pay our respects."

Damien nodded soberly and looked away. It seemed they could not even share the grief of a friend with one another.

Max stared at the parchment in his hand with a curious detachment. He thought he should feel something for the woman who had grieved more than he had for the loss of his own father. The most he could feel was a stark sadness for the friend who had known and loved his mother so dearly.

As for Bruce not standing up with him at the wedding—it didn't matter. Nothing mattered except to get the whole thing over and done with.

PART III

Chapter 22

It was Jillian's wedding day ... the most important day of her life.

As she stood in front of the mirror in her room, again subjected to LadyLou's and Clancy's tweaking and tugging, she vowed that this would be her final grand entrance.

Today, it would all be over, and Max would be hers. Once they were married and alone with one another, she reasoned, it would be easier to convince Max that they belonged together, that she could and would make him happy.

The past six weeks had been a horror as she'd struggled to balance the images of radiant happiness and proud dignity as Max had stipulated, giving him no further cause to mock and censure her. He'd been remotely polite as he'd escorted her through a tedious round of musicales, routs, and theater appearances. And though he'd given every impression of being devoted to her, and Damien had faithfully and protectively kept to her side, she'd never felt more alone in her life.

But today it would all change. It had to. As brothers-in-law Damien and Max would have to get along. As her husband, Max would find it difficult to ignore her on a continuing basis. She and Max would have to become themselves again.

They would truly become a family.

"There we are," LadyLou said, startling Jillian from her thoughts. "You may go now, Clancy." She stood back and adjusted a fold in her gown. "I do believe you look as grand as any queen I've seen, Jillie."

Jillian nodded, bitterness rising in her throat as she studied her reflection. Her gown was all she might have wished for with its Medieval styling of ivory satin underdress and lace sleeveless tunic that spread out behind her in a ridiculously pretentious train that fell from her shoulders. The seed pearls and crystals sewn into the pattern of the lace weighed her down. Oh yes, she did look grand.

She felt beastly.

The strain of conducting a public courtship had exhausted her. Her head ached with the pull of her hair, drawn back on the sides and gathered in the middle of her head into a braid twined with pearls and orange blossoms. She'd held firm on refusing to wear a veil, arguing that she saw no point in covering up a coif that had taken all night to achieve. At least most of her hair hung free down her back, again in the soft spirals that Max had failed to notice the day he'd given her the betrothal ring. Her mother's pearl and diamond earrings pinched her ears and the matching choker felt as if it were strangling her.

To add insult to injury, her monthly course had come two weeks early.

Thank heavens she'd won the battle for a small wedding in the chapel at Westbrook Court. Given his insistence on a large and ostentatious wedding, Max had not been pleased, but he could hardly argue with the results of her victory. Because of the small and very select guest list of the wealthiest and most respectable members of the ton, an invitation to her wedding was more precious than gold. LadyLou had recounted more than one amusing anecdote on the lengths England's aristocracy was willing to go to in order to procure entrance to the nuptials.

They could all go hang.

"Do not frown so, Jillie," LadyLou said, and her

voice seemed far away. "Soon this will all be behind you. You will be happy again."

Jillian shook her head, dislodging the broad assortment of thoughts that had plagued her for weeks, focusing on the only ones that really mattered. "I know. It is Damien who concerns me."

"Damien is grieving. He thinks he has lost his sister and his best friend. One day, he will realize that this has not happened."

That small reassurance from LadyLou gave Jillian a measure of peace. Damien would be all right and so would she. "And what of Max?" she asked, needing more of her aunt's insight and wisdom to carry her through the day. "This whole affair has made him so broody and distant, not at all like himself."

"But it is exactly like himself, Jillie," LadyLou said as she fussed with the small nosegay of orange blossoms Jillian would carry. "Max has always been rather dark in his manner. Only with you and Damien have I ever seen him let down his guard."

"But that's just it, LadyLou. He has become more impenetrable than ever even while he is being so cold-bloodedly *nice* to everyone."

"Somehow, I don't think Max could be happy with anyone but you, Jillie."

She smiled at her aunt, grateful to have her own belief confirmed. In her heart she was convinced that Max couldn't possibly change so much, that he was and always would be *her* Max.

LadyLou's voice broke into her thoughts, reminding Jillian of yet another concern. "It's really too bad Bruce cannot be here. He and Damien and Max have been friends for such a long time."

"Yes," Jillian responded only because her aunt expected some kind of comment. She would miss Bruce and his ability to wring amusement from the most somber occasion. At first she'd thought his departure from the city had been a deliberate act to remove himself from the danger of discovery. It had been a relief in a way, until Damien had told her that Bruce's mother had died. Now, every thought of the friend who had dared so much to help her brought an irrational fear that perhaps a price had been exacted for their deception. He was at Blackwood, mourning alone when his friends should have been with him. Because of her.

Three sharp raps echoed through her dressing room. "Jillie? Are you ready?" Damien called, his voice sounding tight and strained through the wooden door.

"Yes," she replied, barely able to manage the word as one emotion after another jammed in her throat. She wanted to weep with unaccountable sadness, scream with fear, giggle with hysteria. And then, as suddenly as it had appeared, the panic faded and left her with an odd calm that bordered on apathy. By her own choice, it was done and could not be changed.

With a cold hand, she picked up the bouquet of orange blossoms from the bed and slowly made her way to the door.

Damien sucked in his breath as she opened the door, his gaze sliding over her from head to toe. He shifted from one foot to the other, his face pale and drawn. "It is time," he said simply as if he'd come to lead her to the executioner instead of the chapel.

Jillian took his arm and together they left the house through a side door, and crossed the courtyard.

Damien paused at the gazebo and stared at the pattern of morning sunlight falling through the lattice work. "I wish we could go back to the tea party." He met her gaze briefly, then glanced away. "Jillie, I'm sorry—"

"Don't Damien, please don't." She pressed her hands to his lips, silencing him. She couldn't bear this. Not today. If she were to manage at all, she had to hang on to the calm that had washed over her in her room. She had to be the bride that Max expected.

Damien said nothing as they walked on toward the chapel set in a grove of trees.

A footman opened the oak double doors. Cool air scented by dozens of arrangements of flowers drifted out from the shaded building with a gentle and muted melody played on the organ.

Jillian and Damien stepped inside.

And still, she felt as if she were separate from it all, more of an observer than a participant. The pews were filled with the oddest mixture of guests: the other dukes of England, most older and more staid than Max and Damien; a smattering of young Corinthians of impressive lineage with Jasper Reynolds absent; several ladies whose influence at Almacks set the moral and social tone for the ton; a representative of the Prince Regent, whose presence lent an indisputable air of royal approval to the proceedings; and Lady Seymour and Melissa, simply for the pleasure of rubbing her nose in it.

Her gaze was drawn by the click of a door to the side of the altar and everything in the chapel seemed to fade into the distance.

Max emerged from the shadows, his mane of tawny hair shining like a crown of gold as he stepped into the glow of the candles lit about the pulpit, the planes and angles of his face cast in sharp relief by the gilded light. Though he was dressed in the current fashion of formal blue coat and trousers, the color was both more intense than midnight blue and less flamboyant than the peacocks and pastels the younger men seemed to favor. Rather than being somberly plain as was the trend for such an occasion, his waistcoat was striated with gold threads, a deliberate statement to the ton, Jillian thought, that he and his bride were unconventional because they chose to be.

He was beautiful.

Damien mumbled an inaudible curse.

A murmur rippled through the guests as he took his place at the front of the chapel. Matrons' held back their gasps and their bosoms swelled with disapproval, their husbands frowned, most likely to echo the sentiments of their wives. The few young ladies in the gathering quickly hid their sighs behind fluttering fans, and the young bachelors leaned forward, studying Max's attire with great interest.

Recalling her own defiances of acceptable fashion since her come-out, Jillian wanted to grin, but recovered quickly, schooling her mouth into what she thought might be a sweet smile instead. Why Max had chosen to alter his image at this particular moment was a mystery to her, but it kindled a small flame of hope that she had a small influence on him after all.

Somewhere beneath his closed expressions and arrogant manner lay a definite flair for the dramatic.

He turned to face her, standing tall and proud, his eyes glittering like the sapphire stickpin in his snowy cravat as his gaze shot down the center of the aisle and captured hers. Aside from a slight lift of his brows, his expression gave away nothing of his thoughts.

The organist struck a thundering chord and launched into a slow and ponderous processional that seemed too pompous for the small chapel built of mellow gold stone and richly polished wood.

But then, she felt the music inside her, a swelling, like the love she felt for Max, filling her with a serenity she'd never before experienced. Only barely aware of her brother walking stiffly beside her, she moved forward, toward Max, guided by his gaze as the sunlight poured all the colors of the rainbow through the stained glass windows.

The nearer they drew to Max, the farther away she felt from Damien as she took one step, then another through the prisms of color and the misty smoke of the candles. Doubts and fears and guilt scattered like the rose petals she trod upon. The curious and expectant faces around her faded even more into an indistinct blur. She was aware only of Max ahead of her . . .

Waiting for her . . .

Taking her hand . . .

Cleaving only unto her.

Chapter 23

Now that she had Max, Jillian was not quite sure
what she was going to do with him.

The ceremony was over, the wedding breakfast in
progress as Max stood shoulder to shoulder with
Damien, and hand in hand with Jillian, all of them smiling for the wedding guests. No one had seemed to notice the stiff formality with which her husband—*her
husband!*—and her brother had treated one another in
the receiving line. Nor did anyone comment on how little Jillian had to say as she remained with Max and
Damien, feeling trapped, wishing she were anywhere
else.

Max was behaving like a caged lion.

Damien was like a panther with a wounded paw.

She'd felt like a bird they were fighting over ever
since the moment in the ceremony when the bishop had
asked, "Who gives this woman in marriage?"

A second passed and then two . . . three . . . four . . .

The hush of the guests had been so complete that
Jillian imagined she heard the drip of wax from the
candles onto their silver holders. The rustle of the bishop's robes had sounded like the scrape of pumice on
fingernails as he shifted uncomfortably, waiting for a
reply.

Max fixed Damien with a hard stare.

Jillian had dared to turn her head enough to give her
brother a pleading look.

"I do," Damien finally said, his voice low as he

placed Jillian's hand in Max's. And as he stepped from between them, he gave Max a fierce look as if to say: *She is not yours to keep.*

A man in the audience coughed. The bishop continued his rituals.

Those few, silent moments had seemed longer than the entire ceremony.

And now, the wedding breakfast seemed interminable as she and Max accepted the good wishes of their guests. Her feet were pinched within her new slippers, and her stomach twisted with cramps. Her head pounded from too little sleep and too many concerns.

"It's time to leave," Max said as if he'd heard her thoughts.

Damien cut in before Jillian could respond. "Can you not wait until a decent interval of time has passed?" he snarled from the side of his mouth.

"It is not unusual for a bride and groom to depart the festivities early," Max replied.

"She does not have to leave now if she does not wish to," Damien said.

Max ignored him. "Be ready to depart within the hour."

"Jillie, remember that you need stay with him only until your place in society is certain, a few months at most, then you can come home."

And do what? she wanted to ask. Pretend that Max did not exist, that he had never been a part of her life and she did not love him? But she kept her silence as she had done so many times in the past few weeks while struggling against her irritation at Damien and Max. Both acted as if this marriage was something to be worked out between the two of them. Neither had ever asked what *her* wishes might be.

Damien's belief that she would return home after a respectable amount of time was absurd. Max's expectation that she would want to leave him, both maddened and frustrated her. She would never lose Max. He was hers now and she had every intention of keeping him.

Jillian stared at his impassive face and rigid posture, the way he regarded everyone in the assembly with that odd detachment that had been like a battlement between them, keeping her at a distance.

She slipped from between them, anxious to get away. She was so tired of it all.

Thankfully, her rooms were deserted and offered a much needed sanctuary from the social farce being played out in the formal dining room. After defiantly locking her door, she sank onto her bed and stared down at her hands, too weary to do more than allow her mind to drift where it would.

Idly, she traced the pattern of lace in her tunic and watched the sunlight pouring in through her windows and glinting off her wedding band. She'd been surprised by Max's choice. Given the ostentation of her diamond betrothal ring, she'd dreaded the moment when he might slip something equally bold and obvious on her finger, rather than a delicate and simple etched gold band. Still it was the perfect choice, neither overwhelming her small hand nor pushing the look of her large diamond over the edge of good taste.

She held out her hand, turning it this way and that, admiring the way the gold seemed to catch fire in the sunlight and sighing at how right it felt on her finger.

Max's wife.

Jillian whispered the words, first in her mind, then aloud, trying them on for size and again feeling the rightness of the fit. During the course of the day, she'd been referred to in many ways: Jillian Nicole Forbes, Jillian Nicole Hastings, the Duchess of Bassett. But impressive as they all sounded, only one impressed her.

Max's wife.

Startled by the sudden opening of the door connecting her bedchamber to her dressing room, Jillian looked up to see LadyLou bustle in with Jillian's traveling dress over her arm.

"Whatever are you doing, Jillie? I knocked twice, but you didn't answer."

"Oh, I was just woolgathering . . . where is Clancy?"

LadyLou gave her an arch look. "Clancy is otherwise engaged at the moment. Arabella Seymour had the misfortune of trying to hang on to Max's arm and her skirt accidentally caught under my foot. The hem is almost irreparably torn."

"No doubt poor Clancy is being inundated with questions while she stitches up the damage," Jillian said with a half-hearted smile. Lady Seymour had been a nuisance all morning as she gushed over Jillian's gown in one breath and offered her usual oblique insults on her fashion sense in the next.

"Clancy is inundating that beruffled witch with her inside knowledge of how you and Max are meant for each other." LadyLou brushed a bit of lint from the sleeve of the blue gown and matching pelisse Jillian would wear to enter Bassett House as Max's wife.

Oh, but she did like the sound of that.

"Poor Clancy," Jillian said as she obediently stood while LadyLou helped her out of her wedding gown.

"Poor Arabella," LadyLou retorted. "If anyone can set her vicious mind to rights it is Clancy. In any case, I wanted to help you today." LadyLou's voice softened to a wistful tone. "It will be my last time, you know, to take care of you."

Jillian hadn't thought of that, and the realization that from this day forward she would only be a visitor in this house brought her a sudden sense of loss. Life would no longer be familiar. Her days would no longer include nonsensical talks with her brother nor loving hugs from her aunt.

"You were a vision walking down the aisle, Jillie, the most beautiful bride I have ever seen."

"I am glad someone noticed," Jillian said. Neither Max nor Damien had commented on her appearance. It was just one more hurt to absorb and accept. "Max is waiting," she prompted, reminding herself as well as LadyLou. If she did not join Max soon, she feared she would give in to the urge to hide in the cellar.

"I know dear," LadyLou said as she urged Jillian to sit down, and took a place beside her on the edge of the bed. "But before you go we must discuss your duties as a wife."

"You have prepared me well," Jillian replied. "I know what is expected of me. I am sure I will not have any difficulty running Bassett House."

LadyLou fidgeted with the froth of lace at Jillian's wrists. "There is also the matter of children and the physical act that creates them."

Jillian sucked in her breath sharply. She had been so consumed with other matters that she had not even thought of that. Even now when it had been brought to her attention she could not envision children except in the abstract. "We have only been married for a few hours. Is it not a bit early to worry about having children?" she asked reasonably.

LadyLou smoothed her skirts. "Actually, no. Many brides are mothers before their first year of marriage is complete."

Uneasiness slid down Jillian's spine. She wanted a child, several perhaps, but not in the near future. "I do not want to be a mother so soon," she said.

"I am afraid it is not that simple," LadyLou said, taking Jillian's hand in hers. Spots of color bloomed on her cheeks as she raised her free hand to her brow and covered her eyes as if she could not face Jillian while speaking of such things. "Gentlemen vastly enjoy the act that produces children. Max will want to engage in this activity with you as soon as possible."

LadyLou was *embarrassed,* Jillian realized, and her curiosity increased tenfold. There was a great mystery here. She had never seen her aunt so agitated.

LadyLou rose abruptly and paced the length of the room. "How closely have you studied the nude figures you have seen in paintings and sculpture?"

The question discomfited Jillian. "Avidly" did not seem quite the right answer. "Hardly at all," she said.

"Oh dear," LadyLou said as she took a place at the

window. "Did you at least notice the anatomical differences between men and women?"

"Yes," Jillian said quietly, wishing for the discussion to come to an end. Suddenly, she didn't want to know more about this great mystery. The differences LadyLou alluded to had always seemed rather ridiculous to Jillian as she'd studied the statues of males, and she'd assumed that since the figures were of mythical beings that the odd appendages they sprouted in unlikely places were acts of whimsy on the parts of the artists.

LadyLou sighed deeply. "Tonight, Max will wish to join that part of him that makes him a man to that part of you that makes you a woman. The first time is painful, but some women find it pleasurable after a time."

Heat climbed into Jillian's face. Her mouth worked for a moment, yet she could not produce a sound. She could not believe it. For one thing, the part LadyLou referred to was so *small* . . . pathetic really. Surely it was not possible for a man to . . . to . . . do what her aunt said.

"From what Clancy tells me, you are indisposed," LadyLou said.

Jillian sagged in relief. She did understand what LadyLou meant and was immeasurably grateful to Clancy. Surely now, the conversation would come to an end.

"You will have to tell Max," LadyLou said quietly.

Jillian frowned in yet more confusion. "Tell Max what?"

"That you are having your monthly."

Jillian was horrified. She could not tell Max that. Were men even aware of— Oh, she could not! Nothing short of having a horrible accident on the back of her dress would induce her to admit to that most private bodily function and even then, she would think of some other explanation such as she sat on her scissors.

LadyLou turned to face Jillian. "You must tell him Jillian. It will have a bearing on how Max conducts himself tonight. But he must know before he removes your clothes."

Jillian bounded to her feet. "You cannot be serious."

LadyLou nodded her head. "You must understand Jillian, that there is nothing to be ashamed of. It is all necessary if there are to be children."

Jillian had never been so confused and mortified in her entire life. As for Max removing her clothes, well she did not believe it for an instant. He would never do such a thing.

She didn't believe it, and yet LadyLou had never lied to her before.

Max waited for Jillian in the seclusion of Damien's study to avoid the wedding guests still celebrating in the ballroom. He would have much preferred to wait in his carriage. This room and the entire house brought back too many memories.

It was over. Jillian was his wife rather than his friend. All that was left for him to do was to make the best of the situation. As for her infatuation, well it would fade soon enough. All that talk he'd heard over the years about love coming after marriage was pure drivel. The most that could be hoped for was benign indifference. The worst was contempt bred of familiarity.

But he and Jillian had been familiar with one another for years.

Impatiently, he pulled his watch from his pocket and checked the time. Jillian should have been here by now. If it would not destroy all that he and Damien had accomplished, he would leave without her. He did not feel married. He could not connect Jillian with himself in that manner. Nor could he connect himself with the beautiful woman who had drifted down the aisle toward him, her gaze fixed only on him. She'd been every inch the bride in her ivory silk and lace, and her pearls and flowers.

The stars had been back in her eyes.

And they'd terrified him.

He strode to the door and ripped it open. He had to escape this house. Even Bassett was preferable. At least there, nothing had changed. It was numbingly cold, blessedly impersonal.

As he crossed the entry hall, he saw Damien descend the stairs. "Jillian will be down momentarily," he clipped out as he reached the bottom. "LadyLou is having a talk with her about tonight."

Max stifled a curse. All he needed was for Jillian's maiden aunt to fill her head with horror stories.

"You will take care with her," Damien said, his lips curving with disgust.

"I have never had any complaints in the past," he said mildly, though he was irritated that Damien would institute such a conversation. It was not a subject he wanted to discuss with anyone, and certainly not with Damien of all people.

Damien's fists clenched at his sides. "And none had best reach my ears in this instance."

Irritation turned to anger at Damien's persistence. "What passes between Jillian and myself in the privacy of my bed is none of your business and a subject I forbid you to ever broach with me again."

"If it concerns my sister's well-being, I will broach any subject I see fit."

"You go too far, Damien," Max said. "Jillian is my wife. If you interfere in our marriage in any way, I will forbid her to have any contact with you."

Color crept up Damien's neck. "You cannot do that."

"Yes, I can, and you well know it," Max said, sick to his soul that he'd had to resort to such brutal threats. But Damien had given him no quarter since this whole nightmare had begun. If there was any chance at all that he and Jillian might find a way to live their lives in peace, then they must have time in which to find their way together.

"Max, I am ready," Jillian said softly as she slowly walked down the stairs.

Max frowned. Jillian's countenance was unnaturally

pale, and Max wondered if LadyLou's "talk" had anything to do with her pallor.

Damien gathered her close as she took the final step and hugged her fiercely. "I will come to see you tomorrow."

"No," Max said. "Jillian and I will not be 'at home' to visitors for the next few weeks."

"As I said, Jillie, I will call tomorrow to see if you are all right," Damien repeated.

Jillian broke away from Damien and placed her hand on his arm. "Go back to London," she said softly. "I will be fine."

As her gaze darted nervously from Damien to himself, Max knew she had overhead him threaten to forbid her to see her brother. Of course she had . . . and she had taken it seriously. Already it began, he thought cynically. Already, she was willing to believe the worst of him. At this rate it wouldn't take her long to become disenchanted with her ludicrous dreams of romance. Not long at all.

Still it rankled that either Jillian or Damien could think that he would cut them off from one another. They were family for Godsake, the bond between them stronger than any he could ever forge with Jillian under the best of circumstances.

Max took Jillian's hand and placed it in the crook of his arm. "We will return to town in a few weeks," he said stiffly and led Jillian out the door.

He made no effort to assist her into his carriage, but nodded at his footman to see to the task. It was difficult to touch her in even the most casual way with Damien standing on the broad portico glaring daggers at him. Still proprieties must be maintained for the benefit of any guests observing them from the windows, and Max waited until his bride was settled to climb in after her.

The coachman clucked the horses into motion.

Max watched with interest as Jillian neatly folded her hands in her lap and stared down at them, avoiding his gaze. He could imagine what must be running through her mind to bring about such a fit of shyness. At least she didn't appear to be on the verge of a swoon. Perhaps LadyLou hadn't frightened her with spinsterish tales of the carnal side of marriage after all.

The knowledge that he now had the right to do what he'd only envisioned in his dreams was enough to handle without having to soothe virginal hysterics.

He glanced at Jillian from the corner of his eye, noting her unusual silence and downcast gaze, her prim posture and her lower lip caught between her teeth. Her traveling costume was a slate blue with crisp white trim and gloves, her small hat a matching felt trimmed with white silk and a bit of netting that dipped over her brow. She looked like a successful governess traveling to a new post. And then, as she rested her head against the back of the seat and closed her eyes, she simply looked like a very young woman too weary to face the unknown.

She smelled of white lilies today, a sweet, innocent fragrance of spring meadows and new gardens.

A virgin. Jillian was a virgin. Good Lord.

Max stared out the window and watched the scenery roll by, irritated at the way his body stirred at the thought. But this, too, he would master as he had mastered all the elements—both pleasant and otherwise—in his life.

The carriage halted in front of Bassett House and Max cursed as he saw Burleigh and all the servants assembled in a display that he had not seen since the days his father had put in rare appearances here. It was a ritual that Max scorned and had not permitted since he had assumed the title. But then, Burleigh no doubt assumed that the arrival of a new duchess merited a certain amount of pomp and circumstance.

Jillian sat up but did not otherwise move as she waited, her gaze directed at the squabs directly across from her. Max hadn't seen her so still or so quiet since he'd watched her sleep in her cradle.

A footman rushed forward to open the coach door

and Max climbed out, then assisted Jillian to the ground. She stepped from the carriage, her gaze sweeping over the company of laundered and starched servants as if she were greeted by a mob everyday.

"Your Grace," the butler intoned formally, "all is in readiness."

"For what?" Max inquired.

"Burleigh," Jillian said and stepped past Max, effectively ending his exchange with the cadaverous butler. "It has been a very long time since I have seen you." She glanced around the newly manicured grounds. "Everything looks especially beautiful."

Since she had only visited Bassett twice in her life, Max was surprised that she even remembered his butler's name.

"It has been too many years since I have had the honor of preparing Bassett to receive a new duchess. Welcome, your Grace," Burleigh replied confirming Max's suspicions.

Jillian gave a small start as her gaze shot to Max. In spite of himself, he smiled at the absurdity of it. "How does it feel to be one of the graces?"

A little frown creased her brow, and her eyes took on a gleam as if she were looking inward. His breath caught in his throat as her expression became serene, and a gentle smile curved her lips as she raised her gaze to his for the first time since leaving Wesbrook. "It feels right."

Max scowled at her reply. Didn't she understand how ridiculous it sounded? How utterly wrong it was for her to be his duchess? But no, he thought wearily, she wouldn't see it. Not yet. No doubt her head was filled with sugared fantasies of domestic bliss.

It wouldn't last. Even sweets hardened and crumbled given enough time.

"Burleigh, were you here when the previous duchess came to Bassett?" Jillian asked.

The butler cleared his throat. "Ah, yes, I was, your Grace," he replied stiffly.

Max stood back, removing himself from the scene as Jillian tried to pry the details from his butler. He should have known she would seize the first opportunity to solicit a family story. She loved that sort of thing, but she was doomed to disappointment if that was what she wanted. There were no memories here of Max listening to a story at his mother's knee or of a young master sliding down the polished banisters when no one was looking. At Bassett House everyone was on guard against frivolity.

He was vaguely aware that Burleigh must have been here when his mother had come as a bride. But he had never heard the story. He did not wish to hear it now. His mother existed in the memories of others and Max could no more make a connection with her than he could with the fact that Jillian had taken her place as the Duchess of Bassett.

"The rest of the servants are waiting Jillian," Max reminded and took her elbow. Quickly, he guided her along the line of waiting servants, allowing Burleigh to make the majority of introductions. Max knew very few of their names.

At last it was finished, and Max escorted her up the stone steps and braced himself to enter the cold and sterile atmosphere of the house. Even Jillian wrapped her arms around herself. Max hated it here. He always had. He needed to be out in the sunshine where it was warm. All he wanted to do was change his clothes and ride the parkland. Yet he didn't know what to do with Jillian. It was hours before dinner and ironically, he had no idea how to fill the time with her until then. Somehow he doubted she was in the mood for chess.

Impatient at the memory of Jillian blatantly cheating through every game they'd ever played together, he began to climb the grand staircase.

"Come along," he said. "I'll show you to your rooms." His gut lurched at the realization that she would be sleeping so near to him. He had slept under the same roof as her more times than he could count, but he was used to being separated from her by convention and a long hallway.

Back then, the thought of sharing intimacies with her had never entered his mind. Back then he'd spent wakeful moments planning how he would counter her cheating and still allow her to win.

Reaching the top of the stairs, he stiffly led her down the hall and pushed open the door to her room. He backed away, careful to maintain enough distance to keep her body from brushing his as she entered the room.

She stepped inside and Max stood in the doorway. The room was as darkly furnished and dimly lit as his own chamber, seeming to swallow Jillian in its bleakness.

She looked as if she were going to burst into tears as she turned to him with a shaky smile and jerky movements. "I think I would like to see the rest of the house."

"You have seen the house," Max said.

"Yes," she said as she swept past him into the hall. "But it has been a long time and I have never seen all of it."

"Very well. Burleigh will take you on a tour," Max said as the butler emerged from the shadows. With a nod at Burleigh, Max strode toward his chamber to change into his riding clothes.

Jillian didn't need him to discover that the house was filled with nothing but gloom and the remnants of dead civilizations.

She would find no warmth and homey comfort here.

Chapter 24

Jillian stared at Max's retreating back with a painful lump throbbing in her throat. He could not, it seemed, get away from her fast enough. And oddly, she was glad to see him go. It had been difficult enough to be alone with him in the coach, with LadyLou's instructions to immediately tell Max of her indisposition hanging over her head.

She could not do it. She could not even think about what was to come tonight even though it was still murky in her mind. For the first time in her life, her imagination failed her.

"If you will follow me," Burleigh intoned.

She shivered against a chill that had seeped into her bones the moment she had stepped foot inside, then she followed the butler through the rooms of the centuries-old ducal seat of Max's family.

And now it was her family as well.

As on her previous visits, she was struck by the beauty and grandeur of Italian marble and the elaborate relief of molded and intricately painted high ceilings, of imported furnishings and odd ornaments.

If one could find beauty and grandeur in such an absence of life.

In the formal dining room, the mahogany table seemed to stretch to infinity with so many chairs that she did not even want to count them. In a small room adjacent to the dining room a collection of medieval armor and weapons were arranged as if they would be picked up and used at any moment. The walls here were their natural stone, a fitting-enough setting for polished metal and sharpened blades. A drop of blood welled on the tip of her finger as she curiously touched the edge of a war ax. As she sucked on the small wound, she wondered who kept it all so clean and shiny and well-honed.

The formal drawing room was massive and very formal indeed. Certainly not a place where she could imagine herself sitting down with a cup of tea and a good book.

They went through the library and music room where everything was clean and bright with constant care, yet seemed arranged for effect rather than use. Then, they strolled across a ballroom that looked as if no one had ever danced there. Finally they walked through a long gallery inhabited by all manner of sculpture.

She followed Burleigh through one bedchamber after another in the east wing, each room beautiful and perfectly maintained, silent and cold. She saw not a suggestion of a human touch anywhere. For all its rich appointments and pristine surfaces, it seemed like a world apart from the one she had always known. A lifeless world created to be seen and never touched.

Dejected and feeling a pervading sense of emptiness, she walked toward her room with Burleigh at her side, foregoing a similar tour of the west wing. She had seen enough. "Has Clancy arrived yet, Burleigh?" she asked wearily.

"Yes, your Grace, and your personal effects arrived yesterday and have been put away. I will summon your maid to attend you," Burleigh said in that odd whisper employed by all the servants she'd met.

As they crossed from one wing to another, her pace quickened. At least in her room, she would find the comfort of Clancy's presence and the familiarity of her own things about her.

Once inside her chamber, Burleigh lit the candles, bowed, and pulled the door closed as he backed out into the hall. She stood in the center of the room, her gaze sweeping from armoire to bed to a beautifully carved dressing table. Everything was bare—no litter of perfume bottles nor sign of her brush and comb and hand mirror, no finger smudge on the mirrored door of the armoire, no peek of cloth escaping from a drawer. She pulled the bell rope.

Clancy appeared within moments.

"Where are my things?" Jillian asked with a sweep of her hand.

Clancy stared at her feet. "Mr. Burleigh instructed me to put everything in drawers. There is to be no clutter lying about."

Jillian eyed the closed drapes.

"Mr. Burleigh says the drapes are to remain closed. Sunlight fades the rug."

"Oh," Jillian said weakly, knowing that Burleigh's instructions on how the house was run came from Max. "You may go Clancy."

She sank down on the bed and buried her face in the pillows, ignoring the way her hat pushed to one side of her head. She closed her eyes and the hat pulled at her hair and hurt, and she shivered with cold. Dimly, she heard the door open and not wanting to face the sterility of her room again, she neither turned her face from the pillow, nor opened her eyes.

A soft "shhh" comforted her and the pain in her head eased as the hat was pulled away. She sighed as a blanket was drawn over her.

"Sleep, Jillian."

Surely she'd fallen asleep and was dreaming. It couldn't be Max brushing a strand of hair from her cheek and soothing her with soft shushes. She'd heard him earlier, as he'd ordered Sovereign brought around as he'd left the house, abandoning her along with all the other relics of times past.

"Your Grace," Clancy called, shaking Jillian gently by the shoulder. "It is time to bathe and change for dinner."

Jillian opened her eyes, instantly alert and filled with melancholy. She was not at home in her own bed. Sitting up, she glanced around, shocked that she had been asleep for so long. Night had fallen and more tapers had been lit, their yellow light casting dark shadows about the room. "Why didn't you wake me?

"His Grace said to let you rest."

Her heart fluttered in her chest, and her hand flew to her head just as her gaze settled on the small table beside the bed where her hat now rested. Though she hadn't actually seen him, Jillian had a sudden image of Max bending over her and removing her hat then drawing the counterpane over her. It hadn't been a dream.

Max *had* been here, watching her sleep as she had watched him when she was a little girl. And then, her heart seemed to stop. He had come to her room. Even when she was a very small child he had never ventured beyond the threshold of her bedchamber.

"I'll have the blue silk gown pressed," Clancy said.

"Yes, fine," Jillian said and swung her legs over the side of the bed as Clancy left in a flurry. Her gaze shot to the connecting door at the sound of muffled footsteps and faint clinks. Apprehension seized her as she identified one of the muted voices.

Max was in there. His chambers were on the other side of the door. Quickly, she scurried to the other side of the bed putting as much distance between herself and the door as possible, suddenly fearful that Max might come in. But the sounds continued without interruption and she shook her head in disgust.

What was the matter with her? She had never been frightened of Max before. Nothing had changed. Nothing except that they'd been married that morning. Nothing except that, tonight, he would remove her clothes and commit an unimaginable act on her body, and it wouldn't be possible because she was indisposed. Eve's curse had turned into a blessing, granting her a temporary reprieve. Hopefully, in the next week she would be able to come to terms with the knowledge LadyLou had imparted earlier today.

She had to tell Max.

Drawing a deep breath, she squared her shoulders and hesitantly knocked on the connecting door. "Max?"

The door opened instantly. "His Grace is working in his study," Burleigh said.

"Oh," Jillian said and stared past Burleigh's shoulder to the room beyond—not a bedchamber at all, but a sitting room complete with fireplace where no fire burned. Two maids were busily setting a small table for two. "Dinner is to be served here?" she asked.

"His Grace never takes his meals in the formal dining room," Burleigh said as if he were performing a religious chant.

"Oh," Jillian said again, swallowing her disappointment. She had been looking forward to escaping for a few hours. At least in the formal rooms, all the white marble brightened things, even if it was freezing.

"Do you require anything, your Grace?" Burleigh asked.

"No," she said.

He nodded and briskly dismissed the maids, following them out.

Jillian realized she had not asked what time dinner was to be served.

Dismayed, she glanced around the sitting room. It seemed very strange to her that her bedchamber was smaller than this room. And she didn't have a fireplace. But even a bright blaze could not cheer the gloom. Everything was too dark and overwhelmingly masculine. With the heavy velvet drapes drawn against the night, she felt as if she were suffocating.

Behind her the door opened. "What time does his Grace dine?" she asked, assuming it was Clancy bringing back her gown.

"Eight o'clock," Max said.

Jillian started and turned. He was dressed for riding. "I thought you were working in your study."

"I was for a short time."

"After your ride?"

"Yes," he said.

He could have asked her if she wanted to go along instead of abandoning her all afternoon. "Did you enjoy your ride?"

He nodded. "Did you enjoy your nap?"

"Yes, thank you for covering me," she said. Now. She should tell him now.

"You were cold," he said simply.

But she wasn't cold now. Her whole body felt flushed and warm and she was horribly embarrassed. Behind her, she was aware that Clancy had returned with her dress.

"I must go and dress for dinner," she said. She could not tell him. She could not.

"There is no need to dress," Max said.

Jillian stiffened and took a step back. Apparently he didn't intend to remove her clothes at all, but simply expected that she would save him the trouble by not wearing any in the first place. There was no help for it. She *had* to tell him. "Yes there is," she choked.

Her face burned more fiercely than ever as Max's gaze narrowed on her.

"I meant there is no need to costume yourself in formal attire," he said in a careful tone and nodded toward the watered silk gown Clancy had hung on a hook.

"Oh," Jillian said feeling more foolish than ever. "What are you going to wear?" she asked inanely.

"A shirt and a pair of breeches," he said evenly and opened the door to his bedchamber. "If you will excuse me."

A shirt and breeches without the propriety of a coat? she wondered as she wandered back into her own room. Would he forego shoes as well?

"Your bath is ready, my Lady," Clancy said. "Oh, I'm sorry; I mean, *your Grace.*"

"No apology is necessary," Jillian said. "I am afraid

it is going to take us both a while to become accustomed to my changed status."

And as she dressed, Jillian thought that she might never become accustomed to being alone with Max while he wore only a shirt and breeches.

LadyLou had said nothing about that.

Max leaned back in his steaming bath and willed his tense muscles to relax. What in bloody hell had LadyLou told Jillian? That she was to come to dinner naked?

Tonight was his wedding night and he had no idea how he was going to approach his bride. She was a bundle of nerves. She had actually taken a step away from him as if she were frightened of him. Of him! He supposed he could start by kissing her. She certainly hadn't been afraid of that. If she had been, they wouldn't be in this coil now. But how to get close enough to her was the question.

Oh God, he did not want to do this.

With that thought, his manhood stirred and rose above the water, mocking him, reminding him that his mind and his matter were in conflict.

He rose from his bath and let the chilly air dispose of his overeager manhood. After briskly toweling himself dry, he called for his valet.

His concern was unwarranted, he told himself as he submitted to the valet's attention to his appearance. Jillian was his wife and by the combined acts of her awkward attempts at seduction and their subsequent marriage, she had assumed the role of a woman. Therefore, he would approach her with the same consideration and finesse with which he treated any other woman who caught his interest. As he'd told Damien: He'd had no complaints. It was ridiculous to worry over such a basic act of nature.

Except that Jillian would expect more than a pleasant interlude. Her eyes were studded with stars and her expectations were riddled with impossible ideals.

Jillian couldn't have chosen a better man than him to disillusion her. Though there were legends enough about the Dukes of Bassett, not one included a tale of everlasting love and undying devotion. The family crypt was full of the remains of brave souls and cold hearts.

Dressed in a soft shirt and navy superfine trousers, he eased open the door to the sitting room. Wearing a plain gown of bottle green, Jillian hugged a bright yellow shawl close to her body as she sat on the edge of her chair, watching a footman serve their meal. A single long braid trailed down her back.

She had certainly taken him seriously concerning dinner attire. To look at her no one would believe her to be an eager and loving bride on her wedding night.

The footman departed and Max closed the door with a soft click.

At the sound, she rose abruptly, her back ramrod straight, her hand clutching the shawl as if it were a weapon.

"Hungry?" he asked, forcing a light tone as he sauntered farther into the room and halted at the table.

"Not especially," she said, her gaze wide and wary.

"I should think you would be," he said as he pulled out a chair. "You didn't eat anything at our wedding breakfast." He motioned for her to sit, amused that they had been reduced to such trite conversation.

"Neither did you," she said as she sat down.

"I am not the one denying hunger," he said and took the place opposite her. "I am famished." He didn't bother to tell her that food would not satisfy him. All he could think about was unbraiding her hair, removing her gown, taking what was his.

He lifted a cover from a dish. "Ah, lobster. One of your favorites."

Jillian stared down at her plate.

Max returned the cover to their meal and sat back in his chair. "Enough," he said quietly.

Her head snapped up. "Pardon me?"

"Enough of your fear. I want you to put whatever your aunt told you about tonight out of your mind."

Jillian lowered her gaze back to her plate. "Are you perchance referring to the activity that produces children?" she choked.

To Max's horror, heat climbed up his neck. It was on the tip of his tongue to inform her that the correct term was making love. "That is one way of putting it," he said. "I suspect your head has been filled with nonsense."

"LadyLou is not in the habit of filling my head with nonsense," Jillian said, her voice tight with indignation.

"Really," Max said, his lips twitching at the inanity of it all. "What did she tell you?"

"The truth," she stated.

"On this particular subject, it is possible that everyone has a different version of the truth."

Jillian glared at him as if he had defamed her aunt's character. "LadyLou would never convey information of such a nature unless she were positive her facts were correct."

"Obviously she did a poor job of it, or you would not be frightened out of your wits," Max snapped, then forced himself to assume a more patient temperament. "What precisely did she tell you?"

"That you would remove my clothes and insert a part of your anatomy inside me."

Max blinked and leaned back in his chair. By God, LadyLou did deliver the bald facts. "That's a rather cold way to describe something so warm," he said, struggling to contain his own discomfiture.

"How can it be warm when I won't have any clothes on?" she blurted.

"I suppose I could leave them on, but it is a lot more fun without them."

"That is easy for you to say since you get to keep yours on."

"Did LadyLou tell you that?"

"No, but since she did not mention anything to the contrary, I only assumed. . ."

"You should never assume, Jillian."

"You will not have yours on either?"

Max folded his napkin and set it beside his plate. "You will understand when the time comes. For now, I suggest that we finish our meal. Later, we can explore the mechanics of procreation in the comfort of my bed." Abruptly, he reached for the wine chilling in a bucket by his elbow. He couldn't believe he had made such a ludicrous speech. He'd had more finesse at sixteen when he'd first bedded the village milkmaid.

Jillian's gaze fluttered to his, then lowered again. "I can't," she said miserably.

He went cold. "I see. Do I take it then that you are in accord with Damien's ideas of a temporary arrangement between us? Did he advise you against consummating this marriage so that you might apply for an annulment?"

"No, you don't understand. I *cannot,*" she said, massaging her temples with her fingertips. "I am indisposed."

"A headache?" he inquired acidly. "Come now, you can do better than that."

"It is not that at all." She buried her face in her hands and flushed to the roots of her hair. "I am having my monthly."

Bewildered by her distress, he stared at her bent head. "Your monthly what?" he asked.

Her chair toppled behind her as she surged to her feet. "LadyLou said you would understand," she said as if it were an accusation, then fled the room, slamming the door behind her.

Max stared at the door, stunned by such behavior from Jillian. Though she'd been indulged all her life, she'd never been given to tantrums. Sweet little pouts and well-applied guilt were more her forte, but she'd outgrown those tactics years ago. And even so, she'd always been straightforward in stating her purpose. If nothing else he could count on her to be honest. Her monthly what, for Godsake?

Then comprehension dawned, and he felt his face flame. For all his experience with women, he had never had to deal with the advent of a monthly flux. He had never been close enough to any woman to be aware of when that mysterious bodily function occurred, but had always received a discreet little note from whomever he was involved with at the time pleading a "delicate indisposition." He'd neither had to give it any thought nor identify the infirmity in specific terms.

Still, it gave him a strange feeling of possessiveness to be privy to such intimate details about Jillian. Alarm cut the thought short before he could examine it more fully. Possessiveness was the last thing he wanted to feel for his wife. It implied too much in the way of tender feelings and romantic delusions, all sure indications that he was in danger of becoming vulnerable to his loss of her. And he would surely lose her. It only remained to be seen whether Jillian's enchantment with love wore off before he lost all patience with the sham of domestic bliss.

He could not allow himself to fall prey to the emotions that had destroyed more than one poor besotted fool. The happiest marriages he'd seen in the ton were those where both parties sought nothing more than the mutual benefits of material gain, providing an heir to protect their combined wealth, and getting on together with a modicum of respect and congeniality.

Perhaps her indisposition was a blessing after all. He and Jillian needed time to grow accustomed to living in this house together. He may not like the situation, but it could not be ignored and nothing would be served by conflict between them. It was time they reached some sort of understanding about the proper way to conduct a civilized marriage.

He rose from the table and walked to the connecting door. He raised his hand to knock, then lowered it abruptly, stunned by the sound of wrenching sobs coming from her room.

"I want to go home," Jillian wept. "I want to go home."

He hadn't heard her cry since their fathers had died.

All thoughts of comforting her left him, and trying to reach an understanding seemed redundant. She wanted to go home after less than half a day in his house. His new bride was disenchanted already. At last they had found some common ground.

Chapter 25

Jillian's eyes popped open as sunlight poured in through the open drapes. Her first thought was that Mr. Burleigh did not want the drapes to be open. Her second was that the ghoulish butler would probably melt in the sunlight.

Her third was to wonder why her teeth were chattering. If Clancy had been in to pull the window hangings, why hadn't she lit a fire?

But then she remembered that there was no fireplace.

As she sat up and stared around the small room, she realized why. Her bedchamber was not a bedchamber at all, but a dressing room. This wasn't the master suite. It couldn't be. The one at Westbrook had two sitting rooms and two bedchambers with adjacent dressing rooms and she knew that adjoining apartments were normal for husbands and wives.

She might have realized it sooner if she'd allowed

Burleigh to show her the west wing. The master suite had to be there.

Apparently, he had kept the same rooms he'd used during his bachelor days and had hastily ordered his dressing room to be fitted out for her. Her eyes narrowed on the connecting door to his bedchamber. He had a wife now, yet it obviously had not occurred to him that she might have need of a fire. What would be next? Cold gruel and stale bread for breakfast? Leaving the bed—which on reflection was rather hard—she walked across the room toward Max's door. She wouldn't stand for such cavalier treatment, and she would tell him so.

But then she remembered the night before and how she'd run from the room without answering his question or offering any explanations. She had behaved like a child last night, running from Max in a fit and sobbing into her pillow that she wanted to go home.

But she had not been able to stop herself. The day had been too much and her stomach had hurt and Max had been too patient with her, as if she were a half-wit in need of tolerance. As if he'd pitied her. Under the circumstances, she couldn't help but pity herself. And then, she'd been overwhelmed when she'd learned that Max would also be unclothed when they engaged in the act that produced children. It was one thing to envision herself standing before him naked, but quite another to try to imagine *him* naked like the statues she'd seen. Somehow she just couldn't picture Max with one of those ridiculous acorn-shaped appendages growing between his legs.

She had panicked when he had not understood why she was indisposed, and she had not been prepared to explain in precise detail what her monthly was. On the contrary, she'd been counting on Max to explain a few things to *her*. They would certainly have a difficult time of it if neither one of them knew precisely what part of him was to be inserted into which part of her.

She recalled what he'd said to her about not

consummating the marriage so she could apply for an annulment. Of course she knew from her Latin lessons with LadyLou what "consummate" meant, but hadn't known that it was a binding factor in a marriage. LadyLou had indicated that it was more important to men than it was to women.

If it was so important to Max, then it would be equally as important to her.

She had to go to him and explain what she had failed so miserably to explain last night. Her gaze flicked to the clock on the chest. It was only seven o'clock. Too early for him to have stirred. Yet, she reflected, it was the ideal time to talk to him. She could say what she needed to say and be gone before he had time to react.

She'd never been a coward before and this was no time to begin. That she intended to deliver her confession and run was a simple matter of self-preservation.

With a heavy sigh, she tightened the belt of her dressing gown and once again walked to the door. She felt some hesitation at appearing in his room in her nightclothes, then shoved it aside. Considering what was to come later, her modesty was probably wasted. The larger problem was how to tactfully broach the subject of what was to come later.

As she passed through the sitting room that separated their chambers, her mind turned over possible ways to tell him. Last night there had been too much to assimilate at once. Today, she would address only one problem at a time.

"Max, I apologize for my behavior," she muttered under her breath. "It was not my intention to behave in a hysterical fashion." She paused at his door, not sure how to continue. She supposed it would come to her.

She knocked forcefully on his door. There was no answer. She knocked again, making sure she made enough noise to wake the dead.

Still no answer.

Mustering her courage, she pushed open the door, feeling as if she were eight years old again and sneaking into his room to watch him sleep. The room was dark, the heavy velvet drapes blocking out all light. The carpets in here surely must be in excellent condition.

As her eyes adjusted to the darkness, she made out Max's shape in the bed. Since all she could see above the covers was his mane of gold hair, she assumed he was lying belly down, as swathed in blankets as she'd been all night. "Max, are you awake?" she called.

"I am now," he mumbled. "What time is it?"

"Just past seven in the morning."

Suddenly he raised up, supporting himself on his elbows as the bed linens slipped off his shoulders. In the gloom, she saw the outline of his shoulders and back—his *bare* shoulders and back. She sucked in her breath. She had never seen so much of him before. When she sneaked into his room as a child, he had always worn a nightshirt. Last night she could not imagine him unclothed, yet, now she found it very easy to elaborate on what she saw and fill in the details of his broad shoulders and narrow hips and powerful thighs, and how they'd felt against her when they'd shared that kiss on the drawing room sofa.

"What are you doing in here?" he asked as he barely turned his head toward her.

"I wanted to talk," she said weakly.

"Now?" he said incredulously.

Coherent thought deserted her as a fierce quickening spread through the pit of her belly at the way his sleep-rumpled hair reminded her of how she had sifted her fingers through the strands as they'd kissed. And then she thought of sharing such a kiss again, only naked. The sensations she'd experienced that night rushed through her body, pooling in that part of her that made her a woman. A delicious shiver coursed down her spine as she remembered the feel of Max's mouth on her lips and bare throat, the way she had wanted to melt into him and become a part of him. For a few brief moments she had ached for something nameless and indescribable. And she knew without doubt that if Damien had not walked in, she would have allowed Max to do anything he wanted, no matter how shocking.

Abruptly, Max rubbed his head with his hands, then rolled to his back and dragged the covers about his neck. All she could see was his head and his eyes narrowed to slits. "Surely, whatever you wished to discuss can wait until a decent hour," he said tightly.

Jillian swallowed nervously as she realized that while she'd been woolgathering she had lost her opportunity to talk to him while he was still groggy from sleep. He was completely awake and alert. "I—I came to explain about last night," she said in a rush. "You see, LadyLou had assured me that you would not be ignorant of the workings of the female body. I was not prepared to explain in precise detail about—about—"

He stared at her unblinking. "Your monthly?"

She nodded and swallowed her embarrassment.

"I understand," he said flatly. "Is there anything else?"

There was a great deal more she wanted to discuss, but his manner invited neither further confession nor serious conversation. "I was wondering about breakfast," she said.

"Have a tray sent up."

Jillian took a step back. His voice was so cold and distant that it made her feel as if she had ventured into a room of a perfect stranger. Her gaze skittered around the room and she realized that it was like her own, not only in the darkness of its furnishings but its absence of any human touch. Since she had only occupied her room for a night, she understood why it did not have a lived-in feeling. But this room should be stamped with Max's presence. If he had not been in the bed, it would look as if no one occupied this room either. Suddenly, she wondered if he were a stranger. The Max she knew and loved would not live in an atmosphere such as this.

"Is that all?" he inquired as if she were an annoying insect.

"No," she said. She wanted *her* Max back. "Shall I have your breakfast sent up as well?"

"I breakfast in my room *alone.*"

"Not always," she reminded him. "Not long ago, you came to have breakfast with Damien and me in London, not to mention the meals we shared at Westbrook over the years."

"We are not in London and certainly not at Westbrook. Now, if you would be so kind as to leave, I would like to dress and begin my day."

"Of course, *your Grace.* How rude of me," Jillian said and swept from the room, infuriated with his ducal dismissal.

In her room, she yanked hard on the bellpull to summon Clancy. She had never taken a meal alone in her room in her life and she did not intend to start now. One way or another she would make her presence known to Max in ways he could neither ignore nor dismiss.

To that end, she sent Clancy to inform Burleigh that her Grace wished to have her breakfast served in the formal dining room in one hour.

After bathing and dressing with particular care in a lawn gown of lilac appliquéd with white daisies, she left her room without a backward glance.

As she approached the closed double doors to the formal dining room, one of the footmen stationed on either side snapped to attention and ushered her inside. If she had not been so angry with Max, she would have laughed at the sheer absurdity of what she saw. A place had been set for her at the far end of the massive mahogany table and it looked like a small lifeboat floating on the ocean.

The solicitous footman escorted her to her seat. "Coffee, your Grace?" the footman inquired, his voice echoing through the room designed to seat a hundred guests with room to spare.

"Yes, please," she said, smothering her smile as another footman approached with a covered dish. The aroma of ham drifted through the air and she realized she was hungry. Two footmen hovered near her as she ate her meal with relish.

As she picked the crumbs of her scone from her empty plate with the pad of a finger, she leaned back in her chair and wondered what to do next. She was in no hurry to return to her chamber. She supposed she could go to the library and find something to read and take it back to the sitting room that separated her chamber from Max's. At least it was roomier and she could curl up on the sofa.

But the idea held no appeal. The sitting room was as grim as the adjoining bedchambers. Warmth and comfort of any kind were not integral parts of Bassett House. Even the gardens were too formal and perfect to be enjoyed. Heaven forbid if anyone should muss the lawns.

Yet, as she sat among the splendor of the dining room, she imagined how she could make her quarters her own. She would fill it with the Chippendale furniture and the pale yellow counterpane and drapes she had seen in one of the other chambers. In fact, she would move into the master suite if she knew where it was.

In the meantime, she would have fires built everywhere in Bassett House and banish the coldness forever. She would put fresh flowers in every room and convert one of the rooms into an intimate dining room where she and Max could take their meals like a normal family. The medieval room would be perfect.

Realization crept over her like slow moving fog as she became aware that since the moment she had stepped through the threshold she had been making a list of changes in the back of her mind. Still, she was loathe to mention them. It seemed that the routines at Bassett House were written in stone. She didn't even know what Max's preferences were in regard to the running of the house. Given the state of his temper, she had no desire to ask him. But she knew who she could ask.

"Please inform Burleigh that I would like to see him immediately," she said to the nearest footman.

"Yes, your Grace," he said with a bow.

A few moments later Burleigh appeared. "You summoned me," he intoned from the doorway.

"Yes. I would like to know where the master suite is located."

"In the west wing, your Grace."

"Then why are we situated in the east wing?"

"His Grace prefers it."

"I see," she murmured, though she didn't see at all. Still, there were more important issues at the moment and she decided to leave that one for another time. "I would like a detailed account of his Grace's instructions regarding the house."

"His Grace has never given any instructions. I have continued to run the house according to his late father's preferences."

"I see," Jillian said, but she really didn't. She was beginning to feel more and more as if she didn't know Max at all. She had never realized the depth of his indifference to Bassett House. He cared nothing for it. It was as if he was a visitor in his own home. Not that it felt much like a home.

"Is there anything else, your Grace?" Burleigh inquired.

"No," Jillian said, absently. "You may go."

Nothing had been changed since the death of Max's father, a man as cold and indifferent as the house. Absently she motioned for the footman to pour her another cup of coffee.

"Will there be anything else, your Grace?"

"No" Jillian said. "You are dismissed." She waved both of her watchdogs away.

Relieved to finally be free of such solicitous attention, she sipped her coffee and nearly dumped it into her lap as she glanced up at the entrance.

Max leaned against the door frame, his arms folded across his chest. "Playing duchess?" he drawled with a trace of amusement in his expression.

Refusing to let him know how much his mockery stung, she took another sip of coffee. "Actually, I was having breakfast," she said, idly noting his doeskins, high boots and the crop tucked beneath his arm. "Are you going riding?"

"Obviously."

"Would you care for some company?"

"No. I'm going fishing until such time as you are ready to do your duty. Your monthly lasts about five to seven days does it not?"

"What has that to do with fishing?" she asked, striving to sound as casual as he did on the subject.

"If you are indisposed, there is no point in my hanging about." He pushed away from the door frame and slapped the crop against his boot.

No point? What about her? Had things changed so much between them that he could no longer even enjoy her company? Now that they were married was consummation the only reason for them to be together? Was this all they had left?

"I will return in a week or so," Max said, filling the silence, increasing her confusion. "In the meantime, ask Burleigh for whatever you wish."

Jillian gaped at Max, unable to comprehend what, exactly, was happening, unsure as to how she was to behave. *Fishing*. He was going fishing for a week. Somehow, she doubted that it was common practice for a husband to leave his new bride the day after the wedding. Common practice or not, she certainly felt no equanimity for such callousness. She wrapped her hand around her cup, feeling the heat of the coffee, and for a small moment, entertained the urge to fling the liquid in Max's face. Anything to warm him up. Anything to elicit some sign of emotion from him. The urge passed as other considerations came to mind and she removed her hand from temptation and gazed up at him with a dispassionate expression of her own. "Actually, I would like to make a few changes to the house."

"Do whatever you want while you reside here."

"You make it sound as if I am here only on a temporary basis," she said as her breakfast began to churn in her stomach.

"Aren't you? Did I not hear you weeping into your pillow last night that you wanted to go home?"

Jillian lowered her gaze. She had not realized he had heard her. She had barely been aware of what she had said as she wailed into her pillow. "I'm sorry. You know I rarely cry, but I was lonely and homesick."

"Do not apologize. Neither of us wanted this marriage, but it is done. We are stuck with one another and must make the best of it and do our duty."

She closed her eyes as she felt the blood drain from her face. *Stuck with one another.* Dear heaven was it as bad as that? She knew he hadn't wanted this marriage, but she had believed that it was the circumstances and not her that he objected to, that once they were alone their old habits of friendship would fall back into place. Yet, if anything, his coldness and indifference toward her were getting worse as if the bond of marriage had weakened his old feelings for her.

Taking a slow, deep breath, she forced herself to meet his gaze. "In other words, you see marriage as a duty?"

"Marriage is only good for perpetuating a bloodline, Jillian." He regarded her steadily as he continued to slap the crop against the side of his boot as if he were impatient to get away. "Since you are the only wife I will ever have, it falls to you to give me an heir. The sooner it is accomplished, the sooner you will be free to leave."

Rendered speechless by his impassive tone and bloodless sentiment, Jillian could only stare at him. Surely, he had taken leave of his senses. How could he speak of *them* having a child and *her* leaving in the same breath?

"In the meantime," Max continued, "take whatever measures are necessary to make yourself less homesick. Play the duchess. Play house if you will. Pretend that this is your home until Damien comes for you." With that frigidly delivered sarcasm, he turned on his heel and strode away, leaving Jillian in stunned silence.

It was not that he expected her to leave, but that he expected Damien to come and reclaim her. And no wonder, she thought, as she remembered her brother's parting words, *Remember, you need not stay forever . . . you can come home.* Was the expectation that she would leave him the reason for Max's remoteness? Did he believe that she would turn on him as Damien had? And what of all the time he and her brother had spent together in their club lately, fostering public opinion? What else had Damien said to him? Worse, why did Max believe such nonsense? Did Damien think she was so mindless that she would do whatever he wished her to do? Did Max think her too shallow to merit his faith in her?

"Damn them both," she muttered as she shoved her cup away and rose from the table. They acted as if this marriage was something to be worked out between the two of them, and she had no say in the matter. Well she had news for them. This was her home now, and she was here to stay. Damien was no longer her guardian and had no say in how she conducted her life.

With plans emerging in her mind full-blown, she stalked from the room in search of Burleigh. Max expected her to pretend that this was her home, did he? He would be gone for a week, would he? Fine. She could establish very deep roots here in five days.

Max had best be prepared for a long siege.

She found Burleigh standing before the doors of one of the multitude of rooms on the lower floor, a massive key ring in his hand. Before she could reach him, he slipped a key into the lock and stepped inside.

Jillian did not hesitate to trail in behind him, then

abruptly halted. She had not seen this room yesterday, or at any time before.

The drapes were drawn and the furniture was covered. Yet, even in the dimness the room was beautiful; all done in white and gold with small touches of soft pastels in the Aubusson carpet that had surely been custom-made to blend perfectly with the decor.

"Burleigh, why did you not show me this room yesterday?"

The old butler jumped at the sound of her voice.

"I am sorry. I did not mean to startle you."

"It is quite all right, your Grace," he said recovering his composure. "This is the white drawing room. His Grace ordered it closed some time ago."

"Why?" Jillian asked.

"He did not say."

Jillian could not imagine Burleigh asking. Still, she had a feeling the butler had a fair suspicion. "Would you care to venture a guess?"

"No, your Grace."

So much for gaining any insight from Burleigh. "Open the drapes, please," she said.

Burleigh complied without comment.

The room was even more beautiful with sunlight adding a soft sheen to the fine wool of the carpet and a rich luster to the marble fireplace. Excited, she tugged a cover from a white silk chair woven with gold threads into a rose pattern. It looked new as if it had never been sat upon just as the Aubusson rug appeared as if it had never been walked upon.

"I have seen enough," she said with a nod of her head.

Burleigh reached up to draw the gold velvet drapes closed.

"Leave them open," Jillian said.

"But your Grace, the sunlight will fade the rug."

Jillian cocked her head to one side thoughtfully. "Was that one of the late duke's concerns?"

"Yes, your Grace."

"And did the late duke ever use this room?"

"No, your Grace."

"Well I intend to use it, and for that I need light. Leave the drapes open."

Burleigh's bushy brows rose. "As you wish, your Grace."

She walked from the room, confident that the butler was following close enough to hear the orders she tossed out. "I will require a set of keys, then a tour of any other 'closed room.' And then I want to see the gardens." She halted in the center of the high-ceilinged entry hall and faced Burleigh.

He cleared his throat and gazed down at her. "Might I inquire as to what you have in mind, your Grace?"

"Why, I am going to change everything, Burleigh." For the first time in two days, Jillian smiled. "I am going to turn this museum into a home," she whispered and felt warmer than she had since she'd stepped into her new life.

And as Burleigh again guided her through the cavernous rooms of Bassett House, Jillian thought she saw a brief look of pleasure soften the old butler's sunken features.

Chapter 26

Max had clear skies, a clean breeze and not a single hungry fish to disturb his peace—conditions that should have ensured a pleasant interlude to the chaos of his life. But he arrived at his hunting lodge to find it in critical disrepair, remembering too late that he had neglected to either inspect or give orders concerning the lodge since he had inherited the estates.

A layer of dust coated everything in sight, and judging from the water stains marking the furniture, the place had been flooded by rain. Looking upward, he saw why. Evidently the same storm that had damaged the roof at Westbrook several months before had collapsed part of the ceiling here as well, and a large hole gave entrance to sunlight and fallen leaves. The entire scene was an anomaly on an estate that boasted perfection right down to the smallest blade of grass.

At least the bed was dry, and by the time Max cleared a space for himself in the main room, a footman arrived with a wagonload of supplies and clothing. Wanting no company to mar his retreat, he took the foodstuffs and sent the man away with orders to return in three days with a fresh supply of food.

He couldn't return to Bassett House. The past weeks had been a nightmare of social chaos and personal upheaval. Accustomed to order and control in all things, Max knew that he was as disordered as the lodge. Jillian had shaken him more than he'd realized with her awkwardness and tears and then her abrupt recovery this morning from their disastrous wedding night. How sweetly absurd she'd looked sitting alone in the formal dining room dispensing orders and directing servants as if she were entertaining a hundred guests. It had been unsettling in the extreme to realize that while he needed time and distance to regain his equilibrium before facing her again, she had apparently found composure as easily as locating a handkerchief in her pocket.

He couldn't seem to locate his at all. He shouldn't feel like such an ass for what he'd said and done this morning. He had done exactly what he'd planned all along, demonstrating to her what she could expect from their marriage and her foolish dreams of love. Dreams he could not fulfill.

For Jillian's dreams, he wanted a clean, quick kill.

He'd hoped that once he was alone, he'd be able to

withdraw and muster the control that Jillian constantly challenged with her smiles that warmed him, the tears that had shocked him, the simple words of trust she uttered in a way that dispelled the warmth and filled him with cold dread.

There were moments during the next week when he thought he had succeeded.

He followed the small rivers and streams of his estate as he and Damien had done as boys, and rarely bothered to bait his hook before casting it into the water. At night he slept under the stars shining through the hole in the roof with only the lullaby of an owl for company. He had forgotten that such simple pleasures existed.

After a week, he knew it was time to return to her, yet every day he lingered until it was too late to go back. If he worked at it, he could almost believe he was the only person left on earth, with no pile of stones to concern him, no businesses to oversea, and no wife to plague him. It should have been easy to withdraw in such surroundings, even from himself.

For another week, he pursued that goal with relentless devotion, emptying his mind during the day of the dreams that had haunted him in sleep. Erotic dreams of Jillian lying bare-breasted among white roses, her arms outstretched, her lips parted, offering him her kisses, her body, her love.

In those nocturnal moments when the moon had slipped away and he awakened to stare up into the infinity of black sky and fading stars through the hole in the roof, he doubted he would ever know peace again. There was no place to escape to anymore. No place where she did not follow him with her naiveté and high expectations.

Such illusions could only spawn hope that it might last and therein lay danger. He did not want Jillian to find hope in him. She was going to be hurt enough. He knew only too well that even hope could die of loneliness if left unrealized for too long.

And still he lingered, searching for a way to disillusion her without destroying her in the process.

On the fifteenth day all hell broke loose.

Thunder crashed above Max's head, shaking the earth as lightning rent the sky and sheets of rain drove him to seek more civilized shelter. He guided Sovereign in a slogging pace through sodden leaves on the forest floor and across streams dangerously swollen by the onslaught. How ironic it was that nature had driven him away from the complications of his life, and now was just as quickly sending him back to all he wished to escape. And the closer he came to Bassett House, the more he thought of what might be waiting for him.

Jillian, his wife.

The turrets of Bassett appeared through the gloom and he spurred Sovereign on, anxious for the first time in days for a hot bath and a dry bed. He rode directly to the stables, unwilling to subject his mount to any more of a dousing than was necessary. Leaving orders with the stable master for a good brushing and a bucket of hot mash for Sovereign, Max strode toward the closest entrance into the house.

As he let himself into the kitchen, soaked to his skin and chilled to the bone, the cook and the small army of assistants stared at him in shocked silence. He nodded curtly at the assemblage and received hasty and simultaneous curtsies in return as he tramped through the kitchen leaving a trail of water behind him. The tantalizing aroma of roasting meat drifted through the air, clearing his senses of the odors of rain and mud and sodden leaves rotting on the ground. He was ready for a decent meal, if he was not ready for anything else.

He took the back stairs to the second floor and headed directly to his bathing room. His valet was already there, laying his dressing gown and heated towels beside a bath full of hot water. Puzzled, Max stared at the steam rising from the marble tub. How had this happened? His valet was good, but drawing a bath between the time Max had ridden into the yard and reached this room was beyond the limits of human efficiency.

"Her Grace thought you might arrive home this afternoon," the valet offered by way of explanation.

His scalp prickled with unease at having Jillian anticipate his movements and needs. It smacked of too much familiarity and implied an emotional intimacy that was acceptable from a friend but was intolerable from a wife he had not chosen. Especially this wife.

Still, he could not walk away from the comfort of a hot bath and shave and eased his weary body into the tub. Unfortunately he couldn't seem to relax and hurried through the process of soaping, rinsing and shaving, then pulled on his dressing gown and stepped into his room.

The room was cast in mellow light from the fire blazing in the fireplace, and it looked as if more racks of candles had been added.

But as he donned clean clothes, he realized there were not more candles at all. The drapes had been tied back with gold-tasseled ropes to admit the watery light left behind by the receding storm. Frowning, he glanced around and saw other changes. A new counterpane and bed hangings of rich gold jacquard replaced the old ones of dark brown velvet. A hassock of claret velvet ringed with gold tassels had been placed in front of his chair and the book he had been reading lay where he left it.

He strode to the door leading into the sitting room and jerked it open ... and stopped dead, feeling as if he'd stumbled into the wrong wing of the house.

The sitting room was now a bedchamber. A decidedly feminine bedchamber of yellow and white and deep blue. Her bedchamber. He wandered over to the dressing table and fingered the perfume bottles littering the top along with silver backed brushes and a hand mirror. Though Jillian was absent, the scent of perfume still lingered in the air and her presence seemed to fill every corner of the chamber.

She was wearing a wildflower scent today.

Where was she?

Quickly, he made his way downstairs, his senses running ahead of his thoughts, detecting a change in the atmosphere before they registered in his mind. As always, the house was quiet as a tomb, yet there was a warmth in the air that had never been there before. He saw bits of color, yet passed over them as he caught sight of Burleigh in the formal dining room, checking the correct placement of a vase of flowers. The room never had flowers unless guests were present. Other than the Duke of Westbrook, there had been no guests for dinner at Bassett since Max could remember.

"Where is she?" he demanded as he noted that here, too, the drapes were open and lace curtains had been hung beneath them.

Burleigh straightened. "The white drawing room, your Grace."

"What the devil is she doing there?"

"Napping, the last time I checked."

Napping?

"Your Grace," Burleigh said, interrupting further thought, "dinner will be served in the small dining room."

"Bassett House does not have a small dining room."

"It does now, your Grace," the butler said with a short nod toward the medieval weapons room.

Bemused, Max wandered into the room Burleigh had indicated. His gaze skimmed over a round cherry-wood table that was polished to a high shine and the matching chairs upholstered in striped silk of emerald, gold, and dark blue. An arrangement of forget-me-nots and yellow daisies sat on the sideboard and several paintings graced stone walls that held a soft golden hue in the combined glow of a crystal chandelier and the waning afternoon light. Not a trace remained of old armor and weapons and grim tapestries depicting ancient battles.

Max had long since forgotten that this was the room's intended use, not that he had ever taken a meal here. His father had commandeered the space to house his heaps of metal when Max was twelve.

A burst of laughter caught in his throat as he imagined a parade of footmen marching through the house, each staggering beneath the weight of steel and iron while Jillian stood by giving orders like the King's best general. She must have given Burleigh fits this past fortnight.

He had told her to play the duchess and to play house, but he'd had no idea she would do it so well.

And now she was napping in the white drawing room. This he had to see. Turning on his heel, he strolled down the main hall, trying to imagine how anyone could find rest in there without feeling enshrined for posterity.

He paused in the open threshold, his gaze immediately caught by her jet black hair spread about her head like an ebony fan. She lay curled on the sofa, her skirt rucked up around her knees. Strewn around her was a shawl crumpled near discarded shoes on the floor, needlepoint abandoned in a chair, an open book on the table beside a half-finished cup of tea and a mound of tangled embroidery threads.

The drapes were open. Flames danced cheerily in a hearth that before now had not seen a fire in his lifetime.

A priceless vase held an arrangement of daffodils.

His father was probably spinning circles at the bottom of the ocean. Jillian had commandeered his forbidden room and made it her own. She had made the entire house her own.

Her eyes fluttered open. She turned her head toward him and smiled drowsily. "You've come home," she whispered, her voice still husky from sleep.

Home. He had never thought of this place as home. "Yes, I've returned," he replied, too caught up in the spell of warmth and life she'd created here to do more than follow instinct. He walked into the room and knelt on the floor beside her, then brushed a stray tendril of hair from her eyes. "What have you done to this house? It feels as if someone actually lives here."

Jillian's smile spread wider as her gaze held fast to his. "Someone does."

Nothing seemed more natural than to lower his head and accept the invitation offered by tousled hair, sleep-warm skin and drowsy eyes. Her lips parted slightly and Max took her mouth in a slow, searing kiss. She slid her hands up his shoulders and ran her fingers through his hair. Just that quickly, his body stirred, awakened, became alert to its own needs.

His tongue circled hers and stroked the length of it, explored the textures of her mouth and traced the outline of her lips. She pressed herself closer to him, wrapping her arms around his neck, kissing him with the same abandonment as the night they'd gone over the balcony.

But this time he didn't have to stop. She was his.

He wanted her so badly, he hurt.

He shifted and pulled her down with him onto the floor.

With his mouth, he traced a path from her lips to beneath her ear and over her neck, finding the beat of her pulse there. The rug was soft as a carpet of grass beneath him and the blaze in the grate felt like a bath of sunshine on a summer day. His hands worked at the tiny buttons of her bodice. He wanted to see her breasts, to touch and taste them. He wanted to touch and taste all of her and discover if she smelled like wildflowers in a meadow everywhere.

She tensed and pushed at his shoulders as he separated her bodice and loosened the ribbons on her chemise. "Max," she said on a sigh. "The door is open. The servants—"

He raised his head to see a self-conscious blush stain her cheeks. Her eyes were wide, a little frightened, yet her hands held him close and her legs were twined with his. She wanted him. She would accept him here and now if he would but close the door.

All he had to do was relinquish control, forget himself.

Suddenly the carpet seemed scratchy through his clothes and he felt the heat of the fire through the soles of his shoes. They were rolling on the floor like servants stealing a moment of passion while the master was busy.

Oh God.

Appalled at his lack of control, he wrenched away from her and rolled to his feet. What was it that she did to render him so witless? Every time he touched her, he lost all sense of his surroundings.

"You're right," he replied harshly as he yanked her back up onto the sofa. "This is the wrong time, the wrong place."

"What is the right place?"

"My bed."

"Then perhaps we should go there immediately."

"I prefer a woman in my bed, not a chit who hasn't the sense not to lie about with her limbs exposed in an open room."

Without another word or a backward glance, he stalked from the room. Color and light blurred past as he crossed the hall to seek sanctuary in his study. Even there, he found that the window hangings had been replaced and a throw of Irish wool lay casually over the back and one arm of the sofa. In the corner of the room sat the very globe that was once in his schoolroom. He had loved to spin it as a boy.

Damnit! Jillian had not only invaded his life, she was intruding into memories of which she had no part. What was she trying to do? Leave her mark behind? Fill this dead place with life only to take it with her when she left?

He sat in the chair behind his desk and stared at the old globe. It seemed smaller than he remembered and the paint was faded and cracked in places. He didn't bother to spin it but simply sat there as twilight darkened the room and he could no longer see the changes Jillian had wrought.

Jillian had never been so angry with Max . . . until he had walked into the room, his gaze wandering over the changes she'd made, his voice approving rather than censuring. The fifteen days he'd been gone seemed to disappear as if Max had left her only this morning.

She sat with her feet tucked under her skirts until the fire cooled to a bed of coals in the white marble hearth and the sunlight faded to an amber glow in the distance. Yet again, Max had left her with the memory of bitter words to taint the magic he had created for a few short moments.

But now, she knew that he wanted her regardless of how angry and cold he seemed. Exposing her limbs indeed. Max knew better than anyone how well-trained his servants were. Not one of them would dare to intrude into the privacy of their employers whether the door was open or not. The most they would do was discreetly turn their heads the instant they saw that a room was occupied. Of course one glimpse would have been more than enough if one of them had happened by while she and Max were thrashing about on the floor.

Well, not thrashing exactly. Since they weren't naked, she wasn't quite sure how to describe what they'd been doing. Kissing seemed such a pallid term for the quick and sharp stabs of pleasure she'd experienced. She'd felt as if Max would consume her at any moment.

Consume. She wondered if that is what Max meant by "consummate." She'd been wondering about that word ever since he'd used it on their wedding night. She knew what a consummate liar was and that to consummate meant to accomplish something, but she still had no idea what exactly they were to accomplish beyond removing their clothes and connecting certain body parts together. Oh it really was too frustrating trying to reason it all out. LadyLou's explanation struck her as being rather cold and calculated when compared to the sensations Max evoked with a kiss or a touch. There had to be more.

It couldn't possibly be as impersonal and messy as it sounded.

Leaving the drawing room, she strolled into the small dining room she'd refurbished and inhaled the aromas wafting in from the kitchen. She didn't want food.

She wanted Max.

And she was tired of waiting.

After giving orders for a tray to be delivered to "his Grace"—wherever he might be—she climbed the stairs to her room and sent Clancy away. She needed no help tonight and considering what she was about to do, would prefer to have no one witness her preparations.

This was one time that Max would not walk away from her.

Chapter 27

Max did not pause as he passed Jillian's door, but walked on to his own room. Without ceremony, he stripped off his clothes and slid between the sheets. A warm body rolled into him and the subtle scent of wildflowers wafted around him.

"What the devil?" He bolted out of bed, fumbled to don his dressing gown and hastily lit a candle.

She was there, her hair a swath of black silk on the white linens, her face flushed from sleep. Her eyes fluttered open and she raised her hand to shield them from the sudden light.

"What are you doing in my bed, Jillian?" he snapped.

She rubbed her eyes and stretched like a cat. "I should think that is obvious," she said, a slight waver in her voice. "I am your wife. You said this was the right place for me to be."

He heard her nervousness, saw it in the flicker of her eyelids. She was here to consummate the marriage, and had the temerity to turn his own words against him to accomplish her goal. He wasn't ready. Not now, and certainly not like this. He was the man, damnit. It was up to him to initiate the proceedings.

"Only if I invite you," he said. "Go to your room, Jillian."

"No," she said as she scrambled to her knees in the middle of the bed. "I am your wife and I . . . I . . . *demand* that you finish what you began this afternoon in the white drawing room."

"You demand?" Max said in a low voice. "And tell me, *wife,* do you have any idea what, exactly, you are demanding?"

"Of course I do," she replied defiantly. "LadyLou and I have discussed it. You and I have discussed it. I'm tired of discussing it."

"You know nothing," he scoffed. "Making love is more involved than rearranging furniture."

Her hand flew to her chest and she sagged back to sit on her heels, staring at him as if he had caught her by surprise. "Making love?" she said and her voice was soft and wondering.

Bloody hell. How could he have made so stupid a mistake as to say the very word he'd been avoiding? "Yes," he said with desperate harshness. "Making love is a ludicrous euphemism that refers to 'the act that produces children'. An act you have no understanding of."

She rose to her knees again and leaned toward him. "Then teach me, Max. You've taught me all the other important things like fishing and swimming and whistling."

Whistling? His fists clenched at his sides, Max glared at her and received a soft stare in return. She was doing it to him again, infuriating him and shredding his resolve at the same time. Her appearance wasn't helping. Her virginal white nightgown was full and high-necked, with a row of buttons marching down her nightdress like a battalion of soldiers guarding her chastity. He wondered how other grooms over the ages had managed to get past such intimidating reminders of what they'd gotten themselves into.

"Go to your room, Jillian," he repeated. "Better still, go to the nursery," he added, uncaring of what he had to do to get her out of his room before he fell prey to his own vulnerability.

"I'm not a child, Max," she said quietly and lowered her gaze. "I'm your wife."

It sounded so simple. His wife, in his bed, apparently willing and eager to play her role to the hilt. But nothing was that simple. He told himself that any other groom would have sought her out long before now, perhaps even taking advantage of the drawing-room floor in broad daylight. Any other groom would care little that she wore the trappings of a shy virgin who could not quite meet his gaze as she knelt before him in his bed.

Any other man would not hesitate to take what was his rather than stand paralyzed at the memory that the woman in his bed had been his friend long before she had become his wife. The woman in his bed would only be bound closer to him if he made love to her, and her dreams of love would only be fed by the intimacies shared between men and woman in the throes of passion. She was too vulnerable right now. When he consummated this marriage, he wanted her to be completely aware that mutual pleasure was all that would come from it. He had to drive her away and keep her away from him until she had no higher expectations of him.

"Very well, Jillian," he said with the hope that she

would run and end this torture once and for all. "Remove your nightgown."

She glanced down at the row of buttons on the front of her gown. "I will if you will," she said in a shaky voice.

Without ceremony, he untied the sash of his dressing gown and dropped it at his feet. Standing unclothed before a woman was nothing new to Max and usually brought him to a hard state of urgency, but Jillian stared at him in such wide-eyed shock that his flaccid manhood shriveled and retreated closer to his body. It would be the height of irony if her ingenuousness rendered him impotent as well as witless.

"Your turn," he said mockingly.

She swallowed convulsively. She was frightened. Good. He wanted to frighten her enough to leave. He folded his arms across his bare chest. "Are you going to stare at me for the remainder of the night or are we going to get on with this?" he asked impatiently.

She licked her lips nervously and continued to stare at the pathetic display between his legs.

"Get out, Jillian," he grated. With interest, he watched her flinch and lean backward, away from him. "This might be the right place, but you are obviously the wrong woman."

"No!" she said and scrambled from the bed to stand before him. Taking a deep breath, she fumbled with the buttons at the throat of her gown.

God, she was going to do it. He should have known better than to think an insult would put her off. She was too damn good at turning slights against the offender. Too good at seeing challenge rather than fear in his anger.

The first button slipped free and then another and another.

"You're taking too long, Jillian," he said, thinking to further disconcert her.

Her hands dropped to her sides and her eyes

squeezed shut. Now she would run from the room, or so he thought.

Instead, she gripped the sides of her nightrail and slowly the gown inched up from the floor to expose trim ankles and shapely calves. She tugged the gown above her knees. In a sudden movement, she yanked it upward over firm thighs . . .

He reached out to her, intent on what? Pulling the gown back down over her body? Or lifting it from her altogether? He didn't know. At the sight of her thatch of black curls nestled at the juncture of her thighs, his manhood stirred and hardened and rose and the blood surged hotly through his veins. If she didn't run soon, he would make love to her. Here. Now. Before he was ready. His manhood swelled larger, harder, mocking his thought.

Cloth rustled and he jerked his gaze upward to see her minuscule waist and high round breasts. They were incredible and perfect with their pink tips puckered and bobbing provocatively as she wiggled in her struggle to pull the garment over her head.

She had not unfastened enough buttons and the gown caught on her chin, obscuring her face with yards of fabric. It was as if she were nothing but body. He wished he could keep her that way—a body like many others he'd enjoyed over the years. When he made love to her he did not want to be aware of who she was and what she meant to him.

When, not *if.* More than ever before, he was aware of how little power he had over himself . . . over Jillian. With that thought, he acknowledged that Jillian's view of the situation was far clearer than his. They were married. She belonged here. She had no idea of what she was asking for, and it was his place to enlighten her as any other man caught in such a marriage would do. But he wasn't any other man. He'd never been a selfish lover, and he couldn't start with Jillian. He couldn't give her love, but he could give her passion.

And he wanted her. End of subject.

So be it.

Any doubts and reluctance he'd had about making love to her were banished to the back of his mind where he could not hear them. His erection throbbed with an aching fullness as if to confirm the thought.

Buttons flew as Jillian ripped the neck of the gown, tugging it completely over her head and tossing it aside. Her hair spilled over her shoulders and covered her breasts, her puckered nipples peeking through the thick strands. Desire filled him, building pressure until it hurt to breathe and his heart felt crowded in his chest.

Oh God, but she was beautiful.

As her gaze focused on him, her brows snapped together, and her sharp intake of breath echoed through the room as she stared at his erection.

"Scared?" he asked, keeping his voice soft, admitting to himself in that moment that the last thing in the world he wanted her to do was run.

Jillian shook her head, unable to find her voice as she tried not to stare at the object boldly protruding from Max's body—not an acorn at all but something as fierce and intimidating as the rest of him. He stood so sure and confident in his nakedness with the candlelight casting mysterious shadows over him, emphasizing legs that were too hard and strong, a furred chest that suddenly seemed too broad, arms that were too powerful to hold her without crushing her.

Scared? She was terrified. It had seemed a good idea when she had come to his room. She'd felt confident enough in herself to stay when he tried to drive her away with his sarcasm and cruel remarks. She should have listened to him. She should have run while she'd had the chance.

Now she was too panicked to move.

"Don't be frightened, Jillian," he said.

"I'm not," she lied and blurted out the first thing she could think of to cover her anxiety. "It is nothing like a statue or a painting, yet it was a moment ago. I don't understand. Where did it come from?"

"From you," Max said and his voice sounded strained. "It is desire . . . what happens when a man wants to make love to a woman."

Make love . . . such a dreamy and romantic term. It had sounded so wonderful a moment ago. Now it only created more panic as she stared at that part of him that seemed to grow as she watched, angling toward her, reaching for her—Oh dear heaven, how could something of such size and strength fit inside her without tearing her in two? She licked her lips and tried to swallow down her fear. "How . . ." she swallowed again and jerked her gaze upward, focusing on a spot beyond Max's bare shoulder. "How is it accomplished?" she managed to ask, though she was afraid of the answer, remembering too late that LadyLou had said it would hurt.

It had to hurt. She could not imagine how much it must hurt.

"Look at me, Jillian," Max said softly as he stepped closer to her, his size and scent overwhelming her, reminding her that she was naked and exposed. She didn't want to look. She didn't want him to look either.

He cupped her chin in his hand and tilted her head upward until she had to either close her eyes or do as he asked. His face was so close she could see the beginnings of his night beard sprinkled over his hard jaw and strong chin like gold dust, see the separated strands of the forelock dipping over his brow, see her reflection in his blue eyes. He was sapphires set in gold and so fearsomely beautiful she could not look away.

Slowly, he bent his head toward her, his gaze holding hers, his lips parting. "Close your eyes, Jillian," he whispered and his breath was a touch of heat on her face.

His mouth touched hers, lightly, urging her lips to part, his tongue easing into her mouth in a deep, probing kiss, calming her, comforting her. This she understood, and she gave into the familiar pleasure. The tips of her breasts tingled as the hair on his chest brushed her, and her anxiety seemed to dissolve into a pool of liquid warmth in her belly.

He lifted his head. "There is a place inside you that is made for me," he said raggedly and his hand reached out for her, barely touching her legs in the lightest caress. "Here." He dipped his finger into her, just a little. Just enough for her to realize what he would do, and how.

Her eyes snapped open in shock and a cry of renewed alarm was trapped in her throat.

"Trust me, Jillian. Your body already does," he said and his fingers found a place she didn't know existed, his touch jolting her, vibrating through her.

Startled, she shivered and clenched her fists at her side, fighting down the urge to back away. But there was no place to go with the bed behind her and Max in front of her, nothing else to do but trust . . .

His mouth closed over hers again and his fingers touched her more deeply with every stroke, drawing more moisture from her. Pure sensation became a live thing inside her, twisting with a frightening anticipation. Suddenly she didn't want to back away from him, didn't understand why she should fear something that felt so wonderful and thrilling.

She parted her lips more fully, participating in the kiss, copying the strokes of his tongue with her own. His hand left her and he enfolded her in his arms, stroking her back, tracing her spine, teasing the sensitive spot at the nape of her neck. She lost herself willingly, completely giving up thought and fear in the joy of being so close to him, of knowing that he wanted her, here . . . now.

Max's mouth slid across hers, tearing away from her as if it hurt to end the kiss, and it reassured her as nothing else could.

Her fingers spread out as she reached up between them to sift through the gilded mat of hair on his chest, trace the whorls that narrowed into a silky wedge that seemed to catch fire in the candlelight, leading her downward again to that place that made him a man.

Again it seemed to angle toward her, reaching for her. But this time, she touched it, running her palm up his length, surprised and fascinated by the rose petal texture of it.

He stilled, caught his breath, swallowed. "I thought you were afraid," he said and his voice was strained.

"No, not anymore. Not with you," she whispered, her gaze touching him everywhere. She stepped toward him, knowing she should feel shy about her nakedness. Yet she felt nothing but pride and excitement that he appeared to be as entranced with her as she was with him. This was Max. Being unclothed with him seemed as natural as drawing breath. She could feel no shame with him, now or ever again. "Never with you, Max."

He embraced her suddenly, tightly, holding her against him as his mouth covered hers and his tongue plunged into her mouth. She gripped either side of his head, keeping him close. He was hers and she would not let him go.

He groaned and lowered her onto the bed, following her down to lie across her as his lips traveled to her neck, her ears, and lower to her breasts, taking one into his mouth and biting gently. Sensation pierced her and shot down to her belly as he drew on her nipples, one then the other, over and over again. She'd wondered why women had breasts. Now she knew.

His weight on her was hot and solid, surrounding her with the feel of him—crisp hair a soft abrasion on her stomach, hard muscles embracing her, strong fingers stroking her everywhere at once as if he couldn't do enough.

He nudged her legs apart and kneeled between them, caressing the insides of her thighs to her knees and back up again, watching her face.

She was hot, so hot and all she could do was draw

shallow, erratic breaths as she stared back at him. "What are you going to do?" she asked.

He smiled, a slow, wicked smile. "I am going to make you *feel,* Jillian. Nothing else."

Nothing else? It was everything as he pressed his thumb to her, to that same place he'd touched before, driving her wild with his caress. He was doing more than she had ever dreamed about, overwhelming her with the play of his hand between her legs, thoroughly exploring a place even she had never touched except in her bath. Her "privates" Clancy had called it, but Max allowed her no privacy.

With a light touch, he slipped a finger inside her, then two, stroking gently, and then more deeply, drawing a wetness from her that surely bathed his hand. She arched her back and twisted, both fighting the exquisite torture and pressing herself against his hand, wanting more. She couldn't bear the need he was arousing in her. "Max, please, stop."

He paused, his fingers unmoving inside her. Sensation was still thrumming through her, ebbing, flowing, diminishing, leaving her bereft.

"Stop?" he said with his mouth still curved in that knowing smile.

"No! Don't stop," she said, her hips pushed upward, pressing against his hand, searching for the pleasure. "Max, please—" Before she could finish her plea, he began again, tormenting her with his thumb, his fingers.

"Is this what you mean, Jillian?"

"Yes . . . like that," she panted. He increased the tempo and her back bowed and her body tightened, catching her by surprise as everything inside her rippled like waves on a warm shore, spreading outward.

She opened her eyes, unaware until then that they'd been closed, and stared up at Max. He breathed deeply, his chest rising and falling and his gaze was another kind of caress, searing her, melting her. "What was that?" she asked on a whisper.

"That," he said as he slid up her body and settled be-

tween her legs, "was only the beginning." And with
that he covered her mouth with his as another part of
him touched her—the part of him that frightened her
so, only now she was fascinated by the feel of it, the
pressure, the anticipation of more. Thought drifted from
her mind and all that existed in the world was Max,
kissing her again, his tongue thrusting into her mouth
as he eased into her body, but not hard enough. Not
deep enough. She ached for him. Urgency blazed
through her as he raised onto his elbows and moved his
hips carefully, as he entered her a little farther, pushing
slowly, driving her mad as she felt her body stretch to
hold him. Instinctively, she wrapped her legs around
him, to draw him closer, wanting . . . something.

He levered upward, away from her. She wouldn't allow it. Not now. She flattened her palms on his buttocks, pressing him down to her as she arched her hips
upward to meet him.

He sank into her with one tearing plunge.

"Oh!" she cried, the sudden pain stunning her.

He groaned and stilled his movements, his breathing
harsh, his body so tense she could feel the quiver in his
muscles. "Do you always have to be so impatient?" he
grated. His teeth were clenched and his jaw bunched
with tension. "Don't move, the pain will go away in a
moment."

"Are you sure?" she asked, breathless with the stinging burn that seemed to reach up into her belly, overwhelmed by the feeling of being surrounded by him,
filled by him. She couldn't imagine where he'd found
space to put himself.

He propped his elbows on either side of her head and
she heard a rumble in his chest that sounded almost like
a purr. "Quite sure," he said with a wolfish smile.

Even as he spoke, the burning pain became a dull
ache and then all she felt was fullness and heat and a
flowing wetness. Her body relaxed and stretched even
more, holding all of him as if indeed she was made just
for him.

"Better?" Max asked as he rotated his hips.

"Yes."

"Good," he said as his mouth descended on hers. He slid out of her and plunged again, with a slow rhythm at first, then faster and faster. She shuddered and tightened around him and air seemed to rush out of the room, and she was consumed by heat and sensation. And with every push and slide of his body, a delicious friction set off more sensation, more pleasure, until one feeling ran into another and everything faded from her awareness but the feel of his body inside her, the feel of his mouth devouring hers. She arched her hips, needing to feel more, needing to—

Something seemed to shatter inside her and her heart paused, her breathing stopped and as spasm wracked her body, Max tensed, rising above her, sinking into her one last time.

He shuddered and his chest heaved as he closed his eyes, threw his head back, and then it seemed that he, too, stopped breathing. A fine mist coated his body and she realized that she was perspiring, too.

He lowered his head and kissed her gently, his lips lingering on hers as he rolled to his side, taking her with him, their mouths and bodies still joined, their legs entwined. His lips slid from hers. Moments passed and all she could hear was the sound of Max's harsh breathing and the pounding of her own heart.

She opened her eyes and his face was close to hers on the pillow. "Max?"

"Mmm." It was a soft sound in the stillness yet she felt it vibrate in his chest. He looked so beautiful like this, with his eyes closed and his expression relaxed, peaceful.

"That was the end wasn't it?"

"God, yes," he said lazily.

She laughed with the sheer joy of hearing such contentment in his voice.

He slipped away from her then and the emptiness was startling as the night air wafted over her, cooling her dampened flesh until she shivered with the chill in the room.

"Cold?" he asked as he eased her up onto the pillow.

"I think I must be," she said and shivered again.

Chuckling, he drew a counterpane over them both, then lay on his side next to her, his leg across hers, his arm over her waist.

"Max?"

"Go to sleep, Jillian."

"Did I hurt you?" she asked.

"Did *you* hurt *me?*" he said in amazement. "I was not the virgin here."

"I don't suppose that I am either," she sighed.

"No."

"Then we are consummated?"

"Yes," he said with a curious note in his voice.

"Good," she said around a yawn. "Max?"

He didn't answer, but she knew he was awake. She waited a moment, her fingers plucking at the soft velvet covering her. "Max?"

"What?"

Smoothing out the little peaks she'd created in the counterpane, she folded her hands over her midriff. "How often do married people make love?"

"Go to sleep, Jillian."

"Is it too difficult for you to do it every night? If it isn't, then I think we should make love quite often."

"Good night, Jillian," he said firmly as he guided her head to his shoulder and pressed a kiss to her temple.

"Max?"

"Hmph," he mumbled as if he were already sinking into sleep.

"Sleep well."

A soft leg nestled between his thighs, and something tickled his nose. He reached to brush it away, but there was too much of it and it tangled in his fingers. Opening one eye, he peered down and saw hair. Black hair. The stuff covered two pillows and the lower half of his face. And then it surrounded him as the mattress shifted and two breasts bobbed above him.

"Good morning," Jillian whispered and planted a kiss on his mouth. "I'm starving." She rose from the bed, gloriously nude and completely at ease, as if she didn't care a whit that sunlight was streaming in between the drapes he'd forgotten to close and he could see every last dimple on her bottom. One would have thought she'd been prancing around before him with no clothes on for years.

Didn't she know what she was doing to him? Didn't she know how tempting she was with the morning light gilding her satin flesh? Of course she didn't, he answered himself. He bent his knees making a tent with the counterpane to hide his erection. It was too soon. She would be tender from last night and his body was in a demanding mood. He cleared his throat as he sat up and fluffed a pillow behind his back. "Jillian, it is not proper for you to wander about naked in broad daylight."

"Why?" she asked, her brow creased in genuine puzzlement. "I should think that after what we did last night, anything would be considered proper between us."

He opened his mouth and shut it again, finding no argument for her logic. Truth was, he couldn't remember ever feeling so comfortable in any woman's presence after a night of lovemaking. Jillian seemed to fit in so well, as if she belonged here . . . and always had.

It was a concept he dismissed, unable to think it through with Jillian wandering about his quarters, distracting him with her lack of inhibition and happy chatter.

She walked to the French doors that led out onto a terrace and paused in midstretch. "Max?"

Oh no, not again, he thought. He knew that tone. She was about to drive him to distraction with another artless question or maddening statement.

She turned to face him, giving him a view that surpassed the dawn sky. He should have answered her. Her lack of inhibition was a difficult thing to face at such an early hour. If he were fully dressed it would be easier to deal with.

"You have a swing on your terrace," she said as if she were informing him of something he did not know.

"Yes," he replied, surprised that she was only now noticing the swing. Apparently, she hadn't had the opportunity to redecorate the terraces yet.

"Oh, Max, how wonderful of you to think of such a thing. You remembered how much I love swings."

Wonderful, he thought. She assumed that he'd put it in for her, when in fact he'd asked a taciturn old gardener to put it in for him. He'd been eight years old and his friend Damien had a swing. Why shouldn't he? He'd had it built and put up here because his father never sought him out in his private quarters and would not know his eight-year-old heir possessed such a thing. And every time he'd been moved to different rooms in the house, Burleigh had it moved along with Max's other personal possessions. Over the years, he'd found a soothing peace in sitting on the sturdy board seat and swaying back and forth in mindless activity.

He should have torn the damn thing down long ago, but he could never bring himself to do it. It symbolized so much in his life: his defiance of his father and the comfort it had given him, and later, the day he'd caught Jillian from her fall and the trust she'd given him. The swing was the only bloody thing on the estate that he felt was truly his, the only bloody thing that had no rules attached to it. The only thing in his boyhood over which he'd had any control.

No, he would not share such things with Jillian. She'd taken over enough of his life.

From the looks of things, she was about to throw open the doors and try out the swing that very minute. The thought no sooner formed than her hand grasped the knob.

"Come push me, Max," she said.

"I thought you were hungry," he said. "Besides, I have better things to do than spend the morning plucking splinters from your nether parts."

She glanced down at herself and grinned. "Yes, of course you're right." Picking up her discarded gown from the floor she tucked it under her arm and walked to the door connecting their bedrooms. "I'll see you downstairs for breakfast?"

"Yes," Max said, willing to agree to almost anything to get her out of his room and hopefully into a gown that hung on her like a sack and covered her from neck to toes.

And since he had agreed, Max bathed and dressed and presented himself in Jillian's small dining room for the morning meal. She was already there, waiting for him.

"What are your plans for today?" she said cheerfully as she poured him a cup of coffee and added just the right amount of sugar and cream.

"I have correspondence to catch up on," he said vaguely. He wasn't accustomed to relaying his plans to anyone.

"I'll see you at luncheon, then?"

"Possibly." He rubbed his hand over his face in frustration. Too much was happening too fast, and he felt as if he were trapped in a corner. Privacy was no longer possible in a house that was no longer his. He wasn't accustomed to all this sharing of beds and meals and early morning conversation. He needed solitude in familiar surroundings. Downing his coffee and scalding his tongue in the process, he pushed back from the table. "I'll be in my study. I don't wish to be disturbed," he said, finding the statement to be absurd. All Jillian did was disturb him.

"All right," Jillian said brightly. "I'll just knock when luncheon is ready."

Max felt the walls close in on him a little more. He couldn't face breakfast let alone luncheon. Nodding, he rose and strode to the door. He had to get out . . . away

. . . anyplace where he would only have to answer to himself.

Very quietly, he slipped out of the house and called for Sovereign to be saddled and brought around. He needed a good hard ride to clear his mind. At least the parkland and forest were unchanged, giving him a sense of continuity and comfort. But it didn't last. All he could think of was Jillian, how she brought Bassett House to life, how making love to her had been more incredible than his most erotic dream of her.

He reigned Sovereign in and dismounted to give the horse a rest and an opportunity to drink from a stream and graze on the grassy bank. A spot cushioned by the fallen leaves of a dying tree beckoned to him and he sat down, propping his back against the stout trunk. Roots grew above the ground, gnarled and bowed on either side of him, armrests, he mused, on a high-back throne canopied with drying leaves. How appropriate that he should find himself surveying his own little monarchy from a perch that was rotting around him.

His monarchy, where he ruled neither his house nor his wife. Hell, she had even taken over his body. And he had allowed it.

What would his father think of the merger of Westbrook and Bassett through marriage? he wondered. The families had avoided that particular type of association since the creation of the titles. Given recent events, Max could not disagree with the thinking behind it. Because of such a union, every tradition that had prevailed for centuries had been corrupted. Traditions that had worked to the benefit of both the Forbes and Hastings families. Traditions that had given them strength.

Now thanks to the youngest and weakest of the Forbes line, nothing of the past remained except the buildings and the lands surrounding them. The youngest and weakest. What a joke. Time after time, Jillian had proved herself to be equal to any battle he might institute against her, from the day she'd fallen from the sky into his arms she had defeated him. Last night had been the most ignoble defeat of them all.

She'd caught him by surprise, slipping into his room that way and crawling under his skin with her clumsy attempt to disrobe. Though he'd seen parts of her unclothed—or nearly so—he hadn't been prepared for the sight of Jillian standing before him as naked as her naiveté. It had been a shock to see the lushness of her body exposed all at once. How could he have anticipated such a startling and overwhelming response of his own body to the mere sight of her? No other woman in his experience had possessed the power to rob him of control so quickly. It had been all he could do to contain himself until he knew that Jillian, too, would find some pleasure in the act.

And she had found pleasure. They both had.

It would have been better if they hadn't. Her nearness in one way and another had become a habit over the years, a craving to share moments of unguarded companionship and unaffected laughter, of genuine affection and unconditional trust. Now, there was more between them, strengthening the habit, weakening his resolve to break it once and for all.

Joining with Jillian, his wife and now his lover, could only breed an heir who would find no past upon which to build, no alliances from which to draw loyalty and trust as his ancestors had done. The Dukes of Bassett and Westbrook were at one another's throats rather than at each other's backs. The joining of the families could only breed discontent rather than strength.

Finding no answers in such profound thoughts, and determined to shake off his maudlin thoughts, Max gathered the reigns and again took to the saddle. And though he stayed away until late in the afternoon, peace was not to be found anywhere.

Only one conclusion presented itself as he turned toward home. He could not change what was and there would be no going back. All he could do was keep his current course as free of clutter and complications as possible.

He guided Sovereign toward the stables and as he reached the boundaries of the garden, he caught a spot of color on the other side of the hedge. Color meant Jillian, a vivid turquoise this time with ribbon of a darker shade trimming her hem and tying her hair back with a floppy bow. *What scent has she chosen today?* he wondered as he dismounted and handed over the reigns to a stable boy who had run out to meet him.

Max found a shady spot beneath the leaves of a massive oak tree at the edge of the garden. He found a perverse pleasure in watching Jillian snip a long-stemmed red rose and lay it among others in the basket hanging on her arm. His father had never allowed the flowers to be cut. The garden was just one item on an endless list of things that were to be looked at and not touched at Bassett House.

Max swatted at a leaf brushing his cheek and forced such subjects from his mind. Today, he had given more thought to his father than he had since he was fourteen, in an effort, he admitted to himself, to keep from thinking of Jillian. Yet, it was she who had triggered such reflections. She who seemed to be taking over his home and his life more completely than the duke ever had. She, who in the space of a fortnight had turned every rule and tradition at Bassett House upside down and rearranged them to suit herself.

If he wasn't careful, she would do the same to him.

Chapter 28

Jillian snipped a long stemmed red rose and laid it in her basket alongside the yellow ones she had already cut. The arrangement would look beautiful on the dinner table tonight, and she knew exactly which vase to use.

The hair at her nape prickled and the back of her neck felt as if a hole were burning through. She paused, her hand in midair, as a frisson of excitement tingled in her veins. Raising her head, she turned around, her gaze finding the source of her awareness like a bird finding a home.

Max was leaning against a tree, his arms folded across his chest as he watched her.

It was about time.

All day, she had been torn between being angry at him for disappearing without a word and worried that something had happened to him. He could have at least told her what direction he had taken.

Max's mouth slanted in a derisive smile. "You realize my father would have your head if he could see what you are doing to his precious gardens."

"Why?" she asked evenly, her irritation increasing at him for acting as if nothing was wrong. "They are only precious if they are enjoyed."

A frown creased his brow as he pushed away from the tree and strolled toward her. "He believed that some things are not meant to be touched. They are too fragile, too easily destroyed. Aside from that he loathed flower arrangements."

"How very sad for him," she said and snipped another rose. "Do you loathe them also?"

"Hardly. It would be a rather wasteful use of loathing."

How sad for Max that he thought of emotion in terms of efficiency and waste. How difficult it must be for him to separate his feelings along such rigid lines.

He shifted impatiently. "I have work to do," he said abruptly.

"Did you enjoy your ride?" she asked before he could turn toward the house. She still had things to say to him.

"Yes," he said.

"Where did you go, to London and back?"

He regarded her with brows arched in surprise. "Careful, Jillian, you sound like a peeved wife."

"I am a peeved wife," she retorted. "The next time you plan to disappear for the day, I would appreciate knowing your whereabouts."

"For what purpose?"

"In case you fall off your horse again," she snapped. "You may not be so lucky as to walk away with a sprained ankle next time." She placed another bud in her basket. "Do you realize if anything had happened to you today, I would not even have known where to start searching for you?"

"I have looked after myself for nearly thirty years, Jillian. I do not need, nor do I want anyone to concern themselves with my welfare."

"Then you will just have to get used to it, because I have a habit of worrying about my family."

"I am not your family," he said and turned and stalked away.

"Yes, you are," she whispered to his back, barely able to manage the words.

* * *

Jillian retired early, hoping Max would follow, hoping he would knock on her door. He had been too quiet at dinner, but at least he had shared the meal with her instead of taking it in his room. She chose to view that as progress, small though it may be.

She heard him enter his chamber, listened to his movements and the rustle of clothing, the muted voice of his valet and the silence after his man had bid him good night. Max was alone.

She waited for him to come. He didn't. What should she do? There were rules about positively everything. Perhaps she was supposed to go to him as she had last night. But what had seemed so simple in her ignorance last night was far more complicated now that she knew what intimacies would follow. How frustrating it was that now that she knew what questions to ask, there was no one around to answer them. She knew there was a book detailing the proper comportment of servants and thought there ought to be, at the very least, a pamphlet of instruction for wives.

There was nothing for it, Jillian decided, but to follow her own instincts and do what came naturally. She climbed out of bed and walked to the door joining her room to his. Proper or not, she wanted him and she thought he wanted her, too. After all, he hadn't walked away from her last night. And she knew from experience that if she allowed him to put too much space between them, it would take her that much longer to close it again.

With resolution, she knocked on the door allowing that one small concession to etiquette. There was no answer. She opened the door and stepped inside. He was not in his bed, but the doors leading to the terrace were open.

He was sitting in the swing, clad only in his dressing gown as he idly pushed himself with one foot. Moonlight limned his golden hair, giving it an ethereal shine, and his blue eyes were shot with silver as his head jerked in her direction.

"What is it, Jillian?"

"I can't sleep."

"Perhaps you should have a glass of warm milk."

"I don't believe that would work. I prefer your bed. It's much nicer than mine."

"Husbands and wives don't share a bed."

"We did last night."

"For a very specific reason, if you recall."

"Oh, yes," Jillian said, moving nearer to him. "I recall very well."

Max shifted in the swing. "Go to your room, Jillian. Your body needs time to heal after last night."

She felt a blush rising at that as she remembered awakening with a stiff soreness between her thighs. "I took a warm bath and am quite recovered," she said.

His gaze raked over her thoughtfully. "Did it ever occur to you to wait until I invited you to my bed?"

"I'm not in your bed," she replied, as she watched the gentle motion of the swing, mesmerized by a sudden vision of swaying with him, a part of him. Was it possible? she wondered as she glanced at his lap, the part in his robe, the size of the board seat. It was a brazen thought, she knew, but she didn't care. This was Max, and there was no room for trepidation and shame between them. "Actually, I wanted to swing," she said as she crossed the distance separating them and ran her fingers over the rope. "It's been a very long time since I touched the sky."

He glanced up at her with a wary look. "We are two floors up. You would have a long fall."

"Not if you're here to hold me." Mustering her courage, she hiked up her nightgown, pulled it over her head and tossed it away, fighting down her embarrassment, reminding herself that Max had already seen her. This morning it had seemed so natural somehow to walk around naked after waking up that way. Besides, to make love one had to be unclothed. Knowing that, she'd even chosen a gown that didn't have a thousand buttons down the front.

She felt his gaze on her, sweeping over her, then lingering along the way and it was as if he were touching her with a gentle hand.

"I see," Max said, and she heard the amusement in his voice. "Why don't we save time, and our derrieres, and move to the floor now?"

Embarrassment was forgotten with those words. He knew what she wanted. He wasn't objecting. "You have no imagination, Max," she laughed in sheer relief and climbed onto his lap facing him, her legs on either side of him, her breasts pressing against his chest, sliding against the silk of his robe. And the smoothness of the fabric was cool against her bare bottom as she felt him stir and swell, becoming a hard ridge beneath her. Oh, yes, she thought, it was more than possible. Things were so much easier now that she knew what to do and what to expect.

"It's obvious that you have enough for both of us," Max said on a sharp intake of breath. With a sidelong glance, she noted that he gripped the ropes so tightly his knuckles turned white.

Seeing her advantage, she took it and leaned into him, tracing her tongue over his lips as he had done to her the night before. His mouth opened under hers and his arms wrapped around her, taking control in a blatantly carnal kiss. The swing bobbled and tipped forward. Max's hands left her and grabbed the ropes as his thighs tensed and he braced his feet on the stone floor of the terrace to stabilize them.

He turned his head, tearing away from her kiss. "Jillian, we have to move."

"I like it here," she said, clinging to his shoulders.

"I can't do anything in this position." Even as he spoke, he grew harder beneath her, a delicious pressure rising against her. She did this to him; he'd told her so last night. So, why, she reasoned, couldn't she do more? Why couldn't she do it all?

"I can do it, Max." The ache and the need she'd felt last night were back and so was the memory of all that she'd experienced. He'd given that to her. She wanted to give it back to him. She wanted to make love to him. "Let me," she whispered and laced her fingers through his hair, stroking his head as she bent to nibble on his ear. Reaching down between them, she untied his belt and raised herself slightly to part his robe, freeing him even from that meager covering.

She gripped his shoulder with one hand and raised up over him, reaching for him with her other hand.

He planted his feet wider apart and hooked his arms around the ropes to steady the swing, trying to grasp her around the waist and hold her suspended above his lap. "Blast it, Jillian," he groaned, the swing twisting in spite of his efforts. "You cannot simply drop onto me like a stone. You'll hurt yourself."

She gasped as she lowered herself, ignoring his warning, feeling a sharp, thrusting pain. "Don't move, Max. It will go away in a minute," she breathed as the pain eased and her body accepted him.

He pressed his forehead to hers and chuckled. "As if I could." He ended on a rasp as she wrapped her legs around his waist. Again, the swing shifted. "Now what are you going to do?"

"Hush, Max," It was a sigh against his lips as she kissed him fully, her tongue entering his mouth, entangling with his.

With his arms still hooked around the ropes, he flattened his hands at her waist and slid up her ribs and to the sides of her breasts. His thumbs circled her nipples and his hips thrust upward, filling her completely. He broke the kiss and embraced her tightly, holding her and the swing at the same time.

She was glad he had ignored her. She should have known Max would find a way to take control and keep them from falling. They swayed gently in the swing and the motion enhanced the pleasure, the anticipation that awakened and stretched within her. The stars seemed to sweep back and forth above her as she arched her neck, and her hair brushing against her back was another sensation—soft silk in contrast to the rasp of his tongue over her breasts, the nip of his teeth on her nipples.

Entranced, she stared up at the pinpoints of light above them, dizzy with the sparkle of them, reaching for them as he thrust again, then rotated inside her and thrust harder.

"Higher, Max." She tightened her muscles around him and his groan of pleasure was rough in the night stillness. His hand held her hips, one on either side and lifted her until he was almost gone from her, then urged her down.

She was flying, sailing toward the moon.

Again his mouth found her breast, drawing on her as he raised and lowered her hips. Over and over again he withdrew and penetrated and her legs gripped harder around him, helping him, drawing him ever deeper into her. Perspiration formed on their flesh and cooled in the breeze—another sensation growing from the others. The moon seemed so large, so close as Max drove into her harder, deeper, faster . . .

"Higher," she cried and he swallowed the words with his mouth, his tongue plunging into her with the same rhythm as his body. All she could do was hold onto him now, her fingers digging into his shoulders, her head flung back, lost in the urgency of reaching . . . reaching, of the pleasure that took her farther and farther out of herself.

Moisture trickled between her breasts, between her legs. Pleasure mounted and peaked as he surged beneath her. "Yes," she said in a breathy whisper.

She shivered and trembled and stared at the stars that were so close now, bathing her in shattering light and suffusing her with heat; and she was flying, soaring among them, gathering them in her hands and scattering them again like so much diamond dust.

He stiffened and wrapped his arms around her and she knew he followed her higher and higher . . .

"Yes, Max. Touch the sky with me," she cried as pleasure and joy and love exploded inside her.

* * *

A draft of cold air swept over Jillian, chilling her in spite of the sheet covering her. She rolled to her side, her hand searching for Max to warm her, but the bed was empty. He was gone.

Opening one eye, she winced at the sunlight streaming in through the open French doors. It was late, she thought as she measured the angle of the sun. But then they had made love all night, falling asleep only when the stars had begun to fade and the moon was only a memory.

Already dressed in his usual riding apparel, he stood by the doors staring out at the midmorning sky, a piece of paper in his hand.

She pushed herself to her elbow and smiled sleepily at him. "You're up early," she mumbled.

"I've been summoned to London. My solicitor requires my presence at a meeting."

She rolled to her back and gazed at him. He seemed pensive, preoccupied—not at all as he'd been last night, so full of passion and laughter. For the first time in weeks, she'd felt as if she was getting her Max back, and more. For the first time since she'd realized she loved him, she felt as if she might be experiencing her dream.

She pushed the sheet away and sat up. "I'll have Clancy pack my things. How long will we be gone?"

He crumpled the paper in his fist. "It's only for a few days, Jillian. I'd rather you stay here."

"Is that an order, Max?" she asked softly.

"No, of course not." He swiped his hand over the back of his neck. "You may do whatever you wish. I told you in the beginning that our lives will be our own." With that, he walked to the door and disappeared into his dressing room.

She lay in the great bed, swallowing convulsively as Max's voice mingled with that of his valet in the next room. There was something humiliating about having her presence dismissed so easily after a long night of lovemaking.

There was something offending about being left to listen to his preparations to leave her.

It infuriated her to hear the door leading into the hall open and close, footsteps down the stairs, the front door shutting with a loud echo through the house. Just like that, he was gone. Just that casually, he walked away from her as if they had never flown to heaven and back the night before.

Fine, she thought as she threw back the sheet, ran to her room and rang for Clancy. *Do as you please,* he had said, and she intended to do just that.

It took her precisely two hours to pack and follow him. She would keep following him until he stopped running away from her.

Chapter 29

London

It had become impossible to leave Jillian behind, Max realized as he arrived at his townhouse in London. By her very absence, she occupied his thoughts.

The note from his solicitor had seemed like a godsend when he'd received it this morning, and he'd been doubly relieved when Jillian hadn't put up a fuss about coming with him. It was unsettling how she had crawled under his skin, charming him into believing she belonged there. At least in London, his mind would be occupied by problems easily solved, and his time taken up with activities he could control . . .

As he couldn't control Jillian, or himself.

They'd made love on the bloody swing of all places, and when she'd removed her gown and stood on the stone terrace wearing nothing but moonlight, his own imagination had taken flight, robbing him of the will to contain himself.

Smiling grimly at the literal meaning of that, he climbed the stairs to his bathing chamber to rid himself of the grime of the ride to London. Jillian had sapped him all night long until there was nothing left of him to contain. He'd never felt so drained, or so satisfied.

He'd never felt such confusion.

When she'd sought him out last night, he'd been so sure that she was being ruled by passion, taken with the novelty of it all. Jillian was like that, exploring new experiences with curiosity and enthusiasm. It had never occurred to him that he would be caught up in her illusions. So caught up that he hadn't been able to keep his hands off her all night. So caught up that he couldn't get her out of his mind.

With her, he'd experienced a completion he hadn't known existed.

Logically, he knew he couldn't expect it to happen again. But, knowing Jillian, she would believe that such lofty heights of passion could be attained every night and she would dedicate her efforts to proving it. He knew better. He'd had enough mistresses to know that novelty brought excitement and later, familiarity brought boredom. He had to remember that it was only sex and there were only so many ways to make love, that each woman had a technique as unique as her scent, and with time, it began to pall.

Except that Jillian's scent was always spiced with something new and different.

Last night she'd smelled of jonquils.

He'd seen the array of perfume bottles on her dressing table, crowding the surface as she was crowding him.

He stripped off his riding clothes and poured water from a pitcher into a bowl on a wooden stand. Scent be damned. Soon would come the indifference he experienced with so many others.

But what would happen to Jillian when his indifference came? She would most likely ignore it and do her damnedest to change his mind. Hadn't she always? No doubt, she was already confusing his passion with love. Who could blame her?

He glared at his image in the mirror above the washstand. What a fine job he was doing to disillusion her.

All he managed to do was encourage her expectations as well as his own. Like her expectation that he would keep her informed of his movements so she would not worry about him, and like his expectation of returning to Bassett House to find her napping in clutter and contentment. He had to admit that he found pleasure in knowing she waited for him. He had to admit that there was something satisfying about waking up to sunshine and Jillian, knowing that she would still be there when night fell.

Through a trick of fate, Jillian was his wife. She was making the best of it; why shouldn't he? Again he stared at his reflection, studying it as if he might find an argument for his logic.

He saw nothing but acceptance.

After spending all afternoon with his solicitor, Max headed for his club. He walked into the bastion of male exclusivity, enduring hearty slaps on his back and constant questions and comments on marital bliss. Dodging the inquiries with vague replies, he settled for a drink and hand of whist with the least offensive of the curious. Yet, there was a gnawing restlessness inside him that allowed him no respite.

"Thinking about your bride?" a voice asked at his side.

"Bruce," Max said rising to his feet and clapping his friend on the back. "By God, it is good to see you."

"It is a shock to see you," Bruce replied and took an empty chair at the table as Max's whist partner discreetly made his excuses and left. "What are you doing in town?"

"I had some business matters to attend," Max said and arranged the cards in a neat stack. "How are you getting along?" he asked, diverting the conversation away from himself. "I was distressed to hear of your loss. We all were."

"I know. The messages of condolence you, Jillian, and Damien sent were appreciated." Bruce rubbed his hand over his face. "Grief is really a strange thing. Some days you go along fine and other days it weighs you down like a boulder hanging about your neck."

"And your sister? How is she faring?"

"Not very well; she has it in her head that mother grieved herself to death. I brought her to London in hopes that she might put that silly notion aside."

Max didn't know what to say. He knew Bruce was referring to his mother's grief over the duke's death. Yet it was a subject they had studiously avoided for more than ten years.

"We can talk about it, you know," Bruce said, meeting Max's gaze as if he were issuing some sort of challenge. "They're both dead now."

"What is there to talk about?" Max shrugged. "As you said, they're both dead. Whatever was between them is dead as well."

"Perhaps you are right," Bruce said on a deep sigh as if he regretted making the concession. "So tell me, how are you and Jillian getting along?"

"It is best we don't talk about that either."

"It rather narrows the field, doesn't it?" Bruce asked, giving Max an odd look. "I take it you left her rusticating at Bassett?"

Max sighed in defeat. He should have known Bruce wouldn't be put off. He was like Jillian in his tenacity.

"She is turning my household topsy-turvy and playing duchess as if she invented the role," he said, hoping Bruce would be satisfied with that.

"You know, Max," Bruce said as he accepted a drink from the steward, "death has a way of changing one's perspective of what one has gained or lost in life. Trouble is, we often don't know what we have until it is gone."

Uncomfortable with the feeling that Bruce's maudlin clichés were directed at him, Max pushed back from the table. "It's late. I must be going."

Bruce's mouth quirked in a small smile. "Have a care, Max, that you are not late for your own life."

What the devil was that supposed to mean? Max wondered as he climbed into his carriage and directed the coachman toward home. He had no use for sloshy sentiments and useless regrets. As a rule, neither did Bruce, though Max supposed allowances had to be made for sorrow.

The coach lumbered slowly through the traffic and Max settled in, stretching his legs to rest his feet on the opposite seat. He leaned his head back and closed his eyes, battling thoughts of Jillian waiting for him in the country and his sudden urge to order the coachman to drive straight through to Bassett. Instead, he thought of Bruce's sister and her belief that her mother had died of grief—an implication that Lady Blackwood had harbored illusions of love to the end. It was hard to imagine anyone loving his father, much less being convinced that the emotion was returned. Unwittingly, Bruce had justified Max's own conviction that love was highly overrated as a *raison d'être*. If Lady Blackwood had died of grief, then love was not only an unreliable emotion, but a deadly one as well.

Max's fist clenched on his thighs as he remembered Bruce's mother as he had first seen her, vivid and alive as she congratulated her son on completing his courses at Oxford, and later when she had leaned weakly on her son's arm, her face pale beneath her mourning veil at the duke's memorial service.

Damn his father. He had not only plundered the tombs and heritages of dead civilizations in his search for treasure; he had plundered the living as well.

The tower clock struck midnight as Max stepped down from the coach in front of his townhouse. Down the street, a party of nobles and their ladies entered a coach, careful of their finery lest a ruffle sag or a frock coat wrinkle before they arrived at the social function of the evening. They were, Max guessed, the last of the hangers on at the end of the official Season, desperate to be entertained just one more time, needing to see and be seen to know that they existed.

Shaking his head, Max climbed the steps to the door. Had it been only an hour ago that he had been critical of Bruce for indulging in grim profundities?

As if on cue, a wedge of light spilled onto the portico as his butler opened the door, holding a candelabra to light Max's way.

Handing over his hat and gloves, and advising Ripley to dismiss his valet, Max strode to the staircase, intent on seeking oblivion. He'd had precious little rest the last two nights.

His footsteps echoed through the house as he took the stairs, and candles burned in sconces along his path, casting shadows on the walls and ceiling. Conversations and laughter of servants belowstairs faded with every step—a lonely sound that separated him from the rest of the world. It had never occurred to him before how seldom he'd had the freedom to indulge in easy conversation and spontaneous laughter with others. Only with Damien and Jillian had companionship been a natural state of being for him, and he realized how solitary his life was. He'd never minded before.

He wished Jillian were here.

He missed her.

He shoved open the door to his room and walked in, kicking it shut behind him, his gaze focused on the bed and its promise of peace, and felt as if he'd stepped into a dream without falling asleep.

Jillian sat in the center of the mattress, her back propped up by pillows, a book resting on her upraised knees. Her breasts were bare. Her hair was hanging loose in those soft spirals that seemed to magically appear from time to time, flowing over her shoulders and framing her rose tipped nipples. He caught a whiff of heather, a fresh clean scent that invited one to breathe deeply.

He should have been surprised to see her, but he felt only the same acceptance he'd found earlier. He should have known she would follow him. She always did, just as she always brought him a sense of contentment and well-being. Funny how he could admit that now.

"Have you developed an aversion to nightgowns?" he asked mildly as he stripped off his coat and cravat.

"Yes, I think I have," she said and set her book aside. "I never realized how constricting they were. You must have hated sleeping in nightshirts when you visited Westbrook Court."

Max unbuttoned his shirt and dropped it on a chair. "I did, yet it was necessary. I never knew when I was going to wake up to find you standing over me," he said as he unfastened the front of his breeches and stripped them off.

She rolled to her side and propped her head on one elbow as he approached her. "Ladylou caught me, you know, when I was ten or so. She said a lady should never enter a gentleman's bedchamber. At the time I failed to see how that applied to me, or to you for that matter. I was no lady and you were no gentleman."

"I resent that," he said as he slipped beneath the sheets. The mattress dipped with his greater weight and she promptly rolled into him, planting her feet against his calves for stability. "Ye Gods, Jillian, your feet are freezing."

"Why do you think I put them against your leg?" she said with complete unconcern.

Max chuckled and folded his hands behind his neck and stared up at the ceiling. It seemed the oddest thing to him to be lying naked beside her, simply talking. Yet, he didn't feel like making love and he had not seen the barest hint of desire burning in her eyes, nor did she try to touch him beyond warming her feet against his leg.

He hadn't realized how much he'd missed having uncomplicated companionship until now. *We don't know what we have until it is gone.* The memory of Bruce's words was a sharp and poignant pressure in his chest. Jillian was here, a companion in the night, offering him the freedom and comfort he enjoyed only with her. It was a feeling that seemed more intimate than carnal closeness.

"I saw Bruce tonight," he said.

"He has returned to the city?" She flipped over onto her back and mimicked his pose, layering her hands behind her head. The sheet remained at her waist exposing her breasts. He'd never been around a woman as free and open as Jillian, or as giving.

"Yes, from what I understand he wanted to get his sister away from the memories at Blackwood."

"I never did get to meet her, not really. Now doesn't seem the proper time."

"It may be precisely the proper time," Max said. "She may need a friend right now. According to Bruce, she is taking the death of her mother very hard."

"It's strange," Jillian said musingly. "I only met the countess once at the graces's memorial service, but Bruce spoke of her so affectionately, I feel as if I knew her."

"She was a striking woman," Max said remembering the countess's fiery hair and serene countenance.

"She must have been ill even then."

"No, she was grieving for my father," Max said. "She was the only person who did."

Jillian rolled to her side and raised up to stare at Max in wide-eyed shock.

"They were lovers," he explained.

"For how long?"

"Years." Max found himself telling Jillian all about the late Duke of Bassett and his mistress, the Countess of Blackwood. He told her of how he had been drawn to Bruce's irreverence and odd sense of humor, and how, beyond the revelation that a liaison did indeed exist between Max's father and Bruce's mother, they had never spoken of it.

"And you and Bruce became friends in spite of it," Jillian stated.

"Yes we did."

"Max, it is possible that he loved her," Jillian ventured.

"My father never loved anyone."

Jillian did not argue with him but snuggled up against him, laying her head on his arm, and twirling his hair with her fingers. Had he ever felt such undemanding pleasure, such simple comfort? He could not recall and it didn't seem to matter. He was feeling it now.

"It's funny, but even tonight I couldn't bring myself to discuss it with Bruce. Now that they are both dead, it seems all the more pointless."

"Did Bruce want to discuss it?" Her breath was a soft caress on his ear and her fingers soothed as she began to sift through his hair, smoothing it back over and over again.

"Yes, I think he might have."

She was silent then, but her presence said enough, calming him with the sound of her breathing, the brush of flesh against linen as she shifted her leg and rubbed his foot with hers.

He wanted to make love to her, to increase the closeness, to seal them together, but his mind was too full to give way to his body. He had spoken to her as he never had to another living soul, not even Damien or Bruce. He had needed a friend and Jillian had been here, occupying his life as if she'd always belonged. And he knew if he turned to her and took her into his arms, she would come willingly. Friend and lover.

Against all reason and all odds, he had both.

Jillian lay awake long after Max's breathing grew soft and even in sleep. He'd looked so weary when he'd come into the room. Too weary to fight her or to walk away from her. And there had been a melancholy in his eyes that she had never seen in him before, as if he were defeated and didn't really mind. After what he had told her, she'd felt melancholy, too, for all the years Max's spirit had frozen to death in the atmosphere of Bassett House while he'd waited for his father to come home, to perhaps warm his son with a smile. And she felt it for all the times his father hadn't come because he had been with Lady Blackwood.

Max's father and Bruce's mother had been lovers. She had always wondered why Bruce had gone to such extraordinary lengths to help her. Now she knew. No wonder she'd always sensed a special bond between Max and Bruce. In a strange way, she supposed Max and Bruce were family, too, sharing their parents as they had. It pleased her to know that Max had such a friend.

She had jeopardized that by drawing Bruce into her schemes.

Yet, she knew that Bruce would have never consented to her request had he not believed he was doing the right thing for Max. And now more than ever she was certain that it was right. Tonight, as he had greeted her presence in his bed with acceptance, she had known that absolutely. She had been right to follow him, to let him know that she would not give up on him or abandon him. He'd had enough of that in his life with his mother's death and his father's preoccupations and, sadly, with Damien.

She pressed her hand flat over his chest, feeling the steady beat of his heart, lulled and reassured by the rise and fall of his chest.

It was very odd how sorely disappointed she was that he had not made love to her tonight. Yet, it touched her deeply that he hadn't, that he had fallen into a deep, peaceful sleep in the middle of a sentence—about what she couldn't recall. Their lovemaking had become important to her, but she wanted more. She wanted his passion, his friendship, his love. She wanted it all, given freely without more coercion from her.

With a sigh, she closed her eyes and laid her leg over his. She would not initiate any more lovemaking between them, she decided.

If he wanted her, he would have to reach out for her. Perhaps then he would realize that he could reach out and not always come away with an empty hand . . . or an empty heart.

Chapter 30

J illian lay belly down on his bed, her arms and legs flung out as if the world were hers and she would guard it well. He should have known his Pandora would not sleep curled in a protective little ball.

His Pandora. Max had not thought of her in that way since their marriage. But last night, he had rediscovered her, a woman holding hope in her hands, offering it to him. And God help him he had accepted her gift. For whatever it was worth, he would nurture hope one day at a time.

For the first time since their marriage, he felt free to want her, to take her. The knowledge of her love for him was no longer daunting. He knew her strength and her courage. He'd learned that she was no longer a child in need of protection, but a woman sure of what she wanted. She'd never kept her desire for him a secret, boldly coming to him, setting aside her pride and her fears for him. He wanted to do the same for her, to give her all that he had to give—tenderness, passion, pleasure.

He inched the sheet down and ran his hand over the graceful curve and satin skin presented to him.

She stirred beneath his touch and turned her face toward him, then swept her hair from her eyes as she smiled with seductive drowsiness.

"Do you know you have a glorious bottom?" he said, kneading the softness, then tracing her cleft lightly with his fingertip.

"Why thank you, your Grace," she replied primly and rolled to her back. Though her tone was teasing, her eyes were watchful and questioning, as if she were surprised that he had reached out for her.

Lowering his head, he took a nipple into his mouth, circling it with his tongue, pulling on it with his lips as if he could consume her. And then he nuzzled her neck, breathing deeply between biting kisses, remembering how she had slept against him all night, how he had awakened feeling the imprint of her breasts on his back. "You smell like me," he whispered.

"And do you smell like me?" she gasped as she rotated her palm over his flat nipple, then slid her hand down lower.

Raising up, he gave her a lazy smile and ran his finger down from between her breasts to her belly, and lower, sifting through the triangle of black curls. "I think that before this morning passes, I will smell like you. There will be no part of you that I will not know."

She shivered and returned his smile as she parted her legs in a most accommodating manner.

"You are without shame," Max murmured as he dipped one finger inside her, watching her—his curious Pandora, his trusting friend, his demanding wife and willing lover, his most improper duchess with her lips parted and her eyes glazed with desire.

"Only with you," Jillian murmured, and arched her back, her breasts pushing up, full and erect with passion. Her breath snagged as he swept the pad of his finger over her, finding her small nub, stroking it. "Only *for* you, Max," she said, her voice low, her expression solemn.

Only for him. His fingers delved deeper into her, and she went from warm to hot, bathing his hand. He grew larger and harder than he thought possible as her words smoldered inside of him. Meeting her gaze, he recognized the truth in her eyes, felt the truth inside him, accepted it as she opened herself wider for him and arched against his hand, trusting him with all of herself, offering him all that he wanted from her.

She always had.

He had been the one who was afraid to give too much, afraid to give her too much room in his life, afraid he would not be able to fill the emptiness she would leave behind. He'd feared the indifference that would surely come, but if he fought hard enough, gave enough, perhaps it wouldn't happen.

Sliding down the bed, he lay between her thighs, bending her knees, slipped his hands beneath her buttocks and lifted her hips to gaze at her, study the swollen layers of her, opening for him, waiting for him. Only him.

"Max," she breathed, "what are you going to do?"

He inhaled the heady scent that could never come from a bottle, could never be drawn from anyone but Jillian. He wanted to consume her. He gave her a lazy smile and lowered his head. "Feast, your Grace."

"Oh!" Jillian cried out at the warmth of Max's mouth on her. Shock and moisture rushed through her as his tongue swept over her, tasting her. And then he draped her legs over his shoulders, freeing his hands to torment her with deep strokes and circling caresses on a place inside her that seemed to pulse faster and faster as urgency grew into an ache that left no part of her untouched.

Her flesh burned hotter and hotter. Sparks of pleasure shot to every part of her body at the rasp of his morning beard, the flick of his tongue and the gentle scrape of his teeth. He clasped her hips more firmly as he groaned and breathed against her, devouring her.

She strained toward him, and he accepted the temptation, penetrating her, drawing from her. She moved against him, up and down, faster and faster, pressing against him harder and harder . . .

Pleasure exploded inside her.

She gulped air and sobbed as spasms of sensation crashed against one another, overwhelming her, draining her until she thought she would die. With a tenderness that bordered on reverence, he released his hold and lowered her legs to the bed. The spasms eased, her muscles collapsed and her bones seemed to fold within her.

Max raised his head and stared at her as he stroked her belly and her bottom and her breasts with a light touch. He breathed deeply and smiled. "Now," he said softly, musingly, "I smell like you."

"Was that proper, Max?" she asked weakly, thinking that surely it was not. But she didn't really care. It had been wonderful.

"There is nothing," he said and his voice was a low growl. "There can be nothing improper between us, Pandora."

A ripple of pleasure washed through her, sweet and warm and cleansing. Everything was all right now. He had called her Pandora. He had taken all she had to give in an act that she sensed was truly special. And she knew that he had truly accepted her as a part of his life.

Peering up at him she studied his body as he remained on his knees, still between her legs. His appendage—she could not think what else to call it—

rose boldly from him, prompting her imagination, kindling a new blaze of desire. She smiled as she, too, rose to her knees to face him. "Nothing, Max?" she asked as she flattened her palm against his chest and pushed him backward, his legs on either side of her.

His brows rose in that way he had. "Nothing," he said hoarsely as a strand of her hair brushed over his groin.

Bending over, she cupped the tip of him with her palm. "Wonderful," she said and eased her hands beneath his hips, trying to lift them as he had lifted hers, but he was too heavy for her.

"Careful, Pandora," he warned, raising up on his elbows, "this is one box you might not want to open."

Sweeping her mass of hair over one shoulder, she arched her brows, giving him the same expression he often gave her. "Why, sir, I merely seek to break my fast as you have done." She pushed him down again and before he could reply, she closed her hands around him.

He sucked in his breath. "Pandora, your fingernails."

Instantly, she snatched her hands away, feeling clumsy and embarrassed. This wasn't as easy as she thought it would be. Maybe she wasn't supposed to use her hands. Lowering her head, she opened her mouth over him.

"Easy ... your teeth ..."

She jerked away and sat back on her heels, staring at the place her hands and mouth had been. "I don't know what to do," she whispered around her frustration. "Please show me."

"It's all right," he said, giving her a pained smile. "You don't have to do this."

"I know," she said. "But I want to ... for you, Max."

He inhaled sharply as he stared at her for a moment, searching her expression. And then, he pushed backward on the bed to half sit against the headboard and reached for her face, cradling it between his hands as he kissed her deeply, drawing gently on her tongue, then playing with it, circling it and drawing again. "Just like that," he said softly and cupping the back of her head, he guided her back down.

She caught her breath at the kiss and his silent encouragement, his patience with her. She traced the path of hair from his chest to the nest surrounding his manhood and cradled him in her hands gently—so gently—using the pads of her fingers to explore the rose-petal texture of him.

"Yes, sweetheart," he said as his fingers sifted through her hair, clenching and unclenching.

Her confidence restored, she took him into her mouth and tasted the flesh that seemed stretched beyond its limits, then drew on him gently. His body stiffened and he seemed to grow even larger, more rigid.

"Oh, God," he groaned.

She took him harder and faster, using her hands and her mouth to stroke him, to take from him as he had taken from her.

"Stop, Jillian," he rasped as his body seemed to vibrate with tension and his hands gripped her head, holding it as if he were trying to pull her away and draw her closer at the same time. "You don't want . . ."

But she did want . . . something. Her skin felt inflamed and her heart pounded to the rhythm of her movements. She wanted to smell like him and taste like him. She wanted every part of him to be a part of her.

"Damnit, no, stop, before it's too . . ."

His protests trailed off into a groan and he arched upward as his breath stopped, and then hers stopped, too.

And again she felt pleasure, but it was a gentle caress inside her, a deep contentment that she and Max had shared in a way she'd never dreamed of. She didn't understand it, but she knew it was so. He was as much a part of her as she was of him. They belonged to one another now, completely.

She released him and slid up his body, giving him her mouth and taking his. His arms wrapped around her, holding her tightly, crushing her against him as if he would never let her go.

It was victory and the taste of it was sweet.

Chapter 31

For the first time since they had exchanged vows, Jillian felt truly married.

Max sat behind the desk in the study sorting through a stack of correspondence as she curled up in a corner of the leather sofa, watching him in silence, exchanging a private smile with him when he glanced up at her from time to time.

It was perfect—husband and wife in complete accord, sharing moments of peace and contentment with one another. Jillian had pictured it this way, in her mind, envisioning an entire future of such moments with Max. But she'd never imagined that she would be weak from making love all morning, or that she would tremble all over every time she remembered how they had feasted—as Max had put it—upon one another then, later, joined in a perfect and shattering physical union. She'd never felt more like a wife as Max held her in the aftermath of their lovemaking, as they'd entered the small dining room together and shared a late breakfast, as Max had held the door of his study open for her in a silent invitation to join him, seating her on the sofa and then, very deliberately opening the drapes to admit the sunlight.

He wanted her with him.

Her heart was so full, it ached with happiness.

She heard the knocker clap against the front door, but didn't stir. Already society had taken notice that the Duke and Duchess of Bassett had returned to London and during the course of the afternoon, several callers had left their cards. Jillian had no desire to see anyone, nor, apparently did Max. He had not protested when she'd instructed Ripley to inform anyone who called that the duke and duchess were "not at home."

But when she heard her brother's deep baritone greet the butler, she sat up and smoothed her hair. Damien was the one person she wanted to see. How she had missed him. How nervous she had been as she'd fretted over how she would get Max to call on Damien with her, and how once they were all together she would find a way to reconcile the differences between them.

But Damien was here, and certainly that must be a good sign. She should have known that everything would work out. Smiling, she glanced at Max, but he was staring at the open doorway through narrowed eyes as he listened to Damien address the butler.

"Please inform the duke that I should like to have a word with him," Damien said tersely.

All the pleasure drained out of her at her brother's tone and Max's guarded expression.

"I will see if he is at home, your Grace," Ripley said.

"I bloody well know he is at home. Either you summon him or I will find him myself."

Jillian sank back into the cushions, wondering what on earth had happened now.

Before Ripley could respond, Max pushed himself away from his desk. "In here," he called out evenly.

Glancing neither left nor right, Damien stalked into the room, his jaw taut with anger, his gaze riveted on Max. "I told you I would not tolerate your leaving Jillian at Bassett House to rot," he said, his voice low and furious.

"I'm here, Damien," Jillian said as she pushed to her feet. "Why would you think Max abandoned me at Bassett House?"

His expression changed from fury to relief as he turned and crossed the room to gather her into his arms and hug her fiercely. "I didn't know what to think," he said as he pulled back and grasped her shoulders. "Several people informed me that Max had returned to London, but no one mentioned seeing you, and I have not heard a word from you since the wedding. I thought surely if you were here with Max, you would have sent a note around."

"I'm sorry, Damien," Jillian said, her happiness at seeing her brother punctured by guilt. She had been so wrapped up in Max and herself that she hadn't thought of how Damien might be feeling. "We only just arrived yesterday," she said in an attempt to soothe him. He didn't have to know that she and Max had come separately.

Damien nodded, accepting her explanation. "How are you faring?" he asked with a probing gaze.

"I haven't beaten her," Max provided dryly as he leaned back in his chair and folded his arms across his chest, then added in a soft voice, "yet."

Damien stiffened.

"He is teasing," Jillian said as she frowned at Max. He raised an unrepentant brow.

"His sense of humor does not amuse," Damien bit out.

"Nor does your blatant inspection of Jillian for signs of maltreatment," Max shot back.

Jillian's gaze skipped from her brother to her husband. "How is LadyLou?" she asked abruptly, desperate to change the subject. They might not yet be willing to mend their differences but she did not have to endure their baiting of one another.

"She is well," Damien said, then smiled suddenly. "Come back to the town house with me. I know she would love to see you."

"I would love to see her, too," Jillian said and felt another pang of guilt. She had not written to her aunt since the wedding.

"Come along, then," Damien said, grasping her arm and tugging her toward the door.

"Don't forget your cloak, *darling,*" Max said with a wry smile as he absently shuffled through the papers on his desk. "It's chilly outside."

Damien's grip tightened on Jillian's arm and his lips thinned in irritation at Max's proprietary use of the endearment. Jillian suspected it was precisely the reaction Max had intended, since he had never referred to her in such a pretentious manner. On the other hand, Damien had brought it on himself by pointedly excluding Max from the invitation. Still, she would not have them goading each other at her expense.

She angled her head toward Max and with all the insincerity she could muster, fluttered her lashes at him outrageously. "Your concern for my comfort is touching, *darling,*" she said giving him tit for tat.

Max nodded and gave her a small, private smile, conceding the point.

Damien frowned at the exchange between them. "Come along, Jillian," he repeated.

Dislodging his grip on her arm, she stepped away from her brother. As much as she wanted to spend time with him and LadyLou, she knew she was not going under such circumstances. "Damien if you cannot include Max in your invitations, then I cannot accompany you anywhere."

His shocked expression nearly undid her. But Damien had to understand that Max was her husband. To exclude him was the same as excluding her.

"Shall I give LadyLou your love?" Damien asked tightly.

Pain squeezed her heart at his refusal. But, she could not relent now.

"Go with your brother, Pandora. I still have work to do here," Max said in a quiet voice, one side of his mouth tipped up in a warm half-smile of understanding. Max knew as well as she did that Damien would not ask her again. His pride wouldn't allow it. Too much had been forced on him lately. Just as too much had been forced on Max, yet just now, he had set his own pride aside for her. She had never loved him more.

She wanted to go to him and give him a long, lingering kiss. But she wasn't sure Damien would be able to witness such intimacy without making some acerbic comment. "I won't be long," she said, returning Max's smile with a wry one of her own. "And I won't forget my cloak." She tucked her hand in the crook of Damien's arm. "Shall we go?"

Without a word, Damien nodded stiffly and led her out of the room, remaining silent while a footman fetched her cloak and then stepped out into the crisp afternoon.

"Do not be taken in by his smooth manner and solicitous treatment, Jillie," Damien said as they descended the steps. "Max always behaves in that fashion at the beginning of—" he broke off and shook his head.

"In the beginning of an affair?" she asked, not appreciating Damien reducing what was between her and Max to something so paltry and sordid. "Max is not having an affair with me, Damien. We are married."

He cast her a quick slantwise look and then glanced toward his carriage parked at the street curb. "Guard your heart, Jillian. He will break it."

She wished that she could tell Damien how much she loved Max, how happy she was with him. But, she didn't think he would appreciate the significance of such a revelation. Nor was he ready to believe anything but the worst of Max. She slipped her hand from the crook of his elbow and gathered her cloak close about her as they walked the remainder of the way to the coach.

Max was right. It was chilly out.

A footman opened the door of the coach and lowered the steps. Damien offered her his hand in assistance, his brow creased as he stared down the street, as if he couldn't bear to look at her. "Please don't worry about my heart, Damien. It is quite safe," she said, wanting desperately to see him smile.

He didn't seem to hear her. His frown deepened and she realized his expression had nothing to do with her. She followed the path of his gaze and saw Nunnley standing up the street attempting to hail a hack.

Something was wrong. She knew by the taut look on Damien's face that his preoccupation and his ire were obviously aimed at Nunnley.

"Excuse me a moment, Jillie," Damien said abruptly. "I need to have a word with Nunnley." Before she could respond, Damien released her hand and strode purposefully toward the viscount.

What in heavens name had Nunnley done? she wondered. As far as she knew he was guilty of nothing but poor fashion sense and excessive bootlicking.

Unblinking, she watched as Damien reached Nunnley's side. With his legs braced apart and his fists clenched at his sides, her brother spoke what appeared to be one rapid-fire sentence. Nunnley took a quick step away, his eyes growing wide with fear, his lips moving frantically.

Jillian craned her neck and strained her ears, but she could hear nothing of what was being said. She focused on Nunnley's mouth and tried to read his lips, but she could not. Abruptly, Damien sliced the air with his hand, and Nunnley clamped his mouth shut. Again, Damien spoke, his expression filled with contempt. Nunnley gave a few quick, almost desperate nods of his head.

Jillian sighed and glanced away, unable to watch another moment. She felt sorry for Nunnley. Whatever infraction he had committed, she doubted it deserved the tongue lashing Damien was administering. There was nothing for it, but to make her brother understand that she and Max belonged together, whether he wanted to hear it or not. She could not allow him to run around taking out his anger on the world at large.

A hand closed over her shoulder and she nearly

jumped out of her skin. Her gaze crashed into
Damien's. His green eyes were filled with a fury she
had not seen since the night he had caught her and Max
kissing in the drawing room.

"Go back to the house," he barked.

"What is it?" she said and glanced back down the
street. A hack rounded the corner and disappeared. She
assumed Nunnley was inside.

"Nothing you need concern yourself with," Damien
clipped out and marched her halfway up the steps before releasing her shoulder. "I have a matter to see to
at once."

That said, he turned away from her and climbed into
his coach. "Ten Curzon Street," he said to his coachman.

"Damien, wait," she called out, feeling an urgent
need to know what had happened. She did not like the
look on Damien's face at all. There was something
frightening in his eyes and the grim set of his jaw.

Damien only shook his head at her from the window
as the coach rolled away.

The significance of his direction struck Jillian.

Bruce lived at number 10 Curzon Street.

Suspicion crawled over her skin like thousands of
tiny spiders. It couldn't be, yet she had the horrible suspicion that she and Bruce had been found out. Taking
a deep breath, she shook her head and told herself that
she was jumping at shadows. It was not possible to
trace the gossip that had precipitated her marriage to
Max. How many times had she been witness to that
particular fact? But, what else would have sent Damien
haring off to Bruce's as if it were a matter of life and
death? Damien was the most gentle and understanding
of men except when it came to his family. She had
never seen him angry at anyone or anything except
when she was involved.

Fear bit her deeply. Why had she not made it a point
to find out how Bruce had accomplished her ruin?

She had to go to Bruce. If what she feared was true,

she could not leave him at Damien's mercy. If she was wrong, she could explain away her sudden appearance by saying that since she was already out, she'd come to pay a simple call. She could use the same story on Max with a few minor alterations.

She bolted back up the steps, pausing at the front door to smooth her cloak and collect herself. With a calm she did not feel, she gingerly pushed the door open and stepped inside, smiling at the footman who sprang to attention. "Please have the coach brought around," she said politely as she eyed the open doors to Max's study and considered slipping away without telling him where she'd gone.

But, she quickly discarded the notion. It would never work. If he hadn't heard her order, the servants would surely tell him that she'd taken the coach. She had to tell him something. Gathering her courage, she marched into the study.

Max still sat behind his desk. Yet he was not working. His feet were propped on the desk and he seemed to be preoccupied with other concerns. Looking up at her discreet cough, his brows jerked together. "What are you doing back? Where is Damien?"

"He remembered an appointment with his solicitor," she said, feeling like a spider adding more sticky silk to her web. "I—I thought since I already have my cloak on that I would pay a call on Bruce and Kathy."

Max stared at her thoughtfully, and Jillian held his gaze without flinching. Anxiety squeezed in her chest as the moment spun out and he did not respond. It was all she could do not to blink or nervously lick her lips. She reached for the ties of her cloak and toyed with the ends.

"I'm finished for the day," Max said finally. "I'll accompany you."

No! Jillian wanted to shout in panic. Instead, she nodded mutely as her heart sank to her feet. She didn't know what else to do, except pray.

* * *

Jillian was hiding something; Max was sure of it. Her weak explanation for Damien's abrupt departure, and her sudden urge to pay a call on Bruce and Kathy had been curious enough. But, during the ride to Bruce's, she had stared out the window in an unnerving silence, her posture unnaturally still.

"Apparently, Damien decided to pay a visit to Bruce before his meeting with his solicitor," Max said as his coach halted behind Damien's.

"Maybe Bruce was supposed to go with him," Jillian ventured as she twisted the betrothal and wedding rings on her finger beneath her glove.

"Then, perhaps we should just return home," Max said, testing the waters.

"No!" Jillian said quickly, then visibly struggled to soften her voice. "I still would like to see Kathy. Um . . . why don't you just drop me off and send the coach back for me later? I'm sure you don't wish to spend the afternoon listening to two women discussing the latest fashions."

Something was definitely amiss. It wasn't like Jillian to fidget about and start at every sound and movement around her. He couldn't imagine what would put her in such a state, but one way or another he was going to find out. "We'll both see Kathy," he said firmly.

Jillian said nothing as she walked beside him, staring at the front door of Bruce's town house as if it were the entrance to hell. She seemed to barely breathe as he raised his hand and sounded the knocker.

After a long moment, Smithy opened the door. The burly footman muttered under his breath, then quickly stepped outside and closed the door, but not before Max heard Damien's furious shout, "Goddamn you Bruce," followed by a loud crash.

Jillian sucked in a sharp breath and took a step back.

"What the devil is going on?" Max demanded, his gaze skipping between Jillian and Smithy, certain now that either one of them could provide the answer.

Jillian stared at her feet.

Smithy's gaze hopped around like a fish flopping on a stream bank. He swallowed convulsively and folded his arms across his chest. "His lordship ain't receivin' callers," he said.

Irritation replaced curiosity as Max realized he'd run into a solid wall of loyalty. Smithy's to Bruce and Jillian's to Damien. Didn't she know that he had some loyalties too? Didn't she understand that no matter what was in the past, he and Bruce and Damien had shared too much for him to stand by and allow an all-out brawl without knowing the reasons behind it?

A woman's scream pierced the barrier of the solid oak door.

"Get out of my way," he said through clenched teeth.

Jillian clamped her hand over her mouth and closed her eyes.

"Oh, bloody 'ell," Smithy said and opened the door. "Break 'em up, your Grace. They're near givin' Lady Kathy a nervous breakdown."

Leaving Jillian standing outside, Max pushed past Smithy and followed the sound of crashes and curses to the drawing room.

He halted in his tracks at the open double doors, too stunned by what he saw to take another step.

The remains of a porcelain teapot and cups lay broken on the floor and a table leaned drunkenly against the hearth. Damien had wrestled Bruce down on the floor, his fists landing one effective punch after another on whatever body part he could reach. On top of Damien was a flame-haired young woman landing an equal number of ineffectual punches on Damien's back with one hand while pulling his hair with her other hand. Blood streamed from Bruce's nose and mouth and a cut above his eye. A sleeve of Damien's tailored coat was ripped from the seam in back.

"Get back, Kathy," Bruce rasped and rolled his body to the left and then to the right in an attempt to shake Damien off him. But the weight of two bodies pinned him helplessly to the floor.

Kathy ignored her brother. She continued to batter at Damien's back as mindlessly as Damien battered at Bruce's face. Apparently, she didn't understand she was preventing her brother from giving a decent account of himself.

Damien was in a black rage.

If Max didn't stop them, Kathy might well be the only one to survive intact.

He reached them in three long strides, grasped Kathy around the waist and set her aside.

"No, don't. He's killing Bruce," she cried, her arms flailing wildly in an effort to free herself and return to aid her brother.

Bruce wasn't dead yet, but he was so exhausted that he couldn't fight. Max couldn't hold Kathy and help Bruce at the same time. "Be still and stay out of the way," he said.

She struggled more violently, her brilliant blue eyes swimming with tears. "He's killing him," she repeated, her voice rising to a hysterical shriek. "He's killing him."

The depth of her distress unstrung Max as few things ever had. Pity swelled in his heart for her and anger burned in his belly at Damien. She had just lost her mother. No matter what his reasons, Damien had no right to subject her to this.

Suddenly, Jillian was beside him, her face pale and her eyes wide with fear. "Max won't allow it," she said and gripped Kathy around the shoulders. "He'll stop them, but you must not interfere."

Kathy blinked and sagged against Jillian.

Max glared at Jillian, convinced that she knew the reasons why this was happening. He wanted to bellow at her, but there would be time enough later to sort through it all. First he had to end the bloodshed.

Ducking a wild punch, he leaned over and wrestled Damien away from Bruce. "Stop it," he growled as he stepped behind Damien and pinned his arms behind his back.

Bruce raised himself to a sitting position and pushed himself across the floor until his back rested against the sofa. Sobbing, Kathy ran to her brother and began to dab at his face with the hem of her skirt.

"Let me go," Damien said and tried to twist out of Max's hold. "He ruined Jillian."

"What?" Max said.

"It was Bruce," Damien spat out. "He tricked Nunnley into spreading the gossip. He was on the balcony that night."

Bruce? Bruce had spread the gossip about Jillian? Max's grip on Damien's arms slackened as he saw Jillian press her lips together and avoid his gaze. Bruce glanced furtively at Jillian then leaned his head back on the cushions and closed his eyes.

"I think," Max said, controlling his voice and clenching his fists to keep from shaking someone— anyone. "I think that one of you had better explain, now."

"Max," Jillian said quickly, "can't you see that Bruce is in no condition—"

"Damien, I trust you're willing to enlighten me," Max interrupted.

Damien was most willing, and in the next few minutes, Max listened to the most outlandish tale he'd ever heard. Not only had Bruce witnessed his and Jillian's encounter on the balcony, but so had Nunnley, Arabella Seymour and Melissa. Bruce had ensured that neither Arabella or Nunnley would be able to spread gossip in an act of friendship and loyalty.

As Max absorbed the details of Melissa's torn gown and Nunnley's rumpled appearance he had to admit that Bruce's actions had been pure genius. It was vital that Nunnley wed an heiress, just as it was vital to Arabella that Melissa wed a fortune. The threat of Bruce spreading gossip about Nunnley and Melissa would have been enough to permanently seal Arabella's and Nunnley's lips.

It was just what Max would expect from Bruce.

It would have worked. The forced marriage between himself and Jillian could have been averted, despite what had happened between them later that night in the drawing room. Only Damien had witnessed the true source of scandal.

Yet, the following morning, Bruce had apparently had a change of heart and tricked Nunnley into believing that Arabella had already begun to spread malicious tales. When Nunnley had gossiped to his cronies, he believed he was giving a firsthand account of a known scandal.

Again, it was pure genius.

It was pure Bruce. Only he would have the nerve to set such a bizarre chain of events into motion.

It was the last thing Max would expect from Bruce, yet judging from Bruce's lack of protest over the accusations, and his lack of outrage over Damien's physical attack, Max knew it had to be true. Judging from the way Jillian had inched away to stand apart, her hands wringing her gloves to shreds, Max was convinced that she had known all along what Bruce had done.

Shaking his head to clear the haze of rage from his vision, Max stepped away from Damien, and focused on yet another friend who had betrayed him.

Bruce still sat on the floor with his back against the sofa, staring at the toe of his boot. Kathy knelt at his side, seemingly oblivious to the drama unfolding around her as she ministered to her brother.

Max forced himself to remain where he stood, exercising every ounce of self-control he possessed to hold on to his reason, for reason dictated that Bruce would not do such a thing without sufficient cause. A ragged breath escaped him and he felt his chest hitch with the urge to laugh at the sheer absurdity of such a thought. What possible cause could there be to justify Bruce's actions? Still, he had to believe there was some sort of justification. To think otherwise was to know of a betrayal that cut as deeply as the rift between Max and Damien.

"Why?" Max asked flatly.

Bruce met Max's gaze then shrugged and glanced away.

If he hadn't been sure of the truth of Damien's claims, he was now.

Bright flashes of light exploded in Max's head as control slipped too far away from him to be called back. He wasn't even aware that he had moved until he twisted his hands in Bruce's lapels and hauled him halfway off the floor. "Why, you bastard?" Max demanded and jerked him to his feet.

Kathy sprang up and latched on to one of Max's arms. "No! Don't touch him."

"Max!" Jillian rushed him from the other side, and attached herself to his other arm.

Their combined impact threw Max off balance. With a woman hanging off each arm and his hands still twisted in Bruce's coat, he toppled forward. Bruce's hand shot out and splayed against Max's chest as he sat flat down on the sofa. The impetus of Bruce's fall and Max's grip on him yanked him forward, dragging Jillian and Kathy with him as his upper body slammed into Bruce. He could do nothing but bend almost double in an effort to right himself. Just as Max thought his feet were going to leave the floor, the sofa tipped and hands grabbed his shoulders from behind, holding him steady.

"Turn loose of his bloody coat," Damien snarled near his ear as he hauled him backward, pulling Jillian and Kathy upright in the process.

The sofa toppled over and landed with a thud, taking Bruce with it. Still in a seated posture, Bruce cracked his head against the floor and nothing could be seen of him but his feet sticking straight up toward the ceiling.

"Get up, damn you," Max said as he jerked his shoulders from side to side trying to fling Jillian and Kathy off of him. They flopped about like tenacious little terriers who had sunk their teeth into his arms and refused to let go.

"Enough, Max," Damien said. "This has gone too far."

Max stiffened as he realized that Damien still stood behind him, holding his shoulders, a bitter reminder of times past when Hastings and Forbes had guarded one another's backs. It was a wrenching reminder of what was lost and could not be regained. "It will never be enough," he said harshly. "The bastard ruined my life."

"He is a bastard," Kathy sobbed hysterically on his left. "So am I."

"Kathy, no!" Bruce said.

"Max listen to me," Jillian said urgently. "Bruce ruined me because I asked him to. I could not allow Damien to put you out of my life."

"Bruce is your brother," Kathy gasped, "and I am your sister."

The revelations slammed into Max with the force of hammer blows to his head, his midsection, his heart. The room grew deathly silent and receded around him as a red haze clouded his vision and his knees felt as if they would buckle. Bruce was his brother. Kathy was his sister. Jillian had trapped him.

Dimly aware of hands sliding from his shoulders to beneath his arms to support him, Max heard Damien's voice behind him. "Release him."

It was only when his arms were suddenly free that he realized that Damien had been speaking to Jillian and Kathy, the flesh-and-blood anchors that had dragged him into hell with their confessions.

Confessions and unforgivable betrayals.

Betrayals stacked on top of one another like a house of cards.

Cards that now lay scattered on the floor along with all the faith, loyalty and trust Max possessed. A numbing coldness spread through him. His legs became solid again. He straightened his back and Damien moved away from him.

"Max, let me explain," Jillian said, her face bleached

of color, her eyes wide and anxious. Jillian his wife, his lover, his betrayer.

"You deliberately trapped me into marriage. There is nothing else I need to know."

"There is much you need to know," Bruce said as he struggled to his feet. Bruce his friend, his brother, his betrayer.

To Max, it seemed more effort than it was worth to turn his head and look at Bruce. "I have lived my entire life ignorant of your connection to me. Living the remainder of my life ignoring it should not prove difficult. When our paths cross, as surely they will, I expect that you and your sister will keep well away from me."

That said, Max turned to face Damien. For the first time in months, Max saw a softening in his friend's expression. It could have been compassion or perhaps regret. Either way it chilled him, freezing his anger, leaving him with nothing but cold, clear thought.

Damien opened his mouth to speak, but Max shook his head.

It was too late.

With a dispassionate stare, he viewed each of the people in the room, seeing deceivers instead of friends, a stranger rather than a wife. Without a word, he turned on his heel and walked out of the house, wanting nothing more than to put as much distance as possible between himself and these people who had meant so much to him for most of his life. His father's by-blows were easy enough to leave behind. Bruce had deceived him with his silence in the past and his actions in the present. He had never known Kathy. He'd already accepted the severed connection with Damien.

But Jillian was another matter entirely.

Chapter 32

Jillian couldn't move, couldn't make a sound as the door slammed behind Max. Her body was paralyzed, while her mind spun like a weather vane in a fierce wind.

Bruce and Kathy . . . Max's brother and sister.

She stood estranged from the others, suddenly knowing how Max had felt all these years, standing aloof on the fringes of other lives, not really belonging. He'd been alone since the day he'd been born and his mother died. He'd been abandoned by his father and left to freeze in that great mausoleum of a house among emotionless servants and the treasures of dead civilizations.

Damien, his closest friend, had judged him unfairly. And she had compounded that by betraying and deceiving him.

He had been cheated of a family.

Rage flared so hot that she thought she might burst into flame and burn to ash. She hoped the late Duke of Bassett was rotting in hell. As for Bruce, she could not fathom his reasons for keeping such a secret. If she'd known she never would have asked him to help her, never involved him at all.

Her gaze found Bruce and then Kathy, saw their expressions of regret and pity. She looked at Damien and nearly cried out at the accusation in his eyes.

She had not only ruined herself, but everyone she loved. Yet Bruce had Kathy. And Damien had her. Max was alone.

She had to go to him, to explain why she had done it.

She shook off the paralysis and ran outside.

Only Damien's coach stood parked at the curb.

Footsteps echoed behind her and a hand grasped her elbow, swinging her around.

"You love him," Damien stated.

"More than anything," she whispered then touched her brother's face in silent apology. "I must go to him. Would you take me, please?"

"I'm not sure that is such a good idea, Jillie. What you have done ..." Damien trailed off on a sigh.

"I know what I have done," she replied, bracing herself for the questions she knew Damien was sure to ask.

"No, I'm not sure you do," he said simply as he helped her into his coach.

Damien did not ask for further details. He didn't speak at all during the carriage ride home ... toward Max. How odd, Jillian reflected as she stared out the window, that it had taken so little time for her to come to think of Max's home as hers. Or perhaps it wasn't odd at all, because Max was hers as well. She had seen to it.

You have ruined my life, Max had accused Bruce.

Why hadn't she seen it? she wondered. Why hadn't she realized that if Max loved her, he would have eventually come to her on his own? Why had she so foolishly conspired to force his hand when she knew the depths of his pride?

She shuddered at the memory of how he had stared through her a few moments ago, how he had walked away with a terrifying air of finality.

The coach slowed and lurched to a stop. Startled by the cessation of movement, she glanced out the opposite window and saw Max's coach standing by the carriage house. He was here.

"In his present frame of mind, I'm not sure how Max

will react to seeing you," Damien said as he helped her from the coach and escorted her to the front door.

"He won't hurt me, Damien," Jillian said.

"I never thought he would try to hurt Bruce, either."

"He didn't, Damien. If you will recall, he never raised his hand against Bruce. You did," she said and pushed open the door.

The entry hall was deserted. Not a footman was in sight to collect her cloak. Not a sound came from belowstairs.

Trunks were stacked at the foot of the stairs. Max leaned against the banister beside them, his arms folded across his chest.

"Where are the servants?" Jillian asked, resorting to the mundane, fighting down the panic beating in her breast.

"I've dismissed them for the day," he said coldly.

"Are you going somewhere?"

"No, but you are," he said.

"You will not banish her to Bassett House," Damien said.

"I'm not banishing her. Jillian may go wherever she wishes as long as it is away from me."

The words ripped through her, drawing blood. "Please give me a chance to explain," she said, knowing there was only one place to begin. "I love you, Max."

"Really?" he said, his voice impassive. "How inconvenient."

She straightened her spine, refusing to give in to the pain of his indifference. "I will not leave," she said stubbornly. "You are my family, my home."

"Damien is your family. I am merely your husband and I don't want you—at least not for a few months."

Jillian felt an instant of relief, yet it was short-lived as he unfolded his arms and clasped his hands behind his back. "I require some time away from you before we can get on with the tedious business of breeding an heir for Bassett."

Damien shifted behind her. She brought her hand out to her side and presented it to her brother palm out, a signal for him to keep his silence. Thankfully, he complied.

"Of course, that may not be necessary," Max continued. "If you are fortunate, you are already with child and if you are very fortunate, you will give birth to a son."

"And if *fortune* is not with me on either count?" she asked, struggling to match his calm.

"Then, I'll expect you to return to Bassett House and do your duty as my wife. After you conceive, you may return to Westbrook Court and the bosom of your family, or you may establish your own residence. I care not which," he said, giving an indifferent shrug. "Of course, the process will continue until you bear me a son."

She understood that he was lashing out, intent on punishing her. She could endure anything as long as he did not banish her from his life completely. And it was clear he was not going to do that. "All right," she said softly.

His lips thinned at her acquiescence. "It is gratifying to see that you understand your position."

"No," Damien grated. "You will not use her as breeding stock. Divorce her and leave her in peace."

"I can hardly believe you would suggest such a radical solution, Damien, considering Jillian's extraordinary efforts to accomplish this marriage. Not to mention our efforts on her behalf to restore her sullied reputation. Aside from that, I will not have my private affairs bandied about Parliament." He pulled on his gloves with a casual air. "No. Divorce is not the answer. I own her body and soul."

"Don't forget my heart, Max. You own that, too," Jillian said, not knowing how else to reach him.

He approached her and coldly stared down at her. "If you are here when I return, Jillian, I will have you forcibly removed." He paused at the front door. "Send me a note if you find you are with child," he said without looking back, then stepped out closing the door behind him.

She buried her face in her hands, shattered like a piece of crystal hurled against a stone wall.

"You have to divorce him," Damien said as he led her into the drawing room. "Living with the stigma will not be easy, but at least you'll be able to live."

"What if I am with child, Damien?"

"You're not," he said fiercely as if voicing it made it so.

She shook her head, forcing herself to move beyond the pain until there was nothing left to feel but her love for Max and her determination to make him believe it, trust it, accept it. "There will be no divorce."

Damien untied her cloak and slipped it off her shoulders. "You can't mean to accept his terms, Jillie."

"I expected worse," she said as she sank into a chair.

"What could possibly be worse?"

"Divorce," she said wryly. "A complete loss of hope."

"Weren't you listening to him, Jillie?" Damien said as he poured two glasses of sherry from the cabinet and handed one to her. "I have seen him angry before, but not so much so that he could not show it. I have seen his indifference before, but not delivered so cruelly."

Doubts clawed at her from the inside at Damien's words, yet she could not, would not, allow herself to surrender to them. "Imagine yourself in his place, Damien. Not only has he my treachery to deal with, but Bruce's as well."

"That is precisely what I am doing, Jillian. There are some things a man does not forgive and Max is more unforgiving than most. If you remain married to him, your life will be hell." Damien raked his fingers through his hair. "You're not thinking clearly right now. We'll go home to Westbrook Court in the morning and after a few weeks, you'll begin to see that I'm right."

Jillian made no reply. Damien was partially correct.

She wasn't thinking clearly. In fact, she could hardly think at all. As far as returning to Westbrook Court, she had yet to decide on that. She took a sip of sherry and smiled sadly up at her brother. "I betrayed you, too, Damien, yet you still love me. I think that, knowing what you do about my feelings for Max, you have even forgiven me."

"I'm your brother. No doubt I have disappointed you, too, from time to time."

Disappointed. It hurt her almost as much as watching Max walk away to know she had disappointed her brother. But Damien was here, and in time, the wounds she'd inflicted on her brother and herself would heal. "Once or twice you have, in very small ways," she admitted. "But don't you see, Damien? We know what it is like to be part of a family, to love one another enough to forgive thoughtless actions, to understand why they were committed in the first place. Where would Max have gained such knowledge? From stiff old Burleigh? Or from a father who valued him less than a roomfull of empty suits of armor?" She rolled the small glass between her hands and stared at the swirl of amber liquid.

"It's too late, Jillie," Damien said roughly. "Max is what his father made of him. I was there, remember? I watched it happen."

"That's just it, Damien. You understand him and so do I. Max is a warm and loving man. He just doesn't realize it. Who will prove to him that he can trust love if I don't?"

Damien finished his drink and poured another. "How? Look how easily Max accepted my condemnation of him? If he were a different sort, we might have come to terms in time, but . . ." his voice trailed off as he stared at the mantel.

"Do you want to come to terms with him?" Jillian asked softly.

With a grim smile, Damien set down his half-full glass of sherry. "That depends on how he comes to

terms with you," he said and walked to the door. "I will
call my footmen to carry your trunks to the coach. Is
there anything you need to do before I take you home?"

She shook her head and watched him disappear into
the entry hall. She didn't know what to do or how. All
she did know for certain was that she had to talk to
Bruce. She had always felt they were kindred spirits,
but now she knew it went far deeper than that. From
the first, she had instinctively trusted Bruce and now
she knew why. She'd thought before that he and Max
were a great deal alike. Now she understood just how
many traits they had in common.

The tradition of Forbes and Hastings joining together
in a common cause had never really ended after all.
Blood did tell. She and Bruce had been destined to become allies because their battle had been the same all
along. They both were fighting for a place in Max's
life.

She couldn't imagine that Bruce intended to abandon
Max any more than she did.

What a fine mess, Bruce thought as he sprawled on
the sofa with a cold compress covering his forehead
and eyes, and another over a particularly nasty bruise
on his shoulder. He had a clear memory of falling on it
when Damien had knocked him down. Gingerly, he ran
his fingers across his bared chest and probed his ribs.
They were sore, not from any blows inflicted but from
the pressure of Damien's knees boring into them.

He was rather ashamed of himself for allowing
Damien to take him by surprise the way he had. But
who could have foreseen Damien charging him like an
enraged bull? And then to have Kathy adding to
Damien's weight on top of him ... If Jillian and Max
hadn't arrived no doubt Kathy would have had to pour
him into a glass by the time Damien finished beating
him to a pulp. At least he could be grateful that Max
hadn't started in on him or there wouldn't have been
enough left of him to pour into a thimble.

It was still hard for Bruce to comprehend that everything had blown up in his face like a misfired cannon.

Damn and bloody damn. Why did Damien and Max both have to be such hot-headed asses? Kathy would have never blurted out the truth if they hadn't terrified the life out of her. It boggled his mind that after all these years, Max had learned of that carefully guarded secret in the same moment Jillian had blurted out her confession of guilt. But of course, like Kathy, Jillian had believed she'd been saving him from certain death. Bruce would be eternally grateful to the fates that he would not have the opportunity to prove her right.

It was laughably ironic that just last night at the club, Bruce had tried to tell Max the truth. Yet, Max hadn't wanted to talk about the duke and Bruce's mother. His statement that they were dead and so was everything between them had stopped Bruce cold. If only he had made Max listen to him, perhaps things might have gone differently this afternoon. How exactly, Bruce wasn't sure, but at least Max wouldn't have been barraged by so many truths at once.

If nothing else, the events of the afternoon had proven Bruce's theory that too much truth could indeed be dangerous.

The clock on the mantel chimed the midnight hour. Briefly, he considered retiring and sleeping away the throbbing pain in his head and limbs, yet, he had a feeling that Jillian would come and he wanted to know what had happened between her and Max. He'd seen the look that had passed over Max's face when Jillian had confessed all. The man had been destroyed. If he'd had any lingering doubts about Max's feelings for Jillian, he didn't any longer.

Max had been brought to his knees by love.

And that was one tidbit of information Bruce was bloody well going to keep to himself. Jillian would be downright dangerous if she knew just how much power she had over her husband.

Exhaustion insistently pulled at him and he closed

his eyes, letting it take him, trusting that he would hear Jillian's knock when it came.

Bruce felt as if he'd been poked in the eye with a stick, as he jerked awake and realized he had thrown his arm across his forehead inadvertently striking the goose egg that had formed around his eye.

Painfully, he raised himself and peered around the room. It glowed orange with the first rays of morning sunlight streaming in through the windows.

Where was Jillian? Surely, she hadn't attempted to come here on foot again and been accosted on the way. He'd just taken for granted that after the last time, she'd have the good sense to come in a carriage. Yet, now that his thinking wasn't quite so hazed, he realized that might be a bit of a problem for her. There was, after all, a difference between an unmarried lady sneaking out of the house in the middle of the night and a married lady with a furious husband doing the same. Still, Jillian was resourceful. She would manage.

The thought had no sooner formed when a soft rap sounded on the front door.

He swung his feet to the floor and with sore muscles screaming, he reached for his shirt lying across the arm of the sofa. Just because he felt as if he'd been run over by a carriage didn't mean he could receive Jillian half-dressed.

Still buttoning his shirt, he answered the door.

Just as she had a few months ago, she stood on his doorstep with the hood of her cape drawn about her face. Yet, unlike the last time, she was not panting with fear. There was a resolute calm about her and in the dim morning light, Bruce could see dark smudges beneath her eyes that bespoke of a sleepless night.

He glanced out beyond her and saw a carriage parked at the curb, the Westbrook rather than Bassett coat of arms clearly visible on the door. A bad sign. Apparently, a furious husband would not be a threat to this meeting.

"Come in," he said, ushering her in with a wave of his hand.

Without comment she complied, following Bruce down the short hallway to the same sitting room where they'd planned her ruin. It all had a very strange feel to it as they both chose the same seats they'd taken months ago.

"I'm so sorry," Jillian said without preamble, as her gaze swept over him from head to toe.

Bruce smiled, then grimaced in pain. He knew how he looked with his blackened and swollen eye, not to mention his fat lip and bruised cheek. "Don't be. I'm not. My only regret is that we were found out."

"And you paid the price, physically and at the cost of your own secrets."

Bruce glanced away. Leave it to Jillian to boldly jump right in to a subject. He had never talked about his parentage with anyone save Kathy and his mother and he didn't know where to start. The beginning seemed a good place. "My mother was the late duke's mistress," he said.

"I know," Jillian said softly. "Max told me the other night after he saw you at the club."

That both shocked and pleased Bruce at the same time. He doubted Max had ever spoken of it to another living soul. It reinforced his feeling that Max's marriage to Jillian had been a good thing. He winced at the past tense of his thought. "I suppose you want to know the rest of the story," Bruce said.

"No, actually I don't. Max is the one who needs to hear it. I'm sure you had your reasons for keeping it from him."

Did he? Bruce wondered. In retrospect he couldn't come up with a single reason that had any merit. "Explaining to Max is going to be rather difficult when you consider his parting words: 'I expect that you will keep yourself and your sister well away from me,' " he quoted.

"I know," Jillian said. "We are both caught in the same coil."

"I suspected as much, since you arrived in Damien's carriage."

Jillian sighed and nodded her head wearily. "Tomorrow I return to Westbrook Court with Damien. I am to remain there until I know whether or not I am with child." A sudden shudder wracked her body and she blinked her eyes rapidly. "If not, I am to send him a note and when he can stand the sight of me again—" She broke off her words, visibly battling back the emotion that threatened to overwhelm her.

Bruce fished his handkerchief from his pocket and pressed it in her hands, expecting her to burst into tears at any moment.

Yet, she simply lowered her gaze and twisted the square of white linen until her knuckles turned white. "Except for what contact is necessary to produce an heir for Bassett we are to live separate lives."

He wished he could assure her that Max was only venting his anger, that he would never be so coldblooded. But, unfortunately, he couldn't. Given the same set of circumstances, Bruce would probably do the same thing, or something equally harsh. Once bitten, twice shy and all that. "And are you agreeable to that arrangement?" Bruce asked.

Jillian leaned back against the sofa. "I have no choice but to go along with it until he is willing to listen to me."

As always her determination astounded Bruce. But this time, it would do her no good. Even he knew when to quit. A Hastings tended to take betrayal rather hard, particularly from friends and lovers. "You understand, Jillian, that he may never forgive you," he warned gently.

"I don't intend to ask him to forgive me. I would have to feel some regret in order to do that and I have none."

"What is it you seek then?"

"Clemency," she said, lifting her gaze to Bruce. "And eventually, absolution. I don't believe either you or I deserve anything less." She rose suddenly and paced the floor, like a barrister presenting a case. "We are both guilty of betraying him and manipulating him—"

"In other words," Bruce interjected, "we exercised bad judgment for the best of reasons."

"Yes," she agreed. "We are guilty of caring about him, of wanting him to be happy."

"And was he happy?" Bruce asked.

She clasped her hands in front of her. "Yes. I know he was," she said softly, tears springing to her eyes, but once again, she forced them away.

"Go ahead and wail, Jillian. God, knows you have ample cause."

She shook her head. "I cannot. Tears would mean a loss of hope, a sign that I have given up."

The skin on the back of Bruce's neck prickled as he realized that with one coldly delivered edict from Max that afternoon, he had given up. For the better part of ten years Max had been an important part of his life. Yet now that the truth was known, he was allowing Max to call the shots in a bloodless duel of wills.

Whatever was the matter with him? Perhaps Damien's blows to his head had concussed his brain.

Jillian's chin stopped trembling as she met his gaze. "I will never give up, Bruce. I won't allow Max to turn his back on me, or you and Kathy. We are his family, whether he is willing to admit it or not." She returned to the sofa and collected her cloak. "I had best return. I wanted to see how you were faring before I left for Westbrook."

Bruce rose and escorted her to the door, his mind twisting and turning down devious pathways. He had to make Max listen to him, to make him understand why Bruce had kept the secret of his birth from him.

As they reached the door, Bruce leaned down and bussed Jillian's cheek. "Good luck," he said. "One day, he will have to listen, even if I have to tie him to a chair and force him."

Smiling weakly, she stepped outside and walked straight to the carriage without looking back.

Again, the hair on the back of Bruce's neck stood on end. *Tying Max to a chair.* A drastic measure to be sure, yet entirely reasonable when Bruce considered with whom he was dealing. But did he dare literally lash Max down and force him to listen?

Of course he did. Because if he didn't, Max would close himself off to the point where he would make their late father look like a right dandy social butterfly by comparison.

He was already doing it.

Of course the trick would be in getting Max to come to him. That shouldn't be difficult. All Bruce needed was a plan and he had ample time to formulate one. It would be at least a month before he was back in fighting trim. Strolling back into the house, Bruce whistled a soundless tune and wondered if Smithy would be adverse to sitting on a duke.

Chapter 33

All was as it should be. Max's life was again well-ordered, controlled.

Finally, Jillian had listened to him. Finally, she was gone from his life. He was again free to live as he wished, conducting business and reading from the stack of books he hadn't gotten around to, refusing callers and declining the invitations that still trickled in after the close of the Season.

He'd had two blessed weeks of peace as he remained

sequestered in his London town house, accomplishing more work than he had in the last year, increasing his fortune by adding to his fleet of merchant ships and investing in the proposed progress of England. He hadn't even sent for his secretary, preferring to keep busy by doing the work himself.

Today, he'd wished he had been less driven and more sensible. If his secretary were here, Max would have ordered him to open the note from Jillian and discard it. But Max had been alone when the letter had come in the midst of account statements from tailor, butcher and baker. He'd opened it and read it and tossed it aside, feeling nothing, and telling himself that he never would. And then throughout the day, his attention had returned with unsettling regularity to the parchment laying on the far corner of his desk.

Jillian had not conceived.

He would not recognize his feeling of relief and chose to call it disappointment.

He would have to see Jillian again, touch her again, forget her again.

It had been so simple at first, to wipe Jillian from his thoughts, to convince himself that she no longer held a significant place in his life. But the communication from her had been the same as if she had barged into the room and would not be evicted without a fight.

That night he ordered Ripley to play a game of chess with him. The man gave an impressive accounting of himself though he sat on the very edge of his seat and pondered each move as if it might be the last thing he ever did. It amused Max to wonder if his butler contemplated whether he should play to win or to lose.

It was the kind of thing Bruce would do.

Impatient at having such an intrusive thought, he put Ripley out of his misery with a checkmate and sent him on his way. Picking up yet another book, he settled in a chair and stared at the page without absorbing a single word.

The next two weeks were more of the same. Max

worked harder and read faster though he could not remember a single word in the books he'd stacked on the table. He could, however remember every word his oh-so-obedient wife had written to him in the notes he had received every three days, each carrying the same scent she'd worn the night they had touched the sky.

His whole damned study smelled of jonquils.

He began to look forward to the daytime hours when the servants filled the air with the aromas of soap and polish and cooking food and the sounds of activity distracted his thoughts from Jillian. He had learned to dread the moment when he would find himself alone above stairs, listening to the back door open and shut as the day help left to join family and friends, the muted conversations of the live-in servants as they retired into their own world of familiarity and ease.

Prowling around from library to his bedchamber and back to his study again, Max contemplated going to his club for a game of whist with whatever hangers-on he might find still residing in the city—anything to blot Jillian's latest missive from his mind. But fog enshrouded the city, and even the most obedient of coachmen would think twice about venturing beyond his quarters on a night that concealed friend and foe alike.

The hour was yet early and all he had left to read were the Greek philosophers and Shakespeare. He turned his back on them all, wanting nothing to do with deep thought or the Bard's notions of love, misguided or otherwise.

He sprawled in a chair by the fire and stared at the note he'd received from Jillian earlier in the day.

Max,
Since I have not received any response, I can only assume that my previous missives to you were lost. There is no child. Shall we try again?

Love, your dutiful wife, Jillian

Had she no pride? he wondered as he crumpled the note and tossed it into the fireplace. It was incomprehensible that Jillian would continue her efforts to tempt him back to her with her body. His gaze returned to the fire blazing in the gate as the scent of melting wax drifted through the air. She still used great gobs of the stuff.

Max gave in to his temper and slammed his fist down on the table by his chair as he thought of the Bassett coat of arms blatantly emblazoned in the red wax she used to seal the correspondence. Evidently, she had absconded with one of his seals and felt no compunction in using it freely. As freely as she had played with his life, treating it as if it were one of her damned "pretend" stories.

No wonder he'd been frightened of her since the day she was born. Shutting her out of his life was like trying to stop a tidal wave.

A coach rumbled by and the clop of hooves on cobblestones sounded like cannon shot. The shout of a brave—or foolish—driver seemed more like the cacophony of a mob. And then nothing but dying echoes remained in the fog-shrouded streets as the city seemed to give a final sigh and close its many eyes in sleep.

Suddenly he felt smothered in his own solitude.

Lunging from the chair, he hauled a thick volume of plays from the shelf. Perhaps Shakespeare was what he needed after all. A good dose of *Othello* or *Hamlet* ought to remind him of the devastations of female treachery.

He rubbed his hand down his face and swallowed convulsively. He'd never been able to think of Jillian as he did other women. Even now, his own mind played him false, refusing to acknowledge her perfidy as a crime against the trust he'd always given her. And when he dared to close his eyes in weariness, his dreams presented her to him as the embodiment of all that was both innocent and carnal, her body nude and open to him, her hands outstretched to him as her eyes reflected his image in their depths. And as he forced himself to think of her with cold resolve and bitter detachment, his heart and his body remembered her fondly and often painfully.

"Bloody damn," he muttered and poured himself a snifter of brandy.

Separated from the rest of humanity by a wall of fog and silence, he stared at the ceiling—the only thing in his world that did not resurrect memories of Jillian—and with enough brandy and enough determination, he fell asleep in the chair, the note a pathetic little pile of ash smoldering in the grate.

Max jerked awake at the sound of a firm knock on the closed door of his study. Blinking away the grogginess brought by spirits and tormented dreams, he peered at the part in the drapes, and winced at the thin wedge of morning light streaming in. The clock chimed seven.

"Enter," Max called out, ready to deliver a stinging set-down to Ripley. He had left explicit orders that he was to be left alone unless he ordered otherwise.

The door opened and Ripley stepped in, but before the butler could say a word, Smithy sidled past him and stumbled into the room, then tripped and fell on one knee.

Max shot to his feet, intent on personally pitching Bruce's man out on his ear. He'd thought that Bruce of all people would have the good sense to leave him alone. "What are you doing here, Smithy?" he demanded as he waved the butler out of the room. "If Bruce sent you, you may tell him to go to hell."

Still poised on one knee, Smithy removed his hat. "Lady Kathy sent me," he said and struggled to his feet. "His lordship don't even know what world he's in. Talkin' out of his head with fever, he is."

"Inform Lady Kathy that I regret her brother has taken ill," Max said, shoving down an instant pang of concern. "But there is nothing I can do."

The burly servant twisted his hat in his hands, and his face crumpled as tears gushed down his weathered cheeks. "He's dyin', your Grace. Doctor says it's in his lungs."

Max's breath seemed to solidify in his throat as a moment of black fright swept over him. He wasn't even aware that he had moved until he was standing directly in front of Smithy. Inhaling deeply, he caught a whiff of something coming from Smithy's coat—something so pungent it made his eyes burn .... something like a particularly strong onion. "You lie," he said convinced by Smithy's onion tears that Bruce was in no danger of succumbing to a common fever.

Narrowing his eyes, Max studied the man kneeling before him. After the scene in Bruce's drawing room, why on earth would Kathy or Bruce send for him? Why would either one of them believe he would actually pay attention to such a summons? "What is this about, Smithy?" he asked.

Smithy glanced up at him, then his gaze skittered away as he shook his head and shoved his hat down on his bushy hair. "I gotta get back," he sniffed and wiped his coat sleeve across his eyes. "Lady Kathy needs me. She's near out of her mind." With his shoulders slumped, Smithy trudged from the room.

All in all a good performance, Max mused. It might even have worked if he hadn't smelled the onion. He wouldn't be at all surprised to learn that Smithy had been an accomplice in Bruce's and Jillian's plot to trick him to the altar.

What, Max wondered, was Bruce plotting now?

Whatever it was, Max decided that this time, he would not be the last to know.

"Ripley," he shouted as he climbed the stairs and strode to his dressing room. "Summon my valet and have my coach brought around in precisely thirty minutes."

Dressed in stark black and white, the kind of garb he might wear to intimidate the House of Lords, he strode

out of the house and paced about on the front step, irritated that the coach had not yet appeared. As he'd
washed and allowed his valet to give him a quick
shave, he'd become more and more convinced that
Bruce was up to his usual mischief, and that he was the
intended victim.

If being the butt of malicious pranks was part of being a brother, Max wanted no part of it. He ground to
an abrupt halt. *He had a brother.* It was a concept he'd
studiously avoided for over a month. But once said,
even in his mind, it could not be called back. *He had
a brother* . . . one whom he'd respected and trusted as
a friend for over ten years. A brother whose manipulations had taken from Max all that had value in his life.

The coach rolled up and he absently climbed in, too
preoccupied with his thoughts to berate the coachman
for his tardiness.

What had Bruce meant to accomplish in keeping his
silence? he wondered as he sat by the window and
propped his chin on his fist. Had it amused him? Was
it a subtle means of revenge on the Hastings name?
A lesser man would have been shouting it from the
rooftops in hopes of extorting hush money.

But everything he knew of Bruce negated such suspicions. The realization was both harsh and disappoint-
ing. Max did not want to remember how Bruce's pranks
always seemed to benefit someone—usually the victim.
Like the poor sod who had finally taken to bathing reg-
ularly and therefore had made at least one friend that
Max knew of after Bruce had set him up in the billiards
room at Oxford. Max had even congratulated Bruce on
his methods.

Not once that Max could recall had Bruce deliberately set out to injure another person in any way,
though he suspected Bruce could be a nasty piece of
work if he or a member of his family were being hurt
or threatened.

His family. Surely Bruce was not so caught up in the

idea of blood ties that he thought Max needed his interference in his life.

Yet, like it or not, he and Bruce were related.

He had a brother and a sister.

A brother whose intentions, Max knew, were usually
good though he always seemed to find a way to carry
them out and have a bit of fun at the same time.

With a snort of disgust at such magnanimous notions,
Max realized that the coach was rolling to a stop and a
footman had already jumped down from his place at the
rear and was reaching for the door.

Whatever Bruce's motives for his manipulations in
setting Jillian up for certain ruin and now for sending
Smithy to weep at his feet, it had to stop. Max could
and would manage his own affairs without any help
from shirttail relatives.

Determined to set Bruce straight once and for all,
Max left his coach and strode to Bruce's door, rapping
the knocker with more force than was necessary.

"Praise God, you came, your Grace," Smithy said as
he opened the door to Bruce's townhouse, shaking his
head mournfully. "His lordship's just barely hangin'
on."

Max barely held on to his composure, caught between wanting to berate the man's histrionics and give
in to the smile twitching at his lips.

Smithy was brilliant, although a shade too melodra-
matic. Max was tempted to play the thing out to the
end, just to see what outrageousness Bruce had up his
sleeve. But, although he was feeling extremely benevo-
lent under the circumstances, he wasn't quite up to enduring one of Bruce's farces—at least not one
controlled by Bruce.

"Good," Max said, a forced edge to his voice. "It
will save me the trouble of smothering him with a pillow."

Smithy's brow furrowed in surprise at Max's harshness, but he quickly recovered and schooled his features

into a sorrowful mask. "If you'll follow me, your Grace, I'll show you to his sickbed."

It was obvious Bruce wanted Max upstairs. It was the last place Max was going. The game had gone on long enough. "Tell Lord Channing I'll wait for him in the drawing room," he said.

Smithy's mouth dropped open. He shifted on his feet and glanced warily up the staircase.

"Go on," Max prompted, with a wave of his hand. "I'll show myself in." Without looking back, he left Smithy standing at the foot of the stairs and crossed to the drawing room.

A sharp gasp filled the room as he opened the door and sauntered in. Kathy sat in a large, overstuffed chair in a corner, her body perfectly still, her hand splayed over her heart and her blue-eyed gaze wide and wary.

Max stared back at her, unaccountably fascinated by the girl he had seen only twice before—once at their father's funeral and then in this very room just over a month ago. But, he had never really looked at her. Now he couldn't seem to stop, his gaze riveted by a face that was a feminine version of his own from cheekbones to nose to chin. She even had his eyebrows, and her eyes were the same shade of blue as his. He should have noticed such startling similarities. Why hadn't he?

Of course she'd been heavily veiled at the cathedral, and a month ago he had been interested in putting this house and everyone in it behind him.

He stepped a little closer to her, studying the mass of fiery curls that hung to her waist and clear, almost translucent skin—both obvious legacies from her mother.

Suddenly, he felt the same sense of recognition he'd experienced at ten when he'd seen the resemblances—and the differences—between Jillian and Damien ... yet they were more intense now, more personal. He had never thought to see bits and pieces of himself on the face of another, a likeness born of blood.

And he stepped closer still, seeing in her a mixture of

sweetness and wisdom that hurt him somehow. She'd called herself a bastard that day a month ago, and he thought she was too young to be so old, too innocent to be so resigned to the ugliness of life.

He didn't think about what he was doing, didn't try to keep up his guard with her, but for once in his life, he followed the instincts that were screaming inside him for expression. Just this once, he gave in to the dictates of his heart and held out his hands to her. "Hello, little sister," he said softly.

Kathy smiled, and it was brilliant and beautiful. In that moment, he acknowledged that he did indeed have a heart and a part of it would belong to her.

She accepted his grasp and rose from the chair, and as her arms wrapped around his neck, Max understood at last how Damien felt about Jillian. There was nothing quite like holding a sister in your arms.

Chapter 34

I'm relieved to see that I won't be forced to tie you in a chair," Bruce said from the doorway.

Max and Kathy broke apart as Bruce ambled into the room. Of course, Max thought wryly, Bruce looked healthy and vigorous.

"I cannot believe you contemplated such a thing," Kathy huffed.

"Did you really?" Max asked, even though he knew without doubt that it was precisely what Bruce had intended.

"Whatever was necessary to make you listen," Bruce

said. "I gather by your presence here that you *are* willing to listen."

"I can't imagine what else there is to know," Max replied, but even as he spoke, a torrent of questions came to mind. All these years, he and Bruce had shared so many experiences. They had lived parallel lives and Bruce had known the truth while Max had existed in ignorance.

"Come now, Max," Bruce admonished with a click of his tongue. "That you're here at all proves you're still human enough to be curious. Why not ask your questions? The truth might crack open your thick skull and let in a little light."

"Very well." Max strolled to the window and propped his shoulder against the sill, needing suddenly the detachment of standing apart from Bruce and Kathy. "Our late father was a shrewd man, but the mind boggles in wondering how he managed to pass you off as the heir of the Earl of Blackwood," he said, going straight to the heart of the matter.

Bruce sighed. "Anything can be purchased," he said. "Even birthrights for illegitimate issue. All that is required is a young, destitute nobleman who is willing to sell his soul."

It was hard for Max to imagine his father going to all that bother. "Why did my father not simply procure your mother a house and set her up as his—" he broke off and clamped his mouth shut, uncomfortable discussing such a subject in Kathy's presence.

"Leave us for a while, Kathy," Bruce ordered softly.

"Why?" she asked. "Because neither of you wish to say the word 'mistress' in front of me? I understand such things, you know."

"Then you won't miss a thing," Bruce said. "Run along, now."

Kathy opened her mouth with an obvious argument, then shut it again and flounced toward the door, muttering under her breath about men and their silly inhibitions.

"I think," Bruce said as she left the room and shut the door behind her, "that I will take advantage of your bemusement with our sister and tell you a story."

Frowning, Max sat in the chair Kathy had vacated. *Bemusement?* He supposed he was rather dazed. That didn't mean he would allow Bruce to think he had the upper hand. "I trust you will keep it short," he said mildly.

Again Bruce sighed as he swiped a hand over the back of his neck. "As you know, the duke's marriage to your mother was arranged," Bruce said.

Max nodded, although he didn't know any such thing. The circumstances of his parents' marriage wasn't a matter to which he'd given any thought. Now that it had been pointed out to him, he wasn't surprised.

Bruce sprawled in a chair. "As with all such marriages, the duke felt in no way bound by his vows. Shortly thereafter, he was introduced to my mother, a young lady of high birth and reduced circumstances." He gave Max a challenging look. "According to my mother, it was love at first sight."

"Was it?" Max asked, remembering Jillian's suggestion that it was possible that the duke had loved Bruce's mother.

One side of Bruce's mouth lifted in a cynical smile. "What do you think?"

"Perhaps for her," Max said bluntly. "Can you honestly believe that the duke was capable of loving anyone?"

"No, I can't," Bruce admitted. "Anyway, soon she was with child. To save herself from disgrace, my mother was fully prepared to wed herself to another titled and wealthy gentleman who claimed to care for her. She would not have her child born a bastard, and the duke wouldn't stand for the match she proposed."

"So, rather than lose control of her to another man, who just might command her loyalty, he purchased her a husband," Max said.

"Exactly so," Bruce said. "You better than anyone

know that no one touched what belonged to the duke. Mother belonged to him heart and soul and he was determined to keep her attentions for himself."

With that statement, everything became clear to Max. "He owned the earl," Max guessed. "He controlled him."

"Of course he did," Bruce said. "And in exchange for having his fortune restored, the earl gave my mother the protection of his name and agreed that he would ask nothing of her. *Nothing*, Max. She remained faithful to the duke until the day she died."

"But the earl eventually realized he'd made a bad bargain," Max said, remembering the gossip he'd first heard at university. The earl had left England to live abroad, and had not once returned to England since. "That still does not explain why you kept the truth from me all these years," Max added impatiently.

"It was my mother's wish," Bruce replied. "Keeping her secret seemed a small price to pay for the sacrifices she made to secure a place in the world for Kathy and me."

"And what were the duke's wishes on the subject?" Max asked.

"He never expressed any. It was as if you didn't exist."

"Just as you and Kathy did not exist in regard to me. Yet, you were always aware of your parentage," Max said, and the words were bitter on his tongue.

"No, actually I didn't know until I was seventeen." Bruce smiled grimly, his hands clenched into fists. "One day, in a fit of anger, the earl allowed the whole ugly truth to spill out." He rose from his chair and strode to the window, closing the distance between them. "So, there you have it—the unvarnished truth."

"Yes, I believe it is," Max said as he eyed Bruce's rigid posture.

Bruce folded his arms across his chest. "And now that I have satisfied your curiosity, I think it only fair that you answer my questions."

Max wanted to walk away, but he stood his ground. "I can't imagine what I could tell you that you don't already know," Max parried.

"I don't know how things are going along with Jillian."

"That is a subject best left unaddressed," Max said. He may be satisfied with Bruce's explanations concerning their relationship and his failure to reveal it sooner, but that didn't mean he was willing to discuss his private life with him. Bruce was too good at manipulating information for his own amusement. And he may have accepted Bruce as his brother, but he still harbored a good deal of resentment over his interference.

Folding his hands behind his back, Bruce rocked on his heels. "Then let's discuss my part in yet another fascinating tale."

That was precisely what Max did not wish to do. Perhaps in time he would be able to listen to why Bruce had agreed to participate in Jillian's mad scheme, but not now. Not when the mere mention of her name frayed the threads of his control. "I think not," he said.

"The day I saw her in that ridiculous court costume, I suspected she loved you," Bruce said, as if no objection had been voiced. "After her come-out, my suspicions were confirmed."

"She had a school-girl crush," Max bit out, and wondered why he was standing still for this. "End of story." He strode toward the door and opened it, intent on ending it once and for all.

"Smithy," Bruce called out and immediately the servant appeared in the threshold, barring Max's way as he snapped the double doors shut.

A moment later, Max heard the turn of a key, the click of a lock. He glared at the barrier and contemplated how effective his weight would be against the combined bulk of hard wood and Smithy.

"Sit down, Max," Bruce said softly, a spider to a fly.

"Or you will tie me down?" Max inquired as he struggled with his temper.

"If I must," Bruce said simply. "Just because you refuse to look at the trees does not mean the forest does not exist."

Forcing his fists to unclench, Max turned around and walked to the fireplace, thinking that if Bruce came within his reach he would surely toss him into the flames. Negligently, he picked up a porcelain figurine and weighed it in his hand. "Get on with it, then. And spare me your philosophical drivel."

"It isn't drivel," Bruce said as he again sprawled in a chair—this time the one set into a corner. "You're an intelligent man, Max. Surely you know that not everything in life can be ignored or walked away from. One wonders," he mused, "how you find the strength to avoid life so intensively."

Max wondered that himself as he abruptly set the figurine back in its place. "In the same way that you find the resources to try and outwit life," he said, meeting Bruce's gaze.

Bruce stared back at him with a weariness he'd never noticed before. "Yes, in exactly the same way." He arched his brows in a way Max recognized as ironic. "Would you care to wager on whether you outrun yourself before I outwit myself?"

The question struck Max, cracked him open, exposing him to a realization he'd been avoiding. He and Bruce were alike. Bruce understood him, knew him as no one else could. Only Bruce and Kathy knew what it was like to try and walk in their father's footsteps, trying to live up to his expectations, trying to live with the constant sense of being abandoned, and eventually trying to live beyond the duke's shadow. And in the process, they lived on the fringes of their own existences.

"You begin to see," Bruce said almost to himself.

"I fail to see what any of this has to do with Jillian," Max said, knowing only that if he retreated now he would never stop.

"Surely you saw Jillian's list of eligible bachelors," Bruce said.

Max nodded curtly.

"Haven't you guessed yet that it was your name she crossed out at the top of her list, along with a notation that said, 'Jillie loves Max'?" Bruce asked, yet it didn't sound like a question at all. "All that was missing was a heart drawn around the whole thing."

"A name she blacked out if you recall," Max said more to himself than to Bruce. He felt like an idiot when he recalled how furious he'd been about that list, and how he had interrogated Jillian about whose name she'd crossed out. It was like searching for one's hat only to discover it was on one's head.

"I was there when she did it," Bruce said with a grin. "It was really quite adorable."

"And quite schoolgirlish," Max said and decided to take a seat after all. If Bruce's obvious enjoyment of the situation were anything to go by, he was in for a long siege. "Very well, tell me the whole sordid story if you must."

"If I'm not mistaken," Bruce said, his grin stretching wider, "it was your actions that were sordid. I merely attempted to salvage what I could of the whole mess."

"Next you'll be telling me that your reasons were entirely altruistic."

"Actually, my reasons were entirely altruistic. I had the idiotic notion that you would be happy with Jillian."

"Idiotic indeed," Max said tightly.

"Oh for heaven's sake," Kathy said, bursting into the room. Smithy stood behind her and again closed them in. "Why are you being so bloody stubborn about this, Max? Jillian loves you."

"I am being realistic," Max replied, too nonplussed by Kathy's aggressive manner to rise.

Kathy leaned over him and pointed her finger in his face. "Don't you dare behave like our father. He never understood the sacrifices my mother made, because she loved him," she broke off and squeezed her eyes shut, tears seeping from the corners of her eyes. "She bore his bastards and lived a lie for nearly thirty years, because she loved him."

Max's gaze shot to Bruce for guidance. But, Bruce was staring at his sister with an expression of pain.

"She was a woman to be admired, Kathy," Max said, in an attempt to comfort this sister that he scarcely knew. "The sacrifices she made took more courage than most of us possess."

She opened her eyes and gazed at him sharply. "Then you should see that Jillian has made the same sacrifices for you. You should have the same admiration for her courage."

A spark of warmth flickered in Max's chest. He had always admired Jillian's courage and tenacity. He thought of the bombardment of letters he'd received and how tempted he'd been to go to her . . . until he realized that tenacity had turned to manipulation. Jillian knew he wanted her. How could she not? "It is hardly the same thing," he said, recapturing his anger against his wife, insulating himself against memories of her that haunted him with their sweetness and mocked a solitude that had long since grown sour.

"It is exactly the same thing," Kathy said with a little shake of her head. "I would have never been brave enough to run through the streets of London in the middle of the night to ask someone to deliberately ruin my reputation."

"What?" he said hoarsely as his blood turned to ice in his veins.

"You heard me," Kathy said, then turned her furious glare on Bruce. "Haven't you told him anything?"

Bruce shrugged. "Since you've obviously been listening at keyholes, you know that I haven't had the opportunity." He waved his hand in a real gesture. "Go right ahead and don't mind me. You're doing quite well on your own."

"Tell me. Now," Max said through teeth gritted in fear. He knew what was coming—knew it as well as he knew Jillian—and horrifying images blurred past his vision: of Jillian lying broken in an alley; of Jillian being run over by a coach; of Jillian lost in the city and at the mercy of those who prowled the night in search of plunder. He curled his fingers into his palms to hide the sudden tremble of his hands. "Tell me," he said rising to loom above Kathy, to stare at Bruce over the top of her head, hoping for a denial because he couldn't bear to think of Jillian wandering about the streets in the dead of night.

He could have lost her.

Bruce regarded him over steepled fingers. "Jillian crept out of her house, on foot and unescorted, and came to me for help. She was terrified by the time she reached my front door, yet she insisted on returning the same way lest we be found out. It wouldn't have done for her to be compromised by the wrong man—namely myself. And before you contemplate my immediate demise, I'll assure that you that I sent Smithy to see her safely home."

"Do you not see how much courage that took, Max?" Kathy said softly.

It was lunacy! Only the most dire emergency would send him or any other sensible man out into the middle of the night. That Bruce had duped him paled in comparison to the fear that was only now beginning to subside. Fear for Jillian. Fear of losing her. Fear of being truly alone in the world. If something had happened to her he would have been destroyed. Yet she had done it because of him. Because she loved him.

Oh God. She loved him more than her own life.

As he loved her.

It was that simple—as simple as the declaration "Jillie loves Max" scribbled at the top of her list.

And Max loved Jillie.

He loved Jillian.

Numb with the shock of such a soul-shaking revelation, Max slowly lowered himself back into the chair and slumped forward, his hands hanging between his outspread knees.

"She risked everything for you," Bruce said. "Damien's wrath, your wrath, her reputation, her life . . . hell, my life too. No price was too high." He nonchalantly examined his nails. "Though I fail to comprehend why she thought a numskull like you would be worth such drastic measures. I at least would have appreciated her devotion."

"Shut up, Bruce," Max said roughly.

"Don't turn your back on her, Max," Kathy said. "Don't do what our father did. Don't take such a gift for granted as he did." A tear slid from the corner of her eye.

Max reached up and thumbed it away. "There is no need to weep," he said.

"I can't help it, I'm not strong like Jillian. I cannot hold tears inside." She turned her head and blinked furiously. "Perhaps I have given up on her behalf," she whispered.

He stared at the glistening moisture on the tip of his thumb as confusion settled over him like last night's fog. "I don't understand."

"Kathy is referring to Jillian's last visit here on the morning before she left for Westbrook Court," Bruce explained. "I have never seen anyone struggle as hard as she to keep from weeping. It damned near moved me enough to get sloshy in the eyes."

"She said tears would be a sign that she had lost hope," Kathy added as she dropped to her knees in front of him and framed his face with her hands. "Max, do you want to defeat her as well as yourself?"

"Jillian won't be defeated," Bruce said. "But you will, Max, if you keep fighting yourself."

"You can't win that kind of battle, Max," Kathy said.

Blindly, Max pulled Kathy's hands away from his face and rose to walk to the door, staring at the carved wood as he heard Bruce call for Smithy to turn the key and let him out. And blindly, he left the house and found his way to his coach.

All he could think of as he slumped against the

squabs was that one night he had tasted hope in Jillian's arms as she'd listened to him, comforted him, asked nothing of him but to share himself with her. And later, when he'd made love to her, he'd known that nothing or no one but Jillian could fill the emptiness of his soul. Bruce and Kathy were right, he only knew how to fight against himself in a battle that could never be won. Only Jillian fought for him, with her heart as she withstood his cruel indifference, with her pride as she wrote letters to him telling him that she would come to him anytime, anywhere, and for any reasons he cared to hide behind, and she fought for him with her life in a desperate rush to seek help in the depths of night.

No, she would not be defeated. She was too stubborn.

He closed his eyes and thanked God that his Pandora held enough hope in her heart for both of them.

Chapter 35

Westbrook Court

Max stared up at the stone face of Westbrook Court as his coach rolled over the circular drive and halted in front of the broad portico lined with huge urns of flowers. Sunlight poured over the house, burnishing the stone a mellow gold, the late afternoon shadows reaching outward to embrace the gardens after a day of summer heat. All the windows were open with lace curtains fluttering in the breeze, and a melody drifted down from an upstairs balcony where a maid sang as she watered yet more flowers in a window box. In the distance, a group of gardeners laughed and bandied jokes back and forth.

Everywhere he looked, there was life in movement and light, harmony in color and laughter and song. There was welcome.

For so many years Max had come here for all that was missing from his own life, to find in Damien and later, Jillian, a vicarious sense of family and love. Max realized that he had come here to prove that no one had forgotten his existence.

Yet there had been times when Damien and Jillian had spoken to one another, played with one another in their world of family from which he'd stood apart, watching them, envying them and yearning to be a part of that world.

He'd always thought of Westbrook as his escape, his refuge, from a cold and empty life. But it wasn't the place at all. It was Damien, his friend, loyal even in his anger as he'd set aside his own grievances to support Max when Bruce and Kathy had revealed themselves. And it was Jillian, captivating him with her trust, loving him with her heart and soul, tempting him to believe that love was more than heartache and disappointment, that it gave more than it took, that it was as infinite as the sky. Whether it was true or not, he didn't know, nor did he care.

All he knew was that without Jillian, he wouldn't belong anywhere. Even Bassett House, with Jillian's touches of color and light and warmth, would only be a museum for memories of long-dead happiness without her. It could only be a home if Jillian were there to share it with him.

He descended from the coach and gazed upward at the standard flying from the coned roof of a tower, announcing that the Duke of Westbrook was in residence.

He would have to go through Damien to get to Jillian. He should have taken the time to plan how he would approach Damien and Jillian, what he would say to them. For the first time since he'd received Jillian's initial note, he acknowledged his fear that it might be too late, and he had indeed defeated himself by not trusting enough, by not believing enough, by not hoping enough.

A servant scrubbing the front steps glanced up at him as he approached. Her mouth dropped open and her eyes grew wide, then she quickly gathered her bucket and brush and scurried inside, slamming the door behind her.

Max released a weary sigh. It was a far cry from having a gap-toothed urchin hurl herself into his arms while her brother smiled indulgently from the threshold. He slid his hand into his jacket pocket and found a small jagged object he'd retrieved from his drawer with the whimsical notion that it might bring him luck. A silly notion really, to think of such a thing when it had been almost forgotten in his jewel box for over ten years, but it had seemed important to have a part of Jillian with him, to be able to touch it and know it was his. Rolling the small tooth between his fingers, he recalled how she had given it to him so he "would remember the day she touched the sky."

Shaking off the memories, Max released the memento in his pocket and climbed the steps two at a time.

As he raised his hand to knock, the door was wrenched open. Damien stood in the threshold, legs braced apart, his hands fisted at his sides. "What do you want?"

"My wife," Max said simply.

"Why?"

"Her place is at Bassett House."

Damien folded his arms and regarded Max with a narrow-eyed stare. "And where will you place her among all your relics, Max? Will you keep her on display in that made-over dressing room you gave her as a bedchamber? How often do you plan to dust her off and use her?"

Max opened his mouth and shut it again as pride held him upright and the familiar cold spread through him, around him, a pervasive chill that numbed and paralyzed him. An image of the room he'd had prepared for Jillian flashed before his eyes—a small cheerless chamber he'd given little thought to. Had it hurt Jillian so much that she would speak of it to her brother? No, he decided. More likely, Clancy had related the sleeping arrangements to Damien. Jillian did not complain, but rather rearranged things to suit herself, as she had rearranged the rooms of his suite, appropriating the sitting room as her bedchamber. He smiled grimly. He'd thought that having a sitting room would please her and reasoned that since all she did was sleep in her bedchamber she wouldn't mind having her bed consigned to little more than a closet.

He should have listened to Burleigh and moved to the master suite, but he couldn't bring himself to trade his own place in the house for that of his father. He hadn't wanted to take Jillian to the rooms where his mother had died.

But he would not make such explanations to Damien, would not defend his absurd superstitions nor his misguided attempts at thoughtfulness.

"Have you no answer, Max?" Damien asked, cutting into Max's thoughts.

"Where is she, Damien?"

"Under my protection," Damien said flatly. "Divorce proceedings will be initiated soon. Don't ever come near her again." He slammed the door with a crack that rang in Max's ears and raised a gust that ruffled his hair.

He stared at the door, feeling brittle with the cold inside him. *Divorce.* The word echoed in his ears like a dirge. But then he shook his head and walked stiffly down the steps, refusing to believe Jillian would divorce him. He knew Kathy had been right when she'd told him that Jillian did not cry because she would not allow herself to give up. Instead, she overwhelmed him with her tenacity, humbled him with her patience, shamed him with her faith in him.

He had to make sure she never had reason to cry.

He turned to look up at the house, searching the windows, wondering if Jillian might be behind one of them.

The upstairs maid had disappeared back into the house, her watering can left on the balcony. The gardeners had stopped their banter and cast wary glances at him over their shoulders as they walked toward the stables. Apparently, the servants as well as Jillian's family had rallied around her, and would no doubt attack him with rakes and shovels should he overstep. He thought of how his own servants tiptoed around him, how they scurried to do his bidding and escape his presence before he froze them with a look, shattered them with a word. It had been the same in his father's time.

His father . . . He had become as lifeless and emotionless as the man who had kept a mistress for nearly thirty years, taken her love and given her mere shavings of himself in return, then sold her children to another man for the convenience of his name.

It was a tradition among the Dukes of Bassett to stand apart, to look down on others from heights too lofty for mere mortals. And Max had been raised to honor tradition. At the rate he was going, it wouldn't be long before he, too, was as untouchable as the collection of relics Jillian had ordered moved to the cellars.

Jillian had tried to save him from being buried alive in tradition and pride. She'd made him want to save himself.

He continued to stare up at the house, wondering how to gain access. He had to get to her, yet he saw no way to do so short of throwing stones at her window like some lovesick fool. He stooped and picked up a nice round rock from the graveled drive. As he straightened and drew back his arm, he sensed that he was being watched and cursed his lunacy. Even lovesick fools had the wit to use caution.

He jerked his gaze to the right and then the left. LadyLou stared down at him from a second-story window, shaking her head as if warning him not to follow his present course of action.

"Please," he said, his voice cracking. "Where is she?"

LadyLou smiled and leaned out the window. "The gazebo," she said softly.

The gazebo. The place where his life had become irrevocably entwined with Jillian's . . . a fitting place to acknowledge that without Jillian he had no life.

Max skirted the side of the house, taking the path he'd walked hundreds of times before. As he followed the garden wall, it seemed only yesterday that Jillian had skipped around the corner and into his heart. Yet, as he tried to conjure an image of her as a seven-year-old, he found the memory so dim he could scarcely see the little girl she had been. All too vivid in his mind was the woman she had become, seeing life more clearly than he ever had, reaching for it, taking it in her hands and offering to share it with him.

Quickening his pace, he moved onward across the meticulously manicured lawns. He paused at the swing, and thought briefly of the little girl who had dropped into his arms. But, again, the memory blurred, replaced by the image of his wife, naked and seductive in the moonlight with her head thrown back as she flew to the stars and took him with her.

He strode away, and topped a small rise overlooking the gazebo. How bare it looked, its white latticework gleaming too brightly in the afternoon sun without ivy climbing its walls. Then he remembered it had only recently been rebuilt after the storm had destroyed it, and new foliage had been planted. He saw the small plants ruffled around the raised foundation of the structure, a few already clinging to the wood. At least the two tow-ering oaks still stood sentinel, their leaves casting dappled shadows on the faceted roof of the gazebo.

And through the strips of whitewashed wood he saw the contrast of Jillian's black hair being lifted and caressed by a gentle breeze. He drew closer, slowing his steps as he watched her with an ache in his throat, a pounding in his chest.

She sat on the cushioned seat with her feet curled beneath her, her head bent, an open book in her lap. Her porcelain face was pensive as she sat so still, staring down at her book yet not turning the pages. Only her gown was bright and lively, with its tiny red embroidered roses and claret sash that fell over the seat and seemed to waltz with the breeze. He inhaled, and wondered what scent she wore today.

Instinctively, he reached for the tooth in his pocket and drew it out, closing his hand around it as if it were the most powerful of talismans, feeling foolish for the gesture, yet he could not let go of that small part of her that had given him his first touch of warmth so many years ago.

He went to her, his footfalls heavy as he entered the gazebo.

She did not look up when his shadow fell across her, but merely pushed an errant lock behind her ear. "I am fine, Damien," she said absently, as the air ruffled the pages of her book and lifted her hair away from her face, revealing deep shadows over the delicate flesh beneath her eyes and skin that was too pale, almost translucent.

"You look weary, Pandora," he said softly.

Her breath caught and she looked up at him, her body unnaturally still as she watched him. "You have come for me," she said without inflection.

"Yes," he rasped harshly, struggling to control the rush of emotion caused by the mere sound of her voice, resorting to the mundane because he didn't know what else to say. "I thought you might like to take a nap in the white drawing room at Bas—at home."

With trembling hands she set the book aside. "I am ready," she said, her voice a bare whisper of sound.

Pressure built behind his eyes, a stinging, aching pressure that threatened to burst at her soft declaration. *I love you.* The words sat poised on the tip of his tongue but he didn't know how to form them. His mouth worked and he felt as if he were attempting to speak a foreign phrase for the first time. A phrase whose meaning was too great for mere words to express. A phrase he'd never had the occasion to utter before. A phrase that would destroy him if it were to be thrown back in his face.

"Get away from her!" Damien strode into the gazebo, his boot heels crashing loudly against the wooden floor. Before Max could reply, Damien drew back his fist and drove it into Max's midsection.

Max staggered back at the unexpected blow, and his breath whooshed out painfully, but he regained his balance and stood fast, his feet planted apart and his fists clenched at his sides as Damien landed another punch.

"Damn you, Max . . . *fight,*" Damien said fiercely.

"No," Max said, staring at Jillian—only Jillian— refusing to fold, locking his knees to keep them from buckling, tightening his mouth against the pain of his friend's anger.

Jillian stared back, her eyes glazed in shock, her body frozen with one hand covering her mouth in horror.

His head jerked back from another blow and blood trickled from his eye.

"So you do bleed," Damien said, his chest heaving. "You haven't completely turned to stone, yet." He drew back his fist and clipped Max on the jaw.

"Damien, stop," Jillian cried as she leaped from the seat and clawed at her brother.

Damien shook her off and she stumbled back against the cushions. Before Max could react, she reached frantically for her book and snatched it up, brought it down on Damien's head.

With a stunned expression, Damien turned to her and shook his head as if to clear it.

Max could only hold his position and watch her with blurred vision, waiting for his mind to clear, waiting for the anguish to recede.

"Touch him again and I will tear this place down and beat you with it," she said to Damien between deep gulps of air. "Is that what you did to Bruce?" she shouted. "Caught him off guard, never giving him a chance to defend himself? I never realized you fought dirty, Damien."

And as his surroundings came back into focus, the sight of Jillian and Damien glaring daggers at one another disturbed him. Bizarre though it was, the condemnation in her voice disturbed Max even more. He realized then that he could not—would not—come between brother and sister. "He's not fighting dirty, Jillian," he said in a voice that was surprisingly calm, almost removed from himself. "He is fighting to win."

She shook her head. "He attacked you without provocation."

Damien glared at her in stark disbelief. "His mere presence is provocation enough. You know why he is here."

"He is my husband. I belong with him. Why can you not accept that?"

"How can you accept that he wants you only as a brood mare?"

"It's a start," she said with a defiant glance at Max.

The simple statement, devoid of pride and brimming with hope, almost brought Max to his knees. And her defiance almost brought a smile to his lips. Never would she accept such a thing. She had merely been biding her time—was still biding her time—waiting for the opportunity to slip back into his life by hook or by crook. His Pandora could give Bruce lessons in the art of making a victim feel like a victor.

But Jillian was not his enemy and neither was Damien. He took a step forward, toward Damien, yet kept his gaze locked with Jillian's. "I would not use her so, Damien. I had hoped you would know that."

"How would I know that, Max? If nothing else you are a man of your word, and your words to Jillian in London were explicit."

"I would not use her so," Max repeated, having no other defense.

"Then why are you here, Max?" Jillian asked. Her brow furrowed and her lips parted as she held his gaze, her green eyes burning into him, questioning him, hope and dread playing across her features like clouds shifting in the sky.

I love you. The words screamed inside his mind and burned his tongue with their power. And with crystal clarity he realized that if he said the words, he would be giving himself over to her completely. He could not do that, not when he'd fought so hard to break his father's power over him. Not while the slightest doubt as to the endurance of love squirmed inside him. He loved her and he would show her every day in every way, but he could not say the words.

"You are my wife," he said, knowing the answer was inadequate, and he was responsible for the way her shoulders sagged with resignation and the animation left her face as if it required more energy than she could muster.

"If that is your only reason for being here, then it is not enough," Damien said as he gazed out over the lawns, his jaw clenched and his mouth tight.

"It is the only one I need," Max replied, feeling torn in half. He wanted desperately to end the scene and whisk Jillian away right then, yet he knew he owed Damien some assurance that he would not hurt her. "I have every right to take her from here. But, I vow on my honor, I won't." He swallowed convulsively. "Not without your blessing on our marriage," he said, trying to articulate his feelings to Jillian with his gaze.

A slow smile tipped the corners of her mouth and her green eyes softened. She took a step toward him and it seemed forever before she covered the distance separating them. As her arms wrapped around his neck, Max's chest felt as if it would burst. His hands tangled in the satin of her hair streaming down her back, and he squeezed his eyes shut as he buried his face in the crook of her neck, breathing deeply of her, drowning in her embrace and coming to life again with the touch of her breath on his cheek. She smelled of soap and Jillian, a scent as intoxicating as the feel of her body pressed against his. He couldn't seem to hold her tight enough, or long enough. He wanted to kiss her more than he wanted to breathe.

He eased her arms away from around his neck and pressed his lips to her fingers. "Let's go home, Pandora," he said.

"Yes," she replied softly.

He raised his head and straightened, sliding his hands down to lightly grip her waist as hers slipped beneath his coat to do the same. "I'll make her happy, Damien, and protect her as you always have."

"And who will protect her from you?" Damien asked as he bent to pick something up from the plank floor of the gazebo.

"Please, Damien, don't do this," Jillian said, pleadingly. "Max would never harm me. You must trust him."

"Trust him?" Damien said, his voice scoffing as he stared down at the object in his hand with thoughtful intensity. Then he pinned Max with a harsh uncompromising gaze. "A moment ago you vowed on your word of honor that you would not take her without my blessing. I do not recall giving it."

Max's stomach knotted as Jillian stiffened in his arms, her brow creased with apprehension.

A vow of honor. Fully aware that Max would never break his word, Damien had turned his promise against him. "Then do so," Max said, knowing it was a futile request. He had doomed himself with that vow.

Jillian's arms tightened at his waist.

For a long moment Damien stared at them with a stony expression, then gave an emphatic shake of his head. "It is for your own good, Jillian," he said. "Too much has happened. I cannot trust him with you."

"I trust him and that is enough, Damien," she said and buried her face against Max's chest, locking her hands at the back of his spine, pressing herself as close to him as she could. "I love you, Max. Take me home."

"I cannot, Pandora," he said, anguish twisting inside him as he grasped her shoulders, forcing her away from him. "I gave my word of honor."

"Honor? *Honor?*" she spat as she backed away, her gaze challenging. "Is it honor to toss me back and forth as if I were a coin to spend on a whim of the moment?" She rounded on her brother in a whirl of muslin and outrage. "Is it honor, Damien, to give me to Max as his wife, then deny me the right to keep *my* vows?"

Damien said nothing as he continued to contemplate the object he'd picked up and cupped in his palm.

"And you," she said fiercely as she turned on Max and pointed her finger at his chest. "Tell me if it is honorable to make such a promise to my brother without regard to my wishes." A single tear rolled down her cheek and a small whimper escaped her. Still, she continued to point her finger at him, her words tumbling out like pearls from a broken string. "You married me without asking my consent. I honored your wishes— and yours, Damien." Again, she faced her brother, her finger poking him in the chest. "I even honored the rules of your society and endured the insults and cuts of the ton."

"Enough, Jillie," Damien said harshly.

"No, it is bloody well not enough!" she gasped and her shoulders heaved as she turned back to Max, stumbling in her skirts, righting herself before he could reach for her, holding him at bay with the finger she poked at him like a cocked pistol. "I honored you by dishonoring myself. I gave myself to you with honor and g-g-good faith. I thought you t-t-took me in the same way." She swiped at the tears with the back of her hand as she stepped back and lowered her hand to her side.

They stood beneath the roof of the gazebo, points of a triangle, Max thought, separate yet connected by Damien's anger, Jillian's love and his own fear. Fear that chipped away his strength piece by piece, riddling his mind with holes until all he could do was look at Damien, knowing there was a silent plea in his eyes.

Damien stared back at him, expressionless, his body still, looking as if he were waiting ... waiting ...

A leaf fell from one of the oaks and drifted lazily on a pattern of air. A family of birds chirped from their nest. A cloud scudded past the sun.

Jillian glanced from one to the other and her body shuddered, her chin trembled. "There's no hope is there?" she said raggedly, her gaze blank as she stared straight ahead. "Damien will never relent. And you will never break your word." Another tear rolled from one eye, then another and another until they flowed in a silent endless stream—hope draining out of her like blood from a mortal wound. "It's funny isn't it?" she said on a fractured laugh. "My brother loves me too much and my husband not enough. But we all have our honor."

Stark terror shot through Max as her tears doubled, drenching her face.

She had given up on him, on herself, on them all. And in that moment of her defeat, an image crossed Max's mind of himself and Damien in the gazebo, listening to Jillian talk about Pandora as she sat between them, linking them together, showing him what it was like to belong, reminding him of what contentment was like, teaching him that happiness was built one moment at a time.

"Don't," he croaked as he lurched toward her. "No, Pandora, don't cry." He grasped her chin and tilted her face up, forcing her to look at him. "I love you," he whispered, then swallowed and found his voice. "I have always loved you."

"I know," she said, and the tears kept coming. She clutched his jacket and held onto him as she sobbed so hard, Max feared she would break into a million pieces. He bent his head and kissed her trembling mouth, and something splintered inside him at the salty tang of her tears on his lips—the taste of lost hope, the price she paid for his honor.

The cost was too high.

He gathered her closer, cradling her, rocking her back and forth as he glanced at Damien over her shoulder. "I am taking her home," he said quietly. "With or without your blessing."

With tears still flowing, Jillian made a sound that was somewhere between a sob of misery and a cry of joy as she raised her head and gave him a watery smile, a rainbow appearing in the midst of a storm.

Damien angled his head to one side and narrowed his gaze. "And what of your honor, Max?"

"If I must choose between my honor and Jillian, then I choose Jillian."

In less than a heartbeat, Damien relaxed his stance and smiled. "Then, you have my blessing."

The last barrier between them crumbled like a great stone wall and Max could think of nothing but lowering his mouth to hers and taking it in a fierce, possessive kiss. But Damien stood nearby, his hands shoved in his coat pockets as he cleared his throat. "I should be returning to the house," he said, his lips slanted in a melancholy smile. "I'm sure the two of you would like to be getting along home as well."

That was it? Max thought numbly. No anger or bitterness? No warnings or threats? He opened his mouth, then closed it. He glanced at Jillian, but she had turned her head to stare at her brother in open astonishment.

"I had to know that he loves you as much as you love him, Jillie," Damien said simply. "I had to know that he loved you enough to sacrifice as much as you have—pride, honor, family."

Max recognized the note in Damien's voice as resignation, recognized the way his friend stepped back toward the arched entrance of the gazebo in self-imposed isolation. Damien's melancholy smile struck an all too familiar chord in Max. It was the uncertainty of wondering if this good-bye was final or if there would be other times of sharing between them. He knew Damien was feeling like an interloper consigned to the fringes of other lives.

"He's falling, Max," Jillian whispered.

Max looked down at her, the last of his doubts melting in the light of the silent understanding between them. Simultaneously, they each released one arm from their hold on one another and held them out to Damien, inviting him to complete their circle—Hastings and Forbes guarding one another's backs in battle and catching one another when they fell.

Yet, still Damien held himself apart, reaching out only to display, between thumb and forefinger, the object he'd retrieved from the floor. "I think this belongs to you," he said, offering the small hollow tooth to Max.

Jillian gasped as she saw it, but said nothing.

Max dug into his pocket and found it empty, then remembered the tooth had been in his hand when Damien had delivered his first blow. He smiled and shook his head. "You keep it, Damien, a memento of the day you accepted me as your brother-in-law." He waited, cautiously hopeful for a favorable response, yet knowing it might not come.

With a chuckle, Damien tossed the tooth into the air and caught it, then dropped it into his pocket. "A poor trade, my friend, considering that you have my sister."

"No, Damien. You will always have your sister as I will always have my wife," Max said thickly, his last surrender to the truth, giving up his doubts and fears as he would a sword after battle.

A battle he had won.

"Finally," Jillian said happily. "We're a family again."

Damien came to them then, and locked arms with Max and Jillian. For a long moment they stood linked together with Jillian in the middle, releasing the past, embracing the future. "We always were family, Jillie," Damien said. "All we lacked was a blood tie."

"Not any longer," Jillian said softly. "The child I carry has Hastings and Forbes blood."

Max heard her, understood her, yet it took him a minute to fully comprehend her announcement. Somehow, he wasn't surprised. Jillian's scruples, he'd learned, were all too flexible where love was concerned. He glared down at her. "You lied."

"To both of us," Damien said.

"Of course I did," she said, smiling smugly. "It was either that or give up on both of you."

"Why didn't you?" Max asked.

"Because you're my husband and Damien is my brother. Because I love you both." She paused to look at one then the other. "Because we *are* a family."

Epilogue

Max stood with one foot hoisted over his bath as Jillian entered his bathing room, their ten-month-old son on her hip, naked as the day he'd been born and his face covered in strawberry jam.

"There you are," she said, dodging a sticky hand reaching for the sleeve of her immaculate gown. "You were supposed to have been home hours ago."

Home. He knew what that meant now. It meant sun-faded carpets and flowers in priceless vases. It meant feminine clutter scattered from one end of the house to the other. It meant freedom to make love in the swing on the terrace. It meant laughter in the kitchens and an occasional twitch of the lips from Burleigh.

"Have you nothing to say?" she said. "I've had the cook hold dinner so long it is probably ruined."

"It is all Damien's and Bruce's fault," Max said, feeling no remorse for blaming them. He lowered himself into the water. "They insisted on stopping at the Cock and Pussycat Inn for a glass or two."

The baby squirmed in her arms and jabbered incoherently as he held out his pudgy arms to Max.

Jillian promptly set him in the pocket between Max's upraised knees and stomach. "He needs a bath anyway," she explained as she knelt on the floor beside the tub. "So, it is Damien's and Bruce's fault is it?" she continued. "Then I will have a word or two with them for keeping the rest of the family waiting." She tickled the baby beneath his chin.

James Alexander Hastings gurgled and buried his face against his father's chest. Jillian bent over the tub and planted light kisses over his back producing squeals of delight as Max made sure the infant didn't slide from his perch. Laughing, she raised herself and stacked her arms on the side of the tub.

Family. He knew what that meant, too. It meant a wife who blistered his ears for being late. It meant his sweet son, with his eyes the color of pond scum and a cap of golden hair . . . a part of Jillian . . . a part of himself—Hastings and Forbes united in blood. It meant that downstairs, in the white drawing room Damien, LadyLou, Bruce and Kathy were gathered together for no reason other than the pleasure of one another's company.

Contentment stretched inside him, a presence that warmed and soothed him and seemed to grow with every passing moment. Surely, he was the most fortunate man alive. "Have I told you how happy I am that you married me?"

Jillian angled her head toward him and reached out to gently stroke the line of his jaw. "That is good to know, considering that you never asked me."

For a moment, Max was lost in the brilliance of her green eyes, but then his vision blurred as he remembered the day of their betrothal and his refusal to formally propose. Such a simple thing really, to ask the woman who had given him everything to marry him.

"Jillian," he said. "Will you do me the honor of becoming my wife?"

"Yes," she said softly, without hesitation.

He kissed the top of his son's head and then smiled at the woman kneeling at the side of the tub, her hand cupping water and dribbling it over his chest and down the baby's back. A beautiful woman with a glow that hadn't left her face since the day he'd brought her back home to Bassett House. A magnificent woman with courage and spirit and an endless capacity for giving.

She was his Pandora, holding hope in her hands, nurturing it, defying trouble to cross her doorstep.

She was his friend and his lover and his wife.

Her name was Jillian Nicole Forbes Hastings and Max loved her.

Avon Romances—
the best in exceptional authors and unforgettable novels!

MONTANA ANGEL **Kathleen Harrington**
77059-8/ $4.50 US/ $5.50 Can

EMBRACE THE WILD DAWN **Selina MacPherson**
77251-5/ $4.50 US/ $5.50 Can

MIDNIGHT RAIN **Elizabeth Turner**
77371-6/ $4.50 US/ $5.50 Can

SWEET SPANISH BRIDE **Donna Whitfield**
77626-X/ $4.50 US/ $5.50 Can

THE SAVAGE **Nicole Jordan**
77280-9/ $4.50 US/ $5.50 Can

NIGHT SONG **Beverly Jenkins**
77658-8/ $4.50 US/ $5.50 Can

MY LADY PIRATE **Danelle Harmon**
77228-0/ $4.50 US/ $5.50 Can

THE HEART AND THE HEATHER **Nancy Richards-Akers**
77519-0/ $4.50 US/ $5.50 Can

DEVIL'S ANGEL **Marlene Suson**
77613-8/ $4.50 US/ $5.50 Can

WILD FLOWER **Donna Stephens**
77577-8/ $4.50 US/ $5.50 Can